MARK MCGEE
AND
THE GATEWAY TO GOD

BY BILLY STANCIL

PRESS

Mark McGee and the Gateway to God
by Billy Stancil

Printed in the United States of America.

ISBN 9781498475532

www.xulonpress.com

For Rachel, my wife, who encouraged me.

The Gateway, Florida mentioned in this book is a fictional town and is not to be confused with the actual Gateway, Florida. I'm sure the real one is in fact a lovely place and nowhere near as creepy as the one you are about to experience.

Table of Contents

INTRODUCTION

There was no moon out tonight, no stars for that matter. It was dark; it was very dark. The kind of dark that you could actually feel. It was scary dark. Black.

None of that mattered to Gameboy, the little black mutt dog that was running through the woods. He was being guided by his nose, not his eyes.

It had all started with a squirrel chase that led him under the backyard fence, over the small creek and into the forest. The chase hadn't gone as well as Gameboy had hoped. The squirrel had scampered up a tall pine tree and began chattering loudly, telling Gameboy off no doubt. Then, it was curiosity that led him further into the forest. There had been several other critter chases and smell investigations, all of which had led Gameboy further from home. Too far now even, to hear his master calling him home for dinner.

Then it happened. The sky lit up as if it were daytime. The loud explosion followed. Gameboy let out a yelp and took off running in a different direction. Again darkness. Light again, followed by the rumble of thunder. Gameboy ran faster. He had no idea where he was running to, but faster he ran. He wanted his dog house. It was safe there. He could hide at the back and wait out the storm, as he always did. Another flash of light... boom.

Gameboy was an adventurous dog. He loved exploring and playing with his master. He loved to bark at other dogs. He loved to chase cars and bicycles. He even loved to ride in cars with his head out the window. He, however, did not love storms. They were his very most, worst favorite thing.

Unaware of which direction he was running, he kept going. Under branches, over logs, among trees. He was so scared, he just had to get away.

Then the rain started. In seconds he was soaking wet. Flash...boom. Faster, yelping. Where was his house? His master? He was scared out of his fuzzy paws. Flash ...he saw an opening in the forest...boom. He ran for it. Out of the forest he flew, as fast as his little legs would take him.

It was big. Teeth bared claws raised to grab him. He turned to the side without slowing. Another flash. Another creature just as scary. This was too much. He darted around it, running faster. He could almost hear them growling at him over the rain and thunder. Almost sense them chasing him. He was terrified, yelping as he ran. Fearing for his life. Flash...boom.

He needed his dog house. Where was his doghouse? His shelter? His safe place? Flash...he saw a big yard before him and a giant house. He ran towards it. Flash... boom. Another creature, just the head though. A big scary head with sharp teeth that were bigger than him. Water was pouring from its mouth. Again he yelped and maneuvered around it. Straight for the giant house. He ran faster. Were the giant creatures chasing him? He did not look back. Flash…boom. He saw a bridge that he'd have to cross to get to the house. It rained harder. He ran so fast it felt as though he wasn't touching the ground. He darted across the bridge, his nails clicking on the boards as he ran.

Flash…boom. He came to a stop at the giant house. He was under shelter and out of the rain. He whimpered. Where was he? It was a very large house. Gameboy had never seen anything like it. The doors were larger than his master's entire house. Flash…boom. He scratched at the door, yelping. He wanted away from the loud noise. He barked and scratched. Flash…boom. Again he yelped. He was terrified. There were strange creatures out here. Flash…boom. He yelped and scratched. And then, slowly the giant door creaked open. It opened just enough for Gameboy to get in. Flash…boom. He was inside. The door slammed shut.

If anyone had been nearby. Anyone at all, they would've sworn, that over the sounds of the rain and the thunder…they'd heard the screams and yelps, of a little dog…that'd made a very bad decision.

The rain stopped. All was quiet. No more flashes. No more booms. No screams. No yelps. Just darkness. Extreme darkness. Black.

CHAPTER ONE

NEW BEGINNINGS

A total chaotic mess. That was the best description to give Mark's room. Only this time it wasn't his fault. Instead of dirty clothes, games, magazines, shoes and videos scattered about, it was boxes. All labeled. "Mark's room." He had no idea where to begin unpacking. His bed wasn't even put together yet. A total chaotic mess.

Things had been great in Pittsburgh. Mark had been happy. He'd had amazing friends there. His grandparents, who loved to spoil him, had lived two blocks away. He'd lived close to town, not too close, but close enough to ride his skateboard in. He'd even liked his school, though he would never admit that to anyone.

Then things took a turn for the worst. His stepdad lost his job. Things were quite scary for a few weeks after that. They had used up most of their savings. His mom and stepdad hadn't discussed the finance situation with him, but he'd heard them talking, and knew things were not well. They'd stopped eating out, having friends over, going shopping, or basically doing anything that meant spending money.

Mark had come home from his friend Jason's house on a Tuesday and was told that they were about to have a family meeting. His mom had asked him to go get his little sister, Bethany, from her room. He'd known it couldn't be good. Family meetings rarely went in Mark's favor. They were usually ways for him to be informed that he would be having more responsibilities, which meant more chores. Why couldn't they just once have a family meeting and say, "Mark, we're going to Disney World for a week and you're allowed to bring any friend you want." Maybe one day that would happen. He and Bethany had gone to the living room where his mom and stepdad were waiting.

His stepdad excitedly informed them that he had gotten another job. He would be making more money. How exciting was that? He would even have better benefits, whatever that meant. He'd even said they would be able to take vacations more often. Was a family meeting finally delivering good news?

"However." His step dad had said. Oh how Mark hated that word. "However." Mark had never been to church. He'd never studied God or heaven or hell. He didn't even know if he believed in them. He supposed though, that if he did believe in hell, the word "however" must have originated there. "However," his step dad had said. "We have to move away from Pittsburgh." The room had begun to spin at that point. Mark was frozen in time. Move away from Pittsburgh? That was not an option. He couldn't move away. He couldn't leave his friends. Jason and Brad were his best friends. Then there was Tina, a girl, though she was still pretty cool. He couldn't leave his perfect neighborhood, his grandparents, his school, his life. This was impossible. He'd shaken his head in an attempt to get a grip. Maybe by "away from Pittsburgh", he meant just a few miles. Maybe they would still be close enough to see everyone and go to the same school. Maybe just another neighborhood.

Bethany's voice brought Mark out of his fog. "Where will we be moving to?" she'd asked. Mark wanted to cover his ears, as if not hearing his stepdad's answer would change the course of their lives, and keep them in Pittsburgh. He'd heard the answer though. "We're moving to Florida," his mother had said excitedly, "A little town called Gateway, Florida." It was close to Jacksonville, where his stepdad would be working. Now, Mark hadn't been that great in geography, but he knew Florida, and it was nowhere near Pennsylvania. Florida? He couldn't remember much more about that conversation. It was all quite fuzzy.

They had begun packing the next day and pulled away from the only house Mark had ever lived in on the following Friday. It had all happened so fast. Mark had hardly had time to say his goodbyes.

It was now Sunday. His room was a mess. His life was over. Mark Evan McGee. Twelve years old and already his life was over. Of course his mother kept saying how great it would be. They would have a bigger house, he would have a bigger room that would be on the second floor, and he would even have his own bathroom. His stepdad told him it would be an adventure. He would get to meet new friends, go to a new school, and experience new teachers.

He, however, did not feel their excitement. His room was definitely bigger, and yes, he had his own bathroom.

That part was kinda cool. He had no interest in new friends though. It had taken him twelve years to get the ones he had. Now they expected him to make new ones as if they had a machine in the garage where he could punch in his expectations and just make a friend. The whole thing was totally ridiculous. He would be friendless for the rest of his life. Not to mention this small hick town they'd moved to. It was a tiny town between Jacksonville and Georgia, named Gateway. Small wasn't even the word for it. There was no mall, no arcades, no anything cool or fun. His life was over.

His mother came into his room and found him sulking. "Mark Evan McGee!" She was the only one that ever called him by his full name and it was usually when she'd had enough of whatever he was dishing out. "It's not the end of the world, now you make the best of this situation or I'm going to give you something to pout about!"

"But mom!" He started to protest.

"No buts about it, now go help your stepfather put Bethany's bed together," she pointed toward Bethany's bedroom, "and then the two of you can put your bed together."

Working was the last thing Mark wanted to do. "Yes ma'am." He stood and crossed his room to the door.

His mother stopped him by placing a hand on each of his shoulders. She spoke gently to him now, "it really will be okay...you'll see."

"I guess...it's just..." He had to choose his words carefully, get his mother to understand the error of their ways. "We'll never see Grandma or Papa again." There, that would get her.

She smiled, "actually, they've been talking about moving to Florida for years." She slid his hair out of his eyes. "We may see them sooner than you think."

He plodded away. So much for that argument.

"That was a good try though, Mark," she called after him.

Later that afternoon, as his mom was preparing dinner, his stepdad was hooking up the television to the surround sound, and Bethany was unpacking her princess dresses, Mark decided to scope out the neighborhood on his skateboard. He ran downstairs, slung open the front door and jumped back.

On his front porch stood four people. A man, a woman and two boys. One of the boys was around Mark's age and the other one was a few years younger.

"Well, hello!" The woman holding the covered dish in her oven mitted hand said. "We were just about to ring the doorbell."

The man, holding what appeared to be a pie replied, "You must be a psychic."

Mark just smiled at him and then sized up the older boy. Did he look like friend, enemy, or geek material? With his shoulder length blonde hair covering his left eye, his vans shoes, long black t-shirt and rolled up jeans, he was definitely not a geek. That left two options: friend or foe?

"We're the Morgan's." The woman again. "I'm Martha, this is my husband Scott, and our boys Scotty, who's twelve and Davey, he's eight."

"Hi, I'm Mark...Mark McGee...Mom!!" he yelled toward the kitchen.

"What is it Mark? His mom responded, "I'm cooking, dear!"

"We have company!"

"Oh wow!" She came out of the kitchen. "Who is it?" She was wiping her hands on her apron. "Invite them in, Mark! I'm so sorry, please come in."

"Thank you," Mrs. Morgan said. "So sorry to catch you at a bad time."

"No problem at all, oh my, what have you brought?" His mother looked over their dishes. "It smells delicious."

They all made introductions as Mark's stepdad came in. He and Mr. Morgan wandered back into the living room discussing electronics. Mrs. Morgan went into the kitchen with Mark's mom, leaving the boys standing awkwardly at the front door.

"So, what were your names again?" Mark asked.

"I'm Scotty," the oldest one said, "and the dork here is Davey." He knocked his little bother's hat off.

"Stop it Scotty!" Davey said, retrieving his hat. "You're such a moron! Stop acting cool, everybody knows you're the dork!"

Scotty jumped at Davey, who moved away while putting his hat back on.

"Do you have any brothers or sisters Mark?" Davey asked.

"Yeah, Bethany's a little younger than you. She's six."

"A six- year old girl?" Davey responded, "You got anybody else?"

"That's it."

About that time, Bethany came walking downstairs. They all looked up at her. She was dressed as a princess in all pink. She looked adorable with her long blonde hair.

"Oh good grief!" Davey said.

"Go introduce yourself, Prince Charming." Scotty said.

"Shut up, Scotty!" Davey said, walking over to meet Bethany.

"Don't let Gabi hear you say shut up." Scotty said.

"Whatever." He and Bethany headed for the kitchen.

"So how old are you, Mark?" Scotty asked.

"Same as you, twelve."

"Awesome, so where did you guys move here from?

"Pittsburgh, Pennsylvania."

Scotty nodded, "what state is that in?"

"Um...Pennsylvania?"

"Oh, right! I knew that." They both laughed. "Nice skateboard." He pointed to Mark's board, he was still holding.

"Oh, thanks, do you skate?"

"Oh yeah." They pounded fists.

They were quite the pair. Both with hair too long, same style, covering their left eye. Mark's was black and Scotty's blonde. Quite a pair indeed.

"Hey, you want to check out my room?" Mark asked. They headed upstairs. First door on the right. Even though the bed was together, it was still a messy room. Scotty got the picture though, it was definitely a skateboarder's room. Vans and Sketchers shoes strewn about. Skateboarding posters laying around. Video games old and new stacked everywhere. They sat on Mark's bed.

"Cool room." Scotty said.

"Yeah, I even have my own bathroom."

"Sweet! Davey and I have to share a bathroom.

"That's cool, at least you have a brother, I have the princess of pink." They both laughed.

Scotty picked up a stack of magazines and flipped through them. "So," he said, "what brings you to the thriving metropolis of Gateway?

Mark shrugged, "My stepdad lost his job and found a better one here, well, in Jacksonville.

"Stepdad huh?" Scotty asked, "How old were you when your parents split?"

"Actually", Mark said, looking at the floor, "my dad died about three years ago."

"Whoa, sorry man."

"He was in a car accident."

"That sucks."

"The strange thing is, he was on his way to church."

"Yeah, why is that strange?" Scotty asked.

"My mom said he'd never been to church in his life and she had no idea why he was going. He said he would tell her when he got home."

"Only he never did..." Scotty finished his sentence for him. "That is strange."

"So that's why I've never been to church."

Scotty nodded. "We go, but I'm not really into it that much."

"Anyway," Mark said, "here we are in Gateway. What exactly is there to do here in this hick town?"

Scotty grinned, "do you mean to tell me that Pittsburgh is bigger than Gateway?"

"The word Pittsburgh is bigger than Gateway!" They laughed.

"Gateway isn't bad," Scotty said, "there's plenty to do here."

"Okay," Mark waved his hands, waiting for this big to do list. "Like what?"

"Like…Billy Mumpower has a half pipe in his yard."

That got Mark's attention. "Where does he live?"

"About a mile outside the neighborhood."

"Okay, what else?"

"Well, a lot of us go hang out at the Snyder's house."

"Who are the Snyder's?"

"They're a really cool couple. Their kids are grown, but they have an awesome house. Pool table, ping pong, foosball, and a swimming pool. They are so nice too. Sometimes we just hang out over there and watch movies.

"Who is we?" Mark asked.

"Well, our little group is me, Billy, Matt and Gabi."

"Gabi?"

"Yeah, she's pretty cool, for a girl. Kind of bossy. Really sarcastic. She's always yelling at me. I think I like her."

Mark just stared at him.

"We hang out at her house sometimes too. Her family is really cool. Now, they're super involved in church."

Mark stood and walked to the window. "I had great friends too. A great neighborhood. My grandparents lived just around the corner. There was a skate park about two miles away. It was awesome."

"Trust me dude, you'll love it here. I tell you what… how about I come by in the morning and take you around to meet everyone?"

Mark nodded, "Okay"

"Sweet. How's nine o'clock sound?"

"Early…but whatever."

Scotty's mom called him down. They were leaving.

"Aw man," Mark said, "I was hoping you guys were going to stay for dinner."

"Me too, my mom's pies are really good."

"I'm sure my mom tried to convince your parents."

"Actually, we ate before we came over." They went downstairs. Everyone was standing by the front door.

"Thank you so much for the shepherd's pie and the apple pie," Mark's mom said.

"And the help with the surround sound," His stepdad added.

"It was our pleasure," Mrs. Morgan replied. "And welcome to the neighborhood."

"We have lots of pies mommy!" Bethany said.

"We sure do honey, did you say thank you to the Morgan's?"

"Thank you to the Morgan's!" Bethany said.

They all laughed and said their goodbyes.

Once the door was closed, Mark's mother gave him that look.

"What?" Mark asked.

"Well?"

"Well what?"

"Is he friend potential? Scotty, right? He seemed nice."

"He's alright." Mark shrugged, "I guess."

"Uh huh." She smiled, messing his hair up as they headed for the dining room.

After dinner, Mark went to his room. He did some cleaning and put his clothes away. Once his wall was as covered with posters as was humanly possible, he hooked up his X Box and played video games. He loved getting lost in "game world" as his mother called it. She hated the violent games but let him buy whatever he wanted with his own money. After several hours of mind numbing gameage, he brushed his teeth and went to bed.

CHAPTER TWO

THE LEGEND OF THE CASTLE

M ark awoke in the middle of the night. He'd heard a
loud thump. Was his stepdad still working downstairs? He started his new job tomorrow, Mark would
have thought he'd gone to bed early. He heard the noise
again. Definitely coming from downstairs. It was even
louder the second time. Surely someone else would've
heard it too. His mom was a light sleeper. He decided to
go check it out. His Iron Man night light gave off enough
light in his room to find a hockey stick he could use for
protection. He slowly opened his door. It was dark in
the hallway. He peeked out. Another loud bump caused
him to jump back. "Mom!" he called, "Is anybody up?"
He didn't want to wake Bethany up, so he didn't yell
too loud. He wished he knew where his flashlight was
packed away. The light switch for the hallway was on
the other side, a million miles away. He did a quick leap
across the hall and slapped it. Nothing. He was still in
darkness. "Awesome," he said under his breath. "Now
what?" He started to go back to his room and look for his
flashlight but then he felt as if someone were watching

him from the end of the hall. Trying to let his eyes adjust, he saw nothing. Then...

"Mark." A low raspy whisper.

"Who is it?" He was frozen completely forgetting he held the hockey stick. "This ain't funny."

"I'm watching you Mark. I've been waiting for you."

"Stop playing around! Who is that?" He stepped toward the voice, trying to be brave. He raised the hockey stick. "I have a weapon."

There was a low laugh and then he saw the eyes. Two huge, red eyes. They seemed to stare into his soul. "You belong to me, Mark."

He was frozen where he stood. He dropped the hockey stick. He couldn't scream.

The eyes came closer. They were attached to a huge... dragon? Really? There was a dragon in his new house? He knew Florida had alligators and maybe a few big snakes, but nobody had said anything about dragons. It opened its mouth. Huge, razor sharp teeth that dripped blood and drool onto the carpet. The tongue flicked out. It was forked. It swiped his face. He could feel the heat of its breath, the smell of sulfur and sewage. "It's only a matter of time," it whispered.

With every bit of strength Mark could muster, he turned and tried to run. His feet were like a hundred pounds each. He could barely lift them.

The dragon laughed from behind him. "Only a matter of time, Mark!" It roared.

He ran as if in quicksand, he appeared to be sinking into the floor.

"Mark!" The dragon yelled, "It's time to go!"

Deeper he sunk, panicking he tried to call out, no words would come.

"Mark! Let's go!" Mark paused, the dragon's voice was changing. What was... "Dude, get up! Come on, it's nine o'clock."

He opened his eyes with a jump and looked around. The sun was up. He was in his bed, sweating profusely.

Scotty stood there looking at him like he was crazy. "You okay, man?"

"Yeah, ummm, crazy dream." He wiped his eyes.

"Really? I had one too!" Scotty said, a little too excited.

"What was yours about?" Mark asked, wondering for some strange reason if Scotty had been chased by the horrible dragon.

"Well, Roger, the mailman, was driving the ice cream truck and handing people ice cream sandwiches with their mail and..."

"Scotty?" Mark just stared at him. "I should get ready."

"Okay, but I told you it was crazy."

"You're crazy." Mark said, sliding out of bed and heading for the bathroom. "Give me ten minutes."

Fifteen minutes later they were on their skateboards cruising the neighborhood.

"So," Mark said, "Where to first?"

"I thought we could go get Gabi first. I told her we would be coming."

"Does she skateboard?" Mark asked.

Scotty laughed. "Now that's a funny thought, Gabi on a skateboard...no, but she has a bicycle."

"Where does she live?"

"Left at the next street."

A few moments later, Mark followed Scotty up the driveway of a single story home. The sign over the porch read, "The Motes Family." The garage door was open.

"They were the first family to move into the neighborhood," Scotty said. "I really think you'll like them." He rang the doorbell and they both took a seat on the porch swing.

A cute little blonde about Bethany's age stuck her head out the door. "Gabi will be ready in a minute!"

"Okay, thanks Abi." Scotty said.

"Who's he?" she asked, pointing at Mark.

"This is Mark, his family just moved here."

"You live in our neighborhood? Abi asked excitedly. "Where at?"

"Towards the front." Mark replied, pointing in the direction of his house.

"You don't live on the same side as the scary forest do you?" she asked.

"Well, there is a forest behind my house. Is it scary?" He looked at Scotty.

"It's very scary!" Abi replied. "Don't go in there... EVER!" She yelled the last word for effect.

"Okay then," Mark said, sensing her passion on this subject.

"A lot of crazy stuff happens in those woods man." Scotty added. "I'll tell you about it sometime."

"You'll never get me to go in there." Abi said. "Especially with that big castle in there?"

"Castle, huh?" Mark looked at Scotty as if Abi had lost her mind. "What have you guys been telling her?"

"Actually dude, there really is a castle in there. It's pretty far back, but the entrance to the driveway is off the main road outside our neighborhood. I'll show you sometime. It has some pretty cool statues at the gate. A dragon and a knight."

"A dragon?" Mark straightened up, remembering his dream.

"Yeah, it's pretty sweet actually. They have a big iron gate. I'd really love to see that castle."

Mark just stared in that direction. He could still hear the dragon. "You belong to me, Mark." "It's only a matter of time." "I'm waiting for you." Mark got chills just thinking about it. He rubbed his arms.

"You okay man?" Scotty asked.

"Yeah, I'm good."

About that time Gabi came out.

"This is Mark." Abi said, "He just moved here."

"I know," Gabi replied, "Thanks Abi."

"Bye Mark." Abi said, heading back inside.

"Bye, nice meeting you, Abi."

"Hello Mark," Gabi said, standing in front of the two boys.

Mark stood, not sure if he should shake her hand or what. He hated awkward situations. "Hi Gabi, I'm Mark."

"Yeah, I got that." She said, smiling.

He felt like an idiot. He looked for Scotty to help him, but he was only grinning at Mark.

"She already said your name, dude."

"Yeah, shut up." Mark replied." So, where to now?"

"Should we round up the gang, Gabi?" Scotty asked.

"Matt's already at Billy's," Gabi replied, "He called me when you weren't home." She said to Scotty. "Let me grab my bike...and Mark?"

"Yeah?" he replied as she headed into the garage.

"Don't say shut up...it's not nice."

"Yes ma'am," he replied, "I mean, okay." He looked at Scotty who was laughing to himself. "She's kinda mom-like, isn't she?"

"You'll get used to it." Scotty replied.

She came out of the garage on a large black bicycle. "Boys and skateboards," she said, leading the way, "try and keep up!"

Mark smiled as he watched them go ahead of him. Gabi was a little thing, way too small for her large adult bike. Her feet didn't even reach the ground. He thought she was cute too, and could see why Scotty liked her. Her long, straight blonde hair and blue eyes with glasses that made her look smart. Not only was she mom-like but Mark imagined she was a know it all book worm. Then there was Scotty, Mark's blonde twin. On his board next to Mark. Both of them were Mark's age and lived close to him. Yesterday he'd about given up on life, thinking he would never have friends again, and now... he had two really good potentials. Maybe this place wouldn't be so bad. Then again, there was that chilling dream. What was that about?

A half hour later, they were at Billy Mumpower's, sitting in his treehouse. Billy was a tall, lanky, nerdy looking, freckle faced kid. He had short, wavy reddish-blonde hair. He didn't look like a skater, but here he was the one with the half-pipe. Of course, he lived on a bigger piece of property, away from Mark's neighborhood. His house was small and rundown, practically a shack. It was just him and his mom and it didn't appear that they had a lot of money. None of the gang seemed to care though, he had a treehouse and a halfpipe, how rich was that?

Matt Ramsey was the other one in the group. He was a year older than the others, and a lot bigger. The local high school was already looking to get him on the football team. Matt wasn't interested in sports though, he liked music. He'd played piano since he was young and had recently taken up the guitar. Still, he was a head taller than even Billy, and they considered him their bodyguard. Mark, however, couldn't imagine him hurting a fly.

"So Scotty," Billy said, "Did your dumb mutt ever show up?"

"Gameboy? No, we've looked everywhere."

"He probably chased a squirrel into that forest, never to be seen again." Matt said.

"That's what I said," Gabi added, "that forest is so creepy."

"Did you guys try looking in there," Billy asked.

"No! My mom wouldn't let me go in," Scotty said, "But I stood at the edge and called him."

"So what's the story on this forest?" Mark asked. "Why is it so creepy? Did somebody die in there or something?"

"Lots of people," Billy said.

"No!" Gabi gave Billy a look, "You don't know that, Billy." She looked at Mark, "It's been said that if you go into the forest, you're never seen again."

"Well, it's been said because it's true, lots of people have vanished in that forest!" Billy said.

"Oh yeah? Like who?" Mark asked.

"Like Michael Roth," Billy said. "Remember him?"

"Yeah," Matt added, "he was only a couple years older than us."

"I saw him the day before he went in," Scotty said. "He was bragging about doing it."

"Why did he go in?" Mark asked.

"He wasn't real smart," Gabi replied. "He was thirteen in the fifth grade."

"He was crazy," Billy added.

"He was brave to go in there alone," Scotty said.

"I heard he went in on a dare," Matt added.

"Yeah," Billy said, "Todd Johnson dared him."

"Speaking of smart," Gabi said, "I've met rocks with more brains than Todd Johnson."

"So what happened?" Mark asked.

"He said he was going in after school on a Friday," Scotty said. "That night there was a search for him."

"Yeah, when he didn't come out after several hours, his friends went and told his parents," Billy said.

"And they immediately called the police," Scotty said.

"My dad took the call," Matt said, to Mark, "He's a cop."

"They had a helicopter and search teams and dogs," Billy said. "It was so cool. I was even on TV."

"Yeah," Gabi said, "they interviewed a few of his friends."

Mark stood and walked to the window. "And they never found him?"

"Nope," Billy said. "Not a trace."

"How long ago was this?"

"Two years," Matt said, "and nobody's gone into that forest since."

"Do you think the castle has anything to do with it?" Mark asked, turning to face the group.

"It's possible," Billy said. "Nobody seems to know much about that castle."

"Who lives there?" Mark asked.

Billy shrugged, "the only person ever seen going in and out of there is old man Willoughby."

"And he's just a groundskeeper." Matt added.

"Lucius Willoughby," Gabi said. "There's a creepy character. The police questioned him, but he'd been away at the time, somewhere out of the country."

"So," Mark said, pacing around their circle, "how many people do you know of, that's gone missing?"

"Three that I know of," Billy said.

"My dad told me about a fourth one," Matt said. "A homeless boy that wandered into Gateway years ago. The police could never catch him and turn him over to Child Services. One day he was running away from an officer and went right into the forest." Matt held up his hands, "they never saw him again."

"Okay, who else?" Mark asked.

"There were two teenagers about five years ago," Billy said. "They told some friends that they were going to disprove the rumors. They took camping gear, food and all kinds of survival equipment. None of it was ever found."

Mark sat back down. He pondered all of this information. "Has anybody around here, this might sound crazy, ever mentioned having strange dreams?"

"Strange dreams?" Gabi asked. "Like what?"

"That's right dude!" Scotty said, "You never told me about your dream. He nearly jumped out of bed this morning when I went to wake him up."

"Everybody has strange dreams from time to time," Matt said.

"This was different," Mark said, and then he proceeded to tell them every detail. "It seemed so real."

"Okay," Scotty admitted, "that is a little weird. You dream about a dragon and then I tell you about the castle with the dragon statue."

"Exactly what I thought," Mark said. "Especially after having the dream my first night here."

"Come on guys!" Matt laughed. "It's just a coincidence."

"Yes it is," Gabi added, "You guys are just trying to creep each other out."

"Still," Mark said, "I want to investigate this castle."

"How?" Billy asked.

"Let's do this," Mark stood again. "You guys ask around, find people who've been here a while. Find out as much about the forest and the castle as you can. Write it all down. Stories, rumors, everything."

"Great, homework on our summer break." Matt said, "sounds fun."

"And what are you going to do, Mark?" Gabi asked.

"My stepdad is an architect. He may be able to find some records on that old castle. Maybe we can find out who owns it."

"Sounds exciting," Billy said.

"Sounds like a waste of time," Matt said. "What are we hoping to find out?"

"The truth," Mark replied.

It was getting late, so they all headed home. As Mark went up his driveway saying goodbye, Gabi called to him. He stopped as she rode up "What's up?"

"Can I ask you a question?"

Mark shrugged, "of course."

"Are you a Christian?" she asked.

"No way! Why?" He replied, not meaning to come across that harsh.

She nodded, smiling, "You should come to church with Scotty and me. That's all." She pedaled away.

He stood there confused. "Bye!"

A few days later they all met up again in the treehouse to compare notes. Everybody was chatting and carrying on about video games and movies they'd recently played or watched. Mark got Gabi's attention and motioned for her to get things started. She nodded for him to do it, but he gave her his best pleading eyes. She shook her head in disgust and stood.

"Okay everybody! Listen up! We need to go over what we've learned! I'll go first," She paused as they all stopped talking and gave her their attention. "Thank you. I wasn't really able to find out much. Most of the people I asked didn't know too much other than the castle has always been there. Even Mrs. Riles, at church, who is eighty-seven, said that it was there when she was a little girl. She also said that kids had went missing even back then, when they'd entered the forest. That's when they'd first put up the do not enter signs." She looked through her other notes, "I asked her how many people had gone missing, and she wasn't sure, but guessed over twenty in her lifetime. Maybe more."

"Wow!" Billy exclaimed.

"Here's my question," Matt said. "If nobody ever comes out, then why don't people in the search parties ever disappear?"

"I don't know," Gabi said, "but Mrs. Riles did make one interesting observation…only children have ever disappeared in there."

"Yeah," Billy said, laughing, "and dogs!"

"It sounds like a bunch of hogwash to me." Matt said, "Somebody probably started those rumors just to keep kids out."

"What about Michael Roth?" Scotty asked. "We knew him."

"Who knows?" Matt replied, "Maybe he ran away. He was always fighting with his parents and getting in trouble."

Gabi shrugged, "that's all I have, except hold on…" She flipped through her notes. "Lucius Willoughby. Mrs. Riles said that he was the groundskeeper back then, and…" she looked at them all for affect; "He was old then. She said they called him old man Willoughby over eighty years ago."

"He should be dead by now," Scotty said.

"You guys are crazy," Matt said, "That had to be his dad."

Gabi sat down.

"I'll go next." Billy stood and cleared his throat. "I asked my mom, who by the way, has lived right here on this property her whole life. She also said the castle has always been there. She said that her fifth grade teacher tried to find out one time if her class could visit it for a field trip.

"Wow, what happened?" Scotty asked.

"Get this," Billy replied, "not only did old man Willoughby tell her to get lost, but the next day, she was fired."

"What for?" Gabi asked.

"For nothing," Billy answered, "just canned for no reason."

"Yeah right," Matt said. "No offense, but your mom was in the fifth grade. I don't think she would have been told why her teacher was fired. For all she knew, her teacher could've been selling drugs to students."

"Anyway," Billy continued, "she said that if anybody knows anything about that castle, they sure are quiet about it. That it is almost like they are pretending the castle isn't there. And," he paused for affect, "she also said that the search parties have never been allowed into the castle, and that, doubting Matt, is probably why no search party members have disappeared. I agree with Mark. It's the castle, not the forest."

"And why would they cover it up?" Matt asked. "Why wouldn't they get a court order or a warrant and check it out? Why don't they just tear it down if it's so evil?"

"Because they can't," Mark said. Everyone looked at him.

"What do you mean?" Gabi asked.

"I'll tell you when it's my turn," He replied. "I want to hear what you guys found out first."

"It seems like we all have about the same stuff," Scotty said. "It's always been there and a lot of people have disappeared."

Matt nodded, "That's about all I got too. I asked my folks about it last night and my dad told me to drop it. Of course, he's always told me to stay out of the forest too, so that tells me he knows something, but here's my thing, its private property, so mind your own business.

Maybe they're doing government experiments in there and silencing nosey kids."

"Kind of strange though," Billy said, "how he won't tell you more."

Matt shrugged, "That's all I got."

"Me too," Scotty said. "Whatcha got Mark?"

Mark stood and sifted through his notes. "Well, I was able to get into my stepdad's computer when he wasn't around. I started in city records.

"Good idea," Scotty said. "What did it say?"

"Apparently the castle has been there for a very long time…"

"Duh!" Matt interrupted, "we've established that."

"No," Mark said, "I mean it was here even before the town was here."

They all looked at each other, confused.

"In fact," Mark continued," the only record they have is an old Indian legend, dated to just after the Spanish settlers came to Florida."

"What was the legend?" Billy asked.

"Apparently, the very site it's on, was an old Indian burial ground. In fact, it was where all the tribes of that time would travel to, to bury their dead." Everybody listened intently. "According to legend, the Indians would trade with the Spanish when they came here. Sometimes they would leave some of the merchandise behind. You know, things they couldn't carry, like crates and barrels and things. They would bring wagons on the next trip to bring back what they'd left behind, and they only came on a full moon. Some kind of superstition. They believed that the spirits of their dead could only find their way home during the light of a full moon. Well, one month, they came back to get the barrels they'd left behind and bury their dead, and instead of finding things as they'd left it, there was a castle built here…right on top of their burial ground. It had been built in a month."

"Okay, back up," Matt said. "I've seen the size of that castle on Google Map, and it is huge. They couldn't build it in a month with today's technology. So try again McGee, that's rubbish."

"Well, hold on," Mark said, "I'm not finished." He had their attention. "Researchers have since found that it has brothers."

"Brothers?" the others said in unison.

"What do you mean brothers?" Matt asked. "How can a castle have brothers?" He laughed.

"He means there are others like it," Gabi said.

"Wait, here in Gateway?" Matt said, "No way!"

"No, not here," Mark said. "There are three identical castles in other countries, each one with its's own legend."

"What countries? Gabi asked.

"There's one in France, one in Italy, and one in Germany. Nobody knows who lives in them, nobody is ever seen coming or going, except, get this, the groundskeeper." They all stared at him.

"Dude that gave me chills." Scotty said.

"No doubt!" Billy agreed, they both rubbed their arms.

"There's more," Mark said. "Are you ready for this?" He waited for them to settle. "Nobody knows when they were built. They all just, according to each local legend, appeared. The one in France appeared in the middle of a well-traveled road. The people woke up one morning, and there it was. The one in Italy appeared right next to the home of an extremely wealthy family. One day there was an open field next to their house and the next there was a castle. Three days later their son disappeared. A search was made. Nobody could figure out how to get into the castle. There were no windows and only one door. Their axes broke when they tried to break it down, and it would not burn. Anyway, after a while, all the people that were trying to get in started complaining about really bad headaches, and having bad dreams. Within weeks, they'd all died of an unknown disease. A notice was posted for nobody to go near the castle. Over time, statues of dragons and knights and gargoyles randomly appeared on the property."

Matt made the Twilight Zone music with his mouth. "You guys don't believe all that do you? Are you telling me you got all that from the city records site?"

"No," Mark said, "there was a link to a local legends website."

"Exactly! Legends, and hardly believable ones at that."

"Just telling you what I found," Mark said, looking through his notes. "Oh, before you write it all off, there's one more thing you might find interesting. The towns that these other castles are in…the one in France is in a small town named Porte. The one in Italy is in a small town named Ingresso. The one in Germany is in a small town named…" he paused.

"What?" Scotty asked, impatiently.

"Einfahrt" Mark replied.

They all laughed.

"You did what?" Matt asked, laughing.

"It better not stink," Billy added.

"Listen!" Mark said, trying not to laugh.

Even Gabi was chuckling, shaking her head.

"Dude, say excuse me," Scotty said, cracking up.

Mark waited them out until finally they stopped laughing. "It's spelled E-I-N-F-A-H-R-T."

They still laughed. "So," Matt said, "what's the big deal of the town names?"

"The big deal is," Mark continued, "each name: Porte, Ingresso and Einfahrt, all have the same meaning in their own language."

"And what's that?" Gabi asked, leaning forward.

"Each word means...Gateway." He replied.

They were all silent. Nobody moved. Nobody spoke.

CHAPTER THREE

WHAT? CHURCH?

Mark had been proud of his investigation. If true, all the information he'd found, made for an amazing story. He just needed to prove it all. The revelation that all four castles were in towns named Gateway had been the clincher. He knew he had their attention after that. Matt was still skeptical, but they were all in. In what, Mark wasn't sure. At least they all agreed it was worth looking into. He desperately wanted to solve this mystery and in order to do that, he needed to do two things. First, he needed to get in that gate and see that castle, and second, he needed to talk to Old Man Willoughby. Lucius Willoughby may have slipped through the cracks of police questioning, but he wouldn't get around Mark. He would have all the right questions to put this whole thing to rest. Maybe by the end of next week he and Scotty could find a way to get in. Who knows, maybe old Lucius would tell them everything just to shut them up. He might even give Scotty his dog back. Mark laughed at the thought.

He turned his light off and got in bed. It was good to have a plan. This mystery stuff was exciting. It was also exhausting. Mark was so tired. He would sleep well tonight.

Just as he closed his eyes, there was a tap at his window. His eyes shot open. Another tap. This was disturbing since he was on the second floor. There were no trees near his windows, so he knew it wasn't a branch. Again, another tap. It sounded like someone was throwing small pebbles at his window. Or…a dragon was tapping its claws on the glass, trying to get Mark's attention. "Get a grip." He said to himself, and got out of bed. "It's probably Scotty fooling around." He walked over to his window and looked out. There actually was a boy in his yard but it didn't look like Scotty, though he appeared to be about Mark's age. The moon was just bright enough to reveal him. He appeared to be wearing a suit and tie and was staring right at Mark. The hairs on the back of Mark's neck stood up. Who was this strange kid? Mark reached for the window latch, unlocked it and opened it. When he looked out, the boy was gone. Nowhere to be seen. "Am I going crazy?" He closed the window back and turned around. He jumped back against the window with a shout. The boy was standing in the middle of his room, just staring at him. "Dude, really? Who are you?" Mark's heart was pounding.

"You're the one," The boy said.

"The one what?" Mark was aggravated. "Dude, you can't just come in people's houses."

"The destined one," He replied. "You need to go to the castle."

"Wait, what do you know about the castle?"

"Only you can save the children."

41

"What children? What are you talking about? The children that have disappeared over the years?"

"Go to the castle, Mark McGee." He said and he turned around. "You will see and understand." He walked toward the door.

"No, wait," Mark called to him but was frozen where he stood. "Who are you?"

The boy stopped at the door. He turned back to face Mark. "Do not bring the girl." With that, he turned and left the room.

Mark's legs unfroze and he ran out into the hallway, "Wait!" he yelled. He didn't see him. He ran downstairs. The front door was locked, chain and all. He ran to the back door. Locked. He even checked the garage door, which was closed as well. Was he still in the house? He was about to look upstairs again when the doorbell rang. He ran to answer it before his parents came down. He unlocked it and swung it open. To his horror, there on his porch stood the black dragon, blood dripping from its mouth. With lightning speed, it struck at him like a snake. He screamed and jumped out of the way, landing on the floor next to his bed in a cold sweat. It was morning. Another dream.

The doorbell rang. Mark froze. The dragon? Was he still dreaming? Who else would it be? The boy? No, he would just come on in. What day was it? He could never keep up with the days on summer break.

"Mark!" His mother called from downstairs, "Mark! Get up sweetie, Gabi's here! Come on down and I'll fix you some breakfast!"

"Okay! I'm up!" He responded. Why did she have to call him sweetie in front of his friends? He'd have to remember to complain later. He got up and dressed.

Why was Gabi here? He looked at his calendar, it was Sunday. They hadn't made plans. She had mentioned going to the library yesterday, maybe she discovered something about the castle. Still, she could've called. He went downstairs.

His mother was busy preparing breakfast. Gabi and Bethany sat at the dining room table sharing a coloring book. Bethany was explaining that the girl's hair should be pink.

"Good morning!" He said to everyone.

"Good morning sweetheart," his mother said, while buttering some toast. He gave the back of her head a look that pleaded with her not to say that.

"Good morning," Gabi said, not looking up from the book.

"Mark look!" Bethany said. "Gabi colored the dragon purple."

Mark's heart skipped a beat at the sound of the word dragon. He walked over and looked. "She did, huh? It must be a girl dragon."

"Girls aren't dragons!" Bethany said, "Girls are people."

"But dragons can be girls," he replied, getting a glass of orange juice. "Just like you have girl dogs, girl cats, girl...bunnies."

"Gabi," Bethany asked, "can dragons be girls?"

"They sure can," Gabi replied. "The pretty dragons are the girls. The mean ugly ones are the boys."

Bethany laughed, "Yeah, they're mean and ugly."

Mark rolled his eyes, "So Gabi, why exactly are you here?" Then he noticed she was dressed up. "And all dressed up?"

"Because," she said, looking up from coloring. "I came by to invite you to church. It starts in ..." she looked at the clock, "about an hour and twenty minutes."

"Church? Um, what?" Mark wasn't sure what to say.

"I think it's a great idea, Mark," his mother said. "You can even help me out by taking Bethany with you."

"Yup!" Bethany said, "they have a children's church Mark...with puppets!" Gabi had clearly made her sales pitch already.

"Church...what...? I've never even been to church."

"They'll be ready Gabi," his mother said, setting his plate down. When she saw the look he was giving her, she added, "or Mark can help me paint the guest bedroom all day."

"I look forward to going to church with you Gabi, thanks for inviting me."

"By the way, Gabi," Mark's mom asked, "what church does your family attend?"

"Lighthouse Christian Center, it's the big church in the center of town. Pastor Eric Osborne is the senior pastor. My dad is the worship leader."

"Oh neat, I bet it's really good," his mom replied, leaving the room.

"Well," Gabi said, "I'll let you guys get ready. We'll be by to get you in around an hour."

"Bye Gabi!" Bethany said.

"Bye Bethany...hey, you'll get to meet my little sister Abi!"

"Yay!" she yelled as she ran upstairs to get ready.

"See you, Mark," And Gabi was gone.

An hour and a half later Mark was standing at his seat in a pretty big church. There were a lot of people there, but it wasn't packed. The balcony was still empty. The music was rocking, nothing like Mark had imagined. "So that's your dad?" He leaned over and asked Gabi.

She nodded, smiling, "Yeah, the one with the crazy hair!"

He looked like one of the eighty's rockers Mark had seen on his dad's old cassette collection he had. "They're good." Mark looked around wondering if Scotty was here. He'd mentioned going to Gabi's Church. He nudged her, "doesn't Scotty come here?" He was glad the music was so loud nobody could hear him talking.

Again she nodded. "They don't come every week, but this is where they come."

They had dropped Bethany and Abi off in children's church. Gabi said that she had been in there up to last year and still helped out with the kids in there sometimes. Apparently she played the keyboard too.

After about forty- five minutes of really cool music, they were told they could sit down. A young guy got up and introduced himself as Charlie Deberry, the youth pastor. He gave announcements and took up an offering. Then he introduced the pastor. Mark had expected some stuffy old guy in a suit to come out and put him to sleep, but this guy was nothing like that. He wasn't even wearing a tie. He introduced himself as Pastor Eric and asked all the visitors to raise their hands. Gabi nudged Mark and made him raise his along with about fifteen other people. Everyone burst into applause. That was actually pretty cool. Mark was given a pamphlet to fill out that came with a free pen.

"Turn with me, if you will," Pastor Eric said," to the book of Genesis, Chapter 28."

Across the church, pages turned and the room got especially quiet. Gabi snickered when Mark's stomach growled at that very moment.

"We're going to start with verse 10," Pastor Eric said. Mark pretended to look on with Gabi, but couldn't help wondering if she'd found out anything at the library about the castle. He guessed she hadn't, since she hadn't mentioned it. Then Pastor Eric said something that caught his attention. It was in verse 12. Mark read over it again. "He had a dream in which he saw a stairway resting on the earth, with its top reaching to heaven, and the angels of God were ascending and descending on it." Strange, Mark thought, he'd heard the song Stairway to Heaven off of one of his dad's old cassettes but he'd never realized it was in the Bible. Was this for real? Where did this happen? He looked a few verses back. It was somewhere between Beersheba and Haran. It only called it a certain place. Why this intrigued Mark, he didn't know, but he felt that it was very important. Almost like it was going to be on a test. He looked down at the notes in Gabi's Bible. It said that the fact the angels were ascending and descending was a sign that the Lord offered to be Jacob's God. Then it said that Jesus told a disciple that he would "see heaven open, and the angels of God ascending and descending on the Son of Man."

Just then, Gabi turned he page and it brought Mark out of his thoughts. Pastor Eric had moved on to another passage.

Mark wasn't sure what was happening, but this place in Florida was really strange. Dreams of a dragon attacking him and some strange boy coming into his room. That weird castle with it's even weirder legends. Not to mention Mark was actually in church. He'd sworn to never do that after his dad's accident. This was it. He needed to drop all this castle-dragon mania and enjoy the rest of his summer break. There wasn't too much time left and his mom had promised him a trip to a Florida beach. How cool was that? Maybe he could even talk her into buying him a surf board. He and Scotty could hit the waves. Definitely. It was time to forget all this craziness and have some fun.

Pulled from his thoughts, he heard Pastor Eric say, "And finally, look back at Genesis Chapter 28, verses 16 and 17." When Jacob awoke from his sleep, he thought, surely the Lord is in this place, and I was not aware of it. He was afraid and said, "How awesome is this place! This is none other than the house of God. This is the gate of heaven." Pastor Eric continued. "Jacob had found himself at a sort of gateway."

Mark stared straight ahead. A tingling sensation raised the hairs on the back of his neck. There would be no forgetting the craziness, he was being pulled further and further into it.

After church, Gabi's family invited Mark to have dinner with them at the Snyder's house. He had gotten to meet Mr. and Mrs. Snyder at church and they were super nice. Mark had called his mom and she said he could go but Bethany needed to come home and clean her room. They dropped her off on the way.

The Snyder's lived at the back of Mark's neighbor-hood in one of the largest houses. The yard was really big too. While the adults prepared the meal and Abi watched a movie, Mark and Gabi went for a walk behind the Snyder's house. This was a different forest, Gabi had told him, nobody had disappeared in here.

"So," Mark said. "Did you learn anything at the library yesterday?"

"Nothing about the castle," she replied, "it seems every story ever done on it was erased in the files. You click on the link and it says, "We apologize for the incon-venience, but this story has been blocked due to question-able material. It really seems like a cover up. I couldn't even find old news stories about the disappearances."

"What do you think about going to the gate and looking for Old Man Willoughby?' Mark asked, fully expecting her to tell him it was a stupid idea. Only, Gabi probably wouldn't say stupid. It being an ugly word and all. "Maybe he would answer our questions."

"No way," Gabi replied, "Stay away from him. In fact, I even did a little investigating on him."

"Seriously?" Mark said. "What did you find out?"

"I found something very interesting. It seems that when the first settlers of Gateway tried to get a road going from here to Jacksonville, back in the 1800's, there was a man that fought the decision. In fact, the story says he became very violent about it. He made threats and attacked a few of the townspeople that opposed him. In the end, the vote went for the road.

"So what did he do?" Mark asked.

"Apparently, he withdrew to his home in the woods, never to be seen by those people again."

"Okay," Mark said, not sure what this had to do with
Old Man Willoughby.

"Get this," Gabi said, "His name was Lucius
Willoughby."

"Do what? Surely it was a grandfather or something."

"And here's the weird part," Gabi continued.

"Weird huh?" Mark replied.

"Yes, apparently, during the construction of the road,
six workers disappeared, four died mysterious deaths,
and seventeen workers claimed to have nightmares so
bad, they quit their job."

Mark stopped walking, staring at her. "Gabi, this
is crazy."

"I know. I have to admit though Mark, I'm a little
concerned."

"About what?"

"About you. I'm afraid you're going to do something
stupid."

"I'm…" he attempted to talk, but she held up her hand.

"Let me finish, "she said, "I'm afraid you're going to
try and go see that castle and something bad is going to
happen to you. Here's the thing, yes I'm concerned about
you getting hurt or killed, but I'm more concerned with
where you would go if you were killed."

"What are talking about?" Mark asked. "Heaven
and hell?"

"Yes, Mark."

"You don't really believe all that do you?"

"Yes I do, Mark McGee!" She said, hands on hips."
And you'd better believe in them too because they're
real! The Bible says that when we die, we will go to one
of two places, heaven or hell. There is no middle ground

for good people who don't believe. If you die in your sin, you will go to hell."

"Chill out Gabi!" Mark said, backing away. "What sin? I'm a good person. I'm only twelve for crying out loud."

"I didn't say you weren't a good person, Mark. To mine and your standards you're a very good person. However, its God's standards we have to worry about. He's going to judge you, not Judge Judy. God is perfect, Mark. He's holy. He's righteous. He's totally good. We have to be all of these things too! It's the only way we can get into heaven."

"Then there won't be a lot of people in there, Gabi, because nobody is perfect! It looks like we're all doomed to hell."

"You're exactly right." That got his attention. "None of us are perfect. Not one of us deserves heaven. We should all be sentenced to hell for our sin that separates us from God. That, my friend, is where Jesus comes in!"

"Gabi!" It was her mom. "You guys come wash up, it's time for dinner!"

"Yes ma'am!" They began heading back. She looked at Mark, "We're not done with this conversation."

"I didn't figure we were. Just, don't worry about me, okay?"

"Yeah...right." She punched his arm.

"Oh, and Gabi"

"What?"

"Don't say stupid...it's an ugly word."

They had dinner with the Snyder's. The food was delicious. Mark really liked Gabi's parents and the Snyder's. They were all so nice and fun to be around, which was odd because he never enjoyed being around adults. Mr. Snyder even offered to take Mark on his motorcycle, with his mom's permission, of course.

After dinner, they all played games and had a great time. What was it about these people that Mark liked? He could hang out with them forever. Their love for enjoying the moment was contagious. Mark wanted more of what they had.

It was late afternoon when Gabi's parents dropped Mark off at his house. He thanked them for a good time and Gabi told him they would talk tomorrow. As Mark walked up his driveway he noticed Scotty sitting on the front porch with his arms crossed not looking very happy.

"What's up, Scotty" Mark asked as he approached.

"Dude, you tell me!" Scotty said, "Where have you been all day?"

"Well, I went to church with Gabi and then we spent the day at the Snyder's, why? Didn't you ask my mom?

"Yeah, I asked her."

"So what's the problem then?" Mark asked.

"The problem is," Scotty said, standing up in front of Mark, "you've been with Gabi all day."

"Yeah, her parents invited me to have dinner at the Snyder's. Why is this a problem?"

"What exactly are your intentions with her?"

"My what?" Mark asked, "Dude, what are you talking about?"

"Do you like her?" Scotty asked it as if Mark were dense.

"Of course I like her," Mark replied. "She's really cool and she tells it like it is."

"Sooo, what?" Scotty asked. "Are you two boyfriend and girlfriend now?"

Mark stared at him for several seconds. "Is that what this is about? No Scotty, we're not boyfriend and girlfriend. Wow dude," Mark gave him a gentle shove, "jealous much?"

Scotty sat back down. "Okay, cool." He kept his head down.

Mark sat next to him. "Listen dude, let me tell you something I learned in Pittsburgh. I had this friend named Steve Phipps, he was a few years older than the rest of us and really cool. He was nice to us younger guys, let us join in on football games and invited us to his house to hang out. Like I said, he was really cool, until "it" happened."

"What happened?" Scotty asked.

"Girls," Mark replied as if the word was poison. "Now, don't get me wrong, I like girls." He said, holding up his hands. "I think they're pretty and they smell nice and they color in the lines and all. However, as soon as Steve started hanging out with girls, he got all weird. He stopped letting us hang around. He stopped inviting us over. He stopped being nice. All he wanted to do was spend time with girls, always looking in the mirror and being really...weird."

"So what are you saying?" Scotty asked.

"I'm saying, I'm not in any hurry to get weird. There will be plenty of time when I'm older to worry about girls and dating and how my hair looks." They laughed. "No sense growing up now, most grownups I know wish they could be kids again. So I say, let's enjoy being kids.

"Sounds cool," Scotty said.

"Besides," Mark added, "we're two good looking guys. Let's break their hearts making them wait."

"Yeah, awesome!" Scotty said and they fist bumped.

"Let's make a pact," Mark said.

"Like, no girlfriends until we're...fourteen." Scotty said proudly.

"How about sixteen?" Mark asked.

"Sixteen? Scotty's eyes got big. "That's forever!"

"Only four years, and just think, you'll be saving yourself from four years of jealous fits like you just had when I got home."

Scotty thought for a second. "Okay, Mr. McGee," he held out his hand to shake, "you have a deal...no girlfriends until we're sixteen." They shook.

"No matter how much they beg," Mark added and they laughed.

They stood to go in, "Dude," Scotty said "it's like a weight has been lifted from me."

They walked into the living room where Mark's mom and Bethany were watching cartoons. "Hey boys!" his mom said. "Mark, don't forget your Sunday chores."

"Yes ma'am," he replied, then to Scotty, "I'll be right back." He went into the kitchen to take out the trash and load the dishwasher.

Scotty sat down in the living room.

"How are you doing, Scotty? Mark's mom asked.

"Much better, thanks. Mark and I made a pact to not have a girlfriend until we're sixteen."

"And you're happy about that?" She asked.

"Yes ma'am," he replied. "Girls really stress me out. Mark's idea was amazing."

"Did you say it was Mark's idea?"

He nodded, "Oh yeah."

"Mark sweetie!?" She called him but got up to meet him at the kitchen entrance.

"Yes ma'am?"

"I'll finish your chores for you, you and Scotty go have fun." She kissed him on the cheek. He was thoroughly confused. She smiled and whispered, "All those no girl-friend talks I had with you are paying off I see...I'm proud of you."

"Oh," he grinned, "don't tell Scotty it was your idea, he thinks I'm a genius."

"Well, I know you're a genius, now go have fun."

CHAPTER FOUR

SWEET REVENGE

Mark and Scotty had discussed going to the gate of the castle. They would just go up and hit the buzzer and see what happened. "We won't know if we don't ask." Mark had said.

The next morning, they met up at the park in front of the neighborhood and headed out.

"Did you tell Gabi?" Mark asked Scotty.

"Are you crazy?" Scotty replied, "I'd rather tell my parents than her." They laughed.

They were scooting along pretty good on their skateboards when someone yelled Scotty's name. They turned to look and saw three older boys on bicycles coming up pretty fast.

"Aw man," Scotty mumbled. "Not now."

"Who is it?" Mark asked.

Before Scotty could answer, they'd caught up.

"Didn't you hear me call you, Morgan?" The bigger one said.

"Sorry Todd, we're in a hurry," Scotty replied.

They rode along beside them, "who's this, your new girlfriend, Scotty?" He cut in front of Scotty with his bike, causing Scotty to have to bail. The other two guys crowded Mark, causing him to stop.

"Come on guys!" Mark said. "First time on a bicycle?"

The big guy was about to say something when Scotty jumped in. "Hey Todd, this is Mark, he just moved into the neighborhood."

Todd grinned as he sized Mark up. Mark wasn't sure why though, the guy was at least sixteen or seventeen. What threat could Mark possible be to him? He was clearly a bully and attempting to impress his friends.

"Mark," Scotty said, "This is Todd Johnson."

"The king of Gateway," Todd finished and he and his friends laughed. "How old are you Mark?"

"Twelve," Mark said, watching the other two as they pressed in closer, still on their bikes. "Why, are you the census taker?" He looked at Scotty who looked like he was about to lose his breakfast.

"You think you're funny?" Todd asked and they stared each other down. Finally, Todd laughed. "I'm just messing with you guys. This here's Eddie." He motioned to the shorter one. He had blonde greasy hair. He was trying to look tougher than he actually was. He looked a year or two older than Mark. "That's Andy." Andy was Spanish looking, bigger than Eddie but smaller than Todd. Todd was big. Maybe six foot, and well built. He definitely had the look of a troublemaker, with scars on his arms, neck and face. Mark guessed that Todd's dad was probably pretty rough with him.

"So...where did you come from Mark?" Todd asked.

"Pittsburgh," Mark answered, trying to keep it short. He wanted to end this interruption as soon as possible.

"That's up north, ain't it?" Todd said.

"Yeah, it's up north." He tried not to make it sound like he thought Todd was ignorant, "In Pennsylvania."

"I know it's in Pennsylvania, I'm not stupid," Todd said, "Boys, do you know what this means?" He looked toward Eddie and Andy. "We got us a Yankee." They all laughed, except Mark and Scotty.

"Yeah," Andy said, "a Yankee boy!"

Todd laughed even louder, "I like it, Yankee Boy!" They were really cracking themselves up.

"Um..." Mark said, "The war's kinda over guys... I've come in peace."

They stopped laughing, Todd stood up and Mark realized he was much taller than he'd thought. "The war ain't over until I say it's over... Yankee Boy."

Eddie snickered, "Yeah."

"Come on, Todd," Scotty said, trying to break the sudden tension. "We need to go, my mom asked us to run an errand."

"Yeah, I'm sure you and Yankee Boy got important business to attend to." Todd replied. He looked Mark over. "That's a nice board Yankee Boy, let me see it."

"My name's Mark and you can see it from there."

"Well, your new name is Yankee Boy," Andy said, "And you don't want us as your enemies."

"And you don't want me as your enemy, either," Mark said, "Now have a nice day, gentlemen." Mark got on his board and attempted to go around Eddie, who was blocking his way. Eddie moved his bike back to keep Mark from getting away.

"I don't think so, Yankee Boy!" He laughed a cackle of a laugh.

"With that laugh how about I call you Hyena Boy? Now get out of my way!" Mark tried to shove his bike.

Eddie shoved Mark back, "Hey! Don't touch my bike!"

Before anyone knew what happened, Mark had leapt off his board and onto Eddie, knocking Eddie off his bike and onto the ground. He'd had enough. Mark had dealt with bullies before. They only understood violence. Mark straddled Eddie's stomach, holding his chest down with one hand and pounding him in the face with the other. Eddie tried to block his punches and push him off but Mark was a wild man, screaming and swinging. The next thing he knew, Todd had grabbed him and picked him up and threw him into the grass. Todd was laughing.

"Wow Eddie, Yankee Boy cleaned your clock." He laughed, helping Eddie up. Eddie's nose was bleeding.

"He got the jump on me Todd, I can take that punk!" He was practically crying.

"Maybe next time," Todd said, holding Eddie back as Mark stood up. "This time you're just an embarrassment."

"You're not so tough when you can't hide behind your boyfriend, are you?" Mark said, taunting Eddie.

"Anytime, punk!" Eddie's face was red and swollen. He was furious.

Scotty stood next to Mark, dumbfounded, yet ready to help if needed.

"Dude, your bike got banged up!" Andy said, pointing to Eddie's bike. The seat was turned and it was scratched from hitting the road.

"What??" Eddie shouted, "You're paying for this, Yankee Boy!"

"Yeah okay!" Mark said. "Have your lawyer call mine, genius!"

Todd picked up Mark's skateboard. "Well, how about I hold onto this until you pay him? Twenty dollars should cover it."

"That stupid bike ain't worth five dollars!" Mark said, trying to take the board from Todd.

Eddie laughed at Mark's failed attempt to reach the board from over Todd's head. "Is the baby gonna cry?"

"You shut up!" Mark said, turning on Eddie and causing him to jump back.

"Twenty bucks, Yankee Boy!" Todd said, climbing on his bike and motioning to Andy and Eddie that it was time to go.

"Come on Todd!" Scotty said, "Give him his board!"

"Gladly," Todd smiled, "When he pays." They rode off laughing.

"Later, Yankee Boy!" Eddie said.

"Run away with your tail between your legs, Hyena Boy!" Mark responded, he was furious. He turned to Scotty, "Dude, he took my board!"

"It's cool man, we'll get it back."

"I'm not paying him one red cent!" Mark spat.

"Come on, let's just head back home," Scotty said. "No sense going to the gate now." Scotty picked up his board and together they walked back to their neighborhood. Mark was deep in thought the whole way.

They stopped at the park. Scotty sat on a bench. Mark paced. "It is so on." He said.

"Dude, can't you just pay them and be done with it? I'll pay them!"

"No, then you'll be paying them for the rest of your life. They'll never stop doing stuff like this. You have to fight guys like this head on."

"Well, we can't exactly fight Todd Johnson," Scotty exclaimed. "The guy's a beast!"

"I don't plan on fighting him," Mark said. "At least not with fists. As you know, there's more than one way to drop in a half pipe."

"So, how do you plan to fight him then?"

"With my brain," Mark said with a grin. "He clearly doesn't have one. Do you know where they live?"

"Yes, but why? What are you planning Mark?" Scotty was clearly distressed.

"Revenge," Mark replied, "beautiful, sweet revenge."

For the moment, Mark forgot about the castle, the dragon, the boy, Old Man Willoughby, and the mission completely. He had one thing on his mind...revenge... he could practically taste it. His friend Jason in Pittsburg had been jumped by four boys. He was in the fifth grade and they were older, they'd knocked him down, kicked him, ripped his shirt, taken his money and his Gameboy. Jason hadn't fought back or even cried. He did, however, get them back. He'd gone after them one at a time. He'd found something that each of them cherished and destroyed it. Mark still remembered it well, an expensive guitar busted up, a shattered laptop, a split skateboard and a cut up football that was autographed by the 2006 super bowl champion Pittsburg Steeler's team. Jason was suspected but never caught. His revenge had been so sweet. Yeah, Mark was going to enjoy this. Todd, Andy and Eddie would regret the day they'd messed with Mark McGee.

The next night, Mark lay in bed, waiting for his parents to go to sleep. He had his plan. Scotty had shown him where each boy lived. Under his covers, he was fully dressed. All black from head to toe, once he put his ski mask on. He had made sure the back door was unlocked, so that would be one less sound to make when he left.

At exactly midnight he slid out of bed. He grabbed his backpack from his closet and slipped out of his room. He crept quietly down the hall and stairs, thankful that they were carpeted, otherwise he would've made too much noise with his boots. He was in the kitchen and out the door in no time. He had stashed Bethany's pink bicycle on the side of the house, since he had no skateboard. He truly hoped nobody saw him, he'd be more embarrassed about being seen on a pink bicycle than being caught doing what he was about to do.

None of the guys lived in his neighborhood but thankfully they didn't live too far away from it either. He pulled up to Eddie's house first. They hadn't seen a dog when they walked by earlier. Mark parked his bike in the woods next to Eddie's house. He put his mask on, got out the tools he'd need and walked cautiously across his yard. Eddie's bicycle was leaning against the fence that divided the front yard and the back yard. It was chained to the fence but that would not affect what Mark had planned for it. Luckily, it was on the garage side of the house, and nobody would hear him. He went to work with his tools. Fifteen minutes later, the frame of Eddie's bike hung from the fence. Mark had removed everything detachable. He put all the parts he could in his back pack and tossed the rest into the woods. He grabbed his bike and got out of there.

Within minutes he was entering the trailer park where Andy lived. This one would be the toughest because he would be easily heard through the thin walls of the trailers. He lived in trailer number thirty-seven. He cruised past it once, making sure there were no lights on. Everything looked good. He parked his bike in the playground and walked over. Andy's bike was stashed underneath the trailer with a ton of toys and lawn equipment. He had to be fast and quiet. Their neighbors were close and all it would take was one person to catch him. Mark got the bike and walked it back to the playground. He had something special for Andy. He slipped off his back pack and pulled out the can of pink spray paint. His stepdad had bought extra since Bethany wanted everything to be pink. He smiled as he worked. Boy had they messed with the wrong guy. He painted everything pink, even the tires. When he finished, he waited for it to dry. It was glorious. He slid his gloves on and walked it back to where he'd found it. He ran back to his bike and headed for Todd's house. Two down, one to go.

Mark couldn't help but laugh as he approached Todd's driveway. Everything was going so good. He couldn't wait to see these guys' faces tomorrow.

He hid his bike in the woods. Todd had a long driveway, it went back into the woods. Scotty had told him that Todd definitely had dogs, big mean ones. Mark was prepared. He reached into his pack and pulled out the three raw pieces of meat he hoped his mother wouldn't notice were gone. He slid his pack back on and headed quietly down the long dark driveway. It was so dark, he couldn't use a flashlight, he would surely be seen. He had to use the light of the moon alone and tonight that wasn't very bright. The mosquitos were really bad as well, they were buzzing all around him, biting him through his clothes. As if the miserable heat wasn't enough. Maybe he'd been positive too soon.

Then, to make matters worse, he heard the growling dogs running towards him. They sounded big too. He tensed and unwrapped the meat as three large dogs approached him. They began barking. "Shush, shush. Good doggies," he whispered, and tossed one of the pieces of meat. They fought for it and one of them grabbed it and ran, the other two turned back to him. He tossed one to each of them. They were gone. He'd need to work fast.

He hurried up the driveway. His eyes were beginning to adjust to the darkness. As he approached the yard, he noticed that it was very cluttered. Junk cars and appliances strewn about like last week's laundry. Across the yard and on the opposite side of the driveway from the house was his target. An old shed. He headed for it and in his haste, he tripped over half of a motorcycle. He could tell his leg was cut but he had to hurry, no time for pain.

It was an old shed with rusty sliding doors. It would probably make a lot of noise. Mark pulled out a can of WD-40 and sprayed it on the rollers. Slowly he opened the doors. Once he could fit inside he stepped in. Now he could use his flashlight. He pulled it out and clicked it on. Mostly lawn equipment and old boxes. There it was, in the corner, exactly what he was looking for. He made his way back to it and picked up his skateboard, smiling. "Oh Todd, you sneaky devil, you have bullied the wrong guy." He set the board back down, did what he'd come to do and left it there. As he turned to leave, he heard the dogs coming. They were snorting and growling. He stepped out cautiously and closed the doors. He slipped his pack back on and faced them. They stood in front of him, their little nubs of tails wagging. "Hey guys, sorry, I'm all out of meat," he held out his hand and they each licked it. He gently walked past them and down the driveway. They walked with him all the way to the road, where he shooed them back. He hopped on his bike and high tailed it home. "Oh yes", he thought aloud, "revenge is sweet."

Mark set his alarm to get him up early. As soon as it went off he got up and went downstairs to the phone. He called Matt's house.

Matt answered, sounding groggy. "Hello?"

"Matt? Hey, it's Mark."

"Mark? What's up man?" He replied.

"Hey, sorry to call so early, I was hoping to catch your dad before he went to work."

"Yeah, he's here, hold on." He heard Matt set the phone down and holler for his dad.

A moment later, "Hello, this is Officer Ramsey."

"Yes Mr. Ramsey, this is Mark McGee, I'm a friend of Matt's."

"Okay, what can I do for you Mark? Talk fast, I need to get out the door."

"Well sir, that's why I called you," Mark said. "What I have to tell you is work related."

Thirty minutes later, Mark was getting out of a police car at Todd Johnson's house. The dogs were now chained up. There was one other police car already there. Apparently a slow morning for Gateway's finest. Officer Ramsey told Mark to hang back. Todd and a man Mark assumed was either Todd's dad or stepdad were standing on the porch talking to the other officers. Then Mark noticed a third officer coming out of the shed holding several items. He and Officer Ramsey were discussing something.

"Is this your skateboard Mark?" Officer Ramsey asked him, holding up Mark's board.

"Yes sir, my name is on the bottom!" Mark replied. Todd was glaring at him.

The other officer turned it over and they both nodded.

"Mr. Bernat, could you step over here please?" Officer Ramsey called to the man on the porch, who was obviously Todd's stepdad.

Mr. Bernat was a large man with an even larger belly. He walked across his yard in only a pair of jeans. He did not look happy.

Officer Ramsey shook his hand and introduced himself. "Good morning, Sir."

"You can't just go rooting through a man's shed," Mr. Bernat said, "I know my rights."

"Sir, your wife gave us permission before she left for work." The other officer said. "You can feel free to call her."

"Sir," Officer Ramsey said, "we received a call this morning that your stepson, Todd Johnson, might be involved in a theft."

"Boy, get over here!" Mr. Bernat called to Todd angrily.

The other officer walked with him. Mark crept a little closer.

"What'd he take?" Mr. Bernat asked.

Mark McGee And The Gateway To God

"The phone call was in regard to this skateboard, which I just found in the back of your shed, sir." The other officer said.

"I told you!" Todd said, "Mark let me borrow the skateboard? Why are you lying Yankee Boy?"

Mark showed his most innocent face.

"You don't even skateboard!" Mr. Bernat said, he raised his hand to smack Todd but thought better of it with the police there. "How dare you do something to bring the police to my house?" He was spitting mad.

"Sir, we also received a couple of other calls this morning," Officer Ramsey continued. "Which, until now, we thought were unrelated."

"There's more?!" He gave Todd a death look.

"Yes sir, we received a complaint that somebody painted a bicycle pink and stole parts off another bike. What I have here," he showed Mr. Bernat that the other officer held a can of pink spray paint and several bike parts they'd just found in the shed, "is evidence that Todd may be involved with this as well?"

"What?" Todd said. "I don't know anything about that! Hold on!" Todd said. "Where did that junk come from?"

The officer nodded toward the shed.

"No way!" Todd said. "I've been set up!"

"Sir, we're going to need to take your son in for questioning," Officer Ramsey said. The other officer handcuffed Todd and read him his rights.

"Take him!" His stepdad said. "If he stays here, I'll half kill him!" He walked back toward his house. "And shut that shed back up!" He yelled over his shoulder.

Mark smiled and winked at Todd as they led him past.

"You!" Todd yelled. "You did this?" You little weasel, he set me up!" He began squirming as they put him in the car.

"I'm going to need to hold onto your skateboard, Mark," Officer Ramsey said." For now, its evidence."

"Yes sir."

"Climb back in my car, I'll take you home."

He waved bye to Todd as they left. Brains had defeated brawn. He couldn't stop smiling. Revenge was so sweet.

As they drove down the driveway, Mark saw a little girl in a light blue frilly dress standing at the edge of the forest. She waved at him. He waved back.

"Who are you waving at?" Officer Ramsey asked.

"You didn't see that little girl?"

"No, I must've missed her."

Mark looked back and she was gone.

CHAPTER FIVE

BEYOND THE GATE

Within fifteen minutes of Officer Ramsey dropping Mark off at his house, Scotty called him. News had already spread about Todd being arrested.

"Dude!" Scotty exclaimed, "what did you do?"

"Well, it appears that Todd was quite busy in the night," Mark replied. "He apparently dismantled Eddie's bicycle and painted Andy's a pretty color of pink." Mark laughed.

"Pink huh?" Scotty asked. "I wonder where Todd got pink spray paint." He laughed.

"Unsolved mysteries my friend." They both laughed.

"Remind me to never get on your bad side," Scotty said.

"Just remember, dude!" Mark said. "You can never tell anyone about this...and I mean anyone!"

"You mean other than Gabi?" Scotty teased.

"Especially not Gabi!"

Scotty laughed, "my lips are sealed."

"Hey!" Mark had a thought, "We still need to go to the castle, what's better for you, today or tomorrow?"

"Neither," Scotty said. "We're visiting family in North Carolina for five days. We leave in the morning but my mom says I have to pack and clean my room today."

"I've seen your room Scotty, that's at least a two-day job." They laughed.

"Sorry man, looks like you'll have to take Matt or Billy." Scotty said, "Well, gotta go."

No sooner did Mark hang up the phone than his doorbell rang. Mark ran to answer it.

"We need to talk, Mark McGee!" Gabi said, stepping in.

"Huh? About what?"

"I think you know," she said, clearly mad.

"Hold on," Mark said, not prepared for this. "Let's talk out on the front porch." They stepped outside.

"I heard about Todd Johnson and I know you had something to do with that." She gave him a death stare.

"Wh...why do you think I had something to do with it? I'm the victim here!" He got defensive.

"I know Todd Johnson is not the brightest bulb on the tree, but even he wouldn't vandalize his two best friend's bicycles!" She walked over and sat on the bench on their front porch. "Now spill it."

"Spill what, Gabi!?" He tried to sound exasperated, "What are you talking about?"

"You set him up, didn't you?" She asked, giving him a guilty look.

"How did I do that Gabi? Are you saying I vandalized their bikes?" He was really sounding innocent.

"I know you have access to pink spray paint, and you're quite crafty."

"Well thank you very much, but I can't believe you would accuse me of vandalism."

She stood back up and faced him eye to eye. "Look me in the eyes and tell me you didn't do it."

"I didn't do it!" It scared him how easily he could lie.

She sat back down. "Okay, it's between you and God if you did."

"Well, I didn't." He sat next to her.

"Good, because revenge belongs to God, you know."

Mark looked away. If there was really a God, he was in big trouble with him over more than revenge at this point.

"If somebody does you wrong, God will deal with them. So, don't you go playing God!" She said, poking him on the arm.

"Well," Mark said, looking down, "apparently God did deal with him. Todd was arrested and I have my board." That seemed to settle it with Gabi, even though he felt she knew he was lying through his teeth.

"So," she said, "with Scotty out of town for a few days, when do you want to go to the castle?"

"What?" He was shocked, "You know about that?"

"You think Scotty Morgan can keep secrets from me?" She asked. "It's better to take me anyway."

"And why's that?" Mark asked.

"Let's face it, you and Scotty couldn't even handle a few bullies, what are you going to do when you face real trouble, beyond the gate?"

"That reminds me," Mark had forgotten to mention a detail of what the boy had said in his dream. "That dream I mentioned about the boy in my room?"

"Yeah?"

"Well, he said something as he was leaving, right after he told me to go to the castle."

"Okay, what?" Gabi asked, turning to face him.

"He said, "Don't bring the girl."

"What girl?"

Mark shrugged. "Do you think it was you?

"I don't know, it was your dream," she said, trying to act like it wasn't important.

"You don't think there's any significance to it?"

"No, and until we learn more, I'm just going to assume it was nothing more than a dream."

"So how does tomorrow morning sound to you?"

"Come by around nine." She stood to go.

"Oh," Mark said before she could leave, "there's something else I wanted to tell you."

She turned back at the top of the steps. "Okay, what?"

"Scotty and I have made a pact not to have girlfriends until we're sixteen." He let that sink in. "Anyway, I just wanted to let you know in case you were thinking about... you know."

"Thinking about what?"

"Being my girlfriend." There, he'd said it. To his surprise, she burst into a laughing fit. "What?" he asked, totally embarrassed now. "Why is that funny?"

"Oh," she said, trying to stop laughing, "I'm sorry... were you serious?"

"About the pact?"

"No, about me wanting to be your girlfriend?"

"Oh...no, I was kidding."

"Good, because my parents instilled into me when I was eight years old that I didn't need a boyfriend. The whole reason for dating is to find a spouse and I'm sure not looking for one of those anytime soon."

"Okay cool, that's a good plan too." Why did he have to open his big mouth?

She turned to leave, "thinking about being your girlfriend, Mark McGee? HA! I have better things to think about thank you very much!"

"Yeah, whatever!" He said jokingly. "You know you think of nothing else!"

"Except maybe throwing up!" she said as she got on her bike.

"Wow! Pleasant thought!" He waved goodbye, "I love you too!"

"Goodbye, Mark!" She waved, "See you in the morning!" She rode away.

"What a strange girl." Mark said to himself.

He spent the rest of that day doing yardwork with his mom and then after showering and eating dinner, he went to his room to play video games.

Now, he lay in bed, pondering all that had happened since he'd been in Gateway. It had definitely not been boring. He'd made good friends. He was investigating a really cool mystery. He had dealt with a bully, quite successfully. He'd even gone to church, which hadn't been as bad as he'd thought it would. He may not be sure about all that God stuff, but the service hadn't been horrible. The people were very nice. Then there were dreams. He wasn't sure what to make of them. Before moving to Gateway he'd never had dreams that felt so real. This was definitely a different place. He wasn't certain if he liked it here or not yet but it absolutely was not the boring hick town he'd expected. Maybe once school started, things would get normal. Mark remembered normal. Barely.

His mother poked her head in to check on him. "Mark?" She whispered in case he was asleep.

"I'm awake," he said.

She came in and kissed him. "Good night, sweetie," She said. "Sweet dreams."

"Good night mom," he said. "When are we going to the beach?"

"Maybe we can go one day this week," she responded, "I think we could all use a nice day in the Florida sun. See if Scotty would like to join us."

"He's out of town for a while, so he can't."

"Okay, well good night." She closed the door as she left.

Mark lay there for a while realizing he wasn't very sleepy, so he got up and played video games. After about an hour of blowing the heads off zombies, he started getting tired. He shut his game off and sat there for a few minutes trying to build up his desire to get up. Finally, after nodding off twice, he got up, turned around and froze.

There, standing in the center of his room, was the dragon. It took up a large portion of his room. Mark was frightened beyond words. Its skin was shiny black, glistening as if it were wet. Its eyes were a deep dark red, they reminded him of cat eyes. It seemed to be looking right into Mark's soul. Mark didn't know what to do. It brought its face to within inches of Mark's. The dragon's breath was foul. "Hello, Mark McGee," it said in its deep resonating voice. "We meet again."

"Whh..." Mark cleared his throat and tried to sound brave. "What do you want?"

"You, Mark," it laughed. "I want you."

"Wh why do you want me?" Mark asked. "I'm nobody special."

"Oh, yes you are, Mark McGee. I've been waiting for you for a long time."

"What? Why?" Mark was thoroughly confused.

"I have all the answers to all the mysteries, Mark McGee."

"Mysteries? What mysteries? The castle?"

"Yes." The dragon backed away and smiled. "The castle. The forest. The gardener. The battle. The gateway."

"The gateway? What about the gateway, and what battle?" He was still cautious but not scared.

"Soon, Mark McGee, soon you will know." The dragon began to fade away, slowly disappearing.

"No, wait! Don't go!"

"Soon." He was gone.

Mark stood there staring at the empty room. A battle? The gateway? Was he dreaming? "Pinch yourself Mark." He said aloud. As he reached to do it there was loud crash downstairs. It sounded as if a tree had fallen on the house. He darted from his room and ran downstairs expecting to be joined by his parents. They didn't come. "Where are you guys at?!" Mark yelled. "You need to come see this!" The entire front wall of the living room was blown out, as if something big had gone through it. "Mom!?" He ran back to the stairs and called up.

Just then there was a scream from outside. A girl. Mark turned and ran into the front yard. Another scream of terror. He saw the dragon in the street, walking away with what looked like a child in its mouth. A child that was kicking and screaming. It was...Bethany!

"Bethany! No!" Mark tried to run but his feet were sinking in the grass. He was barely moving as the dragon got away with his sister in its mouth. "Bethany! Wait! No! Bethany!"

Someone grabbed him and shook him. "Mark!? Mark! Wake up!" It was his step dad shaking him. He jumped up out of his game chair looking around. He was soaking wet with sweat. "Whoa, buddy!" His step dad grabbed his arms. "It's okay."

"I... What?" It was all Mark could manage, as he panted.

"You were screaming Bethany's name." His step dad said, stepping back. "You scared your mother and me to death."

"Is Bethany okay?" Mark asked.

"Yes, oddly enough, she woke up screaming your name."

His mother came in holding a soaking wet Bethany. "Bad dream," His mother said.

"Are you okay, Bethany?" Mark asked, "What did you dream?"

Bethany's face was buried in her mommy's neck.

"Mark, not now." His mother said.

"It was a dragon," Bethany said, between sobs. "He was eating Mark. I couldn't stop him!" She buried her head again.

"It's okay baby," her mother said, patting her back. "Mark is right here." She left the room. "You can sleep with us, okay."

"So," his step dad said, "what was your dream about?"

"I," if he told the truth, he and Bethany would probably be locked away for people to study. "I don't remember."

"Ok well, get some sleep, and I told you those violent games would give you nightmares."

"Yes, sir." He didn't argue.

"We'll discuss it tomorrow."

"Okay, good night, sorry." Mark said.

"Good night... and sweet dreams," his step dad said.

Mark sat on the edge of his bed. How crazy was that? Him and his sister each dreaming of the other being eaten by the dragon. What was going on? Things just kept getting stranger. Mark left his light on. He was suddenly afraid to go to sleep.

After a couple of hours of tossing and turning, Mark had finally fallen asleep. Thankfully, he hadn't had any more dragon dreams. Having forgotten to set his alarm, he'd awoken just in time to shower, dress and get to Gabi's by nine.

As he sat in her living room waiting for her to get ready, her sister Abi was talking his ears off. He was getting all the latest gossip on everyone in the neighborhood.

Her mom, pregnant and waddling around the kitchen, was preparing breakfast. She tried to convince Mark and Gabi to eat, but Mark was too nervous to think about food. Gabi slathered jelly on a piece of toast, kissed her mom, and they headed out.

She grabbed her bike as Mark rode Scotty's skateboard to the end of the driveway.

"Hold on, Mark," She said as she approached.

"What's up? He asked.

"I think we should pray."

"Okay," Mark replied, unsure of what to do next.

"So, you're okay with that?" She asked.

"I may be willing to face down a dragon today Gabi…
but I'm not saying no to you."

"Ha ha," she said, giving him a gentle shove. "Then
bow your head Mark McGee." He did and she prayed.
"Dear Heavenly Father, I ask that you give Mark and me
favor today. That, first of all, you would protect us from
evil or anything else bad. Secondly, that you would help
us in the investigation of the castle and the mysteries
that surround it. One other thing Father, I pray that you
would open Mark's eyes so that he would see your Son.
In Jesus' name I pray…Amen."

Mark peeked, not sure what to do.

"Say Amen," Gabi said.

"Amen."

She took off on her bike, "Good, now come on,
you're wasting time."

"Yes ma'am," he said jokingly.

On the way, he told her about what had happened last
night. How he and Bethany had both had dreams about
the other being eaten by a dragon.

"That's absolutely crazy," she said when he finished.
"Is Bethany alright?"

"Yeah, she slept with my parents after that," he replied.
"How much further to the gate?"

"Not much," she said. "What exactly do you intend
to do when we get there?"

He shrugged, "we'll see when we get there, but I'm
not leaving without answers."

Ten minutes later they rolled through the entrance that
led to a gate. It was a large circular drive with a big statue
of a dragon in the center. There were two large statues
of knights on either side of the gate. The gate was black

and made of iron. It stood over twelve feet tall and was joined on both sides by the forest. Mark noticed there was no fence. You could easily walk around the gate but you would have to go into the forest to get around it. Maybe the forest was all the protection they needed. It was all quite fascinating, Mark thought, like something out of a movie.

"So, what now?" Gabi asked.

Mark noticed a call box beside one of the knights next to the gate. He walked over to it. There was a keypad and a large red button with a note that read. "Press for deliveries, all others go away." He read it to Gabi. "Fat chance of that." He pressed the button. Nothing happened. Gabi circled the driveway as they waited. He pressed it again. Nothing happened.

"Maybe nobody's home," Gabi said. "What do you want to do?"

So Mark did what any normal twelve years old boy would do. He pressed the button again and again and again and again. Finally, he stopped.

"Who is it!!!" A raspy male voice shouted through the speaker causing Mark to jump back and Gabi to stop her bike. Mark didn't know what to do or say. "I said who is it!!?" This time almost yelling.

"...Um," Mark tried to think, "Mark McGee...sir, I'm Mark McGee and..."

"Press the black button if you're talking for crying out loud!"

Embarrassed, Mark pressed the black button. "I'm Mark McGee, and I'm with my friend Gabi and we need to talk to you, sir."

"Mark McGee, huh?" He asked, a little calmer. "Well Mark McGee, what do you want?"

"We would like to ask you a few questions, sir."

"We?" He asked, sounding irritated, "who did you say was with you?"

"My friend, Gabi."

"Gabi Motes, huh?" He said, "I know her."

Mark looked at Gabi who had a deer in the headlights look. "I didn't tell him your last name."

"I know," Gabi said. "How does he know me?"

"Mark McGee, you may come in and ask me anything you want, but your friend Gabi will have to remain outside the gate.

Mark pressed the button. "I'm sorry sir, but we would prefer to stay together."

Nothing happened.

After several minutes Mark pressed it again. "Sir? Mr. Willoughby?"

To their surprise, the gate opened. When it was fully open, they looked at each other.

"You ready?" Mark asked.

"Let's go." Once inside the gate, they left their bike and skateboard and walked down the long driveway. The gate closed behind them.

The forest bordered both sides of the driveway so they stayed to the center. It seemed to reach for them as they walked.

"So how does he know you?" Mark asked.

"I have no idea," Gabi said. "But that's kind of creepy."

"Everything about this is creepy," Mark said.

"Plus the fact that he didn't want me to come in."

"Maybe he's scared of you like Scotty and I are," Mark teased. She shoved him and he laughed.

"Behave, Mark McGee."

"Can I ask you a question Gabi?" Mark asked. "Are you scared?"

"Why would I be scared?" She asked. "Greater is He that is in me, than he that is in the world."

"What is that supposed to mean?" Mark asked.

"It means, that with Christ in me, I have nothing to fear."

Just then, the castle and the huge yard came into view. They both stopped, mouths open in awe.

"Wow." Mark said.

There were statutes all around the yard. Knights and dragons mostly. A few gargoyles. A huge fountain stood near the bridge that crossed the mote. It was a giant dragon's head that had water pouring from its mouth. The castle was huge. It was made of stone and had a mote circling it. There was a single wooden bridge that led to a massive door.

"This is awesome," Mark said. "Like being in a medieval theme park."

"No theme park I'd want to go to," Gabi said.

"Well," Mark said, as they continued walking toward the bridge, "you're a girl."

"Over here!" The old man called from their right. There was a small shack right at the edge of the forest. He stood in front of it holding a pair of hedge clippers. He was tall with a large barrel chest. Thick but not fat. He had white hair that lay flat on his head. He wore navy blue work clothes that were quite dirty. They approached him cautiously.

"Mark McGee, huh?" He asked. He looked and sounded like somebody from a slasher movie, with his raspy voice and slow speech.

"Yes sir," Mark said. "And this is Gabi. Are you Mr. Willoughby?" He held out his hand.

"I am." He only looked at Mark's hand. "What is it you want?"

"First of all Mr. Willoughby," Gabi said, and he would not look at her. "How did you know my last name?"

"Oh, well," he fidgeted, "small town... not many Gabi's I guess."

"Mr. Willoughby," Mark said, "there's a lot of rumors about the forest around your property."

"I don't know nothin' about no rumors!" He snapped.

"Well, is there any truth to them?" Mark asked.

"If yer talkin about people goin missin', then I guess it could be true," he replied. "But people go missin' all the time, don't they?"

"Yes sir, but it seems that everyone who goes into the forest, is never seen again."

"Well, that ain't true," he said, "I been in there a hundred times, and those rescue workers were in and outta there for days."

"Okay, any children who go in there are never seen again," Mark clarified.

"I don't know," he shrugged. "Might be true, and might not. Rumors ain't usually dependable."

"What about the castle?" Mark asked.

"What about it?"

"Who owns it?" Gabi asked.

"Well that ain't none of ya'lls business." He opened the shack door and set the clippers inside. "I think it's time you left!" He waved his big arm toward the direction of the gate. "I suppose you'll tell people you survived a visit in."

"How old are you, Mr. Willoughby?" Mark asked.

"What kinda question is that?"

"There's people that knew you were an old man fifty years ago." Mark said.

Mr. Willoughby smiled. "They do, do they?"

"Yes sir, is it true?"

"Well son, if I was an old man fifty years ago, don't you reckon I'd be dead now?"

"A normal person would, yes sir, but I'm not certain you're a normal person."

Anger flashed across his face, and Gabi grabbed Mark's arm. "Well what are you sayin' I am if not normal!?!"

"We're sorry, sir," Gabi said. "We'll leave now."

"And don't come back either, little lady! You hear me!?" He spat.

"Leave?" Mark said, "He hasn't answered the first question." Gabi was pulling him back.

"Trust me Mark," she said into his ear. "Let's go."

"How old are you, Mr. Willoughby?!" Mark called over his shoulder as Gabi led him away.

"Old enough boy!" He responded with a sinister laugh.

"What do you know about the other castles?"

"I know you better mind your own business and not stick your nose where it don't belong." He started following them. "Or you could try your luck in my forest." He laughed again.

Gabi pulled Mark along. "What are you doing Gabi?" Mark asked.

"Something isn't right with him, Mark," Gabi said. "Let's just get out of here."

"What do you mean?" Mark looked back. Mr. Willoughby was watching them leave.

"I mean," Gabi said, walking even faster, "I don't think he's human."

Mark gave her a sideways glance to see if she was joking. "What do you think he is? A Martian?"

"Don't be silly." As they reached the gate, it began opening. They grabbed their bike and skateboard and got out to the road as fast as they could, without speaking.

"Well?" Mark asked.

"I think he's a demon," She said.

"You mean, possessed by a demon?" Mark asked. "I've read about people like that."

"I thought that at first, but that wouldn't explain his age. I don't think he's human at all."

Mark let that sink in. "So, when did you realize it? Because you just freaked, I mean, for you."

"Didn't you see his face when he got angry? It was like, he changed."

"He just got mad."

"No Mark!" She said, stopping her bike on the side of the road. He stopped next to her. "For like a second, his eyes, nose, his whole face transformed. I really think." She stopped.

"What?" Mark asked.

"I think my being there stopped him."

"Huh?"

"Think about it. In your dream the boy said don't bring her, and Mr. Willoughby wanted me to wait at the gate. Mark, I think they're afraid of me because I'm a Christian."

"That's crazy."

"Demons are powerful, Mark, but they can't touch God's people. He wouldn't even look at me. Jesus is in me, Mark!"

Mark gave her a look.

"What? I'm serious!" She said. "Think about it! It makes sense."

"Nothing about this makes sense, Gabi!" Mark kicked off, "you're crazy! This whole town is insane!"

CHAPTER SIX

GOD AIN'T WELCOME

M ark had steered clear of Gabi and all his friends for
the rest of the week. Scotty had come by to see him
when he'd gotten back in town but Mark had told him he
didn't feel good. He'd spent his time devising his plan,
tonight was the night. He would sneak out of the house,
enter the forest at a spot he'd seen near the driveway,
go in, get close to the castle, take some pictures, and
see what happened. He might even try to go inside the
castle. He wanted answers and he would get them one
way or the other.

Once again, he wore all black. He had his flashlight, knife and phone. He'd also written a note to put in
Scotty's mailbox, just in case something happened and
he didn't make it out. He outlined his plans in the note.
He also told Scotty to make sure he was dead before he
said anything to Gabi. She'd kill him if she found out.

He'd played video games pretty late and had expected
his mother to tell him goodnight for a while. Was she
still up or had she fallen asleep downstairs? He grabbed
his things and stepped out into the hall. It was all dark
upstairs. He could hear his stepdad snoring. He knew

Bethany was in bed, she'd been sick all week and hardly been out of her room. In fact, she had a doctor's appointment the next day. So where was mom? He crept downstairs. He could see that a lamp was on in the living room and the TV played quietly. He peered around the corner. His mom was lying on the couch facing the opposite direction. She must be asleep. Either way, he'd have to be dead quiet, for she was a very light sleeper. He passed right behind her quietly and slipped into the kitchen. So far, so good. On his way past the stove, however, he hit the handle of a skillet and it spun off the stove. Mark dove for it and caught it just before it hit the floor. He stood there unmoving. He heard her getting up. He gently set the pan on the floor and slipped into the pantry as she came into the kitchen. She turned on the light. He could see her through the slats in the door. She looked dazed and confused. She picked up the skillet and set it on the stove. She looked around suspiciously. "Hello?" Mark held his breath "Oh well." She turned off the light and went upstairs. Mark had put a pillow under his blankets to look like he was in bed, but he hoped she didn't go in for a kiss. He waited for a few minutes in case she did and freaked out. All was quiet. He slipped out of the pantry and quietly opened the back door.

He made his way to the front yard. He would have to jog this time. As he began to cross the yard, he saw movement out of the corner of his eye. He quickly dropped to the ground and looked in that direction. He didn't see anything but would not have been surprised to see a dragon walking across the yard. This town was that strange. He was about to get up when he heard a twig snap around the side of the house. Somebody or something was in his yard. He crouched low and made his way around the corner. Before heading any further, he stopped and pinched himself, "okay, I'm awake." As he reached the backyard fence he saw someone walking toward their shed. Quietly Mark ran toward them, the element of surprise in his favor. He quickly closed the gap between them and realized they were quite large just before he slammed into their back and tackled them to the ground. They grunted in pain and shock. He'd knocked the wind out of whoever it was. He pressed their head to the ground. "Who are you and why are you in my yard?" Mark asked in a loud whisper.

"Ow, man get off me!" He said, rolling over and throwing Mark off. "What are you doing, Yankee Boy?"

"Todd?" Mark asked. "What are you doing? This is MY yard."

Todd sat up, "I was here to get you back man, you're crazy sneaking up on someone like that."

"Well, if my stepdad had seen you, he'd have shot you." Mark said.

"Wait," Todd noticed Mark in all black, "why are you out? What are you up to?"

"Nothing." Mark stood up. "None of your business."

Todd jumped up and had Mark in a headlock before he could react. "Now tell me Yankee Boy, what are you up to?"

Mark struggled, "Nothing, let me go, Todd."

"Not until you tell me." Todd tightened his lock on Mark's neck. "Now spill it."

"Okay, okay," Mark managed, "I'm going to the castle."

Todd released him, pushing him to the ground. "You're doing what?"

"I said I'm going to the castle."

"Yeah right," Todd said. "Why would you do that? You got a death wish?"

"I want to disprove the rumors." Mark said. "Now, you need to leave."

"Hold on, Yankee Boy, the rumors are true!" Todd said, getting serious now. "My friend Michael disappeared in there."

"Well, don't you want to know what happened to him?" Mark asked.

"He vanished never to be seen again!" Todd said. "No trace of him."

Mark stood up. "Well Todd, if I vanish, you'll have your revenge."

"No way, Yankee Boy!" Todd grabbed his arm. "People tried to blame me for daring Michael, I'm not letting you go."

"Nobody will blame you if I disappear, unless you tell them you knew."

"I'm going with you." Todd said.

"What? No way," Mark replied. "Go home Todd."

"So help me, Yankee Boy, I'll wake up everybody in your house." Todd said and Mark knew he would.

"Okay, you can go," Mark said. "But... my name is Mark."

"Fair enough," Todd said, shaking his hand. "What's the plan?"

"Just keep up," Mark said and turned and ran from his yard. Todd followed.

As they ran from the neighborhood, Todd said, "You know, nobody's going to believe us, right? I mean, if we make it out alive."

"Sure they will," Mark said, "I brought my phone, pictures dude." He patted his jacket where it was in the inside pocket.

"Sweet," Todd panted. "Did you happen to bring a gun?"

"Knife," Mark said, as they ran toward the driveway of the castle.

"You think you're pretty brave, don't you, Yankee Boy!?" Todd asked. "I mean, Mark."

"Not really, why, are you scared?"

"I'm scared of watching you die."

"Well don't be, just worry about yourself," Mark said. "And it's not too late to back out."

"No way, if you're going in, I'm going in. I'm not afraid of anything."

"Are you sure?" Mark asked. "I won't tell anybody if you're scared."

"Because you'll be dead." Todd said, "Face it, you need me in there McGee."

"Whatever." Mark said, slowing up as they approached the spot where he wanted to go in. Todd stayed on the road as Mark walked to the edge of the forest and took out his flashlight. "Coming?"

"Lead the way," Todd said, and in they went. It wasn't very thick at first, but after about twenty feet in, they were having to push through the heavy brush. "Dude, this is crazy. What are you trying to prove?"

"I'm proving that there's nothing to fear in this forest."

"And what if there is?" Todd asked.

"Then, we'll know for sure." Mark didn't want to think about that right now.

It was really thick and they were moving super slow. Mark was getting cut up from the thorns and branches.

"Man!" Todd exclaimed. "This is stupid!"

"Stupid isn't a nice word." Mark mumbled.

"What??" Todd asked. "Why did I follow you in here? I shoulda just let you die. I could be in my bed right now."

Mark stopped and faced him. "You can leave any-time, Todd, nobody is forcing you to come."

"And give you the satisfaction? I don't think so."

"Well, it shouldn't be much further," Mark said. "Come on."

After a few minutes of being scratched by branches, tripping over vines and swatting bugs, Todd finally asked, "So if something happens to us, who's gonna know? Did you think of that genius?

"Actually, I did," Mark said. "I wrote a letter for Scotty and..." Mark felt his back pocket. "No!!" he yelled.

"Nice McGee!" Todd said. "Now nobody will even know where to look for us!"

"Well, you kinda threw me off my plan, I was going to put it in his mailbox. Then I ran into you, and forgot about it."

"Sure, blame me."

"Wait, now you HAVE to go back." Mark said. "That way if something happens to me you will know where I was."

"Nice try, McGee," Todd said. "I'm not letting you be the hero. If this legend is going to be put to rest, I'm going to be part of it."

"Suit yourself, just don't blame me when they never find our bodies."

They made their way through the thick brush for another twenty minutes before coming to a clearing.

"Is this it?" Todd asked way too loud.

"Yeah, this is the point where you need to be quieter," Mark whispered. He turned off his flashlight. It was really dark. They let their eyes adjust to the darkness.

"So what's the plan? Todd asked.

"First, we make our way to the castle and check it out, get a few pics."

"Sounds good, lead the way."

They started walking, glad to be free of the forest.

"Whoa," Todd startled. "What is that?"

"Relax tough guy, it's just a statue."

"It's huge, is that a dragon?"

"Yeah, wait until it visits your bedroom, then call me."

"Hey, there's a bunch of them. They're everywhere."

"Yeah, knights, dragons, gargoyles and the fountain with the huge dragon head is pretty sweet."

"Almost like an army of statues," Todd said, "Kind of creepy."

They walked through a garden, with it's labyrinth of bushes, trees and statues. They came to the fountain.

"I need a quick rest," Todd said, sitting on the edge of the fountain.

"Only for a second," Mark replied. "I don't want old man Willoughby finding us."

"Now that's a scary guy."

"Gabi doesn't think he's human.'

"Now that's a scary girl."

Mark smiled, "Definitely different."

"I pushed Scotty in the creek one time, and she came after me. Dude, I'm not afraid of any guy, but that look she gave me. I almost peed myself."

Mark laughed. "Yeah, super scary, we better get going." They walked on a little further, to the driveway he and Gabi had come in on. He crouched down behind a bush and motioned for Todd to join him.

"What is it?! Todd whispered.

"Over there," Mark pointed toward the old shack, "is where old man Willoughby stays. We want to steer clear of that shack."

They stayed behind the bushes, crouching as they walked toward the castle. They came out and quickly ran across the bridge. Todd was about to hide behind some more bushes when Mark told him to hold on.

"Let's take a selfie with the castle behind us." They posed, smiled, and Mark clicked. They then ducked behind the bushes and Mark checked the picture. He gasped loudly.

"Dude, what?" Todd asked, looking at the picture. "Whoa!" They both peeked over the hedges. Nobody was there. They looked back at the screen. Behind them, standing about ten feet away was Lucius Willoughby.

"Where is he?" Mark asked, quite frantic.

"We need to get out of here, McGee," Todd said, "and I mean now."

"But where did he go?" Mark asked.

"I don't care, this ain't fun no more."

"Hold on, let's think about this," Mark exclaimed as Todd began pulling him back in the direction they'd come.

"What's there to think about, McGee?" Todd said, clearly set. "I'm not one of those stupid people in scary movies that keeps going toward the haunted house."

"But he's not here!" Mark whispered loudly, trying to pry his arm free from Todd's grip.

Todd stopped and faced him, "Well, how do you explain that picture? He was right behind us!"

"I don't know," Mark pulled away from him, "but I'm not leaving. I'm seeing this through. Feel free to leave though."

"You're crazy McGee!" Todd said, looking around, a scared look in his eyes. "People die here!"

"We don't know that," Mark said, "Just go, I'll be fine. I have to solve this."

"Who are you?" Todd asked. "Nancy Drew? Live with the mystery for crying out loud, everybody else does. Let's go!" Todd was starting to freak out.

They heard a noise and ducked behind the bushes. Someone was coming. They could hear footsteps on the stone walkway. They stopped.

"I know you're here." It was old man Willoughby. "You ought not to be."

Todd looked like he might pass out. "Dude, let's run."

"You're on private property, uninvited. Show yourselves now, or I'll...unleash my pets." Old man Willoughby had an evil sounding laugh.

Todd grabbed Mark's arm with a death grip.

Old man Willoughby began to walk away. "I'm just glad for one thing." He yelled with his evil laugh. He was getting further away.

"Run!" Todd whispered loudly and they turned to run. They both gasped and fell backwards onto their rears.

Lucius Willoughby stood right there, towering over them with his hands on his hips, smiling.

"I'm just glad you didn't bring that girl!" He laughed again a laugh that seemed to come from within the earth.

"What girl, sir?" Todd asked.

"Gabi?" Mark asked.

"Gabi?" Todd asked, confused. "Is he afraid of her too?"

"Get up," Lucius said.

They obeyed.

"Um, listen sir, we're real sorry," Todd said. "We're just goofin around. We didn't mean any harm. We'll just go."

"You ain't goin nowhere boy....'cept where I tell you," Lucius said. "Now turn around and walk." He pushed them through the bushes onto the driveway. "You wanna see that castle? I'm gonna show it to ya." Another laugh as he pushed them toward the door. "And this time, she ain't here to stop me."

"Gabi?" Mark asked, looking back at him. "Are you talking about Gabi? How could she stop you from doing anything?"

"Shut up and walk!" Lucius yelled.

The two huge doors began to open.

"Oh God!" Todd said, almost in tears. He tried to stop walking but Lucius shoved him forward.

"Where you're going boy!" Lucius laughed, "God ain't welcome."

Gabi awoke with a jolt. "Mark!?" She looked around. She was in her room. She was sweating and breathing heavy. She couldn't remember her dream, but Mark had been in trouble. She knew she had to pray for him. She knelt beside her bed.

"Dear Heavenly Father, I don't understand why I need to pray for Mark right now, but I know I do. Please bless and protect him. He's not a believer...yet. Of course, you know that. I have a strange feeling that he's in danger." (She thought about that). "If he is, please be with him. I pray that your angels would surround him and protect him from the attack of the enemy in his life." Suddenly she felt a peace. "Amen."

She got up and went to the bathroom. When she came out, she walked over to her window. Her room faced the front yard. She saw someone standing in the road in front of her house. It was a boy. He was wearing a suit and he was staring right at her. She blinked and he was gone.

It was in that moment that she knew. Mark had gone to the castle. That's why he'd ignored her calls. That's why he'd been so distant. He'd been planning to go back. Now something was wrong.

Fifteen minutes later, fully dressed, she slipped out her bedroom window. She'd never been one to sneak out or break the rules but she couldn't alert adults yet, not until she was sure. She ran to Scotty's house.

Once at Scotty's, she tapped lightly on his window. Nothing. Again total silence. "Come on Scotty." He'd better not have gone with Mark. She tapped harder. The curtain moved. He looked out and jumped back when he saw her face.

He opened the window quietly. "Gabi? What are doing?" He whispered.

"Get dressed, I think Mark's in trouble."

"What time is it?"

"Does it matter? Come on."

He walked to his dresser. "How do you know he's in trouble?"

"I just do. Meet me at the road." She left him to dress. Five minutes later, he joined her.

"What's going on?"

"We need to see if Mark's home."

"What? Why?"

"Scotty, just trust me."

"We're going to get in trouble."

"You want me to go alone? At night?"

He just stared at her.

"Scotty!"

He snapped out of it. "Ok, let's go." They headed for Mark's house. "Wait, his room is on the second floor."

"I hadn't thought of that," she said. "We'll think of something. Come on, we need to hurry." They ran.

Once there, they hunched down and hurried to his back yard. Scotty located a ladder leaning against the shed. He quietly extended it and set it up against Mark's window. Gabi held it still while he climbed. He knocked on Mark's window and waited. Nothing. Then he noticed that the curtains were slightly open. He peeked in, letting his eyes adjust. Mark's bed appeared to be occupied. He knocked louder. No movement. He checked the window. It wasn't locked. He raised it up. "Mark!?" He whispered loudly. Still no movement. "Dude! Are you alive?" Nothing. Scotty raised the screen and climbed in quietly. He tiptoed over to Mark's bed and shook him. He wasn't there. It was only pillows. Scotty's heart sank. He quickly got out and shut the window. He climbed down and told Gabi. They put the ladder away and headed to the park to think.

"Run for it!" Mark shouted as they approached the door. He went left and Todd went right. Lucius could only chase one. Maybe the other one could bring help. To his surprise, old man Willoughby, just started laughing. That couldn't be good.

Mark crossed the bridge as fast as he could run. Once across, he ran across the yard towards the forest. He saw movement from his right. Was that a statue…moving? He ran faster. Whatever it was, was gaining on him quickly. He looked back. It was one of the knight statues, it was reaching for him. Just then a giant ball of fire shot from the sky and went right through it, knocking it lifeless to the ground. Mark slowed to look and heard Todd scream.

"Todd!" Mark yelled, "I'll get help!"

"No! Let me go! No, please!" He was frantic.

Mark heard something coming toward him. It was a dragon statue. How? Was he losing his mind? He started to run just as another ball of fire shot from the sky. It split the dragon statue in half. Another ball of fire dropped right in front of Mark and turned into a person. A beautiful glowing person.

"Mark!" It shouted. "Run!" It pointed toward the driveway. "Run to the gate!"

Mark obeyed. As he ran, he heard rustling around behind him. There was a fight. More of the light people stood between him and the statues. He ran faster. The gate opened as he approached it. Mark ran toward his neighborhood as fast as he could. He had to get help for Todd.

Gabi and Scotty sat on the swings trying to figure out what to do next. They had prayed as soon as they got to the park.

"I'm going to kill him," Gabi said.

"Let's hope you get the chance."

"He better hope…" She froze. She stood, staring toward the entrance of the neighborhood. Someone was running. "Is that…

"Mark!" Scotty shouted and took off running toward him.

Mark stopped, confused.

"Dude!" Scotty yelled as he approached, "did you go to the castle?"

"Yes!" Mark panted. "He has Todd!"

"Who has Todd?" Gabi asked as she approached.

"Lucius does." Mark sat on the curb to catch his breath. "He's taking him into the castle."

"Why was Todd with you?" Scotty asked.

"I caught him in my yard when I snuck out." Mark could hardly breathe. "He wanted to go with me, when I told him where I was going. He insisted, Gabi! They'll kill him! We have to get help!"

"They?" Gabi asked. "Who else was there?"

Mark proceeded to tell them the whole story, as he calmed. When he tried to show them the picture of Lucius, it was gone. No picture at all.

"This is crazy," He said. "You have to believe me."

"I believe you," Gabi said.

"That's not the crazy part." He went on to tell them about the statues, the balls of fire, and the glowing people.

"Mark, they were angels."

"Well, why did they just save ME?"

"Because we only prayed for you. We didn't know Todd was with you."

"Yeah," Scotty said, "I still wouldn't have prayed for him."

"Scotty Morgan, you'd better pray for your enemies." Gabi said.

He looked at Mark and shrugged.

"We need to get help," Mark said.

"Hold on," Scotty said. "Think of how much trouble you'll be in. Is Todd Johnson worth it?"

"He was so scared. He was crying," Mark said. "We have to help him."

"I agree. We would expect him to help you," Gabi said.

"Yeah,' Scotty said, "fat chance he'd ever do that! I say we know nothing and keep Mark and us out of trouble."

"No!" Mark was already walking. "You guys go home. This is on me."

"No way, Yankee Boy!" Gabi said.

Mark stopped and turned.

"This is on US. Come on Scotty."

"Wait...what?" Scotty said.

"Scotty Morgan!"

"Yes ma'am."

They headed to Matt's house.

CHAPTER SEVEN

SCHOOL'S IN

An hour later, Mark, Gabi and Scotty were at the police station, waiting for their parents to arrive, so they could tell their story for a third time.

Once it had been established that Todd was missing, his stepdad had been called in for questioning. He could be heard all over the station exclaiming how Mark McGee was a trouble maker and how he must've forced his Todd to go to that castle.

It was each of their mothers that showed up. The look on Mark's mother's face let him know that it was definitely not going to be a peaceful day when he got home. Gabi and Scotty didn't seem to be in much trouble, since they were basically helping a friend. Mark doubted Gabi had ever been in trouble a day in her life. He couldn't complain though; she was a good friend.

The police sent two officers to the castle to question Lucius Willoughby. It was basically a waiting game until they got back.

Mark couldn't believe all that had happened. Lucius seemed capable of being in two places at once. Then there were the statues coming to life. Had Mark somehow been drugged? Maybe one of the plants he passed in the forest? What about the balls of fire that actually helped him? Gabi had called them angels but didn't people who hallucinate always say they saw bright lights? Had he only been high the whole time?

Officer Ramsey interrupted his thoughts by asking them all to follow him into an interrogation room. Their moms were given chairs to sit in along the wall and asked to allow the kids to tell their story. Gabi told all she knew up until Mark came into the neighborhood. She left out having seen the boy in the street. She wasn't sure she actually had. Scotty basically agreed with all Gabi said.

Then came Mark's turn. He left out the statues and the balls of fire. He didn't want to be put in the looney bin. He just told them that he went left and Todd went right and Mr. Willoughby went after Todd. He told how he'd heard him screaming as he ran away. "Did you find him? Even a trace?"

Officer Ramsey had been writing the entire time. He set his pen down. "Officer Butler and I went out to Mr. Willoughby's establishment."

"You mean the castle," Mark interrupted.

"Mark," his mother said, warning him with a look.

Mark was tired of everybody treating Mr. Willoughby like an innocent bystander. Why weren't they tearing that castle apart? "He denied everything, didn't he?" Mark asked.

"He denied Todd being there, or at least he said he only saw you. He knew you from a previous visit where he told you and Gabi here, to never return."

"I'm sorry," Mark's mother said." You've been there before?"

"Gabi, you know better." Her mom said.

"Yes ma'am," she replied, "He let us in the gate before. We asked him some questions."

"You know how dangerous that was," Mrs. Motes said.

"Ladies," Officer Ramsey said, "I understand and appreciate your concern, but you'll have plenty of time to discuss this when you get home."

"Yes, we will." Mark's mom said.

"Mrs. Motes," Mark said, "Gabi only went because she knew I was going alone."

"Okay," Officer Ramsey said, "thank you Mark." Once everyone was quiet. "As I was saying, he says he never saw anyone but you and when he approached you, you high tailed it out of there." He sat back. "Now, he is not pressing charges, but asked me to stress that he is a private man and his property is private property."

Mark was livid, "He has Todd Johnson in his castle! Why aren't you searching it?" Mark's chair slid back as he stood. "Why aren't you doing anything to look for him?"

"Mark Evan McGee! Sit your bottom down, right now mister!" His mother said, giving him a death stare only a mother can.

Mark sat.

"Todd has run away before, Mark." Officer Ramsey said." I'm sure he'll turn up. He's probably back home now."

"So I made it up?" Mark said. "Why would I do that Officer Ramsey? So I could come in here and get in a bunch of trouble with my mom?"

"There was no evidence Todd was there, Mark. I need evidence in order to get a warrant."

"And the word of a twelve- year old is squat? I was there. You have to look for him!"

"We are looking for him, and will continue looking for him. His stepdad will make sure of that."

"So, what now?" Mark asked.

"Now," Officer Ramsey said, looking at Mark's mom. "I need you to drop this. No more sneaking out, no more visiting the castle, no more breaking the law." He looked at Mark now. "Can you do that for me Mark?"

Mark just stared at him.

"I can assure you he can do that Officer Ramsey." His mom stood. "He won't have time to do much of anything for the remainder of his summer break. That much I can promise you." She lifted Mark by his arm. "May we go?"

"Yes ma'am, you're all free to go."

Mark's mom had not been joking. His remaining summer break was spent working from sun up to sun down. He painted, cut grass, cleaned gutters, scrubbed floors, vacuumed, washed dishes, he even painted their privacy fence.

He'd had no free time at all. No video games, no television, no friends ever, no phone, he hadn't even been allowed back at church.

Usually he could play one parent against the other in order to get some form of freedom, but they were sticking together on this one. It was horrible.

The only time he got to see his friends was at the school orientation the week before classes started. The whole gang was there. Despite the fact that his mother was watching him like a hawk, he managed to get signed up for all the same classes as Scotty and Gabi. Scotty asked him when he would be off restriction, but as far as he knew, after high school. All he could do was keep his nose clean and hope his parents had mercy on him.

Gabi told him that Todd still hadn't shown up. Of course, he hadn't expected him to. She told him that his stepdad was still looking for him but the police had assumed he'd run away. They expected him to come walking up the driveway at any time. His stepdad, however, had been arrested for attempting to tear down the gate of the castle.

The day before school started, Mark's mom came into his room while he was making his bed. "Mark honey, let's talk."

"Yes ma'am." Mark sat on the bed.

"Mark, I hope you've learned a valuable lesson from all this."

"Yes ma'am, I have."

"You can't just sneak out of the house," she said. "We're responsible for you, Mark. One day when you have children of your own, you'll understand." She slid his hair out of his eyes. "I had no idea you were even out. Do you know how embarrassed I was when that officer called me to say you were at the police station?"

"I'm sorry, mom." He really was, for what he'd done to her.

"With Bethany still not feeling well, and your stepdad working so much, I need you to be more responsible, okay?"

"Yes ma'am."

"Okay." She smiled. "I'm taking you off restriction".

"Yes!"

She kissed his forehead. "The Motes have invited us over after they get home from church, for a kind of back to school party."

"Awesome."

"I'm pretty sure Scotty's family will be there too."

"Sounds great," he said, grinning. Finally, something to look forward to.

The party was amazing. The whole gang was there, including Billy and Matt. They played volleyball, kickball, horseshoes, they swam and even had a water gun fight. They also ate too much food and by Sunday evening they were exhausted.

The parents were inside chatting and playing Pictionary. The younger kids were in Abi's room watching a movie. The gang were all outside sitting by the pool. It was the first chance they'd all gotten to talk since the castle incident.

"So Mark," Matt started in, "what's the real deal with Todd?"

"Exactly what I told your dad. Lucius took him in the castle."

"Dude, my dad was so mad at me for even knowing you after that. Told me to never ask him anything about that castle again. He'd probably kill me if he knew you were here."

"Yeah," Mark said, "no offense Matt, but the cops are definitely hiding something when it comes to that castle. It's like they're terrified of it."

"Do you think he's okay?" Billy asked.

"I don't know what to think," Mark said.

"That place is so evil," Gabi said. She and Scotty had not told the others about the statues or the balls of fire. "Please promise me you won't go back, Mark."

"Okay mom," He said smiling. Everyone laughed but Gabi.

"I'm serious, Mark," she said, giving him that look

"So," Mark said, attempting to change the subject, "is everyone excited about school tomorrow?" There was a collective groan.

"Middle school is the worst," Matt said, "I can't wait until I'm in high school next year." He was a year older than the others.

"At least you guys have all been there," Mark said. "I won't know anyone but you."

"Not true," Scotty said. "You'll know Andy and Eddie. I hear they can't wait to see you."

"Wonderful," Mark said. "Beavis and …

"Mark!" Gabi said. "Be nice."

"So we all pretty much have the same schedule, except Matt." Billy said. "The only difference is, you all have Art and I'm taking Band."

"What instrument?" Gabi asked.

"Snare drum."

"The snare?" Scotty asked. "You can only take one drum?"

"Yes, silly," Gabi said. "Haven't you ever seen a marching band? They don't exactly carry a whole set of drums. Each person has one."

"Usually a bass or a snare," Billy added.

"Oh," Scotty said, "I thought Band was like being in a band, you know, like The Riptide."

They all laughed. Gabi just shook her head.

"What?" Scotty asked.

"Billy's going to miss the seventh grade because he'll be on tour with The Riptide?" Gabi asked.

"No! I meant…Oh never mind."

About that time Gabi's mom came out and told them it was time to start cleaning up. They all helped out and said their goodbyes.

Thirty minutes later, Mark was climbing in bed, exhausted. He was both nervous and excited about his new school and his new friends. He was also ready to put his summer adventures behind him. He'd learned his lesson and would stop meddling. Let somebody else worry about that castle. Not his problem. He'd had enough run ins with the law and with his parents to last a lifetime. If nobody else cared that Todd Johnson wasn't coming back, then neither did he. He fell fast asleep.

Before he knew it, he was walking up the steps to his new school. The sign read Gateway Middle School, Building Minds. There were people everywhere. Running, walking, shouting, sitting, talking, hanging out. Mark wondered where Scotty and Gabi were. They were supposed to be showing him around. He stopped at the top of the steps and scanned the school yard. He didn't see a single person he…wait. At the bottom of the steps was…it couldn't be. It was the boy from his dream. He just stood there staring at Mark. Mark waved to keep it from being awkward. He could've sworn that the boy's eyes flashed red for a split second. Somebody bumped into Mark and he looked away. When he looked back, the boy was gone.

"Strange." He scanned the yard once more for Scotty, Gabi, Billy or Matt. Nothing. He turned to go in and the boy was standing behind him. He wore a suit and his hair was perfectly in place. "Whoa dude, can I help you?"

"Hello, Mark."

Mark blinked. This guy being in his dream was one thing, but actually knowing him? "Who are you?"

"My name is David."

"And how do you know me, David?" He couldn't mention his dream; how weird would that be?

"I told you Mark, you're the destined one."

"Wait, you said that…" Mark leaned in and whispered, "In my dream."

"That's right, I did." He said as if that was perfectly normal. "Why did you run away, Mark?"

"What do you mean?"

"You were so close. You should have let Lucius bring you into the castle. Only you can save the children."

"What? You know about that?"

"Yes Mark, you were so close."

"What about Todd? Is he okay?" Another flash of red in his eyes. Mark stepped back.

"Go to the castle Mark. Go in. Let Lucius take you in and all your questions will be answered. You will learn the mystery of the gateway."

"Wait, the gateway?"

"The Gateway to God Mark…go to the castle." He turned to leave.

Mark grabbed his shoulder and as soon as he touched David, he saw a great pit of fire. Millions of people were burning and screaming in the pit. Mark immediately pulled his hand away, and jumped awake in his bed.

He was covered in sweat, panting. His alarm clock went off. It was time to get ready for school.

At the bus stop, Mark told Scotty and Gabi that he'd had another dream about the boy, and that his name was David. "He said I should've let old man Willoughby take me in the castle."

"Dude, no way!" Scotty said.

When he told them what happened when he touched David's shoulder, Scotty's eyes got big.

"That was hell," Gabi said. "You need Jesus, Mark McGee."

"Wait, what?" Mark asked.

"I'm serious, you're dealing with some serious stuff here, and for some reason the devil wants you bad. You need Jesus. Only he can help you."

"Come on Gabi, give him a break," Scotty said.

"I know you go to church sometimes, Scotty," Gabi said. "But you need Jesus too. You need to encourage Mark."

Just then the bus came. Mark and Scotty took a seat together. Gabi got stuck with Tina Pennington, a chatty girl in the eighth grade, who was talking with two boys in the seat behind her.

Mark turned to Scotty. "Need Jesus? What does that mean?"

"Well," Scotty shrugged, "you ask him into your heart, or, something. It's how you become a Christian."

"Yeah, like it's that simple." Mark said.

"I don't know, ask Gabi," Scotty replied, "All that stuff confuses me."

"Don't you have to get baptized?" Mark asked.

"Yeah, maybe."

"And give money? I only get ten dollars a week."

"Hey, me too."

"How much do you give to the church?"

"Um, I don't." Scotty looked guilty.

"So I guess you're not a Christian." They both laughed.

"I have been baptized though."

"So, what did you think about my dream? Why do you think I need to go to the castle?"

"I think it was just a dream. You should just ignore it. Everybody has dreams. They don't mean anything. Besides, you're just a boy in the seventh grade, it's not like we're going to Hogwarts or anything. It's just Gateway Middle School."

Mark sat back, looking at the ceiling "You're right, thanks Ron…I mean Scotty." They laughed.

After homeroom, Mark, Scotty, Billy and Gabi headed to first period. They had history with Mr. Austin. He was an older man that didn't even look up as they came in. The guys wanted to sit in the back but Gabi wanted up front. Scotty asked her to compromise in the middle, but they took their seats in the front.

The bell rang. Mr. Austin stood. "Everyone take your seats please." He walked around to the front of his desk, holding a notebook. "I'm Mr. Austin and this is seventh grade History. Is everyone supposed to be here?"

"Are you serious?" A girl in the back stood and shuffled out, embarrassed. Everyone laughed.

Mr. Austin smiled. "There's always one…now…I only have a few rules in my class. Be here on time. No phones or gizmos. Do your homework I assign you. History is not a guessing game. It is facts. You either know it or you don't. Therefore, you either make an A or you make an F. I do not believe in middle ground when it comes to History. You will find that I am quite passionate about two things. History…and the past." He walked back around behind his desk. Someone had their hand up. "Yes?"

"What's the difference between history and the past?"

"Exactly, now, I need some volunteers to pass the textbooks out. How about you two?" He pointed to Mark and Scotty.

Scotty gave Gabi a mean look for making them sit in the front.

Mark couldn't believe Mr. Austin actually gave them homework on their first day. Seventh grade was not off to a good start.

Their next class was English and again Gabi had them sitting on the front row.

"Seriously Gabi?" Scotty exclaimed. "This is not helping my reputation."

"Scotty Morgan, I couldn't care less about your reputation."

Their English teacher was young and pretty. She looked like she was fresh out of school.

"Hello everyone," she said, "I'm Ms. Tyler." She turned and wrote her name on the board. "This is second period English. May I have a couple of volunteers to hand out our textbooks?" She pointed out Mark and Scotty.

"Thanks Gabi," Scotty said as Gabi laughed at him. "I was hoping to be teacher's pet in every class."

Ms. Tyler had them write about what they did over the summer break. "I'm especially interested in any adventures you may have had." Mark could've sworn she looked right at him when she said that. He chose to leave out his adventure with the castle. She did not give them any homework.

Next was Math, Mark's least favorite subject. Their teacher was Mrs. Mott, an older black woman with a nice smile. She greeted them at the door, speaking to each of them as they entered. She was so nice, she actually had Mark looking forward to doing fractions.

Once again they sat on the front row and once again Mark and Scotty handed out the text books. Several people laughed when they were asked, but only because Scotty was pouting. Gabi actually laughed out loud.

Mrs. Mott went over their course plan during class and gave them a worksheet to do for homework.

Fourth period was Art. They had to walk all the way out to a separate building. Their teacher was Mr. Stanley and he was a very strange man. He was tall, pale and quite...strange. He wore a suit and sat up straight at his desk. After calling the roll, he gave a brief history of Art and had everyone draw a picture of the apple on his desk.

Mark hoped he didn't talk too much. He talked way too fast and was difficult to understand.

At the end of class, he asked for volunteers to hand out the workbooks. Scotty tried to look busy but he and Mark were chosen, since they were sitting at the front table. Scotty gave Gabi the evil eye. No homework in Art.

Next was lunch.

Matt and Billy joined them at a table outside. Matt complained about having to take Home Economics, but otherwise loved his other classes, especially Music.

"I'm just thankful we only have two more classes," Scotty said.

"Yeah," Mark added, "and P.E. is the last one."

"I hate P.E." Gabi said.

"Why?" Scotty asked. "Because you can't sit on the front row?"

"No Scotty Morgan! It's because there won't be any books for you to hand out!" She laughed.

"Well, well, well! Who have we here?" Someone said from behind them. They all looked.

"Hello, Andy and Eddie," Matt said.

"Matt," they nodded to him, "why are you sitting with this loser?" Andy pointed to Mark.

"He's cool guys," Matt said.

"Yankee Boy is not cool," Eddie said, laughing. "And neither is his girlfriend, Scotty Morgan."

"Wow!" Mark said. "You guys didn't tell me they train monkeys in this school too."

"You think you're funny, Yankee Boy?" Andy asked, stepping up to him. Mark stood. "You better sit down, you don't want to get beat up and suspended on your first day, do you?"

"I don't know Andy, who you got in mind for me to fight? I'm surprised you goons are so brave without mama Todd to hold your hands."

Eddie made a move toward him. Andy held him back.

"Anytime Eddie," Mark said. "You know you don't want this."

Andy pulled Eddie away. "Watch your back Yankee Boy."

"Hey Andy!" Mark called as they walked away.

"Mark, sit down," Gabi said.

Andy looked back.

"How's your bike?" Mark asked, smiling.

"Soon, McGee," Andy said and they left.

"Well, that was smart," Gabi said.

"What?" Mark asked. "They started it."

"And you clearly ended it," she said sarcastically. "Those guys are bad news, Mark."

"They're losers," Scotty said and the bell rang to end lunch.

They headed to fifth period Science.

Mr. Kelly, the Science teacher, seemed quite mellow. After having Mark and Scotty hand out the text books, he had them read chapter one quietly for the rest of class. No homework.

In Gym class, Mrs. Keys, their coach took roll and let them choose between basketball, volleyball, and helping with the banners for the upcoming football game. The guys chose volleyball while Gabi helped with the banners.

On the bus ride home, Mark turned to Gabi, who was sitting alone. "So, what about my dream?"

"I told you Mark, you need Jesus."

"What does Jesus have to do with my dream?"

"He has everything to do with everything. Every single part of your life. You've evidently got something trying to get your attention, Mark. Whether your house was built on that Indian graveyard, or you just eat too much spicy food before you go to bed, I don't know. What I do know is that you shouldn't face it alone."

"Well, I'm not alone. I have you guys," Mark said.

"That's true, but we're not always with you. Jesus is."

Mark smiled and nodded, then turned around. He leaned over to Scotty. "She's really serious about that Jesus."

"You have no idea," Scotty said. They laughed.

It had been a good first day of school. Somewhat normal. Normal was good. Mark liked normal.

CHAPTER EIGHT

THE DAGGER AND THE DECISION

That night, as Mark lay in bed thinking about his first day of school, he couldn't help but wonder about all the strange events since moving to Gateway. He even considered the whole church thing strange. It all kind of went together in his mind. The castle, the disappearance, the dreams, old man Willoughby, the secrets, the scriptures. It was as if someone was trying to tell him something. He wanted to put it all behind him and attribute it to the stress of moving, but he knew better. He'd been there when Todd was taken. He'd heard the screams.

He lay there tossing and turning, unable to sleep or turn off his brain for what seemed like hours. All of a sudden his eyes shot open when someone knocked at this door. He sat up. "Hello?" Nothing. "Mom?" Silence. "Hello?" He swung his feet out of bed, getting nervous. Another knock, louder this time. He jumped. "Who is it?" He walked over and slung it open.

He jumped back. "Is this a joke?" He walked to the door and looked out. It wasn't his house at all. It was as if his hallway had become a cave. The walls were made of stone. The floor was dirt and rock. "Hello?" he called. "Anybody in there?" He heard feet shuffling to the right.

"Mark, come on!" A loud whisper. "This way!"

It was David. "Dude, wait up! Is this a dream?" It had to be a dream. He ran towards him, trying to catch up. He almost ran into him in the dark cave. "Whoa what's going on David?"

"In here." He led Mark into a large room. "Hold on while I light a torch."

It was very dark and damp. Mark could hear something, like chains clanking and…the torch was lit…the walls were lined with children. They were dirty and their clothes were tattered.

"Mark!" A loud whisper. It was Todd. "It's about time!"

"Todd?" Mark said loudly. "You're alive?" There were at least fifty kids in there.

"Be quiet Mark, you must not awaken him," David said.

"Awaken who?"

He raised the torch toward the back corner. There curled up in the dark, was the dragon, sleeping.

"So, what now?" Mark asked. "We have to get them out of here. Is there a key?"

"There is only one way, Mark. You have to kill the dragon."

"What? How?"

David reached inside his jacket and pulled out a dagger.

"Whoa," Mark said. It was beautiful. The handle seemed to be made of ivory or marble. The blade was very shiny. And sharp.

"Plunge that into the dragon's heart, and the chains will be broken," David said.

What about the gateway to God?" Mark asked.

"That was for the lost souls. This is for the living. Hurry Mark! Soon he will awaken."

"Please Mark!" Todd said, "Kill him!" The other children nodded.

Something didn't feel right about this. How were all these kids alive? They'd been taken over decades. How were they still children?

"Mark!" David said, "Now! Only you can do this! You're the destined one!" He pushed Mark towards the dragon. "Do it now."

As Mark walked toward the dragon quietly, he looked into the faces of the children. They were pleading for him to do it. He stood over the dragon as it lay before him. It was breathing heavy. Smoke escaped its nostrils. He looked back at David.

David nodded and pointed to the dragon's heart. "Now."

Mark raised the dagger. The dragon's heart was exposed. It would be an easy kill.

"Slay the dragon Mark!" Todd whispered.

Just as he was about to plunge the dagger, "Mark Evan McGee!" His mother screamed. The dragon's eyes shot open and lunged at him. He jerked awake. His was standing in Bethany's room beside her bed. With the dagger raised over her. Wait, how did he have the dagger?

"Mark?" His mother called, "Where are you?" He cleared his throat, "I'm here Mom!" He called, hiding the dagger under Bethany's dresser. "I thought I heard Bethany crying."

She appeared at the door. "I thought you'd snuck out again." Bethany woke up, confused. "Go back to sleep baby."

She walked Mark back to his room and thanked him for checking on Bethany.

"Yes ma'am, no problem." He closed his door. His hands were shaking. He'd almost killed his sister.

And the dagger! How had he brought it out of his dream? Was he losing his mind? That was stuff out of horror movies. He stayed awake the rest of the night. He got up before everyone else and went to get the dagger. It was gone. He looked all around Bethany's room in a panic. Had someone found it? Was he really losing his mind? It was nowhere to be found.

On his way to the bus stop, Mark couldn't decide whether or not to tell Scotty and Gabi about what had happened. They might agree that he was going crazy.

"Mark!" It was Scotty running toward him. "Dude, let me see your History homework!"

Mark dug it out and handed it over.

"Good morning, Mark." Gabi said.

"Hey Gabi…good morning."

"You okay?"

"Just peachy."

"Oh boy, what did you dream this time?"

"It's not important."

"Let me be the judge of that, spill it," Gabi said.

"Seriously," Mark shrugged, "it was nothing."

"Mark McGee, I woke up at midnight to pray for you, what happened?"

Mark sighed, "I think I'm losing my mind guys." He told them everything.

Scotty was totally fascinated, but Gabi had a seriously worried look on her face.

"Do you still have the dagger?" Scotty was so excited.

"No, it was gone this morning."

"Is it possible you dreamed the part of your mom calling you, and waking up in Bethany's room?" Gabi asked, sounding hopeful.

"No, she thanked me again this morning for checking on Bethany."

"Dude!" Scotty said, "you brought something out of a dream. That's like that Elm Street movie with Jason or Michael."

"It was Freddie." Mark said.

"Oh yeah, my parents don't let me watch those." Scotty said.

"Mark, I really think you should talk to Pastor Eric about this." Gabi said. "It would be confidential."

"No way!" Mark said. "I'm not telling ANY adult that I woke up holding a knife over my little sister. They would lock me away so fast."

"Mark, this is serious!" Gabi said. "What if you don't wake up next time?"

"There won't be a next time," Mark said.

"And how, may I ask, are you planning to stop it?" She asked.

"I'll just, stay awake."

"Forever?" Scotty asked. "Sorry dude, as cool as that sounds, it can't be done. I tried it one time. I lasted two and a half days, then fell asleep on the playground. My mom woke me up that night, freaking out. I'd have rather faced a dragon."

"Scotty, you need to take this serious too," Gabi said.

"Excuse me." It was one of the students wanting off the bus. They were at school.

"We'll talk more at lunch," Gabi said.

"Listen," Mark said. "Don't worry about it. Its's my problem."

"Mark, we're your friends," Gabi said. "We're in this together!"

"No we're not, Gabi!" Mark snapped, causing her and Scotty to stop. "We're not in this together!" He started to walk away, then turned back. "You aren't in my dreams with me. You don't face that dragon with me! Nobody else was there. So just…whatever!" He stormed off.

"What was that about?" Scotty asked.

"Don't take it personal, Scotty," Gabi said. "He's in a battle, and he's totally unarmed."

"Well," Scotty said, "he has a dagger." He smiled as she gave him that look.

Neither of them attempted to talk to Mark before lunch, where they sat outside in the courtyard under and old oak tree.

Mark walked up. He stood there until they both looked up. "Listen guys…"

"Forget it," Gabi said. "Sit down."

He sat.

"Frito?" Scotty asked, holding out a bag. Mark took one.

"What do I do Gabi?" Mark asked.

"Well," Gabi said, looking at him for few seconds, "I'd pray."

"For what?"

"For God to protect you. Mark, you're in a battle."

"A battle against who?"

"The devil."

"Wait, what?" Mark asked.

"I'm serious. There is a literal battle going on for your soul."

"Not just his soul Gabi!" Scotty added, "His life too."

Gabi cut him a look.

"I'm just saying, if he'd stabbed Bethany, his life would've been over. We're talking prison or loony bin or whatever."

"I think we all get that Scotty," Gabi said. "Listen Mark, what you said earlier is true. When you dream, we can't be with you. But God can. All you have to do is ask Him."

Mark thought about that. "So, all I have to do is pray for God to protect me?"

"Asking Him into your heart and becoming a Christian would probably end the whole thing but yes. If you..."

As Gabi talked, Mark looked over her shoulder. There was a really pretty girl staring right at him. She looked goth, wearing all black, with black hair, nails and lipstick. Just then, the bell rang, she winked at him and walked away. Mark had missed most of what Gabi said, but he figured he'd gotten the point. He searched for the goth girl for the rest of the day, but never saw her.

For the rest to the week, Mark tried praying before he went to bed. So far, no more dreams. Maybe there really was something to Gabi's whole God thing.

He also didn't see goth-girl again either. At least until Friday morning. He went to the restroom after first period and when he came out someone tapped him on the shoulder. When he turned, she was standing there smiling.

"Oh!" He blurted, "um hi."

"Hi yourself." She held out her fist, "Name's Angel."

He bumped her fist. "I'm Mark."

"Nice to meet you Mark McG..." She paused.

"Wait, you know my name?"

"Busted...I'm a fan."

"I'm sorry, a fan?'

"Heard about your little trip to the castle, and I must say...impressive."

"More like stupid, it may have gotten Todd killed."

"Maybe, but it still took guts, and I like a man with guts. Listen, this is my class here, it was nice meeting you Mark."

"It was nice meeting you Angel." He watched her disappear into the sea of students. He made his way to English, unsure of what to think about having a fan. "Well," he said to himself, "Gabi said angels would be sent. I just met one."

After English class, Ms. Tyler called Mark to her desk.

"Yes, ma'am?"

"Hello Mark, I just wanted to check on you. How was your first week?"

"Okay, I guess," he shrugged.

"How are you adjusting to Gateway?"

"It's okay." He really hated talking to teachers.

"Well, I know how new places can be extra stressful, I just wanted to check on you. I'm here if you need to talk."

"I'm fine. Thank you."

"Alright then, have a great weekend."

Saturday was a crazy day of skateboarding at Billy's, lunch at Scotty's, swimming at Gabi's and video games at Mark's. There'd been no mention of castles or dragons or dreams. It was a very good day.

Now it was just Mark and Scotty in Mark's room. Scotty was sleeping over and Gabi's parents were going to pick them up for church. They were presently on their fourth hour of video games.

"Dude," Scotty said, "I just had a crazy thought."

"What?"

"What if you try to kill me tonight?"

"Very funny."

"I mean, it's possible.'

Mark shrugged, "I guess."

"What do you mean you guess? Wait a minute!"

Mark laughed. "I'm kidding. I promise I won't kill you." He got up and set up the cot for Scotty. He grabbed the blankets his mom had set out.

"So," Scotty said, ending his game, "nothing strange like this ever happened to you in Pittsburgh?"

"Nope," Mark said. "I don't remember ever having a bad dream."

"That's crazy."

"This place is crazy."

"Maybe, but not before you got here," Scotty said.

"Well obviously, there's a castle full of kids out there, and a town full of people who don't care. If that isn't crazy, then what is?"

"What's crazy is how it's targeting you," Scotty replied.

Mark walked over to the window and looked out at the forest. It was dark and quiet. What secrets were out there? He thought of old man Willoughby leading them to the castle. He could still hear Todd's screams. Those balls of fire...

Mark jumped when Scotty patted his shoulder. "You have to admit dude, there hasn't been a dull moment since you got here."

"Yeah, thanks."

They got ready for bed. They lay there chatting for a while, until Mark heard Scotty breathing heavier and knew he was asleep.

Scotty did have a point. Had it been all of Mark's meddling that had the castle and its occupants after him? What was really going on? Why was he being targeted? He lay there pondering this before falling asleep. He forgot to pray.

Mark woke in the middle of the night to go to the bathroom. Scotty was sound asleep. As he was getting back into bed, something like a pebble tapped the window. He walked over and looked out. There was nothing or no one there. An empty yard visible in the moonlight. He turned to go back to bed and jumped. The boy was standing beside his bed.

"Why didn't you kill the dragon?"

"Dude, there has to be another way to communicate with you. You have got to stop freaking me out like this."

"You were supposed to kill the dragon."

"Don't you mean my sister? Huh? I almost stabbed her."

"If you had killed the dragon, everything would have been better."

"Why am I even talking to you?" Mark asked. "This isn't even real. It's only a dream."

"It's very real Mark, it's more real than anything else you know."

"Okay, why is the dragon attacking the children?"

"It's what he's done for centuries Mark, only now his thirst is unquenchable. His fury is about to be unleashed. You have to stop him, Mark."

"Why is his thirst unquenchable now?"

"Because he is afraid."

"Afraid? Afraid of what?" Mark asked.

"You," David said. "He is afraid of you, Mark McGee."

"Wait. Why would that vicious, horrible, dream stealing, child murdering dragon be afraid of a twelve-year old boy?"

"Well, that's simple. Because of the prophecy, of course."

"What prophecy?"

"You were correct when you told the others about the castle being built on an old Indian burial ground. That is where the Indians would bury their warriors, their wives and their elderly. However, they did not bury their children there."

"Okay, why not?" Mark asked.

"They believed that the spirit of a child could not find its way to the great beyond, because they were too young. They were afraid that if they did not strike a deal with the Great Spirit, that the spirits of the children who died, would be lost forever."

"Wait, the Great Spirit? Who is that?"

"It is who they prayed to. They had a great ceremony where many tribes came together. They cried out to the Great Spirit, they cut themselves, they even offered animal sacrifices."

"And what happened?"

"When they were totally exhausted after three days of no food or sleep and about to give up on receiving an answer... one came."

"What was it?"

"The Spirit appeared in the fire. He told them that he would protect the children when they died, and lead them safely home. He would personally see them reunited with their loved ones. There was a catch however."

"Of course." Mark said.

"They were to build a temple on that spot and worship him there. The ground around that temple was where the children were to be buried."

"Well, that's not so bad."

"He also told them that they would have to sacrifice a child each year on that night or the souls of all the children would be lost."

"They had to kill a kid each year?"

"Yes."

"What did they do?" Mark asked.

"They agreed."

"What? They agreed to kill their own children?"

"Yes, but their wise leader, made one stipulation to the contract."

Mark waited.

"If the spirit ever lied or deceived them, that a boy would rise up from that very temple and strike the Great Spirit dead, and he would set the spirits of all the children free. He would show them, the Gateway to God."

"Whoa."

"That was the prophecy that was set into motion the moment he deceived them."

"So he deceived them?" Mark asked.

"Yes. He killed many of their children and he locked their spirits inside the castle so he could torture them forever."

"So," Mark said, "where do I come in here?"

"That temple, Mark McGee," David said, "Stood on the very spot where your house is."

"Yeah, I kinda saw that coming," Mark said. "But what about the dragon? Wait ... was he the Great Spirit?"

"Very good, Mark." David smiled. "That is why you have to kill him. You are the only one that can." He reached into his jacket and pulled out the dagger.

"Oh no." Mark backed away. "I'm not touching that thing!"

"It is the only way Mark. Nothing else will kill him."

"Well ... I don't know anything about slaying dragons, David. I can't possibly be your guy."

"You are, and I will help you. That's why I'm here, Mark. I'm your guide.

"So what, you'll train me or something?" Mark asked. "Like some kind of dragon slayer?"

David smiled, "Something like that."

Mark thought for a second, then nodded, "Okay, what do we do first?"

"Well, first," David put the dagger back in his jacket, "I have to know that I can trust you."

"Okay."

"Very soon, you're going to be asked to make a very important decision. Life changing even, one that your friends may even encourage you to make, especially the girl."

"You mean Gabi?"

"Yes, and you have to resist, Mark. You have to be our own man. As the old saying goes, Just Say No."

"So, by saying no to this decision, I somehow gain your trust?"

"Yes. That will show me that you are serious and willing to do whatever it takes to slay the dragon."

"Okay, I say no ... then what?"

"First things first Mark, first things first. Now, the first thing you need to do is wake up."

"Wake up, Mark! Mark!" It seemed as if David's voice had changed to sound like ... Scotty's. "Mark!" Someone was shaking him. "Dude! You sleep hard! Get up, I've already showered."

The Motes picked up Mark and Scotty. Bethany wanted to go, but wasn't feeling good.

Mark decided not to mention his dream. He was a little confused. If Gabi and Scotty were for this decision that he was supposed to say no to, then he had to wonder how much he could trust them. He'd just have to play things by ear until he completed this dragon slaying mission. Besides, after he slayed the dragon, set the children free and revealed this gateway to God, they'd have to see that he was right and they were wrong.

"I have a surprise for you after church, Mark," Gabi said.

"Okay."

"Don't you want to know what it is?" Scotty asked.

"Wouldn't be much of a surprise then, would it?" Mark responded, with a distant look.

Gabi and Scotty shared a concerned look. Scotty shrugged.

The church service was good. Mark really did enjoy the music. Pastor Eric spoke on something out of the book of Romans. Mark had drifted off, imagining himself as a dragon slayer. Being trained to fight like Batman or the Count of Monte Cristo.

Mark did wonder about the whole guide thing. He'd never even heard of anybody having one. He shrugged it off though, he was after all, the destined one.

And what about this decision. What would it be? He figured if Gabi was for it then it would have something to do with God. Maybe he would be asked to join the church or get baptized. He could definitely say no to that.

Pastor Eric had them stand and hold hands. He closed in prayer.

"Okay," Gabi said, "meet me in the vestibule in about ten minutes."

"In the what?" Mark asked.

"She means in the front entrance area of the church," Scotty said. "I think vestibule is in the Bible or something."

"Wow, Scotty." Gabi said, "Nobody can accuse you of not reading your Bible." She rolled her eyes and walked away.

"Should I be worried?" Mark asked Scotty. "She seems kinda excited."

"No," Scotty replied, "definitely not worried."

"So tell me Scotty, where exactly do you stand on this church stuff! Do you actually believe any of it?"

Scotty shrugged. "It's alright. I'm just not sure I'm ready to commit. Especially like Gabi has."

"I know that's right." They laughed.

"We should probably start heading back." Scotty said.

"To the vestibule?"

"I'm telling you it's in the Bible, "Scotty said. "Nobody but church people say that."

They met Gabi in the front and she had them follow her down a long hallway.

"So what's going on, Gabi?" Mark asked.

"You'll see."

They stopped at the end of the hall. Gabi knocked on a door to the right that had a sign that read Pastor Eric Osborne.

"Come in." He called. They entered, Pastor Eric was sitting behind a small desk. "Hey Gabi, Scotty, and I assume you're Mark." He stood and shook their hands.

"Yes sir, Mark McGee."

"Well, have a seat." There were three chairs and Mark got stuck with the middle one.

"So Mark McGee, I've heard a little bit about your adventures with our infamous castle in the forest."

Mark hadn't expected him to know about that. He grinned, "Yes sir that was extremely stupid." He glanced at Gabi for saying the word stupid. She didn't even flinch.

"Actually, I was going to say it was quite brave, but sometimes there's a fine line between brave and stupid. How much trouble did you get in with your parents?"

"Enough," Mark nodded. Scotty and Gabi laughed.

Pastor Eric smiled,"I also heard that you got to meet Mr. Willoughby?"

"Yes sir," Mark replied.

"What was that like?"

"Intense." Mark was being vague because he wasn't too sure where this was going. Pastor Eric seemed friendly enough, but David's warning weighed heavy.

"Well, I've never had the pleasure to meet him, but I think I would enjoy it. Well Mark, let's get to the point, shall we?"

"Yes, sir."

"I would love to discuss what happened at the castle sometime in the future and I want you to know that my door is always open if you need to talk, okay?"

"Yes sir." Mark nodded.

"Great, now I would like to ask you a few questions, just to see where you are."

"Okay," Mark replied.

"Okay then, have you ever told a lie?"

"Um." Was this for real? He looked at Scotty who seemed afraid to look at him.

"It's okay," Pastor Eric said. "Just be honest. It's only a question."

"Yeah, sure... hasn't everybody?"

"Okay," he held up his hands, "have you ever stolen anything?"

"I...uh."

"Yes or no?" Pastor Eric smiled.

"Yeah, I mean, it wasn't anything big."

"Stealing is stealing, Mark. Have you ever cheated? On a game, homework, a test?"

Mark gave Gabi a dirty look for getting him into this.

Pastor Eric smiled, "don't worry Mark, what's said in this office, stays in this office."

"Sure, I've cheated, when I was younger, but everybody..."

Pastor Eric held up his hands. "Hold on, this is about you. Now, I don't know what your belief in God is, but let's just say, for the sake of argument, He exists. Let's also say He's perfect and holy and everything the Bible says about him is true. Let's also say that only perfect people can go to heaven to be with Him. Now, you just admitted to me that you are a lying, stealing, cheat. What do you think your chances of going to heaven are, Mark?"

"Umm, I know this is about me, but if that's the rules, then nobody is going to heaven." Mark smiled, he had them.

"You're exactly right," Pastor Eric smiled. "You were paying attention! Nobody could get to heaven Mark! If not for what Jesus did on the cross.

"I don't understand." Even Scotty was fidgeting.

"It is impossible for us to go to heaven, Mark, but with God nothing is impossible. It was for that reason that He sent His sinless Son to the world. Through Jesus, a way was made for us to get to heaven. You see Mark, when Jesus died on the cross, He took your lies, your thefts, your cheats, and any other sins you've committed and He placed them on Himself. That way, when you stand before God, He doesn't see your sin anymore. He sees His son." He paused to let it sink in.

"So, I don't have to do anything?"

"Yes and No." Pastor Eric smiled, noting Mark's confusion. "All you have to do Mark, is acknowledge that you're a sinner, in need of a savior… Jesus. Understand that you can't get to heaven without Him and ask Him to save you."

"That's it?"

"Well, then you allow Him to do His work in you daily, by studying His word, going to church, living for Him. It really is the biggest decision you could ever make, Mark."

And there it was. He could feel Gabi staring at him. Scotty too.

"So, what do you think?" Pastor Eric asked.

"First of all, I find it a little difficult to believe it's that simple."

"Mark," Gabi said, "it's a gift, from God. If you had to work for it or do something, then what would you need God for? He loves you so much that He wants to spend forever with you. It's a gift."

"If Scotty here handed you a big gift wrapped package," Pastor Eric continued, "would you try and pay him for it?"

"Nope." Mark smiled at Scotty. "I'd take it."

"Exactly. And all you have to do is take this gift too."

Mark nodded. It really was quite simple and seemed innocent. However, he knew this was the decision that David had warned him about.

"What do you say, Mark?" Gabi asked.

He looked at her and then at Pastor Eric. "It does seem like a sweet deal, but I think I'll have to pass. I'm just not ready."

Pastor Eric nodded. Gabi sighed. Scotty fidgeted.

"Besides, I'm young. I have my whole life to...accept this gift, right."

"I don't know, Mark, can you guarantee tomorrow?" Pastor Eric asked.

"No, but that's my choice. I'm ready to go." He stood. "I'm sorry Pastor Eric, I'm just not ready."

"Well, I'm sorry too Mark." They shook hands. "Remember, I'm here if you ever need to talk."

"Thank you." He glanced at Gabi and left the office. He'd done it. David would know he was committed to the mission now.

When he got home, the dagger was lying on his pillow.

CHAPTER NINE

TO SLAY A DRAGON

The following day, Gabi had been quiet, but didn't seem to be upset with him. He didn't want to offend her. He truly wasn't ready to commit to something like God right now. Besides, he had a dragon to slay.

After school, he'd gone home and done his homework. That hadn't taken so long, so he'd taken his board to the park. He needed to think. There was nobody else there but a boy sitting on top of the slide reading a book. Mark sat on a swing.

Mark wondered how this would all play out. Would he have to slay the dragon in his dreams or would David tell him he had to go back to the castle? He hoped it would be in his dreams because he did not want to go to the castle. However, he also didn't want to end up hurting someone else, like he almost did Bethany.

The boy on the slide began whistling while he read. It was actually quite loud. He seemed oblivious to Mark being there.

Mark also wondered if David would train him. Would he learn special dragon-slaying skills like in movies and video games? Learning to fight could have other benefits as well, like dealing with bullies.

"As long as I'm around, bullies will never be a problem." The boy from the slide was standing right beside him. Mark jumped. It was David, wearing shorts, a tee shirt and a baseball cap.

"David? Is that really you?"

"Yes it is Mark, please, sit back down."

Mark sat back down on the swing. "Am I dreaming?"

"No, I've made a few changes to our relationship. You won't be seeing me only in your dreams anymore, thanks to your new commitment to our friendship."

"Can other people see you?" Mark looked around.

"No, only you."

"So, it would appear to anyone walking by right now, that I'm talking to myself?"

"Yes, it would." David smiled.

"Great...I'm insane."

"Insanity is more normal than you think, Mark," David said.

"So, am I ready for some dragon slaying?" Mark asked.

"For the sake of the children, I certainly hope so."

"So, what do we do first?"

"Well, first we have to locate the dragon," David said.

"You mean you don't know where he is?"

"Well," David said, "I know where he is, but not who he is."

"Okay, I'm confused," Mark admitted.

"He's not exactly a dragon anymore."

"So, what is he? And why? And how, for that matter."

"He's, a person now, because he knows you're looking for him, and, well, he's a spirit, so the how is really quite simple."

"Wait..." Mark was so confused. "He's a person? What person?"

"Well, that's the question, isn't it?" David responded. "You don't know?"

"I know that he's someone at your school. I know that he will try and get close to you. I don't, however, know much more. And oh, he may be a she, for all I know."

"So," Mark stood and began pacing. "How will we find out who it is? And why will they try and get close to me?"

"We will have to be smart, and they will try and get close to you because, it will be hard enough for you to kill them as it is, but even more difficult if they're your friend."

"Wait a minute!" Mark said, stopping in front of David. "I can't kill a person!"

"You may have to, Mark."

"No, no, no. Guide or not, you're crazy! People still frown on that."

"Mark." David raised his hand to calm him. "The fact that he is now hiding in your school places him in close proximity with a lot of children. His blood lust will strengthen. Not only is it extremely important for you to kill him but you will have to be quite fast about it."

"That's crazy!"

"Mark, he's still a dragon, and when you kill him, there will be no body. He will just vanish."

"Well, I still have to kill a person!"

"You must stay true to this, Mark McGee!" David said. "Otherwise more children will die."

Mark thought for a few minutes. "Could it be somebody I already know?" A twig snapped behind Mark, he jumped and looked back towards the forest behind the park. Scotty was standing there at the tree line. "Dude, you scared me!"

"I live just through there." Scotty pointed through the woods. "I made a path to the park. It's kinda convenient. Your mom told me you'd be here."

Mark nodded and sat back on the swing. David was gone.

Scotty walked over. "Were you talking to yourself?"

"Just thinking out loud."

Scotty sat next to him. "I thought I heard you say something about killing somebody. I mean, it's bad enough to be talking to yourself, but when you're discussing murder, that worries me."

Mark smiled, "If it makes you feel any better. I was trying to talk myself out of it."

"Well, that's good. Keep yourself in line."

"So, does Gabi hate me?" Mark asked.

"No way, Gabi doesn't hate anybody!" Scotty replied. "She was disappointed at first, but then she blamed herself."

"What? Why?"

"For surprising you with it. She thought you'd want it, just because you're our friend."

"Well, I am your friend, but that has nothing to do with God or church."

"Hey, I get it, it's not like I take it all that serious."

"Yeah, well," Mark said, "you should."

"Huh?"

"I'm just saying, nobody likes a fence rider. Get in or get out I always say, and that's about anything."

Scotty nodded, "I guess. I just haven't decided what I believe yet. I mean, I go because my parents make me, but I don't know if it's what I want. I see all the older kids leave church when they get out of school. I mean, if it's so great, why doesn't anybody stay?"

"All of them leave?"

"Most. A few stay and some eventually come back, but it just seems more should stay. They seem to like it, then they leave."

"Well," Mark said, "maybe they're just testing their wings...seeing if they really need God."

"Maybe."

"What does Gabi say about that?" Mark asked.

"The same thing you just said, that they're testing their wings or sowing their wild oats."

"Well," Mark said. "I say if you're going to do something, do it well. That's why I'm not ready to commit."

Scotty nodded. "So, who are you going to kill?"

Mark laughed, "I don't know, any suggestions?"

The next morning at school, Mark sat on the front steps watching everyone. He tried to imagine anyone of them being the dragon. Everybody seemed so...normal. No long tails, no scales, no wings.

When the first bell rang, he got up and went inside. On his way to homeroom, somebody shoved him from behind. He hit the ground hard and his books and papers went flying. He looked back in time to see Andy and Eddie rounding the corner laughing.

"Hey, are you alright?" Angel knelt down and helped him gather his things. The crowds were beginning to die down.

"Yeah, thanks."

"I don't understand it," she said. "Those two have always been such upstanding students."

Mark laughed. "Yeah, I'm sure."

"Tell me, is it true you painted Andy's bike pink?"

"You heard about that?'

"I was impressed by that."

"Yeah, well, it looks like he wants more," Mark replied.

She handed him the last of his papers. "Go get 'em tiger." She stood.

"Thanks again, Angel."

"No problem, maybe I'll see you at lunch," She replied.

"Sounds cool, we sit outside." They went to class.

There was only one person in Mark's first period class that seemed suspicious and that was a kid named Garret. Garret Davidson usually sat at the back of class and drew graphic pictures of gladiators fighting. He even had a few pics of dragons. Scotty even told Mark that Garret had asked about him. He would definitely be one to watch.

After class, Mark made a detour for the boy's restroom. He almost knocked the janitor over when he pushed through the door.

"Whoa! Slow down there, partner!" He was an older man, skinny, short haircut. He had a big smile.

"Sorry," Mark said, "trying not to be late."

"It's okay. I haven't seen you around. Are you new?"

"Yes sir. Moved here from Pittsburgh."

"Well, don't call me sir. Name's Clayton."

Mark was just a little uncomfortable talking to the janitor in the bathroom. He tried to hurry. "Um, I'm Mark."

Clayton was sweeping. "Well, nice to meet you Mark."

"Nice to meet you."

"So, what do you think of our little town?"

Mark shrugged as he washed his hands, "It's alright."

"Quieter than Pittsburgh, I'm sure," Clayton said.

Mark laughed, "If you say so. Well, have a nice day!"

"You too, Mark McGee!"

Mark walked out into the hall and stopped. Had he told Clayton his last name? The bell rang. He ran to English making a mental note to add Clayton to his dragon list.

Ms. Tyler gave them an assignment to work on during class. Mark looked around for other suspects. He caught Gabi's eye and she gave him a look that asked what he was up to. He only shrugged.

Right before class was over, Ms. Tyler asked Mark to take up all the papers. When he went to hand them to her, she asked him to have a seat next to her desk.

"Yes ma'am." He sat.

"How would you like to earn some extra credit, Mark?"

"Um, do I need it?" He asked.

She smiled. "Everybody could use extra credit, but no, I just need somebody to help me with some projects and run errands for me. It would get you out of homework and you would get an A on any projects I give you. Are you interested?"

"Why me? Gabi's way smarter."

"Don't get me wrong, there are a few people more qualified than you. They just, lack your spirit."

"My spirit?"

"Yeah, you're a go getter." Her smile hooked him. She really was very pretty. He couldn't say no.

"Okay."

"Awesome. Thank you, Mark."

"Thank you." The bell rang and he walked out with Scotty and Gabi looking at him. "What?"

"What was that about?" Gabi asked.

Mark shrugged. "I'm Ms. Tyler's new assistant."

"Excuse me?" Gabi said. "How did that happen?"

"Dude, she's the best looking teacher in...ever!" Scotty said.

"All I know is, no more homework," Mark said. They were both quite jealous over that.

"So did she say why she picked you?" Gabi asked, clearly confused over this news.

"She said I had spirit."

"She probably found out about your castle adventure, and wants to keep an eye on you," Scotty said. "And did I mention, she's pretty?"

"Whatever," Gabi sighed and headed into Math class.

Nothing too exciting happened until lunch. Angel came over to their table and Mark introduced her to everyone. She complimented Gabi's back pack and Gabi complimented her hair. Scotty wouldn't stop staring at her black lipstick. She sat with them.

"So, Mark, what was it like at the castle?" Angel asked.

Scotty and Gabi exchanged a look.

"Um," Mark stammered, "it was kinda creepy."

"Well, I think it is so cool that you went there. I mean, how brave is that? Tons of kids go in there and are never seen again, and Mark McGee decides to go have a look."

"Yeah," Mark said, "it was kinda cool."

Gabi rolled her eyes.

"No doubt," Angel said. "You could've been killed. Old man Willoughby is definitely a creeper. I saw him one time in town."

"Really?" Scotty asked. "Where at?"

"He was at the hardware store. He wasn't there long. He drives like a maniac too. Almost ran over a jogger."

"What did he buy?" Scotty asked.

"I don't know, why?"

"It could've been something for a torture chamber or something."

They all looked at Scotty.

"What? It's possible."

"It was nice meeting you, Angel." Gabi stood. "I need to go to my locker." She gave Scotty a look.

"Nice meeting you too, Gabi."

As Gabi left, Andy and Eddie came around the corner.

"There's your buddies, Mark." Angel said.

Mark and Scotty both looked back. "Yeah," Mark said. "I've got something for those bozos."

Friday morning, Mark asked his mom to take him to school early. He'd told her he needed to work on a project.

Andy and Eddie had tried to embarrass him a few times, but other than the push, they'd been pretty quiet. Still, Eddie had slipped a note into his hand after school on Wednesday that said, "The beat down is coming McGee." He had too much to worry about without these losers harassing him. He would get rid of them today.

Before most anybody got to school he had taken care of what needed to be done. Last night he'd asked David for some advice on how to get rid of them. If this worked it would be epic.

He decided to go wash his hands before meeting Scotty and Gabi. Thinking he was alone in the bathroom, he jumped when he saw something move out of the corner of his eye.

"Good morning Mark!" It was the janitor, Clayton. He was holding a broom and dust pan. "Didn't mean to scare you..."

"Clayton!" Mark said, drying his hands. "Do you live in here? I've never seen you anywhere else."

Clayton laughed. "Sometimes I feel like I do, but no Mark McGee, I have a home."

"About that," Mark said. "How do you know my last name?"

"I hear things," Clayton said, shrugging. "So, what are you doing here so early?"

Mark smiled, "I have some important business to tend to...for an assignment."

"Alright, well you be careful, you hear?"

"Yep, have a good day, Clayton." Mark left the bathroom. Be careful? Strange guy.

About fifteen minutes into first period, there were loud popping sounds coming from out in the hall. Everybody jumped up. Some people screamed, some laughed. The halls were filled with smoke. The alarm went off. Ms. Tyler hurried them out of class.

Somebody thumped Mark's ear as they got outside. He turned around to see Gabi giving him the evil eye. "What did you do, Mark?"

"Me? I was in class with you," Mark exclaimed.

"Yeah Gabi! "Scotty said, "Chill out. Wait, did you do that Mark?"

"Wow you guys are crazy," Mark said. He looked towards the parking lot, David was standing there with a girl in a dress. She looked familiar.

"What are you looking at, Mark?" Gabi asked.

"Huh? Oh, I thought I saw something." When he looked back, they were gone.

Later in the day, they found out that Andy and Eddie had set off fire crackers in their lockers and in their book bags, at the same time. Someone even said they'd seen Eddie pull the fire alarm. They were both in big trouble. The police had even been called to the school. Fire crackers are illegal in Florida. Mark hadn't known that.

Gabi gave Mark a knowing look after the news came out. "Coincidences seem to happen with you a lot."

"What does that mean?"

"I'm just saying, every time those guys mess with you, they get in trouble with the police."

"Well, they're not exactly upstanding citizens Gabi, I'm sure their mugshots are on file."

That night Scotty came over for a visit with Mark. They went up to Mark's room and played video games for a while. After about thirty minutes of blowing things up and shooting zombies, Scotty paused the game.

"OK dude, what gives?"

"Huh?" Mark asked.

"How did you do it?"

"How did I do what Scotty, take out that busload of zombie kids?"

"No Mark, how did you sabotage Andy and Eddie? And don't you dare deny it or our friendship is over."

"Scotty, dude, if I had anything to do with what happened today, which, by the way, broke about six different laws...I would probably not want my best friend to have any knowledge of it...you know, in case anybody questions him."

"Good point," Scotty said. "So, how'd you do it?"

"A little trick my friend Steve from Pittsburgh taught me. It's all about the timing." That and an invisible friend doing most of the work, Mark wanted to say, but couldn't.

"I knew it was you," Scotty said. "Those two don't even know how to light a firecracker, let alone sync them to go off at the same time."

"You can't tell Gabi," Mark said.

"She wouldn't tell on you."

"Yeah, but she wouldn't stop telling me how stupid it was either," Mark replied.

"She wouldn't say stupid though," Scotty laughed.

"So, did Angel help you?"

"No, I acted totally alone. That's why I went to school early this morning, wait, why would you think Angel helped me?"

"She came up to me after lunch, laughing, and said "McGee is crazy." I asked her why she said that and she said, "Sshhh!""

"She probably assumed it was me," Mark said. "I never saw her today."

"I think she skips a lot. She always has," Scotty said. "So, where did you get the fireworks?"

"I've had them for a long time. My grandfather gave them to me in Pittsburgh. I'd totally forgotten about them until we moved."

"Well, I have to say, it was epic. One day those morons will learn to not mess with Mark McGee."

"Their kind never learn," Mark said.

"So, what should I tell Gabi if she asks?" Scotty asked.

Mark shrugged, "it doesn't matter, she thinks I'm evil regardless."

"No she doesn't Mark, she's a good friend. She really cares about you."

Mark nodded. "You're right. She is a good friend. A little bossy and controlling, but a good friend."

"Yeah," Scotty agreed, "very bossy and controlling...I'm going to marry her someday."

"Well, good luck with that."

Scotty hit play on the game.

Mark hit pause.

"I need to tell you something, Scotty, but you have to swear to secrecy."

"Okay." Scotty sat up.

"No matter how crazy you think it sounds, or how crazy you think I am, you can't tell a soul."

"Dude, what is it?"

"Promise me."

"I won't say anything, besides, I don't want you plotting against me, that's for sure."

Mark shoved him. "Ha ha."

"So, what's this secret?"

"Do you remember the other day when you walked up on me talking to myself at the park?"

"Yeah."

"Well, I was talking to David...He's real, but only I can see him."

Scotty just looked at him.

"I know it sounds crazy, but hear me out." Mark proceeded to catch Scotty up on everything.

Scotty just listened. He hardly blinked, until Mark was finished.

"What do you think?" Mark asked. "Am I insane?"

"Let's see, an invisible boy that you met in your dreams and almost had you kill your sister is telling you that somebody at your school is really a dragon and you will have to kill them when you figure it out...is that about it?"

"You're right...I am crazy."

"This really sounds like something you should talk to Gabi about."

"No way, she'd probably throw her Bible at me or something."

"Do you really think somebody at our school is the dragon?"

"I don't know." Mark was so frustrated. "David said they would befriend me."

"Okay, who's befriended you? Angel?"

"Yeah, but you guys have known Angel."

"Well, how does it work? Does the dragon become someone new or like, possess a person that already is?

"No clue, David never said, he just said the dragon would become someone, male or female."

"Well, Angel is definitely different," Scotty said. "She used to be so rude...and now that you've come along, she's totally cool.'

"Great," Mark said, "the dragon improved her."

"Is there anyone else?"

"Just one...the janitor."

"Jose?"

"Jose? Who's Jose? I'm talking about Clayton. Older white guy."

"I thought Jose was the only janitor at the school," Scotty said. "And he's pretty cool, sometimes he skateboards with us in the parking lot."

"To be honest, I've only ever seen Clayton in the bathroom near second period."

"You'll have to point him out to me."

After Scotty went home, Mark got ready for bed. He went downstairs and told his mom and stepdad goodnight. On his way to bed, Bethany called him to her room.

"What's up, kiddo?"

"Mark, are you going to church this Sunday?" She was in bed and seemed really tired.

"Probably not...why?"

"I want to go."

"I'm sure the Motes would love to take you. Would you like me to ask Gabi?"

She nodded. She seemed sad.

"Are you okay?" Mark asked, walking over to her bed.

She shrugged, her eyes rimmed with tears. "I guess."

"What's up?" Mark pushed her hair out of her face.

"I think something's wrong with me, but mommy won't say."

"Like what? Too much pink in your room?" He tried to make her smile. It didn't work.

"I think I'm really sick, Mark, that's why I want to go to church. Pastor Jonathan said Jesus heals the sick."

Mark had nothing to say to that. "Well, I'll ask Gabi okay?"

She nodded.

"Good night, Kiddo." He kissed her forehead.

"Good night, Mark."

In order to make an example out of them, Andy and Eddie had been expelled. Mark was not sorry. In fact, everyone that knew them seemed pretty happy. The last Mark had heard, they were being bussed to a school in Jacksonville that dealt with troubled students.

Mark was really enjoying being Ms. Tyler's assistant. She actually got him out of homework in all his classes. Everyone was so jealous, especially Gabi.

"I can't believe we have the same grade in all our classes Mark, and you don't do anything."

"I do plenty," Mark argued, though anyone would wonder if stapling tests and getting Ms. Tyler coffee, merited plenty. Who was he to argue though, she was the teacher.

He and Scotty were putting everyone under the microscope and nobody seemed to be a one hundred percent slam dunk dragon. Not to mention, after two weeks neither of them had seen Clayton.

Mark decided to ask Ms. Tyler about Clayton. He was helping her grade papers during her free period. He was supposed to be in Art.

"Ms. Tyler, can I ask you a question?"

"May I ask you a question, and yes you may." She smiled at him. He almost forgot the question.

"Do you know our janitor, Clayton?'

"Clayton? We don't have a janitor named Clayton, Mark. There's Jose and sometimes his cousin Carlos helps him, but no Clayton."

"But he was in the boy's room, I've seen him a few times."

"There was a man in the boy's room? What was he doing?"

"Sweeping...and maybe mopping. He was wearing a janitor outfit."

"Did he say anything? Do anything?" She seemed truly curious.

"He introduced himself, and oh, he knew my name. He told me to be careful."

"Really? When was the last time you saw him?"

"A couple weeks ago."

She nodded, "Mark, listen to me. There is no janitor named Clayton. If you ever see him again, come get me, do you understand?"

"Yes ma'am."

The bell rang to go to Gym. Mark told Ms. Tyler goodbye. She seemed in deep thought.

After changing into his gym clothes in the locker room, Mark had gone to the restroom. When he came out, everyone was gone. He walked over and closed his locker.

"Well, hello Mark McGee!"

Mark jumped back. Standing behind his locker door was Clayton.

"Sorry buddy, you sure are jumpy!"

"Clayton!" Mark panted. "I haven't seen you in a while."

"I've been around. Are you staying out of trouble?"

Mark nodded. "Yeah." He backed away, "I...need to get to class."

"Okay, well, keep your eyes open buddy!"

Mark ran out the door and almost knocked Scotty over.

"Dude! There you are!" Scotty said, backing out of his way. "What's wrong?"

"He's in there, Scotty, Clayton is in there. Don't let him leave! I have to get Ms. Tyler." Mark darted away.

He returned minutes later with Ms. Tyler running behind him. Scotty was waiting outside the door.

"Nobody has gone in or come out." Scotty said.

Mark led them into an empty locker room. "Clayton!?" Nothing. He looked at Scotty. "Are you sure he didn't leave?"

"No way dude. Nobody in or out, and there's no back door or windows in here." He and Scotty exchanged a look.

"Okay," Ms. Tyler said, clearly not happy about Mark pulling her out of class for nothing. "We'll discuss this later, Mark." She left.

"No more involving teachers," Mark said. "I think we've found our dragon."

"Dude, why DID you get her?"

"She asked me to, and she's pretty. I lost my head."

That night, Mark was at Scotty's house. They were discussing how Mark was supposed to kill Clayton. Scotty's mom called them downstairs.

"Yes ma'am?" Scotty asked when they got in the living room.

"I thought you boys would want to know that someone found a body behind your school this afternoon."

"What?" They both said in unison. "No way!"

"Do they know who it is?" Scotty asked.

"Not yet, but they're pretty sure it was a female. One of the kids on the track team was running on the trail behind the school when he spotted the body."

"Pretty sure it was a female?" Mark said.

"Ew," Scotty said, "I wonder who it was."

"Anyway, Mark honey, your mom called and wanted you home. She saw the news too and doesn't want you out too late."

"Yes ma'am." He and Scotty walked outside together.

"Dude," Scotty said, "do you think this has anything to do with your dragon?"

"It could," Mark replied. "David said it was no coincidence he was at a school. His bloodlust was strengthening."

Scotty's mom opened the door and handed Scotty the phone. "It's Gabi."

"Hello? Yeah, we heard…Mark's here…we were studying…yes we were…okay, bye." He looked ticked.

"What?" Mark asked.

"She's accusing us of messing around and not really studying."

"We WERE messing around and not studying."

"That's beside the point."

"Well, I need to go." Mark left on his skateboard. It was quite dark out with only the streetlights to guide him. He felt as if someone were watching him. The hairs on the back of his neck were standing up. Then he could have sworn he heard footsteps running up behind him.

He jumped off his board and looked back. Nobody was there. It was dead quiet out. "I could use a little help, David!" He called out. "Some guide." He turned to get his board and screamed, jumping back.

"Mark?"

"Clayton?" Mark looked around. "What are you doing here?"

"Just out for a stroll, who were you talking to?"

"N..nobody...myself."

Clayton smiled. "It's a dangerous night, Mark...you should get home."

"Sssooo, you heard, ab...about the body?"

"I knew about it, yes." Clayton said. "A bad thing, murder."

Mark nodded. "D...do you, live near here?"

"Close. Would you like me to walk you home, you seem upset?"

"N...no... I'm good." Mark picked up his board. "I'll see you, Clayton."

"Hey Mark, I was going to ask you, how's Gabi doing?"

"She's, good, why?"

Clayton shrugged. "Sweet girl."

"Well, gotta go."

"Goodbye Mark, and no more talking to yourself."

Mark took off running. After a few seconds he looked back, no Clayton. He ran faster. He needed to get that dagger and keep it close.

When Mark got to his room he turned the light on and yelled. David was sitting on his bed holding the dagger. "Dude, really?"

"Mark, are you okay?" His mom called.

"Fine, Mom."

David smiled. "You called?"

"Where have you been? It's been weeks."

"You have a mission Mark, you're kinda on your own until it's accomplished. You don't need me to hold your hand do you?"

"I think I've found him."

"You think?"

"I've found him."

David handed him the dagger. "Well, if you're sure."

Mark took it and immediately David vanished.

CHAPTER TEN

THE HUNT CONTINUES

Mark got to school extra early again. His mom had said she was proud of all his extra work. If she knew what he was actually doing, she would have him committed. He'd actually brought a dagger to school. Not only would he be expelled if caught, but arrested. Not to mention he'd be going to school with Andy and Eddie.

He had to keep in mind that what he was doing was for the greater good. Somebody had already died and Mark had to stop the killer. A dragon, not a person.

He went to the bathroom where he'd first seen Clayton and waited. He went into the stall and took out the dagger. Could he really do it? Plunge it into the janitor's heart? The thought terrified him.

The bathroom door opened. He heard the mop bucket being wheeled in. He peeked out. Clayton had his back to him. He was whistling. Mark gripped the dagger tightly. Now was the time. He eased the stall door open.

"Good morning, Mark McGee." Clayton never even turned around. He wrung out the mop and slopped it onto the floor.

Mark froze. He didn't know what to say or do.

"What are you sneaking around for?" Clayton asked. His back still to Mark.

"I know who you are," Mark said, trying to sound brave. "And I have to stop you."

"Exactly what do you intend to do with that dagger?" He asked, his back was still to Mark.

Mark stepped out of the stall. It was now or never. "I intend to plunge it into your heart, you filthy dragon!"

Clayton turned to face him. His eyes were flames of fire. His face glowed like a thousand fluorescent lights. He lifted his hand and the dagger flew from Mark's hand to his where it turned to ash.

Mark fell back in fear. He hit the stall door and fell back against the toilet. He hit the floor.

He heard Clayton coming toward him and closed his eyes. He knew it was over. He'd never stood a chance. The dragon would slay him. It would be Mark's body they found today, ripped to shreds in the boy's bathroom at Gateway Middle School. He was cornered between the wall and the toilet with his arms up to shield the blow of death.

"Mark? What are you doing?"

He looked up. "Gabi?" She stood there gaping at him like he'd lost his ever loving mind. "How? Where did you come from?"

She helped him out of the stall. "What is going on, Mark?"

"First of all, why are you here?" He asked.

"I received a call this morning from a friend of yours, telling me that you would be needing to talk to me. That you were in trouble in D Hall boy's room. I needed to get there as soon as I could."

"Wait, a friend of mine? Nobody knew I was coming. What friend?"

"It was a man," she said. "His name was Clayton. Mark, what's going on?"

Mark grabbed his bag and went out into the hall. He looked both ways. Gabi followed him. "Did you see him?"

"See who? There was nobody, Mark. Tell me what's going on. I've been praying for you all night."

"You wouldn't understand."

She grabbed his arm. "Try me!" She looked serious. "I know you and Scotty have been hiding something from me and I get this call that you're in trouble and I find you balled up in a bathroom stall like somebody was just about to hack you up. Now, spill it!"

"There's something I have to do, Gabi," Mark said pulling his arm away. "And when I'm done, I'll tell you everything." He turned and walked away.

Mark was so confused. Why would Clayton call Gabi? Why would he say he was Mark's friend? It was almost like he was trying to help Mark, not, hurt him. Is that what the dragon would do? Was he trying to confuse Mark to stay alive?

"Mark." It was David walking right beside him. "Don't speak, just listen. Clayton is not the dragon."

"Then who…"

"I said listen. You want to look crazy? Keep talking to the invisible boy." He was right, people were starting to show up. Mark went to his locker.

"He's just a decoy sent by the enemy to get in the way. Ignore him and find the real dragon. I really feel like you're close. Do not fail." He vanished.

Mark closed his locker. Angel was standing there. "Wow, people really like to scare me in this place."

"Sorry man. How you doing?"

"I'm good. Where have you been?"

"Around. We should hang out, Mark. I still want to hear your castle story. Did Old Man Willoughby really take Todd?

"Yes he did. Listen I need to run. Have you seen Scotty?"

"Nope, but I haven't been looking for Scotty," Angel replied. "I'll see you around."

"See ya, Angel." Mark headed for homeroom, wondering if Angel could be his new number one suspect.

In English class, Ms. Tyler asked Mark to come up and help her while the rest of the class took a quiz. She had him filing papers for her. Gabi did not look happy about this.

"You're such a good assistant, Mark," Ms. Tyler said, "I'm really grateful for all you do."

"Thanks, Ms. Tyler."

"Listen, I'll be at the school tonight, my computer at home is on the fritz. If you'd like to come up and grade some papers, I'd very much appreciate it."

"Okay, I'll have to check with my mom, but it shouldn't be a problem. What time?"

"Say around seven?"

"Okay."

An already upset Gabi was giving Mark the evil eye over all his extra credit opportunities.

"I don't see what the problem is, Gabi" Mark said.

"I'm sure you don't," she replied. "You get an automatic A on everything."

"You have to admit it, Mark," Scotty added. "You got a pretty sweet deal."

"Yeah, but I have to hang out with Ms. Tyler all the time," Mark grinned.

"Uh, the prettiest teacher in the school!" Scotty said.

Gabi rolled her eyes. "So, you're coming up here tonight?"

"Yeah, she needs help grading papers."

"We were going to study for that History test, or is she going to get you out of that?"

"Ha ha!" Just then Mark saw Garret Davidson, the creepy guy that sat in the back, staring at him. Garret walked away when Mark looked at him. "Hey Scotty, we need to talk." He hadn't had a chance to tell him about what happened earlier yet.

"I guess that's my cue to leave." Gabi said, turning and going to class in a different direction.

"Gabi, wait!" Mark called but she kept going.

"What's up with her?" Scotty asked.

"Something really crazy happened this morning." Mark proceeded to quickly tell him all the events of the morning and how Clayton wasn't the dragon but a decoy. He now suspected Angel or Garret.

"Dude, and my biggest issue this morning was choosing Cap'n Crunch or Fruit Loops."

At lunch they were all sitting together listening to Billy talk about how much he loved being in Band.

"We'll get to play at all the events and, in high school, I'll get to travel with the football team."

Mark saw Angel coming and nudged Scotty. She sure looked the part of a dark dragon in human form:

all black clothes, black hair, lips and fingernails, even black eyeliner.

She came over and sat next to Mark, "O-M-G!" she exclaimed, interrupting Billy. "You will not believe what Mr. Allen just told me!" She seemed very excited.

"Who's Mr. Allen?" Mark asked.

"My English teacher, and only the coolest teacher in the school…anyway, he told me he thinks I have what it takes to win the state poetry competition this year."

"I didn't know you wrote poetry, Angel," Gabi said. "That's cool."

"Yes, and he's entering my latest one into the competition. It's called The Dragon's Blood, and it's about life through the eyes of a troubled boy. He said it was one of the best poems he's ever read. Pretty cool, huh?"

At hearing the title of her poem, Mark and Scotty were speechless.

"That's very cool," Gabi said. "Isn't it guys."

"Yeah, that's great, Angel," Mark said.

"Awesome, good job Angel," Scotty added.

Billy and Matt agreed.

"I have to come up to the school tonight; there's a meeting for all the contestants," Angel said.

"Cool," Gabi said.

"Hey Mark, I heard you'll be up here, too; maybe I'll see you."

"You write poems, Mark?" Matt asked.

"No, I'm helping Ms. Tyler. How did you know that, Angel?"

She shrugged. "I hear things. Well, gotta soar." She was gone as fast as she'd come.

Scotty gave Mark a concerned look.

At the end of gym class, Mark was the last one in the locker room. Scotty had to run to his locker and grab a folder; they would meet up at the bus. As Mark tied his laces up he heard someone come in.

"Scotty? Is that you?"

"Hello Mark."

"David, good, I've narrowed it down to two people. Can you help…?"

"Kill them both Mark; we can't afford to miss him and your time is running out. You have to kill the dragon today!"

"Yeah, but they still frown on murder here on planet Earth."

David gave him an aggravated look.

"What?? I can't just go killing all the creepy people! There'd be nobody left in Middle School!"

"Then figure it out…quickly." He walked up to Mark. "I believe you misplaced this." He handed him the dagger.

Mark put it in his bag. "So, you can't help me narrow it down?"

"Say the name."

"What name? The dragon's name?"

"No…give me a pen and paper."

Mark handed him a pen and his notebook. David scribbled something on it and handed it back. Mark read it: Gesú.

"What is this? Gaysu?"

"No, like gee and then sue.

"Oh, Geesue!"

"Yes, yes…" David turned away. "Say it loud in the presence of the dragon and you will know."

"Know what?"

"If it's the dragon; he will not like that name."

"Why? Whose name is it?" Mark asked.

"An ancient enemy."

"Okay, so that's it? Then what?"

"It's quite simple Mark, if he flinches you plunge the dagger into his heart. Mission accomplished."

Mark nodded, and turned to grab his bag. "It's either my friend, Angel, or this really creepy guy named Garret." He turned back around and it was Garret standing there instead of David. "Oh…hi Garret."

"Mark."

Mark slowly unzipped his bag. "Hey Garret…Gesú!" He reached into the bag.

Garret lifted an eyebrow. "God bless you?" He walked past Mark. "And they say I'm weird." He wasn't the dragon.

"So, Garret, what…what are you doing here?"

"Oh, I like coming in here and hanging out in the boy's locker room after school."

"Okay," Mark nodded, "cool."

"Dude, seriously? I'm working off detention. Coach Kelley has me mopping the locker rooms and painting over graffiti; he says it's a wise use of my artistic talents. Great guy, Coach Kelley."

"Okay," Mark said, "good talk…we should hang out sometime." Mark turned.

"Hey McGee, who were you talking to when I came in?"

"Moaning Myrtle, but don't worry, she's gone back into the pipes." Mark left.

Garret stood there staring after him. "I thought she was killed in the girl's bathroom," he said to nobody. "That was funny though."

Mark and Scotty were on the bus, heads together, whispering about Mark's encounter and Garret not being the dragon. Gabi leaned forward from the seat behind them.

"What are you guys up to?"

"Huh?" Scotty jumped. "Oh, nothing."

"It sure doesn't seem like nothing."

"We're discussing History," Mark said. Technically it was true; anything in the past was history.

"Fine, don't tell me."

"Seriously, Gabi!" Mark said, turning around. "It's nothing."

"You guys don't seem to want me around anymore... whatever." She sat back.

"Sure we do," Scotty said. "Hey, you wanna hang out at my house tonight? We could play video games!"

"Or study for the History test," she said.

"Or that."

"Okay, I'll call you." She seemed to cheer up some. "And don't think you're off the hook, Mark McGee, teacher's pet!"

Mark laughed. "Jealous much?"

Mark knew what he had to do tonight. Get Angel alone and test her with the Gesú thing. Then, he just had to put a dagger in her heart. No problem.

His mom was thrilled that he was earning extra credit helping Ms. Tyler, although Mark thought she seemed a little sad as she drove him to school.

"Are you okay, Mom?"

"Sure honey, why do you ask?"

He shrugged. "You've just not been yourself lately. Is everything okay?"

She paused with a sigh, "Yeah, we'll talk later; nothing for you to worry about."

"Okay." They pulled into the parking lot.

"I'll pick you up at nine, okay?"

"Yes ma'am, I love you."

She smiled big. "I love it when you say that...and I love you too." She gave him a big kiss on the cheek. "I'm so proud of you." She pulled him close.

"Mom." He tried to pull away. "Mom, you're crushing me...I have to go."

"Okay, I'll see you later."

As Mark crossed the parking lot, he saw Angel getting out of a van.

"Whatever!" She yelled. "Just pick me up later!"

"You watch your tone young lady!" A woman yelled.

"You just try and stay sober!" Angel slammed the door and stormed away.

Mark hurried to catch up with her. He had to be quick. They were alone in the parking lot. He caught her at the steps. He grabbed her arm with one hand, holding the dagger in the other. "Gesú!!" She screamed and fell back. She swung her book bag and hit him in the arm.

"What the heck, McGee?!" She panted.

"Gesú!" he screamed at her, raising the dagger.

"Are you on drugs? Get away from me!" She stood and shoved him.

"Gesú!"

"Shut up! Stop saying that! Are you ill?"

"Does it bother you?"

"You're bothering me! What's your deal?"

"Say it. Say Gesú."

"Gesú, you big dork."

Mark was confused. "It's not you?"

"What's not me?" She started walking up the steps, giving him a dirty look. "And what's with the knife, you freak?"

"Oh, um…it's a game. We played it back in Pittsburgh. I…I thought for sure you would know what it was."

"Well, I don't and you're lucky I don't carry mace."

"I'm sorry. That probably freaked you out."

"You think?" She stopped at the top. "Listen, I'm sorry too, I've been fighting with my mom all day and I'm a little on edge."

"So, where you heading? I'll walk you."

"Yeah, in case some freak jumps out and yells Gesú," She laughed. "So what's this game?"

"I'll tell you another time. I'm sorry about your mom… you know…fighting."

"Yeah, I'm used to it."

"Well, anytime you want to come hang out at my house, feel free."

"Thanks, Mark." She said, smiling. "This is me." She'd stopped at her class.

"Okay, cool; I'm right around the corner with Ms. Tyler."

"Later…crazy man."

He laughed, "later." Now Mark was totally confused. Garret and Angel were his only two candidates. Who else could be the dragon? He heard whistling from down the hall behind him. He turned to see Clayton setting his ladder up. Mark headed towards him. He continued whistling. Mark walked right up to him.

"Good evening, Mr. McGee." Clayton said, removing the cover from the light.

"Who are you, Clayton?"

"I thought it was obvious."

"After our encounter the other day, nothing is obvious. I know you're not the dragon, but who are you? And who is the dragon?"

Clayton climbed down and set the cover on the floor. He looked up at the light not working. "Funny thing, light; nobody usually pays it any attention, until it's gone." He looked at Mark.

"Who are you?" Mark was getting impatient.

"I'm the guy trying to keep the light on." He went back up the ladder to remove the dead lights.

"Well, you tell your dragon friend that..."

"Be careful who you listen to, Mark." Clayton was looking down at him. "There's only one Guide...and He's no twelve-year-old boy."

Mark took a step back. "What does that mean?"

Clayton climbed down with the lights. Mark noticed that he didn't have any new ones around. "It means you may not have all the facts."

"I'm beginning to wonder if I have any facts."

"Oh, you do. You just need to stop hunting dragons and start seeking the one who slays them daily."

"Listen, David told me you were just a decoy. David is my friend. He's been there for me and I'm tired of all this confusion. I want you to leave." Mark started walking away, "and tell your..." He turned back. Clayton was gone. The ladder was gone. The cover was back up. The light was on.

Mark stood there staring for several seconds. "Come to Gateway, they said...it'll be fun, they said." He turned and headed to Ms. Tyler's class. "This place is crazy."

Ms. Tyler was sitting at her desk working on the computer when Mark entered the room. "Mark! good, I was hoping you could come."

"Sorry I'm late Ms. Tyler, it's a crazy world out there."

She laughed, "yes it is." She showed him the papers she needed him to work on and where he could sit to work. "I need to run down the hall for a sec, can I get you something to drink?"

"A lite beer, I'm watching my weight, thanks." Mark said, trying to look serious.

She smiled, "Mark McGee, don't you try me...how's a Coke sound?"

"That'll work too." He laughed.

At Scotty's house, he and Gabi were sitting at his dining room table doing homework. His parents were watching television and his little brother was in his room supposedly doing his homework.

During a commercial break on the television a news teaser came on. "Good evening, I'm Christina Bulford, on tonight's news, a Gateway man has found a way to beat this unusual fall heatwave, and also coming up at ten, the human remains found behind Gateway Middle School have been identified, and you're not going to believe what they've discovered."

Scotty and Gabi looked up. There was a video of police searching the field behind the school.

"Local police are baffled and may need our help uncovering what some are calling the mystery of the decade. Join us for news and weather at ten on your local channel six news."

"Mom," Scotty said. "I have to stay up and see who it is."

"I can't believe they're making us wait," his mother said.

Ms. Tyler returned with Mark's Coke. She poured it into a cup of ice for him. "They weren't cold, so I got you some ice."

"Okay, thanks." He took a big sip.

She went to her desk. "How's it going?"

"Not too bad, I'm almost done grading your first period."

"Awesome…what time are you being picked up?"

"9:00."

"I really appreciate you coming up to help, Mark, you're a life saver."

"No problem, I'd rather do this than study for History." He took another drink.

Ms. Tyler's cell phone rang. "Excuse me, I need to take this." She said and walked out of the room.

Mark continued grading papers. He was starting to get tired. All this school work and investigating and dragon chasing was starting to wear him down. He could hardly keep his eyes open. He took another big drink of his Coke hoping the caffeine would kick in.

Just then Mark heard a female scream from down the hall. It was blood curdling. He jumped up and ran out into the hall. Nobody was out there.

"Hello?!" Mark called. "Ms. Tyler?!"

Another scream, Mark took off in the direction it had come from. The school seemed to be abandoned. "Hello?" Mark called.

"Mark!" It was Angel, she sounded terrified. "Mark! Help Me!" she screamed.

He turned a corner and ran toward the sound of her voice. "Where are you?"

"In the teacher's lounge! Be careful!"

The teacher's lounge was at the end of the hall he was on, just past the drink machines. He was so tired. As he got closer he heard her talking.

"Who are you? Please don't hurt me," she cried.

Mark pushed through the door and stopped. The room started spinning. He was so tired. He blinked. Angel stood with her back to the wall near the coffee maker. She looked terrified. She was saying something but Mark's head was pounding, he could hear his blood flowing.

"Angel? What is it?" He asked, covering his ears.

She pointed behind the door. Mark turned to look. The room seemed to tilt...or was it Mark? The last thing he saw before he hit the floor were the bright red eyes of the dragon.

Scotty and Gabi were just finishing up their homework at Scotty's house. Gabi was putting her books into her backpack when she suddenly stopped.

"What's wrong?" Scotty asked.

"We need to pray for Mark."

"Why? What's he done now?"

"He's in trouble, take my hands." She grabbed his hands and bowed her head. He bowed his. She prayed in a whisper for Mark's safety and protection.

The phone rang. Gabi said a quick amen and watched as Scotty's mom answered the phone.

"Hello? Yes...is everything okay...? Of course, it's no problem at all...I'll bring him over here. He can stay with us tonight. Okay, keep us posted...good bye."

"What happened?" Gabi asked Mrs. Morgan.

"They're taking Bethany to the hospital, we need to go pick up Mark."

"Is Bethany okay?" Scotty asked.

"Bethany's very sick Scotty, they're not sure what it is, but it's not getting any better."

Scotty looked at Gabi, "Are you sure we weren't supposed to be praying for Bethany?"

Gabi looked worried. "Mrs. Morgan, if I ask my mom, can I come with you?"

"Yes, but we need to leave in a few minutes."

Gabi called her mom and told her everything. Her mom said she would head up to the hospital now and Gabi was okay to go with the Morgan's if they didn't mind taking her home later.

The school was about a five-minute drive from their neighborhood. The parking lot was empty. There appeared to be no lights on.

"Is anybody here?" Scotty asked.

"Where is everybody?" Mrs. Morgan asked. She pulled up to the front. "Check the front door Scotty."

He jumped out, ran up the steps and pulled on the door. Locked. He knocked and looked into the window. Totally dark.

"Can I help you?" someone called from Scotty's left, causing him to jump.

"Whoa you scared me," Scotty said to the man who approached him.

"I apologize," he said and held out his hand for Scotty to shake. "Name's Clayton."

"Clayton?" Scotty shook his hand and as soon as they touched, Clayton's entire body changed. He glowed like a thousand lights and his eyes were flames. Scotty's knees buckled and he fell on them. He looked away unable to speak. He was terrified.

"Scotty Morgan!" Clayton said, "Pray for your friend Mark McGee! Like you've never prayed before!" He let go of Scotty's hand.

Scotty looked up. Clayton was gone.

"Scotty?" his mother yelled from the car. "Are you okay!?"

Gabi ran up the steps. Scotty was still staring at the spot Clayton had stood, he was still kneeling.

"Scotty? Earth to Scotty!" Gabi said as she approached. "Are you okay?"

"Did...you see him?" Scotty managed.

"See who?"

He looked up at her. "Clayton."

"Clayton? Who's Clayton?" Gabi asked. "There was nobody here."

"Guys?" Mrs. Morgan called. "We need to find Mark, what's going on? Are you okay Scotty?"

Scotty stood. "I'm fine, Mom!" he called. "Gabi, he's an angel!"

"Did you hit your head?"

"He said to pray...for Mark...like I've never prayed before. Gabi! Clayton is an angel!" He swayed and Gabi caught him.

"Come on, let's go to the car." She led him down the steps. They got in the car.

"Is he okay, what happened?" Mrs. Morgan asked.

"I think he got dizzy." Gabi said.

"I'm fine."

"So where's Mark? Did he lie about coming to the school? I swear that boy has ADD!"

"He was supposed to be helping his teacher grade papers. I don't know where he is," Gabi said.

"Mark McGee, helping a teacher? That didn't strike anyone else as strange?" Mrs. Morgan asked.

"It's true," Gabi said. "She made him her assistant."

"Okay, so where is he?"

"Maybe we should try his house," Scotty said.

"Yeah," Gabi said, "maybe they finished early and Ms. Tyler took him home."

They headed that way. Gabi leaned over to Scotty. "Start talking."

He told her the main things: Mark's dreams, the boy David, his mission, who he thought was the dragon.

Gabi was speechless as they pulled into Mark's driveway.

"Doesn't look like he's here," Mrs. Morgan said.

"Let's go home mom, I'll make a few calls," Scotty said. "Angel may know where Mark is."

"We can find Ms. Tyler's number too," Gabi said. They headed home.

When they got to Scotty's house, Gabi got on the computer and found Angel's number. She called it. "Hello, may I please speak with Angel? Oh, okay, thank you, I'm sorry for waking you, ma'am...goodbye." She hung up. "Wow," Gabi said, "she sounded out of it."

"What did she say?" Scotty asked.

"That Angel was at the school. She wasn't too happy that I woke her up so I didn't bother to tell her that nobody was at the school."

"Yeah, I've heard stories about Angel's mom," Scotty said. "Mother of the year contender."

"What about Mr. Allen? Angel's teacher."

"Try Ms. Tyler first." Scotty said.

"I can't find a number for her. She's apparently new to Gateway. Here's Mr. Allen's number." She dialed it. "Hello? Mr. Allen? I'm sorry to call you so late but I'm looking for my friend Angel and she said...oh, okay, so she was there when you left? Well, thank you. Good night."

"Well?" Scotty asked.

"He said that as soon as he got to the school he received a call that his alarm was going off at home, so he left. He told the students he would meet with them tomorrow. He said Angel was there when he left."

Mrs. Morgan turned the television on.

"Maybe the school's website has teacher phone numbers listed," Gabi said. "Let me check."

Scotty walked into the living room as the news came on.

"Here we go," Gabi said; "faculty."

"Gabi," Scotty said.

"I found her picture, but no number."

"Gabi?"

"Maybe it's…"

"Gabi!" Scotty yelled.

"What, Scotty?"

Come here." He was looking at the television.

Gabi walked into the room. That Christina woman was talking.

"To recap, the remains that were found behind Gateway Middle School are apparently the remains of a teacher. They appear to be several weeks old. Now, here is where it gets strange, the teacher they supposedly belong to has not been missing, but has been teaching. At least, someone has been teaching under her name. In fact, this teacher was teaching classes today and authorities are presently looking for her." At that moment Ms. Tyler's picture came up on the screen. "Police are asking anyone with information on the whereabouts of a Ms. Brandi Tyler to call the hotline number listed on your screen."

"Do you guys know her, Scotty?" Mrs. Morgan asked.

"That's our English teacher," Scotty replied in shock. "The one Mark was helping tonight!"

CHAPTER ELEVEN

A NEW FRIEND

Mark woke with a jolt. He had no idea where he was. It was pitch dark, He waited for his eyes to adjust. They didn't. He began to feel around. It seemed he was lying on a stone floor with stone walls all around him. The room was quite small. He couldn't even sit up, the ceiling was so low. He found that out the hard way. He found a small door down by his feet. He banged on it. It was thick wood that was locked from the outside. He began kicking it and screaming for help. He would bang and scream and then stop and listen. Nothing.

Where was he? He tried to remember what had happened. He'd been at the school helping Ms. Tyler grade papers. She'd left the room. He'd heard a scream. He'd followed the noise. Angel. He'd seen Angel. The fear in her eyes. The dragon! What had happened next? He remembered he'd been so tired. His bones had felt like lead. Had he been drugged? The only thing he'd had was…the coke Ms. Tyler had brought him. She'd opened it…for ice, she'd said. Wait…Ms. Tyler? Was she the dragon? He'd never even suspected her. No. She was too nice. Too pretty. There was no way. Where was he? Was he still in the school? Some storage room in the basement? Some hidden room the dragon...no!

He began kicking again. "HELP!!!" he screamed. "Somebody, HELP ME!!!" He knew exactly where he was. Mark Evan McGee had been taken...to the castle.

Gabi got her cell phone out and called her dad. She hoped he would know what to do in this situation. He was at the church practicing late. She told him the basics and asked if he could come to Scotty's. He said he would and as a bonus would bring Pastor Eric with him. "Perfect, she thought, he'll know exactly what to do.

When they arrived about twenty minutes later, Gabi and Scotty had them, along with Scotty's parents sit down in the living room. Scotty proceeded to tell them everything. Gabi told him not to leave a detail out. They all listened quietly. Gabi added a few comments throughout the story.

When Scotty finished, he sat down next to Gabi. "So, what do you think?"

"The McGee's are good people," Mrs. Morgan said, "but that Mark has attention issues."

"You don't believe me, Mom?" Scotty asked.

"I don't think it's about believing you, Scotty," Pastor Eric said. "What Mark's been telling you, is a big pill to swallow."

"Like bringing a dagger out of a dream," Larry added.

"Exactly," Pastor Eric said. "Either Mark has a serious need for attention, like Martha said, or we're dealing with some seriously dark things here. Now, the only reason I'm giving this story any merit is because of this whole Ms. Tyler issue. That's just a little strange."

"I agree," Larry said.

"Now, that said, two things need to happen: One, somebody needs to be with the McGee family through this. I know Gae is up there, but she's pregnant and needs to be with Abi. I will go to the hospital and relieve her. Two, Mark needs to be found. Larry, I'll leave that to you and the gang here. We'll worry about guides and daggers later, let's just find him first."

"Sounds like a plan," Gabi said, glad there were adults on board now.

Pastor Eric left and went to the hospital. Larry took Gabi home. Once Gae got back from the hospital, he would go pick up Mr. Morgan and they would scour the area looking for Mark. If they couldn't find him after an hour, they would call the police. Scotty and Gabi were not happy about being left out, but they did have school the next morning.

Once at the hospital, Pastor Eric had Gae go home. He assured her that he would stay as long as necessary. Apparently Bethany had a rare heart condition and they were waiting to hear from a heart specialist in Tennessee.

Pastor Eric took Mark's step dad and Mom to the chapel where they could talk. It was empty except for one man sitting on the back with his head bowed. Pastor Eric explained that the church was praying for Bethany and he was there for them. He then proceeded to let them know that Mark was missing and he had people out looking.

"Wait," Mrs. McGee said." I dropped him at the school, didn't Martha pick him up?"

"There was nobody there when she went up." He told them about the teacher being found and nobody was sure who the real Ms. Tyler was.

She began to panic but he calmed her down telling her that it was all in God's hands. He asked if he could pray with them. They agreed and he led them in a powerful prayer for Bethany and Mark. He also prayed that God would reveal himself to the McGee family.

Just before he said amen, the man on the back row, wearing the maintenance uniform, lifted his head smiling. He vanished.

Mark had cried, screamed and kicked at the door until he had no energy. Now, he just lay there breathing, listening to the silence. Was this hell? Had the dragon killed him? Was this where he would spend eternity?

No, he was pretty sure he was in the castle. Every time the thought crossed his mind he would start to panic. He had to keep his cool through. He was still alive and until that changed there was a chance of escape.

The thought of keeping his cool made him think of Gabi. She was always cool. Nothing ever bothered her, except maybe Mark's stubbornness. What would Gabi do in this situation? Pray. She prayed about everything. Mark had chosen to not go that route so prayer was probably not an option. Why would God listen to someone who had rejected him? He would probably make

Mark's situation even worse. No, prayer was not an option. There was someone, however, that he could call on. Why hadn't he thought of it earlier?

"David!" He screamed, "David!! Help me!" He screamed until his head pounded and his voice was gone. He finally gave up and lay his head back. David had probably abandoned him because he'd failed to kill the dragon. "I'm sorry, David," he whispered. "Please help me." He closed his eyes and fell fast asleep.

After driving around for an hour, looking for Mark and finding no trace of him, Larry and Mr. Morgan drove to the police station. The police took their statement but since he hadn't been missing for twenty- four hours, they weren't very concerned, especially with Mark's history.

The only thing that gave them concern was the fact that he'd told everyone he was meeting with Ms. Tyler. The officer told Larry he would be in touch.

Gabi had stayed awake hoping to hear something from her dad. She got on her computer and saw that she had an email from Scotty.

"Have you heard anything?"

"Nothing yet," She replied.

"This is so crazy. What are we going to do?"

"What CAN we do Scotty? We don't even know where he is."

"Yes we do Gabi, he's in the castle."

"So what then, go knock on the door?"

"I don't know; we have to do something. I can't just accept his fate like everybody did with Todd."

"I know. For now, just go to bed, we'll talk about this tomorrow at school."

"School? With all this going on? I don't want to go to school."

"You never want to go to school."

"True."

"Good night," she said and logged off. She bowed her head right there at her desk and prayed for Mark and Bethany and then she prayed for wisdom and help from God. "Amen."

"Hello, Gabi Motes," someone said from behind her. She jumped and spun around, gasping. There was a college aged man standing behind her smiling from ear to ear.

"Don't be afraid," he said. "I'm not here to harm you...I'm here to help you."

She stood slowly, looking him over. He wore jeans, a t-shirt, and black converses. "Uh...who are you?"

"My name is Topher." He held out his hand to shake hers. She did not take it.

"And what are you doing in my bedroom in the middle of the night, Topher?" She felt alarmed but not afraid. He didn't seem to be a threat. There was something peaceful about him.

Um," he said and leaned closer to her whispering, "I'm an angel."

"Oh really?" She said, skeptically.

"Really." He smiled and she saw a sparkle in his eyes that seemed to be a reflection of heaven. The glory of God.

Her knees buckled and she bowed at his feet, a sob escaped her lips. "Oh wow!"

He lifted her up with ease. "Don't go bowing; you'll get me in trouble. Like you, I am only a servant of the Most High God."

She touched his hand. "You're really an angel?"

"Yes, I'm a messenger angel."

"But, you're dressed so...earthly."

He smiled, "hey, this is comfortable."

She laughed, "I just picture angels in white robes with wings. Do you have wings?"

"When I need them."

"That is so cool."

"Yes it is," he said, and they high fived.

"So…" she said, getting serious. "What is your message? Is it about Mark, do we need to go to the castle? I'm ready to take on some demons now…or is it about Bethany? Is she going to be okay?"

"Bethany needs a lot of prayer," Topher said. "But I'm not here on her behalf right now."

"Then it's Mark. Do you want me to call Scotty? I have some black clothes for sneaking around in the dark." She turned to her dresser. "I bet getting into the castle will be a breeze with you being with us. Hey, should I get my dad or maybe Pastor Eric?" She turned to face a smiling Topher. "What?"

"You need to sleep."

"Sleep? What? A messenger angel comes to my house to tell me I need to sleep?"

He stepped closer to her. "Mark is in danger, but where he is, I cannot go. For now, we have a mission. Just know that God is with you. Be at peace and trust Him." He put his hand on her shoulder and she felt a warmth spread over her body. "Now lay down. Sleep."

She walked over to her bed and lay down. When she looked back, he was gone. "Topher?" She whispered as she drifted to sleep.

It was the phone that woke Larry up the next morning. It felt as if he'd just gone to bed.

"Hello?" he answered.

"Good morning, Larry, sorry to wake you."

"Pastor Eric! Good morning, any news?"

"I'm still up at the hospital with the McGee's, the doctor came out a few hours ago and said she is stable. She has an extremely rare heart condition that they've never seen in someone so young. Anyway, they're supposed to be contacting a heart specialist out of Tennessee today to get him involved. He's apparently dealt with this condition before."

"Okay, wow. Do you need us to do anything?"

"No," Pastor Eric said, "other than pray. I'll stay here with the family a little longer. Any word on Mark? That's actually why I'm calling."

"No, the police weren't taking it very serious, considering it was Mark, and he hadn't been missing very long."

"Yeah, Mrs. McGee was on the phone with Officer Ramsey a while ago. He was just leaving to work."

"I was going to call in at work and use a personal day, I can help look for him."

"I'm sure that would be much appreciated," Pastor Eric said. "Well, let me know if you find him."

"Yeah, keep me posted on Bethany," Larry said.

Larry showered and dressed and called in at his job. Thankfully it was Friday. He got Gae up so she could get the girls ready for school. He figured he would comb the neighborhood and look around everywhere between Mark's house and the school. He kissed Gae bye and went out the door.

His Toyota van was parked in the driveway. He was looking at the ground as he walked toward it but as he got close he realized there was a man leaning against it. "Oh, hello."

"Good morning, Larry."

"Can I help you?" Larry asked. "How did you know my name?"

"To answer your first question, you can help me; to answer your second question, I know more than your name."

"Okay," Larry smiled, "how can I help you?"

"You and I need to go somewhere," He held out his hand, "by the way, I'm Topher."

CHAPTER TWELVE

THE ADVENTURE BEGINS

When Mark awoke, he had no idea how long he'd been asleep. It could've been five minutes or five days. He had no watch or cell phone to check. He lay there in total darkness.

He kicked the door again. "Hello!" he screamed. "Can anybody hear me?!!" He slid around and sat with his back to the door. He sat there quietly, trying not to panic. It was totally dark and totally quiet. It was maddening.

Something crawled up his arm and he slapped it away. "Aw man, really? Bugs too?" He wasn't afraid of bugs, he just preferred to be able to see them. For all he knew, they were crawling all around him. He began hitting the door with his elbows. "Hello!! Anybody!"

What if this was how he died? What if he was thrown in this tiny cell somewhere in the castle to be forgotten? Nobody would ever find him. He would be just another kid gone missing. Life would go on for everybody else. Scotty and Gabi would miss him but eventually move on with their lives. Going to school. Hanging out, doing homework, living their lives. His family would cry and search and miss him, but one day they would stop looking and just...live. A few months from now Mark McGee would be a memory. He would eventually starve in this little cell and become food for the bugs. Nobody would ever find him.

Just then there was a loud bang on the other side of the door that startled him from his thoughts. He jumped away from the door. He heard a chain rattle. Somebody was unlocking his door. He kicked it. "Hello!?" It swung open and the dim light burned his eyes. He squinted, having been in the darkness for so long. An arm reached in and grabbed his ankle. It pulled him out. He didn't resist. Once he was outside the small cell he looked around. It was a large room lit only by torches that hung on the walls. It was all stone, the floor, the walls, the ceiling.

It was when Mark looked up at the ceiling that he noticed who, or what had pulled him out. He jumped back and slid away from it. It appeared to be half man half snake. It stood on legs like a man and had the shape of a man, but its skin was black and shiny scales. Its face and eyes were also like a snake. Mark could see sharp teeth.

"Stand up!" it commanded him in an extremely deep voice. "Now!"

Mark did as he was told. "Whh...w...what are you g...going to do?"

Mark asked, backing away.

The creature grabbed his arm so fast he almost pulled it out of the socket. He led Mark to the center of the room.

It was then that Mark noticed the table that lay in the center. There was a large drain vent below it, with a dark liquid caked around it. The table had chains at both ends. The creature tossed Mark against the table with one hand.

"Lie down!" it commanded.

"Why? What are you…?"

"Lie down NOW!!" it interrupted him, apparently not wanting discussion.

Mark slid up on the table. "Where am I? Can you tell me that?"

The creature pushed him down to the laying position and proceeded to lock his arms in.

"Is this the castle?" Mark asked. "Answer me!"

The creature then fastened his legs down. Mark couldn't move.

"What are you going to do?" Mark asked. "Do you know David? He's my guide. I'm going to call him."

The creature walked over and brought a cart over next to the table. There were various instruments on the cart.

What are you going to do to me?" Mark started struggling to free himself. "David!" he screamed. "David, come help me!

"Silence!" the creature said.

"David may look small, but something tells me even you aren't a match for him."

The creature actually smiled at that. It really was a creepy sight; all those teeth.

"You need to be more careful what God you pray to boy!" His laugh was so loud it shook the walls.

Gabi jumped awake. She'd been dreaming. Mark…a snake. Mark was in trouble. "Father, please protect Mark.

I just know he's in trouble. Please be with him and give him the wisdom to seek your help. In Jesus' name. Amen.'

It was morning. Her mom poked her head into her room. "You up?"

"Yes ma'am, have you heard anything?"

"Just that Bethany is stable and they're supposed to be talking with a specialist today."

"So nothing on Mark?"

"No, but your dad just left to go look for him."

"I wanna help," Gabi said.

"You have school. Didn't you say you had a test today?"

"Please, Mom, I can't take a test knowing Mark is missing."

"I'm sure he'll turn up, but okay. Just...don't go to that castle."

Gabi nodded and went to shower. She would call Scotty once she dressed. She felt so refreshed, what a good night's sleep. She tried to remember her dream. Something about Mark falling in a hole and realizing it was a giant snake hole. The snake was about to eat him when she woke up. "That boy has definitely brought a lot of craziness into my life." She said to herself and it was right then that she remembered last night. She froze. Had she really seen an angel last night? Had that been a dream also? It seemed real. He had been in her room. What had he said his name was? Tony? Toby? No, Topher, that was it. She showered, still not sure if it had been real.

Scotty convinced his Mom that he didn't have anything important to do at school today so she let him miss. It had been a tiny lie but considering he did it to help his friend, he figured it was okay. He showered and dressed and as he went down to eat something, his phone rang.

"Scotty, I'm taking your brother to school, and going to work. Stay in the neighborhood."

"Yes ma'am." He grabbed the phone. "Hello?" It was Gabi. "Hey!"

"Are you going to school?" she asked.

"No way, I'm going to look for Mark."

"Me too, I'll be right over. I have to tell you something."

"Okay, see ya."

Ten minutes later his doorbell rang. He opened the door and Gabi darted in. "Good morning to you too." Scotty said.

"Yeah, yeah. I had a visitor last night; at least I'm pretty sure it wasn't a dream. I was pretty tired."

"A visitor?"

"An angel."

"Clayton? What did he look like?"

"No, his name was Topher and he was young, like in his twenties."

"Topher? What kind of name is that?" Scotty asked.

"It's short for Christopher, thank you very much!" A voice behind them said, causing them both to jump.

"Topher!" Gabi said, "So, it wasn't a dream!" She ran up and hugged him. "That was the best night of sleep I've ever had."

He smiled, "Awesome."

Scotty just stood there with his mouth open.

"Well hello there, Mr. Scotty Morgan." Topher held his hand out to shake Scotty's.

Scotty took it and Topher yelled, "BOOM!" Scotty jumped back and screamed.

Topher laughed, "Sorry man, just breaking the ice."

"Well, now I have to go change shorts," Scotty said, clearly terrified.

Gabi and Topher laughed, Scotty was not amused.

Topher pulled him into a hug. That seemed to really calm him. "Oh wow," Scotty said, backing away. "Now prove you're an angel."

"How?"

"Do something angely."

Topher laughed and was gone.

Gabi and Scotty looked around. Topher came walking out of the kitchen eating a cookie. "Hey, these are good."

"Dude, that was awesome." Scotty said.

"While I agree that it was awesome," Topher said, "that is not the proper way to test an angel."

"Oh, what is?" Scotty asked.

"You ask them who they serve," Gabi replied. Topher nodded.

"Okay, who do you serve?" Scotty asked.

"I serve the King of Kings and the Lord of Lords! Jesus! Emmanuel! The Lord on High!" And he bowed on his knees.

"Demons fear the name of Jesus." Gabi said.

"Yes they do!" Topher said.

"Okay," Scotty said, "you're an angel, and that's really cool, but what's the plan?"

Topher smiled at them both. "We're going," he paused for effect, "on an adventure."

It was the strangest thing, Larry thought, he and Topher had gotten in the van, pulled out of the driveway and driven maybe fifty feet. He'd asked Topher where they were going and looked over and Topher was gone. He'd slammed on brakes in the middle of the road and the van had stalled. When he went to start it again, he'd looked up. He was no longer in his neighborhood. He was parked in the parking lot of a small church. The sign read Gateway Community Church, Pastor Joshua Guillemette. The strangest thing indeed.

Just then someone tapped on his window and he jumped. There was a tall, well- dressed young man standing there smiling. Larry rolled down his window. "I have one question for you, sir," the man said. "How did you do that?"

"What did I do?" Larry asked, just to make sure what the guy meant.

"Your van literally just appeared out of nowhere. Seriously, I was coming out to change the sign and bang, a van."

"You wouldn't believe me if I told you." Larry said.

"Time traveler?"

Larry laughed, "no."

"Alien?"

"No."

"Super hero? Government spy?"

"Okay, Larry laughed, "maybe you will believe me."

"I just put a pot of coffee on, come in and spin me this tale."

Larry got out. "Okay, cause apparently this is where I'm supposed to be."

"By the way, I'm Pastor Joshua."

"Larry Motes." They shook hands and Joshua led him to the fellowship hall.

"Have a seat, I'll pour." He brought the coffee with the cream and sugar. "So, are you from around here Larry?"

"Um, Neptune," Larry smiled. They laughed. "Yeah, I live in Gateway, I'm actually the worship leader over at Lighthouse Christian Center."

"I thought your name sounded familiar. Now that is interesting. The plot is thickening."

"How so?" Larry asked.

"I've been praying for a worship leader and one literally appears in my parking lot."

Larry laughed. "Okay, are you ready for the story?"

"Hit me," Pastor Joshua said, taking a sip of his coffee and sitting back.

"Does this adventure have anything to do with rescuing Mark?" Gabi asked.

"No and yes." Topher replied. When he saw their confused looks he explained, "No, we're not going to rescue him right now. Yes, what we're going to do, could lead to his rescue."

"So, what are we going to do?" Scotty asked.

"Wait!" Gabi said. "So you know where he is?"

"Yes," Topher said.

"Then why won't you help him?"

"He isn't ready to be helped now..."

"Hold on!" Gabi yelled. "He isn't ready? What if he's killed, he's in that castle isn't he? What's the deal with that castle and why do I have a feeling it's controlled by demons?"

"Gabi," Scotty said. "You do realize you're getting an attitude with an angel?"

"It's okay, her passion is legendary in heaven."

"Wait," Gabi said, softening, "it is?"

"So back to my question, what are we going to do?" Scotty asked Topher.

"We are going to prepare for a battle," Topher said, smiling.

"Wait, a battle?"

"Yeah, it'll be epic!" Topher said. "Now take my hands."

Gabi and Scotty looked at each other, and took Topher's hands. Gabi asked, "What n..."

One second later they were standing in the sanctuary of a church.

"...ow?" Gabi continued. "Whoa!"

"Whoa is right!!" Scotty said. "What just happened?"

Topher laughed, "Isn't that cool? We're in a church in Atlanta, Georgia!"

"Where?" Gabi asked.

"Okay, you're explaining this to my mom, right?" Scotty said.

"Is this where the battle will be fought?" Gabi asked.

"Not this particular battle, no," Topher replied.

"Hey, do I get a sword for the battle?" Scotty asked.

Topher and Gabi just looked at him.

"A dagger? Pocket knife?"

"There's somebody here you need to talk to," Topher said.

"Who is it?" Gabi asked.

"An important piece of the puzzle."

Just then a man walked into the sanctuary wearing jeans and a button down shirt. He had dark hair that was silvering and a friendly face. He wore a smile that seemed to be permanent. He stopped when he saw them. "Well, hello. I didn't realize anyone was here," he said, appearing confused.

Gabi and Scotty only smiled, expecting Topher to speak first. He didn't. When they turned to look at him, he was gone.

Larry explained everything he knew about what was going on with Mark and Bethany. Pastor Joshua had listened intently. When he finished, Pastor Joshua got up and refilled his coffee.

"Well," he said, "it sounds to me like Satan is really waging war on this poor family."

"Absolutely," Larry said.

"And they're not believers?"

"No, but Pastor Eric has been with them at the hospital. Mark and Bethany have visited our church."

"Okay."

"So, what do you think?" Larry asked.

"Well, I'm not absolutely positive, but I think God wanted you and me to meet."

"I agree, but why?"

"I have no idea. You already have a pastor that is taking care of the situation. I've met Pastor Eric, he's a good man."

"And a great pastor," Larry added.

"Let's not talk about that," Pastor Joshua said and they both laughed.

"What about the angel thing?" Larry asked. "Am I crazy?"

"Well, I don't think so," A voice from the doorway said, and they both jumped.

"Oh wow!" Larry said. "Topher!"

Pastor Joshua had spun around and froze.

Topher smiled as he approached. He patted Joshua's shoulder. "Hello my friend."

"Wow, you're really...wow."

Topher laughed and looked at Larry. "By the way, Gabi and Scotty are in Atlanta."

"Atlanta? What? Why?"

"The Father's business, don't worry."

Pastor Joshua poked Topher's neck with his finger. "You're an angel?"

"A messenger," he held out his hand, they shook. "Call me Topher."

"Who do you serve, Topher?" Pastor Joshua asked.

Topher smiled, "Good question. I serve the Alpha and Omega, the Beginning and the End. The Lion of Judah, the King of Kings and the Lord of Lords. His name in your tongue is Jesus the Christ."

Joshua's eyes teared up and he had to sit down. "Wow...just wow."

"So," Larry said. "Not that I doubt you or anything, but why is my daughter in Atlanta?"

"She is preparing, as must we," Topher replied. "There is a lot of work to do." Larry's phone rang.

Mark had been trying to free himself ever since the creature had left. It was no use. The only thing he'd accomplished was tiring himself out. All his strength was gone. He was beginning to panic again. He tried to calm himself. He looked around the room. There were several cell doors like the one he'd come out of. He wondered if anyone else was here. What had become of Angel? He could still hear her screams at the school. How long ago had that been? Hours? Days? Weeks? He had no idea, was anyone even looking for him? His mom didn't need this. Not on top of whatever was wrong with Bethany.

Directly in front of Mark, was a large door. It was the door the creature had gone through. This was all so crazy. Was Mark dreaming? Was this all a nightmare? He hoped so but doubted it. Perhaps the dragon really had killed him and this was hell. Why would Mark go to hell though? He was a good…wait, according to Pastor Eric, Mark would go to hell if he died. You had to be found innocent. Mark had been a liar, a thief, a cheat, he'd even gotten revenge a time or two. Gabi had said that was bad. Okay, maybe this was hell.

It was so quiet. He could hear nothing but his own breathing and his heart pounding in his ears. Occasionally one of the torches would flicker. The longer he lay there, the more scared he got. All those instruments on that cart. What were they for? Would Mark be tortured? The silence was maddening.

His attention turned again to the other cells. "Can anybody hear me?" he called to them. "Are there any other kids in here?" No response. "My name is Mark McGee! Is anybody else in here?"

He was so afraid. It was the uncertainty that scared him most. He remembered his grandfather talking about the war. He'd told Mark that the worst part had been the not knowing. Any second a bomb could go off or a bullet could hit you. The next second could be the last second. The creature could come back and slit Mark open at any second. The dragon could come in and eat him. Or worse...he could just lay here and starve to death.

"David!" he called. Where was his guide? The one who had gotten him into this mess. Was he mad at Mark for failing to kill the dragon? Had he abandoned him to find someone else? No. He'd said Mark was the destined one from the prophecy. Where was he? "David!" This whole situation seemed hopeless. Mark had never been one to give up but there definitely seemed to be no way of escape here.

Just then the bolt in the big door clicked; it was so loud Mark jumped. His heart was pounding. Slowly the door opened. There was only darkness beyond it. Mark squinted to see. He saw movement. He tensed. The fear hit him like a sudden wave in the ocean. "No, No!!" He tried to free himself again, letting the panic take over, as the dragon entered the room.

CHAPTER THIRTEEN

THE MISSION

" **P**lease tell me that you saw him," Gabi said to the man that approached them in the sanctuary.

"I'm sorry," He replied, "Saw who?"

"Great," Scotty said. "Now you're gonna think we're crazy."

"Well," he said with a big smile, "why don't you introduce me to yourselves before I meet your imaginary friend." He laughed.

Gabi and Scotty were speechless. They just looked at each other.

"I'm only kidding," he said. "Seriously, is there someone else with you? Maybe they went to the bathroom or they're hiding."

"I'm Gabi." She held out her hand to shake his.

"Hello Gabi, I'm Pastor Randy." He shook her hand.

"And I'm Scotty." They also shook hands.

"Scotty...Pastor Randy Scalise. I'm the pastor of this small, albeit magnificent church."

"Nice to meet you," Scotty said.

"So what can I do for you, Gabi and Scotty and whoever else may be around?"

"Um," Scotty started.

"We have no idea," Gabi finished.

"I feel a story coming on," Pastor Randy said. "Shall we sit?"

"Yes we shall," Gabi said. "You're about to hear a doozie."

They sat on the back row of the church and proceeded to tell Pastor Randy their entire story, from Mark's arrival in Gateway, until Topher left them here in the sanctuary.

He stared at them. He smiled and looked around. "I'm being punked aren't I?"

"I wish," Scotty said.

"No sir," Gabi said. "I promise that entire story is true."

"So you're telling me that an angel…Topher, brought you here in a matter of seconds, from Florida?"

They both nodded. "Gateway, Florida," Scotty said.

"Parents?"

"I could call my dad," Gabi said, taking out her phone.

"Please do."

She dialed and put it on speaker.

"Hello, Gabi?"

"Hey dad!" She said, not sure what to say.

"Atlanta huh?" Larry said.

"So you know?" Gabi asked.

"Hello, Mr.?" Randy started.

"Motes." Gabi added.

"Mr. Motes, I'm Pastor Randy Scalise of Mableton Church in Atlanta, Georgia. Um, I have a few questions."

Larry laughed. "I'm sure you do, and I can assure you that whatever Gabi and Scotty have told you is one hundred percent true."

"Uh," Pastor Randy said, "even the angel thing?"

"Especially the angel thing," Larry said. "Listen I'm in Gateway, Florida right now Pastor Randy, sitting in the fellowship hall of Gateway Community church with Pastor Joshua Guillemette and...someone else."

"And who might that be?" Pastor Randy asked.

"Well...Topher."

"Are you serious, Dad?' Gabi asked. "Topher is there?"

"Yeah." They heard Pastor Joshua confirm it in the background.

"No offense," Pastor Randy said, "but, I need a little more to go on."

"Hold on," Larry said, and there was a pause. "Okay... this is amazing...Topher says, last night, sitting at your home office, you asked God to reveal your true purpose."

Pastor Randy's mouth dropped open.

"He says," Larry continued, "You should be careful what you ask for, and oh, get ready."

"Get ready?" Pastor Randy asked. "For what?"

"For this!" They all turned around in their seats, and up on the stage stood a man, who as soon as they saw him, lit up as bright as a star. They had to cover their eyes. His wings spread out from wall to wall. His countenance was brilliant. Light shone from his pores.

Pastor Randy let out a moan and fell to the floor.

Topher's brilliance faded and he was back in jeans and t-shirt. "Where'd he go?" Topher asked, looking for Pastor Randy.

Scotty pointed to the floor.

"He isn't bowing to me is he? That would not be cool."

"Thank you Jesus!" Pastor Randy cried out in a loud moan.

Topher smiled, "Awesome. He's worshipping the right one."

Gabi smiled.

"Dude!" Scotty exclaimed. "Why did you leave us? That was totally embarrassing!"

"Dude!" Topher replied, "he had to believe without seeing."

"Yeah, well, heads up next time." Scotty replied.

Pastor Randy continued crying, so they all, including Topher, knelt down in worship of God.

After a few minutes Scotty spoke up, "um, does anyone else hear a voice?"

They all looked at him.

"Oh, wow." Gabi grabbed her phone. "Hey dad, sorry. Yeah, Topher's here. Crazy huh? Okay, I'll keep you posted. Love you." She hung up.

Pastor Randy stood up and gave Topher a big hug. "This is unbelievable."

"Well, believe it!" Topher said. "Because you haven't seen anything yet!"

"So, what's next?" Scotty asked.

"Next..." Topher smiled... "We go back to Gateway."

"Wait..." Pastor Randy said, "What?!" The church was empty. They were gone.

Mark was terrified as the dragon entered the room. He seemed larger than ever. His laugh was a low roar that caused the flames to flicker. Once he was in the room, several of the creatures came in behind him. They lined up around the walls. Mark counted thirteen of them. Mark struggled against his chains. It was useless, they held. Sweat poured from his brow and stung his eyes. He squeezed them shut hoping to awaken from this nightmare. He could hear the dragon as it circled the room. Its breathing was deep and heavy. Its claws clicked on the stone floor. He could hear the tail dragging behind.

"Mark McGee," it said in a voice so deep it hurt Mark's chest. "I told you that you belonged to me." It laughed again.

Mark opened his eyes and the dragon's face was right over him. He could smell his foul breath. "Please let me go!" Mark pleaded. "I'll leave you alone. I'll mind my own business like everybody else! Please! I'll do anything you want."

"Yes you will," the dragon said with a low rumble from its chest. "And what I want, Mark McGee, is for you to die." His laughter shook the walls.

Mark looked away. "Okay!" he screamed, "Okay!" The dragon stopped laughing. "Anything but that."

"The only thing better than you dying, Mark McGee!" the dragon said, "is you dying slowly:"

"No!" Mark screamed as he strained to get loose. "God help me!"

"God???!" The dragon raised its head up high, smoke poured from its nostrils. "There is NO GOD HERE!!!" He roared. The walls shook, a torch fell from its holder and fizzled out.

Mark looked at the creatures; they remained as statues. He squeezed his eyes shut expecting to feel pain at any second. After a few seconds of silence, the dragon began to laugh. Mark opened his eyes.

The dragon was walking around the room again. "Mark, Mark, Mark," he said as he walked. He stopped near Mark's feet. "That girl has poisoned your mind."

"What girl? Gabi?" Mark asked.

The dragon laughed again. "Gabi Motes with her high and mighty self."

"High and mighty? What are you talking about? She's my friend."

"Why is she your friend, Mark? What has she ever done for you except preach at you, judge you and boss you around? What kind of friend is that?" He laughed. "She has poisoned you."

"You liar!" Mark screamed. "Gabi is a good friend!" More laughter. "She cares about me, prays for me, she was the one who went looking for me when I was at the castle!"

"You're at the castle now! Where is she?"

"Wait a minute." Mark thought for a second. The dragon walked up beside him. "Why are you so concerned with Gabi? What about a twelve- year old girl worries you?"

"Worries?" The dragon laughed. "I could crush her in my jaws."

"No, you're scared of her…Lucius was scared of her too…is it her relationship with Jesus that…"

"Aughhhh!!!" The dragon threw himself back, the creatures covered their ears at this roar. His tail slammed against one of the cell doors and shattered it. Mark braced for the death blow.

"Never say…." The dragon began to say but one of the creatures stepped forward and as he did he became David, a boy in a suit holding a flaming sword. "Enough,

Foul Dragon! Be Gone!!!" He sliced the sword through the dragon who exploded in ash right next to Mark.

Mark turned his head from the flash of the blade and the explosion. When he looked back, David stood where the dragon had been, the sword in his hand. He stared at the floor, breathing heavy.

"David! Wow! You're here!" Mark said. Immediately his chains loosened and he was free. He sat up.

David looked at him and smiled. "Of course I'm here."

"I thought you'd abandoned or given up on me." Mark hopped off the table.

"I was waiting for the right time."

Mark looked around. The other creatures were gone. "Where did they go? Is the dragon dead?"

"The creatures will return, Mark," David said. "I need to hide you." He grabbed Mark's arm.

"What? Hide me where? Can't we leave?" Mark was frantic, he grabbed David by the arm.

"Come on David, take me home."

"Mark, calm down," David said, and he walked over to a shelf. He took a small black bottle, no bigger that a salt shaker, down. He walked over and placed it in Mark's hand. "You have to keep this safe until…"

"Until what David?" Mark asked. "What is it?"

"Until you get it through the gateway, Mark."

Mark looked at the bottle in his hand. "Wait, is this…?"

"Yes Mark, that bottle contains the souls of hundreds of children. You have to find the gateway to God and release them."

"Wow," Mark said in awe. "It's so small."

"Souls are only like small seeds. They cannot grow until they reach the soil of heaven."

Mark nodded. "So, where's this gateway?"

"It's hidden somewhere in the castle Mark, I'm afraid only the dragon knew, and now he's dead."

"So we have to search for it?" Mark asked. "What does it look like?"

"You have to search for it Mark. My business is elsewhere for now. As for the gateway, you will know it when you find it. Now go, and beware. The castle has many secrets and many dangers. Oh, and Mark, the four castles connect."

"Wait, David, I can't do this alone. And what do you mean they connect?" David was pushing him to the door.

"In one room you may be in America and in the next you be in Italy or Germany or France. David opened the door.

"Wait, please come with me, I don't have a clue what I'm doing."

"You must look for the gateway, now go, the creatures will return, and this time they will not be so nice."

"Nice? You think they were nice?"

"Go!" David pushed him out the door. "And be wise." He closed the door, and bolted it.

Mark stood in a long hallway lined with torches, old paintings, and suits of armor, various statues, and total silence. He was all alone.

Larry hung up the phone with Gabi. "Wow, I still don't know what's going on, but this is crazy."

"Yeah," Pastor Joshua said, "I need more coffee."

"I seriously don't think anything else could phase me right now," Larry said.

"Surprise!!" Topher yelled as he, Gabi, Scotty and Pastor Randy just appeared right there next to where Larry sat.

Larry knocked his chair over jumping back "Whoa!" He yelled. "I stand corrected."

Topher hugged him, laughing. "I love doing that!" He was so excited. "It's not every day I get to appear to humans."

"And it's not every day we get appeared to," Pastor Randy added.

"Oh, and Larry," Topher said. "God will always have new wonders for you. Be prepared to always be surprised!"

"Wow! I will. Thank you," Larry said.

Gabi hugged her dad. "Isn't this amazing?"

"Yes it is," Larry said. "I keep waiting to wake up."

Topher introduced Pastor Randy to Larry and Pastor Joshua. They shook hands, hugged, made a few jokes, and then turned their attention to Topher.

"Okay," Topher said, "if everyone would just have a seat, I will explain a little bit about what is going on."

"Finally," Scotty said.

"This is so exciting," Pastor Joshua said. "Are we like the Seal Team Six of God?" Everyone laughed.

"Well, I am sending you on a mission," Topher said.

"A mission!" Pastor Randy raised a fist, "my purpose revealed!"

Topher smiled at him. "Pastor Randy, your purpose, like every person is this room is to be Jesus to a lost and dying world, every day, every moment, without exception."

You could've heard a pin drop. Nobody moved or spoke.

"But that goes without saying, now doesn't it?" Topher said, smiling. "Now, the mission."

All of a sudden, Topher froze; he looked up. A dim light showed through his pores. His hair glowed like fiber optic lights.

Pastor Joshua went to his knees in worship. "Thank you Jesus for this opportunity and privilege, to not only witness the beauty and majesty of your creation, but to be used by you." The others bowed their heads, except Scotty, who couldn't stop watching Topher, who seemed to be in a trance, watching the ceiling with a big smile on his face.

Just like that, Topher stopped shining, and turned back to them as if nothing had happened. "The mission!" He said. They all looked up. "Okay..."

"Wait!" Scotty said. "What just happened?"

"Oh, right," Topher said with a laugh. "I was just informed that we need to act swiftly. The enemy is on the prowl."

"So what's that mission?" Pastor Joshua asked.

"There's someone you have to find," Topher responded.

"Find?" Scotty asked.

"Yes, find," Topher replied.

"But you're an angel. Don't you know where they are?" Scotty shrugged. "Just asking."

"You have to find him and convince him," Topher said.

"Convince him of what?" Larry asked.

"The truth...of course."

"Who do we have to find?" Pastor Randy asked.

"His name is John Hoffman and he's an atheist."

"Do you know where he is? "Scotty asked. "I mean, is he nearby?"

"He lives in Germany."

"Germany?!" They all exclaimed together.

"How exactly are we going to get to Germany?" Scotty asked.

Topher gave him a confused look," Really?"

"What?"

"Scotty," Topher said. "We'll be in Germany before I finish this…sentence."

They were standing in an old church building. It was made of stone and wood. Quite drafty. It was night time also. Had it not been for the light coming from Topher's face it would have been pitch dark.

"Whoa!!" They all said collectively.

"I think I need to call my wife," Pastor Randy said.

"Yeah, me too," Larry agreed.

"Mom isn't going to believe this," Scotty said.

"This is amazing!" Gabi exclaimed. "We're in Germany!"

"Listen to me," Topher said. "Time is short. When you speak, they will understand you in German. When they speak, you will understand them. His name is John Hoffman and he is a piece of this puzzle. You must convince him to believe and it will not be easy. I cannot be with you but you will not be alone. When you have succeeded, I will come for you."

"What if we fail?" Scotty asked. They all turned to look at him.

"You must not fail, Scotty Morgan," Topher said. "It cannot be an option." And he was gone. And it was dark.

"Okay, that was intense," Larry said.

"Yeah, and he gave us absolutely nothing to go on but a name," Pastor Joshua said.

"So what is this place?" Scotty asked.

"More importantly," Pastor Randy said, "is, does it have electricity?"

"I have a flashlight on my cell phone," Larry said. "Gabi, come with me to check for lights."

Pastor Randy and Pastor Joshua went to go outside to get a lay of the land but quickly realized it was quite chilly. Pastor Joshua found a closet with jackets in it. They put them on to a perfect fit and went outside.

After a few minutes, Larry and Gabi discovered there was power in the kitchen. Scotty found the bathrooms. Larry got a fire going in the wood burning stove.

Moments later, Pastor Randy and Pastor Joshua returned. "We are literally in the middle of nowhere, Germany." Pastor Joshua said.

"Is that really the name of the town?" Gabi asked.

"No, according to the sign out front, we are in Einfahrt, Germany."

Scotty snickered and looked at Gabi.

Gabi rolled her eyes at him. "Yes, of course, Mark told us about Einfahrt." Scotty laughed out loud. "Oh grow up Scotty Morgan!" she said.

"Well?" Larry asked, "how is it significant?"

"All we know is that Einfahrt is the German name for Gateway, and there's a sister castle here."

"Do you mean to tell me there's another castle like the one in Gateway, here in Germany?" Pastor Joshua asked.

"Yes," she replied, "there are four of them. One in Florida, one in Germany, one in Italy and one in France."

"That's just crazy," Larry said.

"Well guys," Pastor Randy said, "crazy or not, we have a mission. We need to find John Hoffman."

"Should we go out now?" Larry asked. "Or wait until morning?"

"I say we go now," Pastor Randy said. "It looked like this church is in the middle of town we can at least get an idea, maybe find someone with some information."

"Good idea, let's go," Pastor Joshua said. "There's jackets in the closet by the front door." There just so happened to be one that fit perfectly, for each of them.

So they walked out of the church into the small town of Einfarht, Germany on a cool summer evening, in search of a man they didn't know. They had no idea where to begin.

"I wonder if there's some kind of phone directory or something," Gabi said. "Maybe we could get his number or address?"

"Good idea," Pastor Randy said. "And maybe I can call my wife."

"Mr. Larry," Scotty said. "I would prefer it if you would contact my mother." They all laughed.

"Maybe there's a phone booth," Pastor Joshua said. "A brilliant idea Gabi."

They came to a street corner, and looked both ways. There weren't too many people out and about on this chilly night. There were a few, however, at what appeared to be a tavern. They headed in that direction.

"This place looks like it came right out of a Thomas Kinkade painting," Gabi said. "With the cobblestone roads and streetlamps. Beautiful." Everyone agreed.

"Who thought this was where your day would lead you when you woke up this morning?" Pastor Joshua asked.

"Not me," Scotty replied.

A man came out of the tavern as they approached.

"Excuse me sir," Larry said, noting his own German accented voice. "Is there somewhere we could find a town directory?"

"I beg your pardon?" The man looked confused and suspicious.

"Perhaps you can help us, "Pastor Joshua stepped up. "We're looking for a man named John Hoffman, do you know him?"

He took a step back. "What business would you have with Mr. Hoffman?" He asked. "Unless you're in the business of trouble." He eyed Scotty and Gabi and then turned to walk away.

"Could you just tell us where we might find him?" Pastor Randy asked.

He turned back to them. "You do not find John Hoffman...he finds you." With that, he turned and hurried off.

"Does anyone communicate with straight answers anymore?" Scotty asked.

"He looked scared," Pastor Joshua said.

"Yes he did," Pastor Randy agreed.

"So what now?" Scotty asked.

"Well," Larry said, "he said John Hoffman would find us...let's put the word out that we're looking for him."

CHAPTER FOURTEEN

CHAOS AND CONFUSION

Mark wasn't sure which way to go. Both ways looked equally promising and equally hopeless. He decided that at any decision he would choose to go right. That way he could easily back track if necessary. He took a torch off the wall, it felt better to have something in his hands. With that, he headed down the hall. There were no doors or windows, only pictures and various medieval artifacts. After about a hundred feet he came to the end of the hall. He turned right again. It was so quiet, the only thing he could hear was the soft sound of his tennis shoes on the stone floor.

After walking on the second hallway for about twenty feet, Mark came to a door on his left. He stopped in front of it. It was a large brown wooden door with a huge round doorknob. He took a deep breath and turned the knob. The door opened. It was dark inside the room as he stepped in. Only the flickering of the flame of his torch, which caused shadows to dance on the walls. He jumped back thinking it was something moving, then laughed at himself. "Jumpy much?"

He saw a torch bracket on the wall and placed his torch in it. It lit the room good enough. He left the door open for extra light. The room was square, about eighteen by eighteen, Mark thought. Considering his stepdad's line of work, he tended to notice such details. There were paintings on the walls, one was a mountain scenery, a forest, and then there was one of a woman that did not look very friendly. Her eyes seemed to follow Mark as he walked. There was no furniture in the room except for a thin table against the back wall. It was an old wooden table about four feet long. It wasn't, however, the table that caught Mark's eye. It was the magnificent Indian head dress that sat upon it. It was beautiful and extremely colorful, with feathers and beads that shimmered in the dim light of the room. It was quite a sight. As Mark stared at it, he remembered David's story about the Indian burial ground. Then he thought of the souls in the bottle he'd placed in his pocket. He had no idea what he was looking for but could this headdress be the gateway? He reached out and ran his fingers through the feathers.

As soon as he touched it, the door behind him slammed shut and the torch went out. He jumped and spun around. To his surprise, he was no longer in the room. In fact, it appeared that he was in a forest at night. He could see the starry sky through the trees. He could hear the normal sounds of a forest also, crickets, frogs, the wind blowing. Then he heard a twig snap. He looked in that direction and could see people and shadows moving quietly through the forest. He moved closer for a better look. There was a lot of people, and they were walking in single file, not speaking or making a sound.

He couldn't make out any details in the dark but with their head gear they appeared to be dressed like Indians. He decided to be brave and find out what was going on. He stepped out into their path. "Excuse me, can you help me?" He asked a passing woman. Nothing. "Hello, can anyone help me. I just…"

"They can't hear you."

Mark jumped and spun around; it was David. "David! I thought you…

"I had a moment and thought I would check on you."

"Where am I?" What's happening?"

"Follow me." He led Mark to a clearing where they were all gathering around a huge bonfire.

"What's going on, David; why are they dressed like Indians?"

David laughed. "They ARE Indians. You are witnessing history."

Mark watched as they began to play music. Some beat on drums, some had shakers, others danced and made noises with their mouth. It seemed like a sad event to them but it was beautiful to watch.

"It is a burial ceremony," David said. "For several children."

"That's sad," Mark said, looking for the bodies. "How did they die?"

"They haven't yet."

Just then a large man led five children up to the front where an old man that appeared to be the chief sat. Mark noticed that he was wearing the headdress from the table.

"What do you mean, yet? What's happening?" Mark panicked.

"Just watch," David said calmly.

Mark saw something move along the tree line behind the chief, as the chief spoke to the children. It seemed to be a large shadow moving closer, then as it came into the firelight, Mark saw the eyes. It was the dragon.

"David! I thought you killed him!" Mark said, grabbing David's shoulder.

"Mark, this happened many years ago, just watch."

The chief spoke to the group. Everyone bowed with their faces to the ground. Then the chief appeared to be praying. As he did, the dragon raised up behind him. He closed his eyes and seemed to be smelling the air. When the chief finished praying, the large man that had led the children out, walked up behind the first one and put his arm around him. Mark couldn't see what he did, but the boy collapsed to the ground. He did this with each one.

"What is he doing?" Mark asked.

"He's cutting their throats," David said.

"What?!" Mark exclaimed. "Why??" But when Mark looked over, David was gone.

The dragon laughed an evil laugh that shook the ground. Nobody seemed to notice it but Mark. Everyone seemed to be in prayer and oblivious to the huge dragon that was leaning over the bodies. Just then the dragon looked up and right at Mark. At the same time there was a sound behind him. He jumped and spun around. When he did, he was no longer in the forest. He was back in the castle, standing in the hall just outside the room he'd just been in. He was holding his lit torch.

Billy Mumpower was eating dinner with his mom and her boyfriend, Harold. Meatloaf and succotash. Billy hated succotash. His mother insisted it was good for him but he found it difficult not to heave when he put it in his mouth. Normally he would make other arrangements to have dinner at a friend's house when he knew his mother was making succotash. Tonight however, he couldn't locate any of them. Matt's mom had said he couldn't come to the phone, and she'd seemed quite upset, which was not normal. Matt's mom was always really nice. Since he'd found out that Mark's sister was in the hospital, he assumed that's where Mark, Gabi and Scotty were, since none of them could be found.

"It's so terrible what happened to Ms. Tyler," Billy's mom was saying. "Such a pretty woman, and so young."

"Yeah," Billy said, "and what's weird is how she's been teaching class all this time, while being dead."

"Well, it must've been someone else Billy. You never have been one to pay attention to what's going on around you."

"Mom, she introduced herself, wrote Ms. Tyler on the chalk board. That's her on the news!"

"It can't be Billy, she's been dead for weeks, tell him Harold."

Harold, however, was watching the sports channel and not even listening.

"Oh for heaven's sake, you both have your head in the clouds," she said, getting up to clear the dishes.

As soon as she looked away, Billy scooped his succotash back into the pan.

Just then there was a knock at the door. "I'll get it mom!"

"You finish your succotash!" she yelled from the kitchen.

"I did." He was already at the front door. He opened it to find Matt standing there looking out of breath. "Matt?"

"Billy," he panted, "we need to talk."

In their attempt to get the word out, there hadn't been many people to tell that they were looking for John Hoffman. They'd covered as much ground as they could and it was getting late.

"We need to find a place to spend the night," Pastor Randy said.

"And I doubt our money is any good here," Pastor Joshua added.

"What about the church that Topher brought us to?" Gabi asked.

"That's actually a great idea Gabi!" Pastor Joshua said.

"Yeah," Scotty said, "and it's warm there. I'm not a fan of this cold German summer."

"Florida boy!" Pastor Randy teased. "Let's go and see if it's still open."

They headed back to the church, having wandered further than any of them had thought. It took over an hour to get there. As they walked down the back alley that led to the church, they stopped short. Someone was standing on the steps of the church. He appeared to be a large man, smoking a cigarette, and looking right at them.

"Who do you think it is? Scotty asked.

"One way to find out," Pastor Joshua said. Taking the lead, he walked toward the man while the others followed. "Excuse me sir, would you happen to know…"

"You are looking for John Hoffman," the man interrupted in deep, raspy voice. It was a statement not a question.

"Yes sir, we are," Pastor Joshua replied.

"You will stop."

"Excuse me?"

The man walked down the steps slowly, looking toward the ground. He stopped at the last step and flicked his cigarette onto the ground. He adjusted his hat and looked at Pastor Joshua. "You will stop...or you will die." He proceeded to walk away.

"But, we really..."

"Good night to you all," he called over his shoulder. "Enjoy the lovely Einfarht and all of its hospitality." With that, he disappeared into the shadows.

"Hospitality?" Scotty asked.

"Let's go inside," Pastor Randy said, and he led them all up the steps. The door was still unlocked and they all went in.

"Well Topher was right," Gabi said. "It's not easy."

"Yeah," Larry replied, "but he also said we couldn't fail."

"Well I don't know about the rest of you," Pastor Randy said, "but I'm exhausted."

"Definitely," Gabi agreed.

Scotty was already lying on a pew, using his jacket as a pillow.

As the rest of them prepared for bed, Pastor Joshua walked up to the old podium. He placed his hands on either side of it. "Heavenly Father, we come to you in Jesus' name." He paused for a moment. "I'm not really sure where to begin Father. We've all kind of been thrown into this crazy mission. We have no idea why you've chosen each of us. I'm sure you have a reason. Anyway, we sure do need your help. I pray first of all, that you give each of us a good night sleep. I also ask that you be with Mark and Bethany McGee, whom I've never met, but because of them, my life is being forever changed." Another pause. "Father I thank you for these friends that you've given me today. I pray that you would bless our mission tomorrow. That we would find John Hoffman, the mystery man. I also ask that you would begin to work on his heart tonight. That you would prepare him for our meeting." After a long pause. "In your son's holy name we pray…Amen."

"Amen," the others said in unison.

They all found a place to lie down. Within minutes they were sound asleep. The church was quiet. Only the wind and branches hitting the windows could be heard. Inside, nothing moved. Nothing stirred. Total quiet. Except, of course, for the two towering angels that stood guard just inside the door. They were mighty warriors. Legs as thick as tree trunks, arms bulging with muscles. Hands holding swords that were larger than the door they blocked. Daniel and Brandon were guardians of old, soldiers of Michael, of the army of God. They had protected God's people for centuries. From the ark of Noah to the Ark of the Covenant. From the lion's den to the tomb of Christ. From the apostle Paul to Billy Graham. From Jerusalem to a small church in Einfarht, Germany. Nobody would be bothering this group tonight. Nobody.

Mark continued down the hall totally confused. The hall appeared to go on forever. He assumed it had something to do with what David had said about the castles connecting. The next door he came to was on his right. It was a bright red door. "Open it!" He heard a girl's voice say and he whipped around. Nobody was there. "Hello?" He called down the hall. All was quiet. He could've sworn it had sounded like Gabi. He shrugged and turned back to the door. Just as he reached for the knob he heard a growling sound coming from the direction he'd been heading. In the faint light of the torches hanging along the hall, he could just make out what looked like a large black wolf. Teeth bared, drooling. "Awesome," Mark said to nobody in particular. The wolf began slowly walking toward him. Mark quickly reached for the knob and as he did, the red door vanished. Before he had time to register it, the wolf began running toward him, growling viciously. He turned and ran as fast as he could, knowing he could never out run the wolf. He could hear it gaining quickly. Everything looked different as he ran the direction he'd just come from. There were obstacles in his way. Columns lay across the hall, he had to jump over them. A statue of a huge raven lay in his path. He pushed past it, looking back to see the wolf leaping over the column. Just then he saw an entryway to his right that led to a huge spiral staircase. He had to make a split second decision to go up or down. Figuring he could run faster going down, he chose that. He ran down those stairs as fast as he could go. Round and round and down he went. He couldn't hear the wolf over his own panting and footfalls. Just when he started to think he was heading to the center of the earth, he rounded the corner and slammed into a huge wooden door. He dropped his torch. It went out. He was in total darkness. He could barely see the slight flicker of a torch burning about five stories above him. He dared not go get it for fear of the wolf. He listened intently for any sound of still being followed. He heard nothing above his own breathing. He leaned against the door panting, attempting to catch his breath. Then he heard it. A low growl. It sounded as if the wolf was right there in front of him. Slowly he reached for the door knob. He couldn't find it. He checked both sides. Nothing. Perfect. The growling intensified. "Nice doggie." He said, hoping his voice would at least confuse the wolf. "Pretty boy... or girl." The growling seemed to get closer and Mark pressed closer to the door. When he did, the back of his head touched something. He reached over him and felt a metal ring. What was it? It felt like a door knocker like the one at his grandparent's house. "Okay, here goes." With his back pressed to the door, standing on his tip toes, arms over his head, he knocked three times. The door clicked open and he fell backwards, fully expecting the wolf to leap on him. But nothing. No more growling, no sound at all, just total darkness. Slowly he felt for the door and closed it behind him. He now stood in a pitch dark room, with no idea what to do next.

As his eyes began to adjust, he could make out a faint light coming from somewhere about ten feet away. It was almost like a light was covered up or in a box. He slowly walked towards it, hoping he didn't bump into anything. Especially anything alive. For all he knew, there were fifty monsters in the room with him trying to figure out the best way to eat him. He made it to the light. There appeared to be a table with a box on it. A small chest. He opened the latch and lifted it. It was like a bright LED light filled the room. He had to turn his eyes for a few seconds. When he did, he saw that he stood in what looked like a storage room or a junk room. There were paintings leaning against the wall, statues, knights in armor, furniture setting about, shelves lined the entire wall to the right. They were mostly full of books but contained a few boxes. "Is there a gateway in here?" He asked the room, hoping he didn't get an answer. Then he looked down into the box. It was filled with small figures of knights and horses and dragons and various mythical creatures. The one that caught Mark's eye the most, was the one that was actually the light. It was a figurine of a unicorn. A bright white glowing unicorn. It was beautiful. Mesmerizing. He was afraid to reach in and touch anything after what happened with the Indian headdress. "You're so beautiful, I want to pick you up," he said to the unicorn. "Could you possibly be the gateway?" He did a quick look around the room and decided to go for it. He reached in and picked it up.

Everything around him immediately changed. He was in the hallway of his school, only it wasn't his school now. It appeared that he'd gone back in time. Everything looked new, except the banners and posters were all real cheesy looking. "Don't forget picture day!" One read. Another said, "Tropical Dance Night 1959." There was… wait…1959? He really had gone back in time. Just then the bell rang and students began to pour out into the hall where Mark was. Wow, their outfits and hair were ridiculous. Mark had to laugh. Apparently it was the end of the day, they were getting out of there quick. Mark followed the majority of the crowd out the front doors. He couldn't believe how different and clean everything looked. He was just wondering what he was supposed to be witnessing when he saw David across the street. David was following two girls down the sidewalk and hadn't seen Mark. He ran to catch up, almost getting run over by a huge round car that was as big as a bus. Mark jumped out of the way before he realized that it probably would go through him since nobody could see him. It was like being in a dream. David and the two girls he was following were way ahead now. He ran to catch up. "David!" he yelled and David looked over his shoulder and flashed Mark a smile. Mark passed several other students walking as he ran up beside David. "Hey, what's going on?" He panted. David put his finger up to his lips to tell Mark to be quiet. They walked along right behind the girls. It was as if David were listening to them. They were talking about some guy named Mackie that was sooo dreamy. After passing the next big intersection, the girls went to walk through a big empty field. If Mark wasn't mistaken, a Walgreen stood there now. There were houses on the other side of the field and trees along both sides. Mark looked over to see what David was going to do and he was gone. He looked all around. David had vanished. Mark assumed he was supposed to stay with the two girls since he'd come this far so he ran to catch up with them. They were now debating who was cuter, that Mackie boy or someone named Philip. Just then, one of the girls gasped and stopped dead in her tracks.

"What is it Melanie?" The other girl asked. Slowly the first girl, Melanie, raised her arm and pointed to a beautiful white horse next to the tree line on their right. "He's beautiful."

"Oh wow," the other girl said. "And he's loose, I wonder whose he is? Maybe Mr. Shepherd's? I've never seen that one before. He's so white, almost glowing."

Melanie was slowly walking toward him, when the horse looked up from grazing. All three of them gasped. It was no horse at all.

"Is that…?" the second girl asked.

"It's a unicorn!" Melanie said. "So beautiful." She seemed entranced.

"But that's impossible, Melanie," the other girl said. "There's no such thing as unicorns."

"Well, you see it don't you?" Melanie responded. "Come on Maria." Again, she walked toward it.

Mark had a bad feeling about this. Even though unicorns were pretty and kind of the symbol of all things girly, he had a feeling something bad was about to happen.

"No, Melanie!" Maria yelled. "This doesn't feel right. Let's get our parents."

"Oh come on you big baby, what's going to happen? It'll probably just run away!"

Maria stayed put though. She, like Mark, knew this wasn't right.

Melanie slowed as she got close to it and it stayed there, eating the grass or whatever unicorns eat. "Hello there?" Mark could hear her say. "Wow, you are sooo beautiful. Who do you belong to?"

"Come on Melanie, I'm going to go get my mom!" Maria called.

"It's fine, look!" Melanie yelled. "He's friendly!"

With one swift motion the unicorn lifted its head, turned and thrust its long horn right into Melanie's chest and tossed her like a rag doll. She never even screamed.

Marie, however, did scream. Loud and long. She ran as fast as she could toward the houses.

All Mark could do was watch as the unicorn tore off after her. Mark knew she would never make it. He looked around, "David!" he called. "David! Help!" When he looked back, Maria lay dead in the field. The unicorn turned and looked toward Mark, its horn was now blood red. It lowered its head and charged him. He turned and ran, calling for David. He was running fast. Screaming at the top of his lungs. "David! Help me!" Just as he reached the sidewalk, a hand hit his shoulder and pulled him back. He looked back, it was David, running behind him.

"Mark, easy…Its okay!" David called.

Mark stopped. He was panicked and panting. "Dude! Where were you? Did you see what happened? There was a unicorn! He killed those girls! Where were you?"

"It's okay man, this happened a long time ago."

"What? Unicorns are real?" Mark asked.

"And dragons too," David said. "Keep up, buddy."

Mark bent over with his hands on his knees to process the whole thing and when he looked back up, he was standing in the room holding the unicorn figurine. He quickly dropped it into the box. He was so confused. More than ever. What did any of this mean? Why did he see that? Where was the gateway? He could literally spend years in this castle searching for it. Was that the plan? Was that why all the children went missing? They were wandering around the castle on some lame mission to find a trinket that didn't exist? Maybe this really was hell. Maybe he would never see his family or friends again. A sense of hopelessness consumed him. He sat in a nearby chair and put his head in his hands. He couldn't cry. He wouldn't cry. He had to beat this.

He heard a scraping sound and looked up. There on the table, next to the box stood one of the dragon figurines. It had just been in the box. Now it stood on the table, staring right at Mark. "I know you aren't the gateway!" Mark yelled at it. "So what's your game?" Nothing. "Oh whatever!!" he yelled and reached up and grabbed it.

Everything went dark and his back was pressed to a wall. He was no longer in the same room. Someone coughed over to his right and it caused him to jump. It sounded like a kid. "Who's there?" he asked before it hit him that they wouldn't hear him. He heard chains rattle and heard a sniff. Someone was crying. "Let us out of here!!" A girl screamed, chains rattled again. "Lori," someone whispered. "Be quiet, maybe they'll forget."

Their whisper was cut short by a loud clang. A door was being unlocked. Straight ahead of Mark a large door opened and light spilled in. It was one of those creatures. It walked in carrying a torch. It placed the torch in the bracket and turned to face the three children that were chained to the wall. There were two boys and a girl. Each of them appeared to be a little younger than Mark. The creature walked over to one of the boys and stood in front of him. The boy was dirty with torn clothes. He looked like he'd been there a while. The other two were just as bad. "I'm sorry," the boy said, "we'll be quiet." The creature unlocked his chains and he fell to the floor. "Please don't hurt me." "Don't hurt him!" The girl yelled. "We're sorry!" All three began crying. Mark could only watch it play out. The creature grabbed him by his arm and pulled him out of the room, taking the torch with them. Mark ran out of the room before the creature slammed and locked the door. The boy was screaming for mercy. They were back in the room Mark had started in, with the table in the center. The creature picked up the boy and set him on the table. "No!!" the boy screamed. "Please!" He caught his flailing limbs and strapped him down.

"Why am I seeing this!?" Mark screamed and tried to grab the creature. He went through him like a ghost. "David!" Help me!" Nothing. No help came.

The creature stood over the boy doing something that made him scream louder. Mark refused to watch. He could hear the boy struggling and gasping and then... nothing. The room went silent.

Mark swung around to see what had happened and he was no longer there. He stood at the top of the spiral staircase holding his torch as if he'd never gone down. He quickly looked around. No wolf, no creature, no children. He was all alone.

"Mom!" Billy yelled, "its Matt, I'll just be outside!"

"Don't forget you're supposed to ..." she was saying as he closed the door.

"What's up man?" Billy asked, "Are you okay?"

"Not really," Matt panted, sitting down on the steps.

"What happened?"

"I started asking my dad questions about the castle," He said, catching his breath." He kept brushing me off, so I accused him of hiding something."

"Yeah?" Billy was shocked, Matt never caused trouble.

"Well, needless to say, that went over real well."

"What'd he do?"

"Sent me to my room, screaming, telling me to mind my own business. Forbid me to ever hang out with Mark again."

"Wow, that's intense," Billy replied. Matt's dad was usually pretty calm too.

"I know, right? Well then the news about Ms. Tyler came out and Mark was supposed to have been with her at the school and now he's missing too."

"Wait, Mark is missing?"

"Since last night dude, apparently that's why nobody was at school today, Mark, Gabi or Scotty. They're out searching for him, I guess."

"No wonder I can't get in touch with anybody. I thought they were all at the hospital."

"No, he's missing and I snuck out to go help find him."

"You did what!?" Billy was shocked.

"Yeah, I rode my bike around the neighborhood and, you know, down to the castle."

"Dude!?" Billy exclaimed. "You went to the castle??"

"Well, to the gate."

"And?"

"And I buzzed it, not knowing what I'd do or say, but I really wanted to find Mark. I had a real bad feeling about him."

"What happened?"

"Dude, the gate opened as soon as I buzzed it."

"No way!"

"Way! I freaked. There was no way I was going in there alone."

"So what did you do?"

"Well, as I was trying to figure out what to do, I heard footsteps and looked down the driveway. Old Man Willoughby was coming straight at me, walking pretty fast. "

"No Way!!"

"Dude, I've never moved so fast in my life!" Matt said.

"Did he say anything?"

Matt shrugged, "Don't know, I got out of there. About half way here I looked back and he wasn't behind me but I kept peddling as fast as I could."

"So you came straight here?"

"Yep. It was the closest place. I had to tell someone."

"Dude, that's crazy!" Billy said.

"It was so creepy like out of a scary movie creepy."

CHAPTER FIFTEEN

FEAR NO EVIL

G abi awoke to the smell of bacon and eggs frying. For a brief moment she thought she was home in her bed and all the previous day's adventures had been but a dream. No such luck. She opened her eyes to find Scotty staring at her from the next pew up. "So it wasn't a dream."

"Nope," he responded, knowing exactly what she meant.

"Who's cooking?"

"Pastor Randy and Pastor Joshua," Scotty replied. "They really seem to be hitting it off. They've been cooking and praying all morning."

"A match made in heaven," Gabi said, sitting up, "literally."

"Yeah, those guys are prayer freaks. They pray about everything."

"It's called prayer warriors, you goober."

"Whatever," Scotty replied. "By the way, what were you dreaming about last night?"

She thought for a second. "Um, I don't remember...why?"

He shrugged, "I got up to go to the bathroom and when I came back, you said, 'Open it!' really loud. I thought you were talking to me so I said, 'open what?' of course, you didn't respond, so I assumed you were talking in your sleep."

"Open it?" she asked.

"Yep. That was all you said."

"Hmm, I don't remember anything."

"So, I was wondering," Scotty said.

"Hold on, I have to go to the bathroom." And she left.

Scotty went into the kitchen with the others. Larry was pouring the o.j. and the coffee. There were eggs, bacon and toast. It smelled delicious.

"So," Scotty said, "what are we going to say when the pastor or priest of this place shows up and finds us here?"

"We're planning to send them money, when we get back home, to cover all our costs," Pastor Joshua said.

"For now, we're going to assume this is God's provision," Pastor Randy added.

"Amen to that," Pastor Joshua said. "Is everyone ready to eat?"

Gabi came in about that time. They all sat. Pastor Randy prayed a blessing over the food and over their day, and then they dug in.

"So," Gabi said, "you were about to tell me something, Scotty."

"Oh yeah," Scotty said. "I was thinking."

"Well that's dangerous," Pastor Joshua said, winking at him.

"It usually is," Gabi said, "but sometimes he's actually helpful."

"Well," Scotty continued, "I don't know if this is exactly helpful, but I was wondering where the castle is? You know, the one that's supposed to be here in Einfarht."

They all stopped eating and stared at him.

"What?" Scotty asked.

"You're right Gabi," Larry said, "sometimes he CAN be helpful." He tussled Scotty's hair. "Good idea Scotty."

"Well," Pastor Randy added, "it sure gives us a place to start. After we eat and clean up, we'll find out where this castle is."

They finished breakfast and cleaned up. Scotty had found a shower and each of them took turns washing up.

"Oh, I feel so much better!" Pastor Randy said. "Ready to face the day and defeat the devil!"

"Yes!" Pastor Joshua added. "I was just outside. It's a beautiful day, the sun is out. Of course, it's chilly, but it's beautiful."

"Is everybody ready?" Larry asked. "Where's Scotty?"

"Present and accounted for," Scotty said, coming in from having showered last. "Thank you guys for saving me so much cold water!"

They all laughed. "You can go first next time," Pastor Joshua said.

"Hopefully there won't be a next time," Larry said. "Maybe we can convince Mr. Hoffman today, and get out of here."

"Well, let's pray for God's favor one more time," Pastor Randy said.

"How can you guys pray so much?" Scotty asked.

"Well, like I've always said," Pastor Randy commented. "What you feed grows, what you starve dies."

Pastor Joshua and Larry gave amens and Gabi nodded.

"I don't get it," Scotty said.

"Basically," Gabi said, "the more you pray and seek God, the more you want to."

"What about the dying part?"

"Well hopefully that would be your fleshly desires," Pastor Joshua said. "Let's say you really love playing video games."

"Yeah!" Scotty said, "let's say that!"

"If you stopped playing, cold turkey, at first you would be going crazy. All you would think about is figuring out a way to play. But, the longer you didn't play, the easier it would get. New things would consume your thoughts."

"Yeah, but that would take a real long time…you know…if I played video games."

Pastor Joshua laughed. Gabi didn't.

"So you're saying God doesn't want me playing video games?" Scotty asked. "I don't play the violent ones."

"Only because your mom won't let you," Gabi added.

"Absolutely, God wants you to have fun!" Pastor Joshua said. "Just be careful not to let 'things' become more important to you than Him."

"It's called having idols," Larry said. "And God is very jealous. He wants to be the most important thing in your life."

Scotty nodded, apparently deep in thought.

Pastor Randy led them in prayer. When he finished, he asked, "So this castle, it's obviously evil?"

They all nodded. "Why do you ask?" Larry said.

"Well," he said, "the Lord is my shepherd, I shall not want. He makes me lie down in green pastures; He leads me beside quiet waters. He restores my soul; He guides me in paths of righteousness for His name's sake. Even though I walk through the valley of the shadow of death, I fear no evil, for You are with me; Your rod and Your staff, they comfort me. You prepare a table before me in the presence of my enemies; You have anointed my head with oil; my cup overflows. Surely goodness and lovingkindness will follow me all the days of my life, and I will dwell in the house of the Lord forever."

"Hey I know that!" Scotty said. "Where's it from?"

"Psalm 23," Larry answered.

"You know what I love about that? Pastor Joshua asked. "I love that it shows us as sheep. Helpless, useless, defenseless sheep."

"And how is that good?" Scotty asked.

"Because, Scotty," he replied. "God is our Shepherd. All we have to do, is obey His commands. Didn't you hear it? He makes me, He leads me, He restores, He guides me, He's with me, He comforts me, He prepares a table, He anoints me, He does all the work. We just obey Him and follow Him."

"And yet, we always try to complicate it," Pastor Randy added. "Just follow Him. Isn't that what He said to the disciples? Follow me!"

"And remember guys!" Larry said. "No matter what happens today, or at any point in all this…fear no evil, for He is with you."

They left the church and headed back into the main part of town. There were several shops open and people were out and about.

"Excuse me ma'am," Pastor Joshua said to a lady passing by, apparently in a hurry. "We were told there was an old castle in this town, and I was…"

She turned to walk away. "Stay away from that castle young man," she called over her shoulder, "especially with those children."

"Okay, thank you!" He called after her.

"Listen," Pastor Randy said, "there's several shops on each side of the street. Why don't Pastor Joshua and I take this side and you three take that side?"

"Somebody has to know something," Larry said. And off they went.

"After you, my good man," Pastor Randy said to Pastor Joshua and they stepped into a bookstore.

What none of them noticed were the two hooded figures standing near the entrance to one of the alleys, watching them. "Remember, stick to the plan," the smaller one said to the much larger one.

"But I want the girl too," The larger one said.

"Of course you do, but orders are orders."

"Why can't we get both of them? You don't think he would appreciate that? I bet he would!"

"Just stick to the plan!"

"How are we going to separate him from the others?"

"We wait."

"Yes, he IS here, as a matter of fact," Billy's mom said as she walked into the living room. They were watching updates on the Ms. Tyler story on the news. "Matt, your mother would like to speak with you."

Matt took the phone and headed down the hall to Billy's room. "Mom, let me exp…" he nodded. "I know, but…mom!" After several seconds. "No! I'll ride my bike back! No, I need..." She'd hung up. He went back into the living room and handed Billy's mom the phone.

"Everything okay?" Billy's mom asked.

"My dad is coming to get me," He replied. "I snuck out to help find Mark."

"Matt Ramsey!" Mrs. Mumpower yelled. "What were you thinking?"

"Something isn't right!" he said. "With what happened to Ms. Tyler! Mark was supposed to be with her last night and now he's missing!"

"Well, it's hardly the business of a thirteen-year old. Your father and the police can handle this."

"That's just it, they're not handling it!" he said. "I have to go!" He headed for the door.

"What!? Wait just one moment, Matt!"

"I can't, I'm sorry." He ran outside. "Tell my dad I'll be home later!" He jumped on his bike.

"Matt Ramsey!" she yelled. "You come back here!"

"I'm going with him mom!" Billy ran past her and grabbed his bike. He took off after Matt, his mom on the porch screaming at both of them.

"So!" Billy yelled, "now that we're both grounded for life, what's the plan?"

"We need to go to the school!" Matt said. They sped off in that direction.

As they got close to the school they could see there were a few police cars in the parking lot. Matt and Billy slowed down. "What now?" Billy asked.

"Good!" Matt yelled, "she's still there!" He took off toward the school.

"Who?" Billy yelled, trying to keep up.

"That reporter lady."

"Okay."

"We need to talk to her."

"About what?" Billy asked.

"About what's going on, if we can get her on our side, maybe she can investigate and help find Mark."

"Well, we better hurry, your dad is going to put an APB out on us!"

They rode into the parking lot. There were two police cars and the news van. The reporter lady was talking to police officer Matt recognized.

"Dude, what's her name?" Matt asked. "I think it starts with an A."

"I never watch the news," Billy said.

"Angie? Andrea? Alice? No…Alicia? Anna? Ann…?"

"Christina!" a guy yelled across the parking lot, and she looked his way. "We're on in five!" She headed towards him.

"Dude," Billy said, "you nailed it with the A."

"Christina!" Matt yelled, and she looked over. "We need to talk to you! It's very important!" She waved, but kept walking.

"It's about Ms. Tyler!" She stopped.

"I have to go on air!" she called to them as they got close.

"Trust me!" Matt said, "you'll want to hear this!"

"This will only take a few minutes, meet me by my van." She headed over towards her camera man.

"Dude!" Billy said. "We gotta hurry! Those cops keep looking over here." One officer headed towards them.

"Evening officer!" Matt waved.

"Hey, are you Ramsey's boy?"

"Gotta go! Come on Billy." He pedaled away.

"Hey!" the officer yelled. "Get back here! Call Ramsey, Jack, I think we found his son!"

Christina, who was about to go on air, turned when she heard the commotion. "What's going on officer?"

"Nothing, just some kids up to no good." He got in his car and went after them.

Billy followed Matt to the back of the school. "Dude! What now?!"

"We have to talk to Christina; follow me!" Matt yelled. The back parking lot was taped off from where the crime scene was. Once they got around the corner. Matt stopped. "I need a pen and paper, you got anything?"

Billy checked his pockets. "Gum wrapper." He handed it to Matt.

"Now I need something to write with." They both searched the ground. Nothing. They heard the cop car before they saw it. "Come on!" Matt said. They rode along the back wall of the school, slowly so Matt could check to see if the doors were locked.

"Hey! Stop right there!" the officer yelled, and shined his spotlight on them.

"Dude, go!" Billy said.

"Pay dirt!" Matt yelled and the next door opened. He rode his bike right into the classroom. "Come on! Lock it behind you!" Billy followed him in and closed and locked the door. Matt rode up to the teacher's desk and found a pen. He scribbled a note on the gum wrapper.

"What's the plan?" Billy asked.

"I need to get this to Christina. Come on." They went out into the hallway. The exit signs were the only lights on. "This way!"

"Matt! Billy!" It was Matt's dad. He was in the school. "You two better stop where you are!" He yelled from behind them somewhere. They only pedaled faster.

"How are we going to get out?" Billy whispered loudly.

"No idea, I'm winging this," Matt said. They turned the corner toward the front entrance.

"It's going to be locked," Billy said. "We're trapped.'

"Matthew Ramsey!" His dad was gaining on them. "Stop this instance!"

They saw a light outside the front door. A flashlight. Someone was outside it. Just then, the front doors opened wide and two officers stepped into the dark school. As they did, Matt and Billy zoomed past them and flew down the front steps.

"Hurry!" Matt said. "To the news van!" They rode around to the side parking lot as fast as they could.

"Matt Ramsey! Stop right now!" His dad was outside and running hard.

Christina stood beside the news van, it looked like they were about to leave. She looked up when she heard Matt's dad.

"Take this!" Matt said as he blasted past her. He held out the note and she grabbed it. He and Billy were out of the parking lot in seconds. Matt knew all the police cars were behind the school, by the time they got to them, he and Billy would be gone.

Matt led Billy to the trail that led to Billy's treehouse.

"Dude, your dad is going to kill you!" Billy said.

"I know, and you better come to my funeral," Matt said. They climbed up to the treehouse and sat.

"So," Billy asked, "why are we here?"

"This is where I told Christina to come for the story of her life."

"Wait, that reporter lady is coming here!" Billy asked.

"And hopefully soon," Matt said. "It won't take my dad long to figure out this is where we are."

They kept watch for over an hour. Matt was afraid to check his phone. He'd turned it off. A squad car had driven by but not stopped at Billy's house. They'd most likely called Billy's mom. Several cars had gone by, but no sign of Christina.

Just then there was a knock on the trap door. They both jumped and looked at each other, knowing the jig was up. Another knock and the door raised up. They both crouched down.

"Hello?" It was Christina.

"You're here!" Matt yelled. "Oh wow, she's here!"

"How did you get back here so quietly?" Billy asked. "We didn't see or hear you."

"Hey, I'm a country girl. Give me some credit."

"Thank you for coming," Matt said, offering her a chair.

"Yeah, well this better be good, I had to lie to my crew and the police to get here."

"Oh, it's good," Billy said.

"I just hope you believe us," Matt said. "Now let me tell you everything before you call me crazy." They all sat and Matt told about Mark's investigation into the castle and what happened with Todd and how the police were keeping everything quiet. He told her about how Mark was supposed to have been at the school with Ms. Tyler and now they were both missing.

239

"Angel's missing too," Billy said. "And she was at the school last night too."

"We just want to find Mark…Angel too, and hopefully they're together. Can you help us?" Matt asked.

"Wow," Christina said. "That's some story."

"We're not making it up. I've literally risked my future tonight. One of those cops is my dad," Matt said.

"Yeah, I know, and I want to believe you." She stood up. "It all sounds too much like an episode of X-Files or something."

Billy laughed.

"I know," Matt said. "It's why I didn't want to believe it at first either. Trust me, I gave McGee a hard time about all this."

"So what if I do believe you?" she asked. "What am I supposed to do? Go on the news with that? I'd be run out of town."

"Investigate it!" Matt said. "Isn't that what you do? Look into it. Our friends are missing! A teacher is dead! Everybody acts like we're crazy or too young to have a clue, but they're the ones ignoring all the signs!"

Billy nodded his agreement.

"Okay," Christina smiled. "I'll look into it. You've peaked my interest."

"Thank you!" they both said.

"But no promises. Here's my card. Call me if you can."

"Just, please don't put it off," Matt said. "They could be in serious danger."

"Okay, now you two need to go fess up to your parents." She stood to leave.

"Don't remind me," Matt said. They all left the tree house. Christina walked to her car parked up the street.

Matt rode his bike home. Billy walked right into his house and faced his extremely angry mother.

Mark decided to go the opposite direction this time, though direction seemed to not matter in the castle. After walking for a few minutes, he came to another red door. He faced it, almost afraid to touch it. He looked both ways. Still no wolf. As he was about to reach his hand out, he felt something on his foot. He looked down and screamed. The entire hall floor was covered with snakes. Big ones, small ones, slithering all over each other, all over Mark's feet.

"Please tell me I'm seeing things," he said to himself and closed his eyes. "Don't be real. Don't be real. Don't be real." He opened his eyes. They were real.

Just then, a large king cobra raised up between him and the door causing Mark to fall backwards on top of the slithering snakes.

"Open the door, Mark!" He heard a girl's voice again. He could've sworn it was Gabi.

"Gabi! Is that you?!" he called out, as the snakes began crawling over his legs. "Are you in there?" Help me!!"

He tried to reach for the door but the snakes underneath him began moving him down the hall, away from the red door. They seemed unfazed by the flames of his torch, though none of them attempted to bite him. They continued to move him down the hall.

"Somebody help me!" he called out. Nothing. The silence was maddening. Even the hisses of the snakes were quiet.

Then he noticed an open door up ahead. They slid him closer and closer. None of the snakes seemed to be going into the room. He needed to get in there. When he got close enough he rolled into the room while holding the torch up. The door slammed shut behind him.

He stood quickly and placed the torch on the bracket. He let out a yell when he saw someone looking at him and then realized that the wall was a mirror. In fact, the entire room was a mirror. Even the door, the ceiling and the floor. He was standing in a mirror box. His reflection went on and on in every direction.

"Well, this is cool." He said out loud. "I should do this in my room." He walked to the center. He turned slowly, wondering what he was supposed to do in this room. There was nothing to inspect. Only his reflection.

Just then, Mark noticed something strange. All of his reflections turned the same way. There were literally hundreds. They all walked to the back wall. They went from the floor, from the ceiling, the right, the left, all of them. They became one person. Him. Then, if that wasn't strange enough, that one reflection walked around the room and then right out the door. Mark looked around. He had no reflection. "Well, that was crazy," he said out loud.

He walked over to the door. "Am I supposed to follow?" He grabbed the door knob and as soon as he did, everything shifted. He fell back from the dizziness. He expected to hit the hard floor but landed in the dirt.

Quite confused, he looked around. He was on the playground at the front of his neighborhood. He was just about to get excited when he heard loud laughter. He jumped up and turned around. Andy and Eddie were standing by the swing set laughing at him. They each held half of his skateboard in their hands. It had been broken in half. He was about to say something when he noticed the crowd behind them. It was literally everyone in his school. They were all laughing at him. Scotty and Gabi were even there.

"You're such a loser, Yankee Boy!" Andy yelled. Everybody laughed.

Mark was so confused. He wasn't sure what to do. They could actually see him here? It felt more like a dream. He half expected to look down and be in his underwear.

"Look!" Eddie said, pointing at him." He's going to cry!"

"Cry baby, Mark!" Andy added and everyone laughed louder. "What are you going to do about your skate-board, Mark?"

"You gonna run tell mommy?" Eddie laughed and was joined by everyone else. Scotty high- fived Eddie.

Mark desperately wanted to beat the fire out of these guys. He tried to figure out his best course of action.

Just then someone tapped him on the shoulder. He jumped and spun around. Everybody laughed. It was a young girl.

"Now Yankee Boy's afraid of girls!" Eddie called.

Mark looked back, "shut up Eddie, you ARE a girl!"

The girl took Mark by the hand and led him away. "Come with me Mark McGee," she said, smiling up at him. She was younger than Mark by a few years and very pretty. Curly blonde hair with a light blue frilly dress.

"Wait, I know you," Mark said.

"We've never actually been introduced but you definitely know me," she replied, leading him to the edge of the playground.

"You were there at Todd's house as I was leaving in the police car. Who are you?" He could still hear everyone laughing. Andy and Eddie were yelling things at him.

"The important thing, Mark McGee," she said, "is who you are." She looked over his shoulder at the crowd. "I don't think they know."

He looked back. "What don't they know?"

"Who you are, silly!" She gave him a light shove. "You're the destined one. You're Mark McGee! Destined for fame!"

"I am?" He was so confused.

"Not to mention you're quite powerful," she added. "If they only knew."

"What are you talking about?"

"Look at them, Mark," she said and he turned to face them. They were pointing and laughing. Andy and Eddie were trying to be funny at his expense.

"What would you like to do to those two?" she asked.

"I'd like to knock them into Monday," he replied.

"Okay, that's good, but think…grander."

"Grander?" he asked.

"More, shall we say, creative. If you were all powerful, what would you do?"

"Okay," Mark thought for a few seconds. "I'd make all their hair fall out and their ears would double in size."

"Done." She clapped her hands.

"Wait, what?" Mark turned around and she was gone. Everyone was laughing harder than ever now. He turned back around and saw that they weren't laughing at him. Andy and Eddie stood there staring at each other with bald heads and huge ears.

By the third shop, it seemed nobody wanted to discuss the castle. Scotty looked across the street. Pastor Randy and Pastor Joshua were also coming out of their third shop. Pastor Randy threw his hands up. No luck either.

"Only two more shops to go," Larry said. "This will be the one."

"I hope so, "Scotty replied. "These people seem terrified to even talk about that castle. I mean, we only want to know where it is. We're not asking if we can get a room."

They entered what appeared, and smelled, to be a bakery.

"Oh wow," Gabi said. "Smells delicious."

"I'm not even hungry and I want something," Scotty added.

"May I help you?" a short pudgy man, wearing a white apron and very large mustache, asked.

"Yes," Larry said, "we were actually needing some information."

"Information?" he seemed disappointed. "I have the best bread in all of Germany, and you want information?"

"Yes, I'm sorry. Perhaps later I can get some bread. It smells amazing."

"What information?"

"I was wondering if you could tell us where the castle is."

"Castle?" he said a little too loud. "There are lots of castles in Germany! Which castle?"

"Well, it would be local. Everybody seems to be afraid of it."

The man turned and walked toward the back room. They assumed they'd lost him. He closed the door and quickly came back. "You are not from around here? No?" he said quietly.

"No sir," Larry replied.

"Well," he leaned over the counter, talking low, "listen to me." He looked around. They all gathered close. "That castle is evil. The home of the devil, they say. People do not go there. Children especially!" He looked at Gabi and Scotty.

"Why do you think it's evil?" Scotty asked.

"Many children have disappeared there. Never to be seen again."

"But you said people don't go there," Scotty replied.

"Some people are not so smart," he replied. "Teenagers especially. As you can see, there are not many children in Einfarht."

"So, it's only bad for the children?" Gabi asked.

"Not so much," he replied. "Adults die there. They are found, though. A reporter once, some hunters. Not many in my lifetime."

"Can you just tell us where it is?" Larry asked. "We just want to see it."

He stared at Larry for several seconds. "Only to look?"

"Yes. We've heard so much about it," Larry said.

"It is south, maybe one kilometer. Turn left at the crossroad. You will see signs warning you to stay away. About a half a kilometer on your right will be a dirt road with a gate. Do not go past the gate! You can see the castle from there."

"Wow, Dad," Gabi said. "It's close."

"You will stay away?" the baker asked.

"Thank you very much, sir." Larry said. "Your bread smells delicious."

"Do not go down that dirt road!" he said loudly. They turned to leave. "Do not go down that dirt road!"

"Do you think we should go down that dirt road?" Scotty asked, once they were outside.

"Scotty, this is serious!" Gabi said. "People here died in there!"

Larry ran across the street to get the pastors.

"We're going to the restroom, Mr. Motes!" Scotty called to him.

"There's the public restrooms at the end of the street!" he called back. "We'll meet you there"

He and Gabi headed that way, each going to their respective restroom.

The smaller hooded figure looked both ways before slipping quietly into the ladies' bathroom. He was immediately met by a blinding light that knocked him back. A giant hand picked him up by the throat and threw him back out into the street. Once he was able to refocus, he looked up at the hulking figure of the angel standing over him, sword drawn.

"Ah, Brandon!" the small, hooded figure said. "We meet again."

"Exactly what do you think you're doing, foul stench?"

"I was only going to borrow the girl for a bit."

"I would absolutely love to see you try again," Brandon said.

"Temper, temper! Come now Brandon! I'll give her back! I'm just trying to win some points with the boss."

"Be gone, sewage!" Brandon raised his sword but the figure vanished before he could drop it. He turned around. Gabi was coming out of the bathroom, tossing a paper towel in the trash bin. Brandon smiled at her, the faithful little warrior. She stood there waiting for Scotty. Scotty? Brandon was in the men's room in a flash. No Scotty. He soared through the roof and scouted the area, looking in every direction. The one going after Gabi had been a decoy. Scotty was gone. "Daniel!" Brandon called. Daniel was immediately next to him. He'd been guarding the pastors. "The enemy has Scotty."

"You know what to do," Daniel said. "I'll stay with our friends." Brandon vanished in a flash of light.

Larry and the pastors were walking to Gabi. Daniel stood behind her, unseen, sword drawn, looking back and forth down the street.

"Scotty in the bathroom?" Pastor Joshua asked.

Gabi nodded.

Pastor Joshua pushed the door open and went in. A few seconds later he came out. "He's not in here."

"We went in at the same time," Gabi said. "He wouldn't have left me."

"No, he wouldn't." Larry said. "He's been watching her better than I have."

"Scotty!" Pastor Randy yelled. They all began calling him.

Hundreds of angels began arriving. Daniel gave them orders, telling each where to look.

"What about the castle?" An extremely large angel asked.

"That is my main concern," Daniel said. "Why don't you scout it out, Adam, and then stand guard at the gate?" Adam nodded and vanished.

"Someone should go with him," Brandon said.

"Adam can handle a thousand demons, I promise you," Daniel replied. "He was Peter's guardian angel."

"Whoa!"

"Yeah, the Master knows how to pick them."

Gabi, Larry, Pastor Joshua and Pastor Randy had walked to the other end of town calling Scotty. He had not been found.

"Well, this is strange," Pastor Joshua said.

"Dad, what are we going to do?" Gabi asked. "Scotty would never just wander off in a place like this."

"Well," Larry said, "maybe he went back to the church for something he forgot."

"Yeah," Pastor Randy said. "Good idea, let's all go together."

"I say we all STAY together from now on," Pastor Joshua added.

They headed back to the church where there was no sign of Scotty.

"I'm really getting worried," Gabi said, sitting down. "What if he's been taken to the castle?"

"Let's pray," Pastor Joshua said, and they were about to hold hands.

Just then Gabi jumped up and yelled, "Open the door, Mark!" Everyone froze and stared at her. "Okay," she said, "that was weird."

"Are you okay?" Larry asked.

"Yeah, but Mark was in trouble. I just know it."

"What door, Gabi? Pastor Joshua asked.

"I don't know, it was red. He was on the other side." She sat back down and buried her face into her hands. "What's going on?"

"Come on guys," Pastor Randy said. "Let's pray for them both."

"Yeah," Pastor Joshua said. "We're in quite a battle, and our mission seems to be going nowhere. Scotty is missing and Mark is, well, who knows?"

"God knows," Pastor Randy said. "Let's pray." And pray they did. Joining hands, they sought the hand of God in their lives. Each one in turn praying, lifting up Mark, Scotty, Bethany, even John Hoffman. As they prayed, the angels began to go into action. They surrounded the hospital where Bethany was, the families of all involved were being protected. Each castle was even being surrounded by armies of angels. A battle was about to begin. The host of heaven was being strengthened by their prayers.

"Whoa!" Mark yelled, staring at Andy and Eddie. "Now that's funny!" He walked towards them. "Who's laughing now you hairless monkeys?" Everyone was pointing and laughing at them. They were beginning to panic.

"What have you done, McGee?" Andy yelled. "I'll bash your face in!"

Mark laughed. "Then maybe I'll make your noses fall off."

"No!" Eddie yelled. "No Mark! Shut up Andy!"

"Yeah, it's cool Mark!" Andy yelled. "You got us good!"

"Yeah man! Change us back," Eddie said. "We won't mess with you again."

"No!" Mark replied. "You guys are bullies. You always pick on people weaker than you! You gang up on people and try to look tough. Well, you don't look so tough now!"

The crowd cheered him on, and when he looked, he saw David walking through the crowd, smiling at him.

"David!" Mark yelled and went to run toward him. He'd lost him. He pushed through the crowd. "David! Wait!" The crowd seemed to get thicker. At first they were cheering him and patting him on the back, then they began pushing him and shoving him.

"Get out of the way, McGee!" One hard push made him lose his balance and he fell to the ground.

"David!" He yelled and looked up. He was back in the hallway again. No crowd. No snakes. All alone. Holding his torch.

Back in the center room of the castle where the sacrifices are made, stood a little girl. She had blond curly hair and wore a light blue frilly dress. She stood before her master.

"You've done well," he said, from the shadows.

"Thank you Master," she said. "It was quite simple actually. Mark McGee has always had a weakness for revenge."

"Still," he said, "you played him perfectly; Pride has taught you well."

"Well," she said, "you have to think pretty highly of yourself in order to take revenge. After all, that is the job of God."

"Yes it is," he replied. "Now go, stay very close to him. Mark may very well need your assistance again, before his time is up." He laughed. "Do not disappoint me Vengeance. My sweet, sweet Vengeance."

CHAPTER SIXTEEN

AN ANGEL APPEARS

O nce again, Mark was walking down the hall. He was beginning to get very discouraged. The hall seemed to go on forever. No doors or windows. There were pictures, knights in armor, mirrors, burning torches, and an endless hall as far as he could see in both directions. Finally, he decided that walking was taking too long. He began to run. A jog at first but he slowly picked up his pace to a full on sprint. Nothing changed, though he ran in a straight line, it felt like he was going in a circle. After several minutes of running, feeling like the Olympic torch runner, he stopped. He bent over to catch his breath.

"Hello."

Mark jumped and spun around at the sound of a woman's voice. Right behind him, not five feet away, stood an older woman in a long, thin, peach colored dress. Her dark hair was pulled back tight into a bun. "Hey, I've seen you somewhere before! Who are you?" He stepped back a few steps.

"We've never met," she said, eyeing him suspiciously. Mark noted her strong German accent. "But you look so familiar."

"Perhaps you've seen my portrait," she replied. "It's somewhere in this dreaded place."

"That's it!" he exclaimed, a little too loud. She stepped back now. "The first room I went in. You were the cree... your picture was in that room".

"So, what is your purpose here?" she asked.

"What do you mean?"

"Everyone here has a purpose," she replied. "We all wander these halls seeking something. What is it you seek?"

"You mean you're searching for something too?" Mark asked.

She smiled, "what task has he given you?"

He saw no harm in telling her. Maybe she could help. He reached into his pocket and pulled out the vial. "I'm looking for the gateway to God," he said.

"Are you now?" she said, her face stern.

"Yes, you haven't seen it have you? I have no idea what it is."

"Of course you don't. It doesn't exist," she said. "Don't you see, he's toying with you, giving you purpose and hope only to make his victory sweeter when he takes them away."

"No, no!" Mark said, correcting her. "David saved me! He's helping me."

She stepped closer to him. "What is your name?"

"Mark...Mark McGee."

She smiled. "I see."

"What is your name?"

"I am Zweifel." She responded.

"Zweifel? What is Zweifel?"

"It is my name."

"Oh, okay…how long have you been here, Zweifel?"

"Oh, a very long time. I don't even know the meaning of time anymore."

"What are you searching for?"

"It no longer matters, Mark McGee. Can one ever catch the wind?"

"I don't understand. How did you get here? Were you taken?"

"Continue your search Mark McGee," she said. "Find your gateway. I will not destroy your hope. Just because no one else has ever found a way out of here, does not mean you can't."

"There has to be a way out!" Mark exclaimed. "The dragon and David left. Old Man Willoughby took my friend Todd through the front door! We just have to find the front door! There has to be a way out!"

"Oh, there is a way out," she replied. "Though it is not a way I would recommend."

"Where?" Mark asked. "Where is it?"

"Should I tell you?"

"Yes, please!"

"You will learn it soon enough," she smiled. "When he comes for you."

"Learn what? Who's coming for me?"

"Death, Mark McGee!" she said, and she began to fade. Mark could see through her. "It is your only escape." And she was gone.

Mark again, stood there in the hall, all alone. Her words echoed in the hall. His hope was fading.

Daniel and Brandon flew to the front gate of the castle. There was an epic battle being fought there. Hundreds of demons surrounded Adam and about ten other warrior angels. Adam's sword was cutting them down as fast as they appeared, though there seemed to be no end to the amount of demons that poured over the gate and out of the surrounding forest. Daniel and Brandon met them at the tree line. Their swords blazed with the power of the prayers of the saints. A fire hotter than molten lava. The screams of the demons could be heard throughout the spirit realm.

"Adam!" Daniel called, "have they brought the boy this way?"

"No sign of him!" Adam replied as his sword pierced through the chests of six demons at once. "But I HAVE been quite occupied!"

"So he COULD be in the castle?" Brandon called as his sword blocked a barrage of flaming arrows from the sky.

"Anything is possible!" Adam called. "They attacked as soon as I arrived! They were waiting for me!"

"They've been pouring out like fire ants on honey!" called another angel named Shane.

"We were expected!" yelled Daniel. "According to Topher, they've surrounded the perimeter of all four castles...as well as the mountain!"

"What are your orders, Captain?" Brandon called to Daniel, as more angels arrived in flashes of light, striking demons down in every direction.

"We must retreat!" Daniel yelled for all to hear.

"Retreat?" Adam screamed. "Never Captain!" He spun out of the way of a black axe and cut the demon swinging it in half. He never had time to scream.

"Adam, my friend!" Daniel said, "we must regroup and prepare!" He wrapped his giant hand around the throat of a charging demon. He squeezed his hand until his fingers touched his palm.

"Prepare for what, my Captain?" Adam asked, soaring into the air and slicing several passing demons right out of the sky.

All of the angels flew up to join him, including Daniel. They all looked to Daniel for his answer.

"Prepare for war!" And they were gone in a flash.

The remaining demons were left to cheer their victory, though no angel fell.

Gabi and the others had just finished up their prayer. She walked over to the front door of the church. "Don't go anywhere Gabi," her dad said.

"I'm not, I'm just looking out to see if I can see Scotty." She opened the door and as she did, a large man pushed his way through, almost knocking her over. "Oh, excuse me," she said, stepping back.

Several other men followed him, all in suits, various ages from mid-twenties to mid-forties. There were seven in all, then an eighth one stepped in behind them. He wore an extremely expensive suit, and a large ring on his pinky finger. He looked to be in his late fifties. Black hair slicked back with a jet black goatee, clearly colored. He stepped to the center of his group with the other men all around him. They had to be his bodyguards.

"Hello," Pastor Randy said, holding out his hand to the older man. The man ignored it. "I'm Pastor Randy Scalise from the United States of America. I can explain why we are here in this beautiful…"

"Please sit down," the older man said with authority. Nobody moved.

The man stepped up to Pastor Randy and stood only inches away from him. He was quite intimidating. Pastor Randy held his gaze without blinking. Finally, the man smiled. "Please, let us all sit." Everyone found a seat except two of his men stood by the door. "I apologize for our intrusion, Pastor Randy from the United States." He paused, eyeing the others. "May I ask the names of the others?"

"I'm Pastor Joshua Guillemette."

"Another pastor?" he commented. "Are we not fortunate?"

"I'm Larry Motes and this is my daughter, Gabi Motes."

He glanced at them all for a moment. "When someone comes into my town and begins to ask questions about things that concern me, I get…curious."

"I'm sorry," Pastor Joshua said, "we didn't get your name."

He looked quite aggravated at having been interrupted. "Again, my apologies, Pastor Joshua." He took out a cigar and clipped the end. One of his men stepped forward and lit it. He took several puffs, and exhaled.

"Um," Gabi said, clearing her throat. "You shouldn't smoke in church."

He laughed, his men laughed. They seemed to find Gabi's comment quite funny. "Gabi, is it?" he asked, looking at her.

"Yes, sir," she replied, clearly annoyed and getting impatient.

"To you, this may be a house of God," he said. "Yet I can assure you, no god dwells here...there is only us."

She wasn't sure if he meant in the building or no God anywhere, however, "Oh, He's here sir...and you should show respect."

Her dad placed his hand on hers to calm her.

"Where is he?" He flicked his ashes on the floor. "Tell me! I do not see him. I do not feel him. I do not hear him." He placed a hand to his ear. "Perhaps he is in the bathroom?" His men laughed. "Enlighten me, Gabi."

"Oh, He's here," She replied. "He may not be as flashy and loud as you are, but He's here. Greater is He that is in me, than he that is in the world."

Larry and the pastors sat back and shut up. They just hoped God would protect them because clearly, Gabi was not concerned.

"And you may sit there acting like you have everything figured out, but you don't. One day you're going to die." She stood up now.

Larry looked over, Pastor Randy and Pastor Joshua were smiling. None of them would have gotten away with talking to him like that. They were definitely enjoying this.

"And how will your money and your power help you then?" She pointed right at him. "All the money in the world won't grant you one second in the presence of a Holy God. It WILL send you to the fires of hell though. You see, there's only one thing that will grant you access into heaven." She was pacing now, and when she turned to face him, he held up a hand, smiling.

"Perhaps another time." He motioned for her to sit and he glanced at Larry.

"Hey," Larry said, holding his hands up, "you told her to enlighten you."

"We still haven't gotten your name," Pastor Joshua said.

"You American Christians are a strange group," he said to them all. "Always wanting to add names to the roll." He paused and stood. "Do you get points for how many people you preach to? Is there some kind of prize?"

"Well, actually…" Pastor Randy began but the man held up his hand to stop him.

He turned to face them all. "I like this one." He pointed to Gabi. "So I will let you all live." They each glanced at one another, wondering if he were serious. "You see, this is my community, my town, my village, my …world. My name, Pastor Joshua, is John Hoffman." He paused for effect. "Hear me when I say this: if you are still here in the morning…" he slowly looked at each of them. "I will have you killed."

Mark sat down in the hall with his back to the wall. Zweifel had taken away all his hope. He needed to rethink things. Was there any point in searching for the gateway? Had David lied to him or was he on his side? Did the vial he held really hold the souls of children? It sounded kind of silly now that he thought about it. Of course, so did talking to dragons and seeing killer unicorns, so who was he to call anything silly?

He thought of his family. He missed them. He actually missed Bethany, she was a good kid as far as little sisters went. Most of the time she left Mark alone, playing in her own little world. He missed his mom and stepdad as well. They'd practically become strangers since moving to Florida. His stepdad stayed busy with work. His mom was busy getting the house in order. Mark and Bethany had school and friends. He wondered if they were going crazy looking for him.

He missed his friends too. Scotty and Gabi were good friends. The best. Matt and Billy too. They'd taken him right into their group. He could see Scotty, Gabi and him being friends forever. Graduating high school, going to college, they would have to go to Penn State of course. He imagined that Scotty and Gabi would get married. He would meet a girl in college, fall in love and marry her and the four of them would grow old together. They could all live in his old neighborhood in Pittsburgh. Their kids would play together. They would have barbeques and go to church together, Gabi would make sure of that. That's how Mark saw it, though if he didn't get out of this castle, he would never see it. Was it hopeless? Was there no way out?

"Mark?" He jumped at the sound of a girl's voice.

"Whoa! What?!" He jumped up, not believing his own eyes. "Angel?" She stood not ten feet away.

"Is it really you, Mark?" She was nearly in tears.

"It's me, is it you?" She ran to him and threw her arms around him almost knocking him over. She started crying.

"Thank God!" she said. "Oh I can't believe it! I thought you were dead." She stepped back. "This place is so crazy!"

He nodded in shock. "Yes it is."

"I'm starting to think there's no way out of here," she said. "I keep coming back to the same place."

"So what happened, Angel?" he asked. "How are you here?"

Fear filled her eyes. "It was Ms. Tyler!" she said. "She saw me in the hall and asked me to help her with something real quick in the teacher's lounge. The next thing I knew she was coming apart. Her skin began to melt away, and...that's when I screamed. She turned into a dragon, Mark. Then you come in with that old man and..."

"Wait..." Mark said, "what old man?"

"I don't know, some old guy with a work uniform on, like a janitor. I'd never seen him before."

"He was with me?" Mark asked.

"Yes, you don't remember? He said something just before the dragon struck."

Mark tried to remember, but he could not remember seeing Clayton there. "What did he say?"

"Those who call upon the name of the Lord will be saved.' I remember because when he spoke, it brought me peace. But then everything went dark. I woke up strapped to a table."

"Call upon the...what?" Mark was confused. "What does that mean? Why didn't he help us?"

She shrugged. "Maybe he tried. I can't remember. You really don't remember him at all?"

"I know who he is but I don't remember him being there, no," Mark replied, leaning back against the wall. He looked at Angel. "What happened to you on the table?"

She leaned against the wall, not appearing to want to think about it.

"Was it the dragon?" Mark asked.

She nodded. "I was terrified. It was going to kill me."

"So why didn't it? How did you get away?"

"I was screaming and begging for my life. The dragon really seemed to enjoy that," she said. "It's foul breath in my face." She was in deep thought. "I've never been so scared."

Mark leaned against the wall beside her. He waited for her to finish.

"Then it gave me a choice," she said. "I could be put out of my misery then or I could be given a task."

"What task?"

"I have to find a locket."

"A locket?" Mark asked. "What locket?"

Angel shrugged. "It's gold and expensive and it's been lost in the castle for a thousand years."

"It could be anywhere," Mark said. "What are you supposed to do when you find it?"

"He said if I find it, to put it on my neck, and I would be home."

"Okay, we can help each other."

"I don't know. I'm starting to think it doesn't exist. That maybe, this may sound crazy, but maybe this is hell."

"Have you been talking to Zweifel?" Mark asked jokingly.

"Yes, how did you know?" She looked surprised.

"Because you sound as encouraging as she did."

"But what if she's right, Mark?" Angel was panicking. "What if there's no way out, ever?"

He took her hand. "We have to believe there is. The dragon gets in and out, we can too."

"So, what do you have to find?" she asked and he proceeded to tell her his story.

"Wow," she said when he finished, "at least I know what I'm looking for, you don't even know what this gateway is."

"He said I would know it when I saw it."

"Well," she said, pushing off from the wall, "we're not going to find anything standing around yacking."

"Yeah, let's get moving," Mark said.

"Hey, good idea with the torch," Angel said, "That would've come in handy a few times."

Mark laughed. "Yeah, I like having something in my hand and everything else you pick up in here causes the world to go crazy."

They walked along the long hall. There were no doors as far as they could see. "So, what creepy things have you seen so far?" Angel asked.

"Let's see, a wolf, a million snakes and a unicorn.

"A unicorn?"

"A deadly unicorn."

"Awesome, all I've seen is a giant rat and a big hairy spider."

"I hate spiders," Mark said. "How big was it?"

"Not as big as the rat but the rat was as big as a Volkswagen. I guess about as big as a house cat."

"Whoa! No thank you"

"Oh look!" Angel pointed ahead. "A door." They ran up to it and stopped.

"Ready?" Mark asked.

"Let's do this." She turned the knob and pulled the door open. It was pitch dark inside. Mark stepped in with his torch. There was nothing in the room. It was just four walls with a set of empty shelves at the back. They stepped inside and as soon as they did, the door slammed behind them. Angel screamed and jumped, causing Mark to jump. "Sorry," she said.

"No problem."

Just then a light come on at the top of the shelf, revealing the bust of an old man. They walked towards it. It appeared to be made of black stone. He had a beard and his hair was long. He looked wise like an old wizard or someone from Bible days.

"Should we touch it?" Mark asked.

"Who is it?" Angel responded.

"I have no idea."

"Do you think it's your gateway?"

"One way to find out," Mark said.

"We should probably touch it together."

"I agree," Mark said and they reached out their hands and touched the bust. Both had closed their eyes, not knowing what to expect. Nothing happened. "Usually something happens."

"Maybe we can't touch it together," Angel said.

"Maybe you should turn around," came a man's voice from behind them, causing them both to jump and scream. There, standing behind them, was the old man from the bust. He wore a long gray robe that went to the floor and a rope was tied around his waist. He had long silver hair and a matching beard that went down to his chest.

"Who are you?" Angel asked.

"I, my dear lady, am Torheit," he replied.

"Hello Torheit," Mark said,

"What exactly is a torheit?" Angel asked.

The old man chuckled. "It is my name, and I," he patted her shoulder, "am your best friend."

"Is that so?" Angel asked, pulling away from him. "What exactly makes you my best friend?" "Well, for starters, you would not be where you are right now without me."

"That doesn't make you our best friend," Mark said. "That makes you our enemy."

"My dear boy," Torheit smiled, "every decision you've made your entire life has led you to this moment." He walked over and picked up the bust. He stared at it. "It really is a peculiar thing, isn't it?"

"I guess," Mark said, looking at the bust.

"Life, I mean, not the head," Torheit replied.

"I'm, sorry," Mark said. "Can you help us get out of here?"

"Of course my dear boy...of course." He set the bust back down and walked to the door. He opened it and looked back at the two still standing there watching him. "Coming?" They both shrugged and followed him back out into the hall. "There, that was simple wasn't it?"

"Um, I meant out of the castle, not the room," Mark said.

Torheit looked at him and smiled. "One step at a time, Mark, my friend."

"You know my name?"

"Of course I know your name, Mark Evan McGee!" He laughed. "I told you, I'm your best friend!" They began walking in the direction they'd been walking when they found the room.

"So, BFF," Angel said, "where exactly are we going?"

"Yeah," Mark added. "How do we know we can trust you?"

"I'm not sure what a B…F…F is, but I've gotten you this far haven't I?"

"Yeah, I still don't get that," Angel said. "How have you gotten us this far?"

"I am, a guide, so to speak, a life guide."

"Do you know David?" Mark asked. "He's my guide."

Torheit smiled and rubbed his beard. "David is more of a personal situation guide. I am the one who has guided you from the time you were old enough to understand until now."

"Does everyone have a guide?" Angel asked.

"Oh yes, some people call it their conscience, or God or other names, but everyone has a guide."

"So, you're like Jiminy Cricket?" Angel asked.

"Make no mistake, young lady, I'm no cricket." Torheit said. "I am the one that you have listened to your entire life when making decisions. I am the one you have put your faith in."

"I don't exactly believe in faith," Angel said.

"Exactly," Torheit said. "Now follow me." He walked ahead. They followed.

"What do you think?" Angel whispered to Mark.

"We'll follow him for now," Mark said.

After several minutes they came to another red door. Torheit walked past it.

"What about this door?" Mark asked. "What's up with the red ones?"

Angel looked confused. "You've seen other red ones?"

"Oh yeah, I usually hear Gabi tell me to open it and then bad things happen."

"You don't want to open that door, Mark McGee." Torheit said.

"Why not?" Angel asked. "It may be the very thing we want to do."

The old man shrugged and clasped his hands in front of him. "You have a free will, though you go against my wishes. Open it, but don't say I didn't warn you."

"What will happen?" Mark asked.

"Nothing I should like to witness, I can assure you," Torheit replied. "If you open this door, I must leave you."

Mark stepped up to it and put his ear to it. Nothing. Just a door.

"Mark, maybe we should wait!" Angel said. "We can always come back to it."

"Words of wisdom!" Torheit said, "if ever I've heard them." And on they went.

As Mr. Hoffman's entourage headed out the door, Gabi stood. "Mr. Hoffman!" she called.

He stopped at the door but did not turn around.

"We've come a long way to find you!"

"That is unfortunate for you."

"No sir, it's unfortunate for you!" She walked toward him.

"Gabi," Larry said, "please be careful."

Pastor Randy and Pastor Joshua were praying for her.

Mr. Hoffman turned. Only he and the man holding the door for him remained inside. "I'm listening."

"Good," Gabi said as she walked up to him, "because the God you mock sent us to find you."

"Young lady…"

This time she held up her hand to silence him, "You said you were listening, so listen. Now, I'm not exactly sure what's going on, but we were sent here to find you and we have. Just a minute ago, I was about to tell you that there is only one way to heaven, well His name is Jesus Christ!"

"Now you listen to me..." he attempted.

"My time is short, Mr. Hoffman!" she yelled, pointing her finger at him. "My friends are missing and for some reason I have to spend my time looking for you! Now hear this!" She walked over to the door and spoke to the man holding it open. "Would you excuse us for a moment please?" He shook his head no.

"It's okay Hans," Mr. Hoffman said, "I'll let her have her say." Hans stepped out and closed the door. "May I first ask you a question, Ms. Gabi?"

"Yes sir," she said, clearly in the zone.

"Who exactly asked you to find me?"

"I did." Everyone jumped and turned to find Topher standing on the stage, dressed in normal clothes.

"What is this trickery?" Mr. Hoffman asked, stepping back. "Men! Enter at once! Hans! Come n..."

The door burst open and Mr. Hoffman's seven body guards stormed in to find an empty church.

"...ow!" Mr. Hoffman finished his sentence and fell back on the floor. He was in a different place. He looked around. "What is this magic? Dark magic!?" He stood. The others stood nearby letting him get his bearings. "Where are we?"

"Florida," Pastor Joshua said.

"Impossible!" He sat. "Florida? America?"

"America," Topher answered.

Mr. Hoffman stepped up to Topher. "Who are you? Explain yourself! Do you know who I am!?"

Topher gave him a big smile, looked over and winked at Gabi and vanished.

Mr. Hoffman fell back again. This time Pastor Randy caught him. "Let me go! I have been drugged!" He ran out of the kitchen of Pastor Joshua's church. They waited, hearing him yell from the sanctuary. Moments later he returned, slinging the door open, he stood in the entryway eyeing each of them, panting. "Where is Germany?"

They laughed. "You are in Gateway, Florida, Mr. Hoffman," Pastor Joshua said. "Now if you'll come in and sit down, we will explain what is going on."

"Very well, but I fully expect to be taken back home," he said, walking over to one of the chairs. "This is a kidnapping."

"First of all," Gabi said, once he sat down, "that young man that vanished was Topher."

"Topher? What is Topher?"

"Actually," Pastor Randy said, "I believe Topher is short for Christopher." He noticed they were all looking at him. "But that's not the point."

"Topher is an Angel," Gabi said.

"Nonsense!" Mr. Hoffman replied. "Don't be silly!"

"I guess you don't have to believe your own eyes if you choose not to. How else do you think you got from Germany to America in under a second?"

"I do not believe in...angels!" he said, still trying to sound like he was in charge.

"Well sir, just because you don't believe in something, doesn't mean it doesn't exist." Gabi added, "you must think pretty highly of yourself."

He gave her a mean look, and crossed his arms.

"Now," Gabi continued, "for some reason, he wanted us to find you, which we have. I have no idea why you are so important in this situation. As far as I'm concerned, you're just an angry old man, who seems to hate everyone and everything."

He stared at the table.

"However," she said, "there are angels and there is a God, whether you choose to believe in them or not. Regardless of how important you think you are; you are NOT the final say on what exists." She gave him a moment to digest that. "So, now that we've determined that there is a God…"

"Young lady…" he started.

She held up her hand. "We have to assume He has a plan for us. For you." She poked him on the arm. "He loves you Mr. Hoffman." He looked at her. "He loves you so much He sent His only son, Jesus Christ, to die for you. He came down to this miserable place and died a horrible death on a cross for your sins." Again she poked his arm. "Why would He do that, Mr. Hoffman? Why would a perfect, sinless, loving God, care so much about a grumpy, mean, sinful, hateful, violent, money and power hungry old man like yourself?" She paused for a few seconds and then, "because He loves you. He loves you so much He can't stand to be separated from you." He looked at her again. He uncrossed his arms and put his hands in his lap. "Have you ever loved someone that much?" she asked. "So much, it didn't matter what they did, you still wanted to be near them?" He looked away, his eyes pooled with tears…and he nodded.

"My…" he cleared his throat, "my daughter." Larry handed him a Kleenex. He put his head down on the table and began crying.

Pastor Joshua took the seat on the other side of him and began quietly praying. Pastor Randy and Larry prayed behind him.

Mark and Angel continued following Torheit down the hall. Both of them were getting impatient. They had been walking for what seemed like hours. They'd passed several doors, even more red ones that Mark had been tempted to open. Torheit had told them to keep up each time.

"I'm so tired," Angel said. "It feels like I haven't slept in days."

"Yeah this is crazy," Mark said. "How much further Torheit?"

"Not much further," he replied. "Just a little bit more."

"Are you sure you're leading us out of here?" Mark asked. Torheit did not respond. Mark stopped, as did Angel. "Where are you leading us Torheit?"

Torheit stopped and turned to face them smiling, he said. "How long, Mark McGee, has folly been your guide?" He spread out his hands and vanished.

"What just happened?" Angel asked.

"I have no idea," Mark responded. "But I have a sneaky suspicion that this isn't the way out."

"Are you serious?" She looked ready to cry. "This is hopeless."

"It's not hopeless until we're dead; come on, let's go back."

Just then they heard a blood curdling scream. "No!! No!! Get away from me! Put me down!!" They heard shuffling of feet and then a door slammed. Silence.

They had both froze. "What do we do?" Angel asked.

"Either someone is in trouble or that was a trick," Mark replied.

"It came from the way Torheit was leading us," she said.

"Come on," Mark said. "If it was me, I would hope someone would help me." With that, they continued in that direction. About fifty feet later they came to a turn on their right. They looked that way. There was a big door.

"That looks like…"

"Yes it does," Mark said. "But it can't be!" They walked over to it and gave each other a look. Mark opened it, holding his torch out in front of him. "Yep." It was the room they'd started in. The sacrifice room with the table.

"No way," Angel said. "Are you serious?" Nobody was in there though.

"Is anybody here!?" Mark called. He walked over to each cell door and kicked them, calling out. "Anybody here!" He heard a muffled scream.

"This one," Angel said.

"We need to bust through it."

"I don't know, Mark, they're pretty solid."

Mark looked around for something heavy. Finally, he found an old battle axe leaning in a corner next to a table. He could barely lift it. "This should do it." He carried it over and was about to swing it when Angel grabbed his arm.

"Or we could use these." She held up a ring of keys.

"That'll work too."

The third key she tried, clicked the lock. The door pushed open quickly from the inside; they both jumped back, as someone popped out.

"Mark!!"

"Scotty!??"

CHAPTER SEVENTEEN

A FALLEN ANGEL

Matt had a problem. After last night, he had a lot of problems, but one in particular. He needed to call Christina. His mother had put him on restriction last night, and the phone was off limits.

His father hadn't exploded as bad as he'd expected. He'd actually remained quite calm when Matt walked in. Of course, Matt had apologized profusely the moment he'd stepped inside the door and tried to explain that his friend was in trouble. His father had simply led him out on the back deck and sat him down. They'd talked it out. His father knew he was a good kid but there'd been no excuse for his rebellious behavior. He explained to Matt that there were things about the castle that he didn't understand but would need to trust his father in that area. Matt knew that arguing would be useless so he just sat there nodding and saying "Yes sir" to everything.

His mother had not been so calm. As soon as he stepped back inside, the hammer fell. No television, no video games, no free time, no cell phones or any phones for that matter, no computer other than to do homework. He would go to school and nothing else. He'd handed over his phone, watched her turn it off and put it in a drawer in the kitchen.

He needed to get to that phone. He wanted to know if Christina had found anything out. He hated himself for thinking it, but he had to get the phone, sneak it to his room and call her. He had to know what was going on.

He went downstairs. It was Saturday morning and his parents were watching some dumb home improvement show. He told his mom he was getting a snack and going back up to do his homework.

"Okay," she said flatly. She was still upset.

He went to the kitchen. He got a bag of Doritos out of the cabinet and then quickly opened the drawer, grabbed the phone, slid it in his pocket and turned around. His mother was standing in the doorway watching him. Busted.

"Matthew Allen Ramsey!" she yelled. "You are not too big for me to take you over my knee! You put that phone back in that drawer right now, young man!"

"But mom, I just…"

"Now!" she yelled, pointing at the drawer.

"Yes, ma'am." He opened the drawer. "Can I still get a snack?"

"Take your chips, get a soda and go do your homework." She opened the fridge and got him a drink.

He closed the drawer, grabbed the soda and went upstairs to his room. He closed and locked the door and took his cell phone out of his pocket. He hoped she didn't check the drawer, as he powered it up.

It seemed like his phone was taking forever to turn on. He tried to cover the speaker so his parents didn't hear it but it didn't help. Somehow it seemed louder. He had two texts, both from Billy. "Dude, my mom was so mad. I'm grounded until I'm 30. She forgot 2 take my phone. R U alive?" The second one was just sent thirty minutes ago. "OMG Matt!! I just called Christina, you won't believe where Scotty and Gabi R, dude she found out that they are in Germany. According to Mrs. Morgan, they're in Einfahrt. Dude, there's a castle there. How much trouble are U in? We need to talk!" Matt had tried to show Billy how to shorthand text like every other teenager, but his mom told him that he couldn't text unless he did it correctly. His lame attempts were amusing. The fact that Scotty and Gabi were in Germany was not amusing. How did they get there? Were they alone? What was going on? Matt needed answers and he wouldn't get them from his bedroom. He quickly texted Christina and Billy. "Meet @ skool 30 min." He muted his phone, and dressed.

"Matthew Ramsey!" his mother screamed from downstairs. He tripped trying to get his shoes on. "Get down here right now!" She was onto him. He tied his shoes. "Now!" He opened his window and heard her coming up the stairs. He climbed out as she yelled, "I know you have that phone!" He heard her try his door. "You open..." He jumped to the soft grass below, rolled back up to his feet, grabbed his bicycle and was gone. He took the back roads in case they looked. Even his father wouldn't forgive this one, but things were crazy and he just knew he needed to help his friends. He hoped Christina had answers. He hoped she would meet him. He stopped at the corner across from the school and checked his phone. A text from Billy. "Oh man!" They would both be in so much trouble. There was nobody at the school. He rode his bike around to the side and hid behind some bushes where he could see when the others arrived. He texted them both again. "R U coming?" Just then he saw Billy crossing the street on his bike. Matt stood up and waved to him. Billy crossed the parking lot quickly and hid with Matt. "Dude, I am so dead!"

"Yeah, me too." Matt said. "What do you know?"

"I'll try to remember everything," Billy said. "You know how I get when pretty girls talk to me."

"Yeah, you're a basket case."

"Christina talked to Scotty's mom and said she had to pry information out of her. All she would say was that Scotty, Gabi, Mr. Motes, and two pastors she didn't know, were in Germany."

"Germany? How did they get there so fast? Doesn't it take like a whole day to fly there?"

"I don't know but she said Mrs. Morgan sounded freaked out like she was really confused. That's all she would tell Christina."

"Why would they be in Germany?"

"All I know is, Einfahrt is where one of the castles is at. It has to have something to do with that. Maybe if they go in here, they come out there."

"Did Christina say anything else?"

"She said nobody at the hospital would tell her anything. That's where Gabi's mom and Mark's parents are. Mark's parents are too freaked out over Bethany right now, she's not doing too good."

"Wow, one kid missing, one in the hospital."

"Apparently they're trusting Mr. Motes to find Mark, while they deal with Bethany. I think they suspect he's just run off on his castle investigation and will turn up."

"Uh oh!" Matt said, "stay down." A cop car turned into the parking lot driving slowly. "It's my dad." He was coming their way. "Quick, around the corner." They crawled around the corner, staying low behind the bushes, then jumped up and ran to the back of the school just as his dad rounded the corner. "This way!" They ran along the back wall, checking all the doors. They were all locked. "Oh man." They were exposed. He would see them when he rounded the corner. Matt looked back and saw the front of the squad car coming into view. At that moment, a door opened and a hand grabbed his shirt and pulled him into the school. He and Billy fell on their bottoms as the door slammed shut. They looked up into the smiling face of an old man in a janitor's uniform.

"Whoa!" Billy exclaimed." Who are you?"

"How did you even do that?" Matt asked. "I weigh like one fifty."

"Hello boys, name's Clayton, I'm a friend of Mark's."

"Mark is friends with a janitor?" Billy asked. "No offense."

"None taken." He pointed towards some desks. "Have a seat." They both got up and took a seat.

"Do you know where Mark is?" Matt asked.

"Before we discuss Mark, we have to discuss you two." Clayton said. "First of all, lying to and disobeying your parents, not cool. When this is all over, you both need to deal with that."

"When what is all over?" Matt asked.

"I have a job for you."

"A job?" Billy asked, "I'm not scrubbing toilets."

"I'm not really a janitor Billy, you need to let that go." Clayton said.

"Then what are you?" Matt asked.

"I'm an angel."

They both laughed. Clayton just stared at them. "I'm Santa Claus," Matt said. "Billy here is the tooth fairy."

"Hey, I'm Captain America! Come on dude!" Billy exclaimed.

"Matthew Allen Ramsey and William Belvedere Mumpower! I can assure you I am an angel!"

"Wait a minute," Matt said, holding up his hand. "Dude, your middle name is Belvedere?" He was looking at Billy.

"It was my grandfather's name!" Billy said.

Matt smiled, "and I thought Mumpower was bad."

"Wait a minute!" Billy said. "He knew our names."

"Yeah," Matt said, "but that doesn't mean he's an angel. He could've accessed the school records."

"Do you mean to tell me you don't believe in angels?" Clayton asked.

"I don't even believe in God," Matt said. "So either prove it or we're done here."

Instantaneously light exploded into the room, blinding both boys temporarily. They turned their heads when they looked back at Clayton he was about two feet taller, younger looking, glowing like a fluorescent light and had wings that filled the room.

"No way!" Matt said, sliding from his seat, to his knees.

"Shut up," Billy said, doing the same.

"Oh, get up!" Clayton said, going back to normal. "I'm only an angel."

"Angels are real?" Matt asked, awestruck. "So…"

"God is real!" Clayton said. "And Jesus Christ is the King of Kings and the Lord of Lords! Demons tremble at the mention of His name and you, my dear boys, are neither Santa Claus or Captain America!"

They both got back in their seats.

"Wow," Billy said. "Mark is friends with an angel and he never told us."

"We wouldn't have exactly believed him, now would we?" Matt added.

"Mark was unaware of my angelic status," Clayton said, with a grin. "I was just trying to keep an eye on him."

"So what happened to him then?" Matt asked. "You didn't seem to protect him very well."

"He made it quite clear that he did not want me around."

"Yeah, well maybe if he'd known you were an angel," Matt said.

"It wasn't time for him to know," Clayton said.

"So what's this job?" Billy asked, suddenly interested.

"First, I want you to go to the hospital where Bethany is and find Pastor Eric Osborne. Ask him to explain the plan of salvation to you. After that, here's what I will need…" he spent about fifteen minutes laying out his plan. "And don't worry about your parents. I've got that covered."

Their parents had both been contacted by the school janitor saying they'd been found on school property and were being put to work for the entire day.

Both boys just sat there, neither believing what was happening. "Dude, this is huge," Billy said.

"Yeah," Matt said looking up at Clayton. "Biblical." Clayton smiled and vanished. Matt got a text from Christina just then: "Heading to the castle."

After having explained the plan of salvation to Mr. Hoffman and leading him in the sinner's prayer, the gang had celebrated and then decided it was bedtime. Larry and Gabi had gone home.

Pastor Joshua had invited Pastor Randy and Mr. Hoffman over to his house. They had agreed to meet back at the church in the morning and figure out their next step. Topher would be needed.

They were now gathered in the fellowship hall having breakfast. They'd all slept like a rock and were now in chipper moods. Especially Mr. Hoffman, who had the biggest smile on his face.

"When I woke up yesterday morning in my bed...in Germany, I would have never guessed I'd be waking up the next morning in America, in a pastor's home, a believer!" They all laughed at his excitement.

"That's how God works sometimes," Pastor Joshua said.

"Okay Topher!" Gabi called to the ceiling, "you can come out now!" Everyone looked at her. She shrugged. "It was worth a try."

"Yeah, he needs to explain our next move," Larry said, "cause I'm really confused."

"And I really want my friends back," Gabi said. "This is crazy."

"Tell me about these missing friends," Mr. Hoffman said.

"Mark McGee and Scotty Morgan," Gabi began. "We believe they may be in the castle."

"Oh my," He said, looking down.

"What?" Gabi asked. Everyone was looking at him.

"It is not good if they are in the castle. When children go in...they are never seen again."

"What do you know about the castles?" Larry asked. "We know very little."

"I know there is evil in them," He replied. "An evil so foul, all the murderers of the world do not compare." He paused as if in thought. They all waited. "Many years ago, I was a very bad man. I was young...and stupid. There was another young man in my village, the same age. He was rich. I was poor. He had everything I wanted. Money, women, cars, nice houses, and power. His father was a very wealthy and powerful man. He ran his father's business. I went to him for a job. He took me in, like a brother. I did small jobs for him at first. Driving him around, washing his cars." He was thinking back. "Then I was promoted, given more money. I became his assistant, his right hand man, telling others what to do. Sometimes I delivered packages for him. All over the world I traveled. I had everything I wanted. I was respected. My life was perfect." Another pause. "It was during that time that I met a woman. Anna. The most beautiful woman I had ever seen. We fell madly in love, and married." Another pause. His eyes were tearing up. "She died giving birth to our daughter. I grieved. I never knew such pain existed. I only wanted to die." He looked up at them. "It was then that my friend took me fully into the business. He showed me things that I could have. More money than I ever imagined. Such power. All I had to do..." His voice caught. "How could I??" He cried. Gabi placed a hand on his shoulder. He looked at her and smiled, tears in his eyes. "Your God washed it all away, Ms. Gabi...all the bad."

She smiled, "He's your God too Mr. Hoffman.

He nodded, "Yes. Yes, He is."

"What did you have to do Mr. Hoffman?" Pastor Joshua asked. "I think this story is an important piece to our puzzle."

He nodded, in deep thought. "I became the muscle of his operation. He had a lot of enemies, my boss. I helped them to see things his way."

"So you roughed people up?" Pastor Randy asked.

"Yes, but that is not the bad part," Mr. Hoffman said.

"Did you kill people?" Gabi asked.

"Not personally," he shook his head, "but I'm responsible for many deaths." He put his head down on the table. They waited for him to continue. Each one praying silently. "That is not the bad part either," he finally said, looking up. He looked at each of them. "They required children."

"What?" Pastor Joshua asked. "Who did? What does that mean? Required?"

"My superiors...I don't know why. I learned early on to not ask questions. Just do what you've been told and you will be greatly rewarded. At first we only had to supply them with one a month. We would find a homeless child or one from a poor family. We would deliver them to the castle. They would never be seen again. Thousands of dollars would appear in my bank account. Then...they wanted a child every week. It became difficult to find enough children to satisfy their need. Sometimes we had to kill the parents just to get the children. They became so demanding." He stood and walked to the sink. He poured a cup of coffee. His hands were shaking. "I began to ask questions. They threatened me. I was so proud. I thought I was untouchable. I threatened to report them if they didn't give me answers. I wanted to know what happened to the children." He sat back down with a distant look in his eyes. "That is when they took her."

Gabi gasped, "not your daughter?"

He nodded slowly. "They took my baby. She was only six years old. So innocent. So beautiful like her mother. They made me watch as they led her into the castle." He cried again. "She was smiling...waving to me. They told her she was going somewhere magical."

"How long ago did that happen?" Gabi asked.

"About twenty-five years ago. I've never seen her since."

"Did you keep working for him?" Larry asked.

"NO" He shook his head. "I was a broken man after that. For several years I stayed hidden away from everyone."

"What do you do now?" Pastor Randy asked.

"Basically," He replied, "German mob." He hung his head. "I'm not much better than they are, but I do not harm children."

"Well," Pastor Joshua said. "You're in the Jesus mob now." He stood up. "We really could use Topher about now."

"Well, look no further!" Topher said from right behind him, causing him to jump.

Mark gave Scotty a big hug, he was so glad to see him. He backed away and looked at him. "So, you're really Scotty?"

"Of course I am! Who else would I be?"

"You never know in this place!" Angel said, patting Scotty on the back. "Welcome to the fun house. How'd you get here?"

"Well, I went to the bathroom in Einfarht and was jumped by this really big guy in a hoodie. The next thing I knew I was flying like Superman. I guess I passed out or something because when I woke up they were bringing me into the castle. I tried to get away from them but they're quite strong."

"Did you say you were in Einfarht?" Mark asked. "Germany?"

"Yes. Long story. Oh, we have a new friend and he's an angel. His name is Topher. He flew us there...like in the blink of an eye."

"Scotty Morgan," Angel said, "what have you been smoking?"

"I'm serious!" Scotty exclaimed.

"Angel," Mark replied. "Considering all we've seen, is it really that hard to grasp."

"True...but an actual angel?"

"Yeah, and he's really cool!" Scotty said.

"So, why exactly did he take you to Einfarht?" Mark asked.

"We were supposed to find some guy named John Hoffman," Scotty replied.

"We?" Angel asked.

"Yeah; me, Gabi, her dad, and two pastors we met. One of them is from Atlanta...we went there too."

"Who is this John Hoffman?" Mark asked.

"No idea. Topher just said we had to find him. That's what we were doing when I was attacked. So, I guess they brought me back to Gateway, to put me in here with you."

"Not exactly," Mark said. "David said that all four castles are connected when you're inside. That room is the center. All four countries are in this room. France, Italy, Germany and America."

"Weird," Scotty said. "So how do we get out of here?"

"That's the million-dollar question, now isn't it?" Angel answered.

Just then the door swung open and one of the creatures stepped in. He stopped when he saw the three of them standing there. "Well, well, well…what have we here?"

"Oh, nothing," Angel said with a laugh. "We were just leaving." The three of them moved towards him.

"Not so fast!" He held up his hand. "My orders are to kill that one." He pointed at Scotty. "Looks like I get a bonus."

Mark lifted the axe up. "You can try."

The creature laughed, and drew a sword.

"Sorry, but I have a gateway to find, then I'm outta here."

"Sounds like you made a deal with the father of lies. You're going nowhere McGee!"

"No, I made a deal with David, my guide." Mark swung his axe and the creature stepped back. He moved out of the way as the creature's sword came at him. Scotty grabbed instruments from the table and threw them at the creature.

"I am not of your world, human!" he screamed at Scotty. "You cannot harm me!" When he looked at Scotty, Mark made his move. As fast as he could move, he jumped toward the creature and swung the axe with all his strength. The creature raised his arm to block the axe with his sword, but the axe met him at the elbow, slicing through it with ease. His arm and the sword hit the ground.

"Run!" Mark yelled. Out the door they ran. Mark looked back before he closed the door. The creature's arm was reappearing. He smiled at Mark.

"Your death will be sweet, McGee!!" Mark slammed the door and ran.

As they rounded the first corner, an alarm sounded. It was like a giant bell gonging. It was horribly loud. They had to cover their ears as they ran. Angel was saying something to the boys but they couldn't hear her. She pointed behind them. There were several creatures chasing them about a hundred feet back. They got to a spiral staircase and Mark insisted they go up. They took them as fast as they could. Mark slowed just enough to grab a new torch. He had to drop the axe, it was too heavy to run with. Up they ran. There seemed to be no end. They couldn't hear the creatures for the bell alarm. They had no idea if they were still being followed, but didn't want to slow down and find out. Angel was pointing up now. There was a door at the top about three more spirals up. They reached it, slung it open and slammed it shut behind them. The bell sound died away.

"Thank goodness!" Scotty said, panting. He was facing them. Their backs were to the door. "That was so loud!"

"Scotty, hush!" Angel whispered, looking behind him.

He turned around slowly. In the center of the room, about seven feet away from him was a giant ball of string. It appeared to be moving. "What is it?"

"Is that what I think it is, Mark?" Angel asked.

"Yes. A spider sack."

"Wait," Scotty said, "those things moving are…"

"Spiders." Angel finished.

"Not a big fan," Scotty said.

"Me either," Mark and Angel said together. There were thousands scurrying around inside it, and they were as big as full grown tarantulas.

"Those are the babies?" Scotty asked, backing up.

"Yeah," Mark looked around for a way out.

"And mom is…"

"I don't care to find out," Mark said. He looked up. It was a high ceiling. Something shifted in the shadows. Just then the door behind them swung open and hit them in the back. They pushed it closed, hearing the grunts of the creatures on the other side. Scotty locked the bolt.

"Now we're locked in!" he said.

Angel screamed. One of the spiders had broken through the sack. Slowly it crawled out. Then another. They lowered themselves to the floor. They began to pour out.

"Mark," Scotty said, clearly terrified." What do we do?" Some of the spiders were coming their way. The creatures were pounding on the door behind them. It was a really intense situation.

"I think I would rather face those demon creatures," Angel said.

"Yeah, me too." Scotty agreed, kicking away a spider that was bigger than his hand. Mark was pushing them back with his torch. He threw the torch under the sack hoping to kill some.

"Quick get in that corner!" He pointed to a dark corner just inside the door. The creatures were shaking the door trying to get in.

"Mark!" Scotty pointed at Mark's feet. There was a spider on his pants leg. He shook it off.

"Get ready!" Mark said, grabbing the door handle. "One, two…" he unlocked it and slung it open. The creatures fell in. There were three of them on the floor. Spiders immediately covered them. They were screaming. "Go!" Mark screamed. Mark heard movement above, as he stepped out he saw a spider the size of his mom's minivan drop onto the creatures. They were screaming as he closed the door. He ran to catch up with Scotty and Angel, grabbing another torch.

When they reached the bottom they cautiously looked both ways before stepping out into the hall. There was nobody or nothing out there. Mark grabbed a new torch.

"Which way? Scotty asked.

"Who knows?" Angel replied.

"Let go of me!" a woman screamed. "Let me go now!" She sounded scared and angry. They ran back to the corner that led to the sacrifice room. They peeked around. "And you better not have hurt Troy. Stop! That hurts." Four of the creatures were attempting to drag a young woman into the room. She was struggling pretty good. One of them grabbed her by the throat.

"Hey, isn't that the news lady?" Scotty asked.

Mark stepped out into view. "Hey!" He waved his torch. They all froze. The creatures looked at him. "Let her go!"

One of the creatures laughed. "Take her to her cell. I'll crush that one."

Mark realized he had no way to fight this creature. It came at him quick. He stepped back as it charged with its sword. Just then, Angel stepped out in front of it and the blade went through her stomach and out her back. She grunted and fell to the floor. Mark screamed. "No, Angel!" The creature laughed. Scotty jumped out and leaped onto the creature from the side. Mark slowly pulled out the sword. With a fierce vengeance, he spun around with one strong swing, and sliced the creature in half. Scotty and the creature hit the floor. The creature vanished. The other creatures had abandoned the woman and were coming for Mark. He stood ready, sword in hand, panting. He would kill them or die trying. "Scotty, get the news lady!" he yelled. She was in the room and Scotty couldn't get to her with the creatures between him and the door. "Never mind! Help Angel!"

"Mark, she's..."

"Help her!" He swung his sword at the first creature and missed. He wanted to slice them all in half. Just then he saw the little girl behind them. She was smiling. She shrugged. At that moment he imagined each of the creatures bursting into flames. All of a sudden their black shiny skin began to glow red. They began screaming, dropping their swords. Within seconds their bodies melted to the floor. Mark stood panting. The little girl smiled and waved and vanished. The news lady came running out. Mark turned to Angel. She lay limp on the floor, her stomach covered in blood and a pool of blood beneath her. More creatures were coming. Scotty shook Mark, motioning that they needed to go. He couldn't leave Angel. "Mark, they're coming!" The news lady looked terrified. But Angel…his friend. "Mark, she's dead! Run!" He couldn't move.

Scotty then stepped between Mark and the charging demons. He bowed his head, took a deep breath, looked up just as they closed in and screamed, "be gone in the name of Jesus Christ!!!" Each of them covered their ears and dissolved into the air.

Mark jumped back and looked around. "What just happened?" Scotty helped him up.

"You don't hang around Gabi Motes as long as I have and not pick up a trick or two," Scotty said. "The only thing demons fear…the name of Jesus."

"Wait, those are actual demons?" Mark asked.

"Obviously," Scotty said. "And we need to get going."

"So, you're Mark McGee and Scotty Morgan?" the news lady asked, clearly baffled.

"In the flesh," Scotty said.

"Is that Gabi?" She pointed to Angel.

"No, her name was Angel," Mark said.

"Oh…I'm so sorry Mark."

"Let's go," Scotty said, grabbing their arms.

Mark grabbed his torch. The swords had all vanished.

"NOOO!!" Angel screamed as they walked away. Mark spun around and ran to her. She was panting. "No!" She had a look of sheer terror. "Don't let them take me there, Mark!"

"Who, Angel?" Mark cried. "Take you where?" He held her head. Tears were pouring from her eyes.

"No!" She screamed. "Please God, no!"

Scotty knelt beside her and took her hands. "Angel," he said softly, trying to calm her. "Listen to me." He was in control and it impressed Mark. "Those were demons you saw...okay? The Bible is real. It's starting to click for me, and you need to accept Jesus into your heart... do you understand me?"

"Scotty," Mark said, "we don't have time for this. We need to save her."

Angel nodded, touching Mark's face. "Sshhh. I think he is." She looked at Scotty. "I understand." She coughed blood. "Lead me..." She coughed more blood. "Scotty."

"Okay...repeat after me." Scotty said, trying to remember every salvation prayer he'd ever heard in church. "Father in heaven."

Coughing. "Father in heaven."

"Please forgive me of all my sins."

"Please..." coughing.

"Scotty!" Mark said.

"Forgive me of all my sins," Angel continued.

"I invite Jesus into my heart," Scotty said, sweating.

"I invite Jesus..." she choked and tried to turn on her side. They helped her. She spit out blood. "Into my heart." She was crying.

"To be my Lord and Savior."

"To be my Lord and Savior," she said through her sobs.

"In Jesus" name I pray."

"In Jesus...name...I pray!" She broke down, Mark stroked her hair, crying.

"Amen...ohhh...thank you Jesus!" she cried out, then her body tensed.

"Angel!!" Mark screamed. "No! Angel!"

She went limp and fell back onto her back.

"No Angel!" Mark cried. His body shook. "Noo!!"

"Mark." Scotty put his hand on Mark's back. "Mark, look at her."

Mark opened his eyes and through his tears he saw it. Her face shone. She was smiling. "Oh Angel..." he cried. "She saved my life."

"Um, guys..." the news lady said. "There's more coming."

"Mark, we need to go!" Scotty stood.

"We can't leave her." Mark said.

"We can't take her." Scotty said. "Come on!" There were literally hundreds running toward them. "Mark!"

Mark snapped out of it and looked. He jumped up and grabbed his torch. They took off around the corner to the right.

They ran as fast as they could. "So you're that news lady!" Scotty said.

"Christina!" she replied.

"Hi Christina, nice to meet you!"

"So, you say those things are demons?" she asked, looking back at them.

"Yes. So how did you know who we were?"

"Your friends have been looking for you...we thought you were in Germany and assumed Mark was in the castle!"

"I WAS in Germany...this place is complicated." The demons were gaining on them.

"Where's Gabi?" She asked.

"Still in Germany, I guess...no idea! Mark...where are we going?"

"To the first door we can find!" Mark yelled.

"I see one, ahead!" Christina said. "There on the right!" They headed for it.

"Be prepared for anything!" Mark yelled as they got closer. They quickly ran into the room and locked the door. It was a well-lit room and seemed to be someone's living room. There was a couch with a coffee table, a wing back chair, several lamps, pictures on the wall. "Well," Mark said, "this is different." They walked over and sat. Mark and Scotty on the couch and Christina took the wingback. There was a cup of tea on the coffee table.

Scotty picked it up. "Um, this is still warm."

"So how did you end up here, Christina?" Mark asked getting up to put his torch in a bracket.

"Well, do you know Matt Ramsey and Bill Mumpower?" She asked.

"Yes," Scotty said. Mark nodded and came back to his seat.

"I kind of ran into them last night while doing my story on Ms. Tyler."

"By the way," Mark said. "She was the dragon."

"No way!" Scotty exclaimed. "That explains everything then!"

"Wait," Christina said, "a dragon?"

"No worries, he's dead." Mark said nonchalantly.

"Dead?" Scotty asked. "You killed him?"

"Not exactly. He was about to kill me and David showed up and killed him."

"So David could kill him all along? Scotty asked, confused.

"I guess so." Mark shrugged. "Anyway, back to your story Christina."

"Well, Matt and Billy risked their immediate futures to get me to investigate your…situation," she said. "I was intrigued, so I looked into it. The deeper I dug, the crazier it got."

"Tell me about it," Mark said.

"So anyway, my cameraman Troy and I went to the castle this morning and were really surprised when Mr. Willoughby buzzed us in. We drove Troy's van up the driveway and got out. The next thing I knew, someone threw a sack over my head and picked me up kicking and screaming. I have no idea what happened to Troy, I heard him yell and then nothing...and then I heard a door slam and they removed the sack. There were all these creatures carrying me down a corridor, then you guys showed up and here we are."

"Here we are..." Mark said, "without Angel."

"Dude, are you okay?" Scotty asked, putting his hand on Mark's shoulder.

"She just jumped in front of me...there was nothing I could do."

"I know. I couldn't believe she did it." Scotty looked down. "She died for you, Mark...just like Jesus did."

Mark shot a quick look at Scotty.

"What?" Scotty asked.

"Whose living room do you think this is?" Christina asked.

"Jesus died for me," Mark said.

"Yes. He did," Scotty said.

"Gesú'" Mark said. "I bet anything it means Jesus."

"Okay." Scotty was confused.

"Here's a picture of a man and a little girl," Christina said, standing over by a shelf. "Looks old."

"David didn't say it, he wrote it." Mark said.

"What?" Scotty asked.

"Gesú...you said demons are afraid of the name of Jesus, right?"

"Yes, they are."

"Hey, there's a door over here." Christina said, not paying the boys any attention.

"And when I said Jesus in the sacrifice room, everything went crazy...that was when David showed himself...and took over. He changed the subject."

"What are you saying?" Scotty asked.

Christina walked over and got the torch. "I'm going to see what's behind that door. Somebody may live here."

"One, that David isn't who I thought he was and two..."

"Um...guys..." Christina said.

"If a person needs Jesus in their heart to get to heaven..." Mark continued. "Jesus may just be the..."

"Guys!" She screamed. They both looked. She was backing away from the large door on the far end of the room. It was open.

"Christina?" Scotty asked. She looked terrified. The torch was shaking.

"I thought you said he was dead."

The dragon stepped through the doorway.

CHAPTER EIGHTEEN

HISTORY REVEALED

"So, what's the plan, Topher?" Gabi asked.

"Our plan is to defeat the plan of the enemy," He replied.

"And what exactly is the plan of the enemy?" Pastor Joshua asked.

"Basically," Topher said, walking to the middle of the room." To steal, kill and destroy."

"You couldn't be a little more specific could you?" Pastor Joshua asked.

"I could...hold on." Topher held up his hand and turned his head as if listening to someone speak. "I have to go."

"Wait...and see ya!" Pastor Joshua said as Topher vanished. "Okay, we should pray...I'm getting irritable."

"Agreed," Pastor Randy said and Pastor Joshua gave him a look. "That we should pray, not that you're getting irritable."

They all went into the sanctuary.

"So, what exactly are we to pray for?" Mr. Hoffman asked.

"Guidance, direction, purpose," Larry replied.

"Yeah," Pastor Joshua said," for somebody to finally put this puzzle together."

"Well, I know I would love to know my part in all of this," Mr. Hoffman said. "It is all quite exciting." They all found a place to pray.

"Don't forget about Mark, Bethany, Scotty and Angel," Gabi said.

And pray they did, for over an hour they sought God's will for their lives and for His protection over their friends.

Outside the church, placed strategically at each entrance and on the roof, were massive powerful angels of war. Swords drawn. Prepared for an attack of the enemy.

As they finished praying, they each made their way back to the kitchen. Pastor Joshua had made coffee and found some stale donuts in the pantry.

They sat and enjoyed fellowshipping. There seemed to be a peace. A peace like none of them had experienced before. They laughed and they told stories of God's grace and mercy. Each of them shared their testimonies. They were encouraged.

"I suppose I should make another pot of coffee," Pastor Joshua said.

"Please, allow me," Mr. Hoffman said, standing and going to the counter. "Besides, your first pot was too weak." They all laughed.

"Too weak?" He acted hurt. "I'm surprised you noticed with all that cream and sugar."

"I usually drink it black my friend," he replied. "What you made was not coffee, it was hot, muddy water."

"Yeah, sorry Pastor Joshua," Gabi said. "Even I thought it was weak and I hate coffee."

Again they all laughed.

"Good, you're all still here!" It was Topher, standing at the door.

"We didn't know what else to do," Pastor Joshua said.

"Well, that's all about to change," Topher said. "But first, I have bad news and I have good news."

"How do you react when an angel says those words to you?" Pastor Randy asked.

Mr. Hoffman walked back to his seat. "We are listening, Topher."

"The bad news is," he paused and looked at each of them, "Angel has died."

"What?!" Gabi gasped, standing up. "No!"

"Angel?" Mr. Hoffman asked. "This is the girl? The friend?"

"Yes," Larry said, putting his arm around Gabi.

"What happened?" Pastor Joshua asked.

"All I've been told is she laid down her life for Mark. She was a hero."

"So the good news is that Mark's alive?" Pastor Randy asked. Gabi looked up.

"That is good news," Topher said, "but not THE good news. Before she died, Angel gave her heart to Christ… YES!" he screamed excitedly. "She was saved."

"Are you serious?" Gabi asked, with tears in her eyes. "That's so exciting!" They all agreed. Topher took her hand. She looked up at him.

"Gabi, Scotty was the one who prayed with her."

"Scotty Morgan!?" She asked. "No way!"

"Wait!" Larry said, "Scotty is with Mark?"

"Yes, and he is okay. If it wasn't for your witness in Scotty's life, Gabi, Angel would not be in heaven right now. You gave him the wisdom and the boldness, through Christ of course."

"Oh wow!" Gabi said, sitting back down. "Her salvation is so much more exciting than her death is sad." She looked up. "Is that bad to say?"

"No it is not." Topher said. "For now, she is truly alive…and oh the reception she received in heaven! A party for the books."

They were all smiling.

"Now," Topher said, walking over to the counter and smelling the brewing coffee. "That's disgusting."

"See!" Pastor Joshua said, "no angel ever said my coffee was disgusting!" They all laughed.

"How do you people drink that?" Topher asked.

"It's an acquired taste," Larry said.

"It's delicious," Mr. Hoffman said, "when properly made." He gave Pastor Joshua a wink.

"Anyway," Topher said, holding up his hand. "There is work to be done." They all got quiet.

"A great battle is about to be fought in the spirit realm. The souls of thousands of people are in the balance. Each of you have important jobs to do. Larry, I need you to go get Pastor Eric, he's at his home. The two of you need to go to the hospital. First, there will be two young men looking to speak with him. They are very interested in what he has to say about salvation. Second, begin to pray over Bethany. A curse has been placed on her. Even now, a battle is beginning to be fought for her life."

Larry stood and headed for the door. Topher reached out and grabbed his arm. "Pray as never before." Larry nodded and left.

"Gabi?" Topher said and she sat up straight. "Be prepared...and know that no matter what is about to happen...Jesus will never leave you nor forsake you."

She nodded unsure at what he meant. She looked at Pastor Joshua and he shrugged.

"Now, the rest of you!" Topher continued, sitting in the chair Larry had just left. He looked at each of them. "As you know, there are four castles around the world, just like the one here in Gateway."

"Right," Pastor Joshua said. "Here, Germany, Italy and France.'

"Exactly, well these castles came about from a curse that happened long ago, it's not something you will find in scripture, it's just something that happened. Each castle has its own legends and some of them are a little crazy, but the truth is...there was a battle in..."

"Heaven?" Pastor Randy interrupted. Topher gave him a look. "Sorry."

"Switzerland, actually," Topher said.

"Didn't see that coming," Pastor Randy said.

"It was a spiritual battle that started when four Dark Priests made a pact with Satan hundreds of years ago. They wanted to give him a way to travel the earth a little quicker, so he could be more effective. Do you remember the scripture in Job where it says that Satan was roaming the earth to and fro?" They all nodded except Mr. Hoffman. "Well, they wanted to help him get to and fro faster.

"I am following you," Mr. Hoffman said.

"Satan told them that he needed their prayers. For their prayers would strengthen him and his army in battle. There was only one thing that would allow Satan this type of travel on earth, and that was to possess Jacob's ladder."

"The one from Jacob's dream in Genesis 28?" Pastor Randy asked.

"Exactly," Topher said. "Well, they got as many people as they could on their side and prayed. They had literally thousands of followers. They gathered on a designated mountain at a specific time and prayed for Satan and his armies. Satan went to war with the angels of God. The angels had no one praying for them."

"So what happened?" Pastor Joshua asked.

"Satan won," Topher said. "He captured the ladder. Well, he captured a portion of the ladder, but it was all he needed. He returned that night to that mountain where there was a huge celebration for their victory. He, of course, made it sound better than it was."

Pastor Joshua was about to ask a question but Topher held up his hand.

"He took the four Dark Priests aside and gave them each a gift. A rung from the ladder, for he had only captured four rungs. He told them that wherever they go with those rungs, he would be able to travel freely to. The rungs would connect regardless of where they were. So the plan was for each of them to return to their homelands and set their affairs in order, then they were to take the rungs to the four corners of the earth. Satan would then be able to travel the world undetected.

"I'm sorry," Pastor Randy said, "but aren't you guys able to travel quite quickly anyway? We got to Germany in what, just under a second?"

"Yes, but our means of travel leaves a trail that other demons or angels can see."

"One other point." Pastor Randy said. "If my geography is correct...Italy, France and Germany are pretty close to each other, not exactly the four corners of the earth."

"Good point," Pastor Joshua said.

"You are correct...that is because Satan's plan did not go so well. Because Satan had stolen the rungs from heaven, they were cursed objects. Three of the priests died in their homelands before they could leave Germany, France and Italy."

"And the other?" Pastor Joshua asked. "He came to America?"

Topher smiled, "Actually, on his way home to Ireland, he met a man, a believer, who told him that because he had made a deal with the devil he was about to die, and be judged by God. He repented right there and gave his life to Christ."

"And the rung?" Gabi asked.

Topher laughed. "He hid it in a barrel in the Spanish town he had stopped in. It ended up on a ship bound for a new land."

"It came over with Columbus?" Pastor Joshua asked, astounded.

"Ponce De Leon actually, and through their many trades with the Indians it ended up in Gateway, where it revealed itself as one of the castles."

"So why exactly do children have to die?" Mr. Hoffman asked.

"Good question," Topher said. "You see, realizing that humans couldn't be used to run or even guard the castles nor even trusted to pray for his strength, Satan had to use demons and foul creatures for these tasks. And as for keeping his strength, sacrifices were required. He prefers children because they're innocent and as close to Christ like as one can be."

"And now for the million- dollar question," Pastor Randy said. "What does this have to do with us?"

"I'm glad you asked. You see, there's only one thing that can break the curse, and basically destroy the rungs, castles and all."

"And that is...?" Pastor Joshua asked.

"An heir of each Dark Priest that is, in Christ, or saved, must stand together, holding hands and praying at midnight of the anniversary of that horrible battle."

"We do not know those heirs...do we?" Mr. Hoffman asked.

"The names of those Dark Priests were Jacob Hoffman, Antonio Scalise, Pierre Guillemette and Angus McGee..." he paused for affect. "You gentlemen, along with Mark or Bethany McGee, are those heirs."

"Whoa!" Pastor Joshua said.

"That's crazy," Gabi said.

"And when," Pastor Randy asked, "is this anniversary?"

Topher stood. "Midnight tonight, Switzerland time."

"How long do we have?" Pastor Randy asked.

"Six hours."

Gabi stood quickly, knocking her chair over. They all looked at her. She faced the wall as if seeing something. "I have to go!" she said, and ran straight at the wall.

"Gabi!" Pastor Joshua yelled, and she vanished just before hitting it. "Wow!!" he exclaimed. "What just happened?"

"She just went where angels cannot go," Topher said. "But God is with her."

"You don't actually think you've figured anything out do you, Mark?" The dragon hissed.

"You're supposed to be dead," Mark said.

The dragon only laughed.

"It's Jesus, isn't it?" Mark asked, backing away as the dragon walked slowly toward them. He noticed the dragon tense at the mention of the name. "He's the Gateway to God, isn't He?"

"That name is to never be mentioned here!" the dragon growled. "Say it again and I will tear you and your friends to pieces."

"I'm right through, aren't I?" Mark asked, standing in front of the others.

"It's a talking dragon," Christina mumbled as if just being able to speak. She was clearly terrified.

"Yeah," Scotty replied, "welcome to being friends with Mark McGee."

"It really doesn't matter if you're right or not, Mark McGee," the dragon hissed. "You're never getting out of the castle."

"Well," Mark said," we'll just see about that."

The dragon laughed. "While you're wasting time looking for the front door, I'll be visiting your little sister in the hospital."

Mark stopped, "What?"

"That's right, you didn't know." He laughed. "Little Bethany is lying in a hospital bed as we speak, just waiting for me to come...finish her off."

Mark looked at Scotty.

"He's right, Mark!" Scotty said, "The last I heard she wasn't doing good. A specialist was supposed to be flying in."

The dragon laughed louder. "Oh, her specialist never made it, he was held up...when his plane exploded just before takeoff." More laughter. "A lot of people are dying because of the McGee family!"

The dragon had backed them up against the door. "Guys, we should probably go." Christina said, her voice shaky. The dragon came closer, his red eyes glowing. Christina put her hand on the door knob. "Just say the word," she whispered, close to tears.

"Let's see..." the dragon continued, "we have the good doctor, there's your pathetic friend Angel." He laughed.

Mark grabbed the torch and held it in front of him. "You're the pathetic one! You slimy lizard!"

"Then we have Todd Johnson, Ms. Tyler, and let's not forget your father..." He smiled. "I enjoyed taking his life, Mark."

Mark froze. He was so confused. The dragon stepped right up to him. "Mark, let's go." Christina whispered."

"That's right Mark," The dragon hissed. "A friend at your father's job had invited him to a men's prayer. He'd

planned to just make a quick stop to be nice, but I knew…
he had to be stopped."

"What are you talking about?" Mark asked. "Why did
he have to be stopped?"

"I suppose it wouldn't hurt to tell you now." The
dragon, filling the room, raised his head. "The McGee
family has a special curse, Mark."

"Why?" What curse?"

"Because of a deal struck with the devil, we'll
say!" The dragon leaned close. "And I'm the keeper of
that curse."

"What did you do? He was in a car accident!"

"A drunk driver ran a stop light." The dragon laughed.

"Yes, he died instantly!"

The dragon laughed harder. "Don't believe everything a distraught mother tells a child. He most certainly
did not die instantly. I had the privilege of…"

"Liar!!" Mark threw the torch at the dragon. "Now,
Christina!" She slung the door open. They ran out into
the hall closing the door. The dragon's laughter shook
the walls.

Again the alarm sounded. They looked to the left.
There were several creatures running toward them.
Christina covered her ears looking panicked. Mark
grabbed her arm and motioned for her to follow. They
ran to the right. For several minutes they ran as fast as
they could, the creatures about fifty yards behind them
and gaining. Up ahead, Mark saw several doors. It was
the last one on the left that caught his eye. Bright red.
Something told him that was the door he wanted. He
approached it, pointing at it, so the others would know
his plan. Just as he reached for the knob, it swung open

and someone came through it and slammed into him. He hit the floor hard. It was also at that moment that the alarm stopped, Christina screamed and Scotty tripped over him and whoever hit him.

"Mark!" The person yelled, sitting up.

Mark opened his eyes, "Gabi!" he screamed louder than he'd meant to.

"What!?" Scotty said, rolling over.

Gabi looked over and saw the creatures closing in. She smiled real big, and stood. "Oh no you don't, you foul beasts!" She walked toward them. They stopped dead in their tracks. "You get out of here in the name of Jesus Christ!" They immediately evaporated into thin air.

"I should've done that!" Scotty said.

"Yes, you should have." Christina replied, quite impressed. "By the way, does that work on dragons… talking ones?"

Gabi turned to face them and gave Mark a big hug, then Scotty. "What happened to you, Mr. Morgan?! She asked.

He smiled, "I got lost in the bathroom. Where'd you come from?"

She turned to Christina, "Hi, I'm Gabi."

"Christina."

"Channel 13?" Gabi asked.

"6," Christina replied.

"Boy, some people will do anything for a story."

"That's me." Christina laughed.

"Mark!" Gabi said. "I'm so sorry, I heard about Angel."

"Really? How?"

"Topher, our angel friend." Gabi said.

"How did he know?" Scotty asked.

"Apparently he was there when Angel got to heaven," Gabi replied. "And I hear you're to blame for that." She punched Scotty's arm. He grinned. "I'm proud of you, Scotty Morgan."

"Gabi, I figured it out," Mark said. "Jesus is the Gateway to God!"

"Really?" Gabi said sarcastically. "I had no idea."

"So why ARE you here, Gabi?" Scotty asked. "You obviously weren't brought kicking and screaming like the rest of us."

"Apparently you needed rescuing," she said. Then she told them everything Topher had told them about the castles and the curse.

"So the dragon may not have been lying, Mark." Scotty said. "Your family IS cursed."

"So you're saying we only have about six hours to get out of here and be on a mountain top in Switzerland?"

"Yep..." Gabi said. "Now, where's the front door?"

"I'm wondering where that red door went," Scotty said, looking at the solid wall where the door had been.

It appeared that all the doors they'd just passed were gone. "Let's just keep going the way we were heading," Mark said. They started walking.

After a few minutes of walking in silence, passing paintings and torches and suits of armor, Christina broke the silence. "So, there really is something to this whole Jesus thing?"

Gabi stopped walking and looked at her. "Um, what did you just witness?"

"Well, how do I know I haven't been drugged? Maybe I'm not even awake, this could all be a dream."

Gabi reached over and pinched her arm really hard.

"Ouch!" Christina rubbed her arm. "You're crazy!"

"Yeah, well you're in danger of an eternity separated from Christ. We could all die at any second." They walked on but before they did, Gabi looked behind them.

"What is it, Gabi?" Scotty asked.

"Nothing. I thought I saw someone back there." On they went.

"It's just..." Christina said, "I've spent my entire life doing things my way. I'm the success that I am because I haven't been blown in the wind by every breeze that comes along."

"Well," Gabi said, "there's a wind coming alright. The Bible says that the storms are going to come, and the winds and waves are going to crash into our lives. Those who have built their house on sand will lose everything, but those who have built their house on the rock of Jesus Christ, will stand the test. They will survive."

"But Christians die every day. They have problems just like everybody else," Christina said, as if she'd just ended the argument.

"I know," Gabi said. Christina looked at her. "I just said, the storm hits those on sand and rock. It wasn't the storm that was different between the two, it was the foundation. Jesus is the solid foundation, and only Jesus. We suffer, we bleed, we fall, we die...but then, we live forever." She saw that Christina got it. "And you can too. Jesus loves you so much, Christina. He wants to spend forever with you."

"Gabi," Scotty said.

She noticed the boys had stopped, then she saw what they were looking at. Something was moving in the hall ahead of them. It appeared that the wall was alive. "What is that?" she asked.

"Spiders," Mark said.

"What?" Christina said.

"Not a fan," Scotty added. "Somebody do something!"

"Wow," Gabi said, "That's a lot of spiders." There were thousands. They were on the floor, the walls and the ceiling. They were coming fast.

"I guess we go back," Mark said and then they noticed that there was a wall right behind them as if it just appeared. "Whoa!"

"Hey, we just came from that way." Scotty said.

"Suggestions?" Mark said.

"Father, we need your help," Gabi said as the spiders got closer. Some of them were already dropping on them. They swatted them off.

"Hey look!" Christina said. "A door appeared." It was just to their right.

"Another red one," Mark said. They quickly opened it and jumped in. Christina screamed, a very large spider had landed on her head. Mark knocked it off. It scurried away. The door slammed shut.

It was a small room, brightly lit, though there were no lights to be seen. The walls seemed to shine, though not so bright you couldn't look at them.

"Oh pretty," Christina said. They all looked around. There was nothing in the room, yet it was very peaceful, relaxing.

Mark noticed a door on the other side and walked over to it.

"No Mark," Christina said, "do we have to leave? What is this place?"

"I think it's an answer to Gabi's prayer," Scotty said.

"Yeah, there's something different about the red doors," Mark said. "Something bad kept happening every time I tried to go in one."

"Oh yeah," Gabi said. "I saw you standing by a door in my dream. I told you to open it!"

"And I heard you!" Mark said. "I thought that was strange...but strange is my life here lately.

"I think they're God's WAY," she said.

"God's way out?" Scotty asked

"Yes and no...the Bible says that God will make a way out of a situation where there seems to be no way. I think the red doors are HIS way out of bad situations in the castle."

"And you came in from one," Christina said. "Is that in the Bible?"

"We can't just stay in here though," Mark said. "I'm going to peek out this door. Who knows, maybe it leads out of the castle." They all agreed he should peek. He opened it just a little and looked out. He closed it back immediately.

"What is it?" Christina asked.

"There's like a million demons out there," Mark said, backing away. "So, spiders or demons?"

"Oh, I got this!" Scotty said, going for the door and snatching it open before anyone could stop him. There were about twenty demons standing in a large room. They all turned and faced Scotty. He stepped into the room with them, "In the name of Jesus Christ, I command you to go!"

Some of them vanished with a scream, some of them vanished with a roar of anger, and some of them vanished quietly but ALL of them vanished.

"Well done Scotty!" Gabi said, patting him on the back, as they all came into the room.

"That was awesome," Scotty said. "It's like having the best gun in a video game."

"I think you're finally getting it!" she said. "Jesus isn't just a story…his name is like Kryptonite to demons."

"Good analogy, Gabi." Christina said, and just then there was a loud crash. The door at the other end of the room burst open. They all jumped back.

Standing in the doorway stood a large man. He was tall and thick and wore overalls. His ham sized hands were balled into fists.

"Lucius Willoughby," Mark said calmly.

He started walking toward them slowly. "Play time is over kids, it's time to die."

Scotty stepped forward, "In the name…" Lucius shoved him back.

"Not with me, punk! You should've fasted and prayed."

Gabi stepped forward, "I did."

Lucius stopped. "You? When?"

"Hold on, Gabi!" Mark said. "Lead us out of here Lucius, and she won't disintegrate you."

"All I want is McGee," Lucius said. "Give me McGee and I'll show the rest of you out."

"Not a chance," Gabi said. "I don't make deals with the devil."

He smiled. "I'm not the devil…I'm his gardener."

"Either way, I come against you in the name of Jesus Christ!"

He cringed.

"And I command you to go!"

He was gone in an explosion of light.

"Wow!" Christina said. "You're no normal Christian, Gabi...you're like Special Forces."

"The Bible says "NO weapon formed against me will prosper," Gabi replied. "All Christians have this potential, but most are too lazy."

"Well," Scotty said, "most Christians don't exactly get chased by demons, dragons, spiders and evil gardeners through a castle either."

Gabi just gave him a look. "We need to get moving."

There were doctors, nurses, visitors and patients all moving about in the halls of the Gateway Community Hospital. Everyone was busy. Everyone had a job to do or a person to see or a procedure to have done. Not one of them was aware of the large dragon that walked through them, past them, by them. He too had a job to do. Kill Bethany McGee. Her brother Mark had turned out to be a bigger pain than he was worth. He hoped Mark was dead now. That would leave only Bethany and without those two, the castles were forever safe.

As he approached her room, he saw a group of people standing outside it. There was her mother, her stepfather, and he froze. It was Gabi's pastor, Gabi's father, and Gabi's mother. They were all as bad as Gabi, though he rarely dealt with adults. That was someone else's territory. He approached cautiously, seeing their angels standing nearby looking as arrogant and regal as usual. They saw him and placed their hands on their swords.

He would love nothing more than to stay and fight them but he had a little girl—to shred. He slipped through the wall and into her room. There was a doctor with his back to the door. He would need to wait for him to leave or he may try and save her. Now that he thought of it, he was a rather large doctor. His head almost touched the ceiling and his shoulders were quite wide.

"You should probably go," the doctor said.

The dragon looked toward the door but nobody was there.

Just then, with a flash of bright light, the doctor turned. His wings filled the room and his sword was at the dragon's throat. "Or I could end you."

"Easy, easy...Adam," the dragon said as calmly as he could. He knew who Adam was. One of Michael's fiercest warriors, known for his high count of demon kills. Of course, demons didn't die, they just went to hell and regrouped. Still, he wasn't one to be messed with. "They must really be taking this serious to have you guarding her."

"Absolutely, and the prayers are strong. You will not touch her on this night."

"We will see Adam," he said as he retreated, "we will see."

CHAPTER NINETEEN

THE REVELATION

B efore they really had any time at all to comprehend what had happened to Gabi, Topher brought Pastor Randy, Pastor Joshua and John Hoffman to a mountaintop in Switzerland.

"Whoa!" Pastor Randy said, as Topher handed them each a coat.

"I will never get used to that," Mr. Hoffman said. "No sir."

"So this is the place?" Pastor Joshua asked.

"This is the place, "Topher replied. He pointed to a circle of stones. They gathered around them. "The priests were right here when they prayed to Satan."

"Wow, our ancestors were here," Pastor Joshua said.

"Yeah, praying to Satan," Pastor Randy said. "That kinda takes away the cool factor."

"So we have like six hours," Pastor Joshua said."What are we supposed to do now?"

"You pray," Topher said. "A very big spiritual war is about to take place, and your prayers are vital."

Mr. Hoffman walked over to the edge and looked out. "So beautiful here."

"Yes it is," Pastor Randy agreed.

"Hey, what is that?" Pastor Joshua pointed to the valley below. There appeared to be something moving. It looked like ants moving quickly together, heading for the mountain.

"The enemy is gathering," Topher said.

"The enemy?" Mr. Hoffman asked. "Who is the enemy?"

"Demons," Pastor Randy said. "And it looks like hundreds."

"Look that way," Topher said, pointing to their right. Coming down from another mountain were more. In fact, in every direction they looked, the mountain was being surrounded.

"Try thousands," Pastor Joshua said.

"Millions," Topher replied. "Satan has invited everybody. He likes his castles. He doesn't want to lose them."

"This is crazy," Pastor Joshua said. "We need to pray now." They walked to the stones.

"Pray for Mark and Bethany. The enemy is trying to kill both of them at this very moment," Topher said. "Without them, our plan fails. Now, I have to go."

"Go?" Mr. Hoffman exclaimed. "We are surrounded by demons. You mustn't leave us alone!"

"Alone?" Topher smiled. "Look up."

They each looked up and in unison said, "Whoa!"

"So, Christina," Gabi said as they walked down the long dark corridor, "Are you ready to ask Jesus into your heart?"

"I...I think so," she responded.

Gabi stopped and faced her. "You have to know."

Christina nodded slowly. "Okay, I'm ready. What do I have to do?"

"Confess that you're a sinner and in need of HIS salvation. Ask Him to come into your heart and be your Lord and Savior."

Christina waited for more. "Wait, that's it?" She was really confused. It couldn't be that easy.

"That's it...as long as you mean it."

"It's too simple."

"Actually, the price for your salvation was paid on the cross by Jesus, so that it could be simple for you. Without His sacrifice, we would all be on our way to hell."

Christina nodded. "Okay." She closed her eyes and bowed her head. She began her prayer. Gabi and Scotty closed their eyes as well.

Mark kept watch. He looked behind Gabi and Christina and saw a woman peeking out from behind a gargoyle statue. He was about to say something when all of a sudden, something grabbed him.

Christina finished her prayers with a shaky amen. Gabi gave her a hug. Scotty squeezed her hand.

"Now, what about you Mark?" Gabi asked, turning around. "Mark?"

"Where is he?" Scotty yelled, in a panic.

"He was just right here," Gabi said, turning in place. "Mark!?"

"What could've happened to him?" Christina asked.

"He's the only one not protected," Gabi said.

"By what?" Christina asked.

"By God," Scotty replied. "Mark hasn't asked Jesus into his heart yet. We need to pray for him."

Gabi gave him an impressed look. "So pray."

"Okay then…" he said. They all joined hands. "Father, we need your help. Mark has been taken, by…by the enemy. We need to find him. Please help us…amen?"

"Amen!" Gabi and Christina said.

"We should find the central room," Scotty said.

"The what?" Gabi asked.

"The central room, it's where they take the kids to torture and kill them. It's in the center of the castle, kind of where all four castles join. I have a feeling that's where he's going to be."

"Okay," Gabi replied, "so how do we find it?"

"I have no idea."

Once again Mark found himself chained to the table in the torture room, surrounded by demons. "Let me go!" he screamed. "In the name of…!" The demon closest to him shoved a piece of cloth in his mouth. It was wet and tasted horrible. Mark gagged. He tried to spit it out but couldn't.

Just then he heard the door open and the chilling laugh of the dragon. "Well, well, well…what have we here?" He walked up next to Mark. "The troublesome Mark McGee." He laughed again. "I've just come from your sister's hospital room. She doesn't look very good, Mark. Probably won't survive the night. Of course, neither will you!" More laughter. "You see, my only job for the past two hundred some years has been to make sure the McGee family never found God. The other's failed. I never fail!" He leaned in close. "My demon here," he motioned to the one who had put the cloth in his mouth, "is going to peel your skin off, Mark." He laughed. "And he's going to do it slowly." More laughter and he backed away. The demon stepped up and produced a really long knife with a curved blade. Mark could see his reflection in the blade as it came close. He squeezed his eyes shut preparing for the pain. He thought of his family. His mom, stepdad, Bethany. His grandparents. His friends, Scotty, Gabi...immediately a bright light flooded his mind. Was he dead? He'd felt no pain. Then...he was standing on a large hill. People were shouting. He didn't understand the language, but they seemed angry. He strained to see what they were looking at and made his way through the angry crowd. He saw several people to his right that were gathered together. They appeared to be crying and holding each other. Then...he looked up. He couldn't believe what he was seeing. There were three men on crosses. He couldn't stand to watch, but found it impossible to look away. The two men on the outside were bruised and bleeding but the man in the middle...was it even a man? It looked as if his skin had been run through a shredder. He was covered in blood. His face was beaten and swollen. His eyes barely slits from the swelling. He was totally disfigured from his head to his feet. The thorns...and the nails...dear God. His hands and feet were nailed to the wood like so much artwork...and...his eyes...he was looking at Mark. This brutally beaten man that was nailed to that cross, surrounded by hundreds of people, screaming, crying, shouting, wailing; and he was staring at Mark.

In the blink of any eye Mark was face to face with him. He wasn't sure what was happening. It felt like a dream, for he was floating in midair, but he could feel the warm wind blowing. He could smell the blood and sweat of the man only inches away. He could see him trembling from pain and agony. And then…the man smiled. No, no, no, why? How could he smile? Mark choked out a sob. A tear slid down his cheek. Then, the man spoke…two simple words that were barely audible. Mark's world would never be the same.

He opened his eyes as the demon was about to slide the knife down his chest. The cloth fell from his mouth. "Father, I surrender my life to your son, Jesus Christ!'

"No!!!" The dragon roared, shaking the walls. The demon fell back with a look of horror.

"I give you my life, Jesus! Thank you for saving me from hell!" Mark sobbed. "Come into my life!"

The dragon was writhing. "SHUT UP!!! Nooo!" His tail whipped around the room knocking over the table of torture devices and tools.

"Be my Lord and Savior Jesus!" Mark actually laughed, and the chains that held him down shattered like glass. He sat up…the demons were fleeing the room. The dragon was backing away.

"You will regret this, Mark McGee!" He roared. "I will shred your family!"

"Whatever, loser!" Mark said, hopping off the table. "Just Go!" And the dragon vanished. Mark fell to his knees. He laughed and he cried. He had passed through the Gateway to God.

Topher joined Clayton in the hospital parking lot. "Hello, my friend!" They hugged. Hundreds of people were out there. It was quite a gathering to have been put together so fast. Some people had even taken the time to make signs. "Pray for Bethany" or "God Bless Bethany," they read. Some people were gathered together praying. Some were gathered in groups, fellowshipping. Some of the teenagers were handing pamphlets to people that read "Pray for Bethany" with a picture of her and an explanation of what was going on with her. "Very impressive my friend," Topher said.

"All I did was tell them what they needed to do," he nodded toward two boys. "They put it together."

Matt and Billy stood under a tree with Pastor Eric, Larry, Gae, and Mark's stepdad.

"So they prayed the prayer!" Topher said excitedly.

"Isn't it great!?" Clayton replied.

"I know! There was quite a celebration!" Topher said.

"Well, let's go see them," Clayton said and they walked over.

"Clayton!" Billy yelled as they got close. He ran up and gave Clayton a hug.

"Topher!" Larry said.

"So, this is Topher?" Matt said, staring in awe. All the introductions were made.

"You boys have done a great thing here!" Topher said. "I can feel the prayers."

"We got saved, Clayton!" Billy exclaimed, and everyone laughed.

"Yes you did! Oh how the angels rejoiced!'

"Seriously?" Billy asked.

"Oh yeah," Topher said. "Guilty."

"Hey," Billy said, "can I show you guys off to my friends?"

"No," Clayton said with a smile. "Let's keep this about Bethany, with the focus on Jesus."

"Before I go," Topher said to the group, "let me say this. Continue to pray for Bethany, Mark, Scotty, Gabi and Christina!"

Larry gave him a confused look, "Gabi?"

"She is on a rescue mission in the castle," Topher replied. "God is with her, though I cannot be."

Larry smiled." Those poor demons."

"And who exactly is Christina?" Pastor Eric asked.

"Christina Bulford," Clayton answered. "News lady, Channel 6...stumbled into the castle. Gabi has actually led her to Christ now and she is working with them."

"That's my girl," Larry said.

"Carry on my friends!" Topher shouted. He and Clayton vanished.

Gabi, Scotty and Christina were moving down the halls at a fast walk. They checked every door, closing them immediately if they weren't the room they were looking for. "This place is endless," Christina said, clearly getting frustrated. "We have to hurry."

Gabi stopped, "Let's pray." They joined hands and she led. "Father, once again we need your help. Mark is in trouble and we need to find him. Please guide our steps, and oh...keep him safe. In Jesus' name, Amen."

"Amen!" Scotty and Christina said.

When they opened their eyes, there standing about thirty feet ahead of them, stood the dragon.

"It's him," Christina said. "The talking dragon."

He laughed a low rumble of a laugh. Gabi stepped forward. "Your prayers are worthless Gabi Motes."

"What are you talking about?" she asked.

"Mark McGee is dead! Bethany McGee is dead!" He laughed. "The castle is safe!" More ground shaking laughter.

The three of them stood there speechless.

He stepped towards them. "Now, if you three surrender to me, I will not go after your families...however, if you don't..."

"No!!" Gabi yelled and took a step closer. The dragon blinked. "You're a liar!" She pointed at him. "Show me his body if he's dead!" she yelled.

"His body was destroyed," the dragon said, trying to remain in control.

"A likely story; he's alive you lying lizard! What? Did he give his life to Jesus? You couldn't touch him? Now you're trying to manipulate us so that you can get to him!" She stepped right up to him.

"Gabi!" Scotty said.

"In Jesus name! Tell me the truth!" she shouted poking him right on the snout.

"I told you!" the dragon roared. "He's d..." His mouth clamped shut.

Gabi smiled. "Where is he?"

Just then the entire castle shook violently. It was like a massive earthquake. They all leaned against the wall. Dust was falling from the ceiling. There was a loud rumble. There was fear in the dragon's eyes as he backed away. "You've done it now!" And he vanished.

"Wait!" Scotty yelled. "What've we done, Gabi?"

"Come on!" Gabi said. "We have to find Mark!" They ran as fast as they could with the ground shaking beneath them.

"How did you know he was lying?" Christina asked.

"It's what they do," Gabi said. "They lie!"

"So you talk to a lot of dragons then?" Christina asked.

"He's just a demon, a devil...they lie!" Gabi replied. "We need to call out for Mark!" Each of them began yelling Mark's name out as they ran.

The castle felt as if it lifted up off the ground and literally turned sideways. Each of them slammed into the wall on their left and hit the ground. Another violent shaking followed. Pictures fell off the walls, suits of armor toppled over. Debris fell from the ceilings and walls.

"It's like the castle is trying to kill us!" Gabi yelled. "Get against the wall!"

About twenty feet ahead of them the floor began to crack from one wall to the other. Then it began to split.

"We need to go!" Scotty yelled, pointing at the crack that was slowly opening up.

"Run. Now!" Gabi yelled. The crack was already more than four feet wide when Scotty reached it first. He made it easily, but it was widening. Gabi jumped and made it but Christina hit the edge at her shin. She'd been too close to Gabi. She slid down trying to find something to grab. Scotty grabbed her arm just as she slipped. They both looked down. It appeared to be bottomless.

"Please don't let go Scotty!" Christina yelled. Gabi joined him and together they pulled her up. The opening kept spreading.

"We should go; are you okay Christina?" Gabi asked.

She rubbed her shin, "I'll be fine, let's go!"

Gabi squinted back from the direction they'd just jumped. Through the dust and debris there appeared to be someone standing in the hall. When she blinked, they were gone. Scotty grabbed her arm and pulled her on, they ran as fast as they could down the hall.

Mark had never felt so peaceful. Here he was in the middle of the devil's lair, surrounded by demons and dragons and all manner of evil and you couldn't slap the grin off his face. Was this joy? He had no idea, all he knew was, he was not worried. The dragon had threatened Bethany, that didn't even worry him. He just knew God could handle it, she was in His hands. Somehow, letting God worry about things felt right.

He had gotten up from praying, left the center room and just started walking. He'd asked God to help him and just knew he'd be okay. After walking for several minutes, he'd heard a horrible growling sound and the entire castle had shaken. At least the part he was in had. He'd just grabbed a torch bracket and held on. It had only lasted about a minute.

Now, he was walking a little faster, calling out for his friends hoping to find them soon. He was excited about telling Gabi the good news.

Just then, the ground began to rumble again. He was knocked off his feet. He tried to roll up against the wall but it wasn't easy, the castle felt like it was being ripped apart. Dust and rocks were falling from the ceiling. Mark covered his head with his arms. He heard what sounded like a chain clanking but he couldn't see anything. Each time he worked himself up against the wall, he seemed to slide away with all the shaking. Then he felt a tightening around his ankles. Had something fallen. He tried to look

but dust got in his eyes. He reached his hand down there.
A chain? Chains were wrapped around his ankles. All of
sudden he was being pulled down the hall on his stomach
feet first. He tried to find something to grab a hold of but
there was nothing. He could barely open his eyes. The
castle still shook. He reached down to try and break free
from the chains but it was useless. It was as if the chains
were alive and gripping his legs. Helplessly he groped
for something to grab. Completely covered in debris, all
his hands could find were chunks of rock that crumbled
to dust when he would grab them. Just then something
grabbed his wrists and squeezed them very tight. For
a moment he thought help had come but could barely
make out through the dust and debris that it was more
chains. They pulled him in the opposite direction that
his legs were being pulled. At that exact moment, the
floor caved in and fell away from below him. "Jesus!
No!" The chains stopped pulling yet Mark was in quite a
pickle. There he was being held over this hole by chains.
If the chains released him he would fall to his death, if
they held him he would, well, be trapped. "Thank you,
Jesus, but…"

"Hello Mark McGee." It was a girl's voice but he
couldn't see. "Who's there?" The castle had stopped
shaking and the dust began to settle.

"I see you've gotten yourself into quite the situation."
Then Mark knew by her voice that it was the girl with
the dress. He didn't know her name.

"I'm sorry," he said, "I never got your name."

She giggled. "I never told you my name, silly."

"Well, is there any way you could help me out?"

"Perhaps you can help yourself, Mark McGee." It sounded like she was pacing along the edge of the hole. "Have you already forgotten about your special talent?"

His ankles and wrists were really starting to hurt.

"You see," she said, "the castle has turned against you, it is trying to kill you. What it doesn't realize is that you are just as powerful as it is. All you have to do is tell those chains to break, and they have to."

"Seeing how the chains are the only thing keeping me alive right now, that would be a really bad idea."

Again she giggled. "You have a point, I suppose, but you see what I mean. You have the ability to control your situation."

Mark really liked what she was saying, but somehow it felt wrong.

As if she could sense his doubt, she said, "everyone has abandoned you Mark…except me. David is gone, your friends are gone, your family is gone…and apparently your God is gone." Something about the way she said the word God gave him pause. It was as if the word tasted bad in her mouth. "You could probably even close the hole up and then break the chains Mark. Show me you can."

"No!" Mark said. "Your mouth is the only hole that needs to shut up! It's not about me anymore! I surrendered my life to Jesus Christ, and my rescue is His responsibility!" When she didn't respond, he said, "hello? Are you still there?" From the best he could tell, she was gone, and that was fine with him. "Okay Lord, I trust you to get me out of this…Please hurry though, it's starting to hurt." It was at that moment that Mark heard a loud clanking sound. It sounded like someone was banging pots and pans against the floor and walls. It got louder and louder. He couldn't see anything though whatever it was got really close, then it stopped. The sound echoed down the cavern below him. "Hello? Who's there?" There was a loud bang and the chain holding Mark's feet broke and he slammed face first into the wall, being held up by the chains on his arms. He looked behind him and there stood an army of knights in armor. He looked up. Another army. Apparently the ones behind him had broken his chain with an axe. One of the knights above him lifted him up. His arms hurt so badly. "Who are you? Friend or enemy?"

Pulling Mark by his chains, they led him down the hall, back the way he'd come.

"I'm guessing enemy…listen, I don't have time for this…how did Gabi do this…In the name of Jesus, I command…" They were gone as soon as he said the name. Even the chains were gone. "Wow," Mark said. "Just, wow." With all the clanking of metal and chains gone, it was very quiet now, Mark thought. He leaned against the wall to figure out what to do next.

It was then that he heard a faint sound in the distance. He looked in the direction that the knights had been leading him. He couldn't see anything. "Hello?" he called. "Gabi?" It was getting louder, a humming sound. Clicking. Buzzing. Then he saw movement like a darkness closing in. "What in the world is…" He turned and ran as fast as he could. He wasn't sure what kind of bug it was but there were a lot of them. He knew they were catching up because they got louder. He looked back. Flies? No, locusts? No, grasshoppers? No, not even bees. Just then one dropped on his hand. It was a cockroach.

He shook it off and realized they were all over him. He slapped them off as he ran, but they were overtaking him. Looking ahead, he now had a new problem. The hole he'd been hanging from was coming up. Could he jump it? The roaches were upon him. Flying in the air, crawling on the floor, the walls, the ceiling. The hole looked about seven feet across, he had to try. "I need your help, Jesus!!!" He yelled as he got close. Just then a fog come up out of the hole, Mark jumped through it going as fast as he could. What was that smell? He landed on the other side and hit the floor in a roll. He looked back. All the roaches were dropping into the pit. Bug spray. That's what Mark had smelled. Bug spray or some kind of gas had come out of the hole and killed the roaches.

"Thank you Jesus!" he shouted. He hated roaches. They were so nasty. He stood up and checked himself. No roaches. Other than bruises on his wrists and ankles, he was fine. He started down the hall, checking behind him frequently for any roaches that may have made it.

Mark's mom and stepdad sat in Bethany's room with Pastor Eric. Bethany wasn't conscious and they were all three sitting quietly watching her. They were appreciative of what was going on outside for Bethany, but didn't fully understand all the praying.

Pastor Eric had talked with them about God and sensed that they were close to making a decision for Christ. Right now they were both just too emotional. They had Bethany close to death with an unusual heart condition, where the only experienced specialist in the

country died on his way to help her. They had a missing
son that they were trusting complete strangers to find.
They had media breathing down their neck for a story.
Was there any wonder they were so emotional?

Still, they sat there in silence, Pastor Eric praying. They
could hear the activity outside. They could see Bethany's
chest rising and falling slowly as she slept. What they
couldn't hear or see were the three angels posted around
her bed or the one at the door, swords drawn.

"So the castle is trying to kill us?" Christina said.
"Are you kidding me?" She was running with a limp.

"Yes," Gabi replied. "Well, the ruler of the castle is,
but apparently he can manipulate the castle.

"The ruler?" Scotty asked. "You mean…?"

"Yes," Gabi said. "Satan."

"Whoa! Are you serious?" Christina asked. "Satan
himself?"

All of a sudden they heard a scraping sound like stone
sliding on stone.

"What is that?" Scotty asked, slowing down. They
all stopped.

"Um, guys," Christina said. "Is it just me or are the
walls closing in?"

"Run!" Gabi said. They ran.

"Where are we going?" Christina yelled, hobbling
along. "There's no doors ahead."

"There has to be a way out!" Gabi yelled. The walls
were closing in fast. After about two minutes of running,
they had to run in single file: Gabi, Scotty and Christina.

"Gabi!" Scotty yelled. "What do we do?" They had to turn sideways. "We're going to be squished! Are you praying?"

It pressed tighter. Scotty got stuck first, then Christina couldn't move, because he blocked her. Gabi grabbed Scotty's hand and tried to pull him. He was stuck.

"Aw, man," Christina said, "I'm claustrophobic!"

"Okay, don't panic!" Gabi said. The walls had stopped, everything went quiet.

"Now what?" Scotty asked.

"Please pray, guys," Christina said, "I can't even move my arms. This is bad, I'm about to panic."

"Okay," Gabi said, "Father, we…"

"Shush," Scotty said. "Listen." There was a clicking sound. "What is that?" It got louder.

They still had light from torches that had fallen to the floor as the walls had closed in. Christina and Scotty's head were stuck looking in the direction they'd been heading. Because Gabi was smaller, she could look both ways.

"Something's coming from behind me!" Christina sounded like she was about to panic.

"Oh, please don't be spiders," Scotty said. "Anything but spiders." He looked at Gabi, "Can you see?"

Gabi tried to see around them and then she saw what was coming. "Oh…wow."

"What? Wow what?" Scotty asked.

Christina just closed her eyes and breathed. She silently prayed.

"It's not spiders," Gabi said as they got closer.

"What is it?" Scotty asked, slightly relieved.

"Scorpions…and there's a lot."

"Scorpions!? That's worse than spiders!!" Scotty said. "No! No! No!"

"Scotty, shut up and pray," Christina said. One dropped in her hair. "They're on me," she said.

"Be very still," Gabi said. "Maybe they'll just go on by."

Christina was crying. Gabi could see that they were covering her, and beginning to get on Scotty.

"They're on me Gabi, pray!" Scotty whispered really loud.

"Jesus!" Gabi yelled. "We really need your help!"

The floor below them began to tilt.

"Gabi," Scotty whined. "What now?" Slowly they slid down. "What's happening?" They dropped slowly and fell one floor down, landing with a thud. Scotty frantically swatted at the few scorpions that were on him.

Gabi helped Christina get them off of her calmly.

"Are they off me!?" Scotty yelled.

"Scotty? Really?" Gabi said. "Christina has like a hundred and she's calm. You had maybe three."

"Well, they were a big three," Scotty said. Some scorpions were still dropping down so Scotty moved away.

"Thanks for your help Scotty," Christina said. "My hero."

"Sorry! I hate scorpions! They have stingers," Scotty said. "And they look like spiders."

"How's your leg, Christina?" Gabi asked.

"Well," she looked at it, "that fall didn't help, but I can keep going."

They looked around. This hall was much wider. The ceiling was a little higher too. There were no pictures on the walls or decorations at all. The torch brackets were set into holes in the walls. Gabi pulled a torch out.

Just then there was a ground shaking rumble and sound that made them cover their ears. It lasted for about twenty seconds and was deafening.

"What was that?" Scotty said, looking behind them.

"It sounded like a siren and a baby crying," Christina said, "mixed together. It was horrible."

Again it screamed and the ground shook. It sounded as if something was coming.

"Aw man!" Scotty said. "What now? A T-Rex?"

They walked backwards, keeping an eye behind them to see what was coming. "Christina, you go!" Gabi said. "We'll catch up." She gave Scotty a concerned look. Beyond fifty feet behind them, the hall was dark.

The steps drew closer. They saw something move and then the deafening sound again.

"What is it?" Scotty yelled.

"Who cares?" Gabi replied. "Run!" They turned and ran. The rumbling moved faster too. They looked back and saw a giant lizard, tongue flicking toward them. "A lizard?"

"It's a Komodo dragon!" Scotty said. "They're awesome creatures!" He slowed to look. It screamed again. He covered his ears and ran faster. "Of course, they're usually not as big as an airplane...or trying to eat me!"

They caught up to Christina who was hobbling along at a good pace. "Big lizard," She mumbled.

"Komodo dr..."

"Don't care!"

It screamed again, getting closer.

"Look!" Christina yelled, pointing ahead. "A red door!"

"Go to it!" Gabi yelled and stopped. "I'll hold him off!" She turned and held the torch up.

Scotty stopped as well, "Gabi!?"

"Run, Scotty!" She yelled.

"Not without you!"

The lizard stopped, not seeming to like the fire. It screamed again.

Gabi and Scotty walked backwards holding it off.

"Guys come on! The doors open!" Christina yelled.

They walked backwards faster. As they drew close, they heard the door slam shut. When they turned to look, it was gone.

"Christina!" Scotty yelled. "Christina!?"

"She's gone, Scotty!" Gabi said.

"But why? Where?"

"It was a red door, hopefully she's fine!" Gabi said.

"What do we do?" Scotty asked.

"Run!"

CHAPTER TWENTY

A LIGHT IN THE DARK

Mark had been walking for what seemed like hours since the roach incident. It had probably only been about twenty minutes. There had been no doors, windows or even any turns. Just torches, statues of goblins, demons, dragons, and a few pictures. The hallway seemed to be endless. Mark was beginning to feel he would never escape this castle. "Okay Lord, I need to find my friends and get out of here…this is crazy!" With a burst of energy, he took off running. After several minutes at a full sprint, he saw something ahead. It looked like an opening. As he got closer, he saw that it was the entryway to a staircase.

He looked in. There was a spiral staircase going up and down. He had no idea where he was in regard to ground level. He looked up. Dark and scary. He looked down. Dark and scary. "Hello?" He called and his voice only echoed. He had no idea which way to go. Finally, he decided he would walk down for a bit and if it didn't look promising, he would walk back up. Down he headed, grabbing a torch off the wall. "Guide my steps, Jesus."

After about ten minutes of spiraling downward and seeing nothing below him, he stopped. Should he try up? Down was easier. He looked behind him and almost fainted. The steps were gone. There was only dark open space. Total blackness. He took a step down and the step he was just on vanished. "Well, down it is," he said and started down again.

About twenty minutes later, still walking down, he felt as if he was heading for the center of the earth. "This place is insane!" he said aloud. "Jesus, I need you!"

Just then a warm breeze blew up at him. His torch went out. "No! No! No!" He stopped. It was pitch black. He could see nothing. He put one hand on the wall and held the flameless torch out in front of him and walked down. The further he went, the more hopelessness consumed him. He started to believe he was dead. This was his hell. Had he been fooling himself about being saved? Was Jesus really the Gateway to God? He heard something and stopped. It had sounded like a shoe sliding on the stone floor. He listened intently. "Is anybody there?"

The armies of heaven were gathered above them. They were innumerable. After seeing them, Pastor Randy and Pastor Joshua had fallen on their faces in worship. Mr. Hoffman just stood there staring in awe. "This is unbelievable," he said. He walked over and looked down. The mountain was completely surrounded by demons. There were tens of thousands of them. They came in different shapes and sizes, from the size of a small dog to some that reminded him of King Kong. "So many demons," he said. "Yet, I'm not afraid."

"If God is for you, who can be against you?" It was Topher, all smiles.

"Topher!" Mr. Hoffman said. "This is amazing!"

Topher saw the pastors praying and smiled. "Their prayers are felt."

"What about Mark and Bethany?" Mr. Hoffman asked.

"No word on Bethany. Mark however, is now a Christian!"

"Praise God!" Mr. Hoffman said.

"Hundreds are gathered at the hospital to pray for Bethany!" Topher said. "Continue to pray. Our time is short. Mark has still not found his way to us!" He vanished.

Mr. Hoffman looked at his watch, one hour left...

Topher joined Clayton in Bethany's room. There were other angels with them but they alone were in human form. The family had gone outside at Pastor Eric's prompting. They were being encouraged by all the people.

"How is she?" Topher asked.

"Safe," Clayton responded, "thanks to Adam and the others. There are hundreds of demons just waiting for the right moment to sweep in."

"Any improvement?"

"No, but we're trusting the Great Physician here."

"Yes we are," Topher replied.

"Guys!" A woman screamed behind them. "It won't open!"

Both angels turned, swords drawn, with Adam at their side in less than a second. Wings filled the room.

The woman screamed and spun around from facing the wall. "Whoa!" She backed away.

They put their swords away and Adam vanished. Topher and Clayton smiled and changed back to human form. "Sorry," Topher said.

"Who are you?" She asked.

"I'm Topher and this is Clayton and we're…"

"Angels!" she said and began to cry. "Oh wow."

"This is Bethany," Clayton said, pointing to her. "Mark's sister."

"It's good to see you Christina," Topher said, placing a hand on her shoulder.

"Y…y you know who I am?"

"Of course, we were at the party celebrating your salvation."

At that she smiled. "Really?"

"Oh yeah," Clayton said. "And you're going to have quite the story."

"Like anyone would believe it." She laughed.

"Still, it must be told," Clayton replied.

"I know two boys outside that would just love to see you," Topher said.

"Matt and Billy? They're here?" She lit up.

"Look out the window," Topher said.

She walked over and looked out. "Oh my! What are all those people doing?"

"Praying. Fellowshipping. Encouraging," Clayton said.

"All for Bethany?" She asked.

"And Mark," Topher said. "And Gabi and Scotty. And…you."

Then she saw her news van. "I have a story to tell."

Gabi and Scotty were running as fast as they could. The Komodo dragon was quickly gaining. There were no doors, windows, or turns; just straight hallway for what looked like miles.

"He's gaining on us Gabi!" Scotty yelled. Every muscle in his body was aching. "I can't keep running!"

"Keep running!" Gabi yelled.

There was another eardrum shattering scream. They covered their ears.

"That is the most horrible sound ever!" Gabi yelled. Scotty nodded in agreement.

Up ahead they saw someone. At first, Scotty thought his eyes were tricking him. There were several suits of armor, but standing in the middle of the hall was a woman. She was waving them on. As they got closer, she held up one of the knight's spears. "Go past me!" she yelled. Just as they reached her, the lizard's tongue lashed out and tripped Scotty. He slammed onto the floor; it stopped and picked him up by the leg and with one shake of its head, smacked Scotty against the wall. He hit the floor with a thud and Gabi screamed. The woman threw the spear into the lizard's mouth. It let out a gargled scream and retreated backwards down the hall.

Gabi ran to Scotty, "Scotty! No!" She knelt beside him. She lifted his head. He was alive, but unconscious.

"Is your friend okay?" the woman asked.

"He's alive… thank you!" Gabi said. "You saved us."

"Just another day in hell," The woman said.

"Who are you?" Gabi asked. "What are you doing here?" She sat down and put Scotty's head in her lap.

The woman shrugged. "My name is Tammy." She kept looking back and forth.

Gabi was patting Scotty's chest. "Wake up Scotty," she whispered.

"Are you the one I saw following us earlier?" When she looked up, the woman was gone.

"Scotty," Gabi sniffed, rubbing his hair. "Please wake up." She cried. "Jesus, I need your help again. We have to get out of here. We're running out of time." A tear rolled down her cheek. She looked down. Scotty was looking up at her.

"Were you crying for me?" He asked.

"No!" She got up causing his head to hit the floor. "Dream on!"

"You were!" he said, "I saw a tear, you were crying over me!"

"Whatever you want to think, Scotty Morgan!"

"Need I remind you, Gabi Motes, that I will not be having any girlfriends until I'm sixteen?"

"Whatever! Let's go!" she said, walking away.

He caught up to her. "So why were you crying then?"

"Hmm, I don't know Scotty! Maybe because I don't know how we're going to get out of this crazy demonic castle, and everything we do, every turn we take, seems to get us further from where we need to be!" They stared at each other.

"Nah, you were crying over me."

"Oh good grief!" She turned and stormed away.

"Wait a minute, Gabi," Scotty said, catching up and passing her. He stood in front of her.

"What?"

"Who was that lady? And," he looked around, "where is she?"

Gabi shrugged. "She said her name was Tammy, and then she vanished."

"Tammy? Did she kill the Komodo?"

"I guess...he left."

"Oh no!" Scotty said, grabbing Gabi's hand, "Run!"

She was afraid to look back but didn't have to when she heard the scream. The Komodo dragon was back! They ran as fast as they could. He was gaining on them though. Again it screamed and it didn't sound happy. He had been denied his dinner once. Gabi put her hands over her ears and squeezed her eyes shut as she ran. She didn't see the overturned statue that Scotty leapt over. She hit it full on and slammed down face first on the stone floor. Before she even realized what happened, there was a searing pain in her leg. She was lifted into the air. She could hear Scotty screaming no over and over. She could smell the lizard's breath. Her body shook. She tasted blood and her whole insides felt icy cold.

"In Jesus' name!" Scotty screamed. "Nooo!!!"

There was a bright flash of light, an ear splitting scream of the lizard, and then Gabi felt as if she were falling and falling and falling.

"Hello?" Mark said into the darkness. Nothing. He could only hear his own breathing and the beat of his heart. It was so dark and so quiet. "This is not cool." He was standing on a staircase that vanished as he walked, so he couldn't go back. He waved the flameless torch in front of him to see if anyone or anything were in front of him. "I could really use your help, Jesus!"

"It would be quite nice if you stopped using that foul name!" A deep voice said from just below him. Mark gasped.

A finger snapped and torches were immediately lit to reveal a large room adorned with treasures. Gold, silver, precious stones. Statues of solid gold. Piles of coins as far as Mark could see and standing in front of him...

"David?"

"Hello, Mark." The deep rumble of a voice did not belong to the boy before him.

"What's going on, David?" Mark was quite confused.

David smiled. "Have you enjoyed my castle, Mark?"

"Um, your castle?" Mark was even more confused.

"That's right, Mark McGee, MY castle, and I really have grown quite accustomed to having it, there is just no way I'm going to let you or your sickly sister destroy it."

"But...I thought..."

"Allow me to introduce myself Mark," David said, taking a step forward and becoming a tall, thin, pale man with slick black hair and a trimmed beard. He wore the same black suit. "My name isn't really David. Actually, I have many names...Abaddon, Apollyon, I've been called the beast, that dragon, Beelzebub, Diablo, Satan, The Angel of Light, the Prince of the Power of the Air. My original name, however, was Lucifer, the Morning Star." He laughed a deep laugh.

Mark got very cold and felt as if he had no hope at all. He wanted to die. "You're just a snake," he said weakly.

David laughed louder, "More true than you know!"

"A slimy, good for..."

"Silence, Mark McGee...now bow your knees to me, you fool! Show me a little respect. Your own Bible calls me a god, a king, a prince…it even refers to me as a father!" He laughed.

"Father of Lies!" Mark yelled, mustering strength. He couldn't remember where he'd heard it, maybe Gabi, but he remembered hearing someone call Satan the father of lies.

"I said show me respect boy! I'm the Gateway to God!"

It was Mark's turn to laugh. "You'll be getting no respect from me you counterfeit! You're nothing more than the gateway to hell!"

Very well then, Mark McGee, I come against you with all the power of hell, destruction and death. You are about to pass though that gateway!" he shouted. He stepped towards Mark.

Mark closed his eyes and took a deep breath, "And I come against you in the name of Jesus Christ!" He opened his eyes and pointed at Satan. A bright light exploded in the room causing Satan to stumble backwards. The light came from behind Mark. Every jewel and coin and statue in the room turned to dust. Satan backed away covering his eyes.

"No!!" he screamed. "Not you! This is my house!"

A bright, brilliant ball about twice as big as a basketball passed through Mark from back to front and stopped between him and Satan. Mark felt stranger than he ever had. Something was changing. Satan stepped back and the ball of light moved. Mark took a step towards him. Suddenly there was a shield of gold attached to his left arm. He felt as if he were growing. Another step back for Satan, the ball, and Mark. A sword of radiant light appeared in Mark's right hand. With each step, something appeared. A breastplate over his chest, armor covered his legs and feet, and a helmet covered his head. He looked down. He stood at least ten foot tall and was quite muscular.

Satan cringed in a dark corner, shaking. A tiny gremlin with its ears up. He looked pathetic.

The light glowed brighter. "I am the Holy Spirit of God. You have done well, Mark McGee. There is still more to do." He began to rise up toward the ceiling. As he did, the ceiling caved in. Debris began to rain down all around Mark. He held up his shield. Stone, boards, pictures, statues and furniture fell. It was as if the entire castle was coming down. The light shown brighter. Mark looked up. He couldn't believe what he saw. In the midst of all the debris, floating slowly toward him, were Scotty and Gabi, as if they were held in a giant hand.

"We're almost out of time!" Pastor Joshua said to the group. We need a McGee!"

"Keep praying," Pastor Randy said. The three of them joined hands in a circle.

The army of angels were still gathered in the clouds above them. The legions of demons still surrounded the mountain. There was tension in the air.

"Dear Heavenly Father," Pastor Randy prayed. "Once again we come to you, in the name of your Son, Jesus Christ..."

The sun was starting to set at the hospital. Matt and Billy were chatting with a few friends about the reason they were doing this. Several people had already made decisions for Christ because of this gathering. Billy was just finishing up telling them what all God had done when someone tapped him on the shoulder. He glanced back and screamed like a girl, "Christina!" He and Matt wrapped their arms around her. "Oh, thank God you're okay!"

"Thank Him, indeed!" She replied. She'd cleaned up as best as she could inside the hospital. "Well, you guys are a sight for sore eyes." She looked around. "So, you decided to have a party without me?"

"This is for Bethany mostly, and Mark and you and Gabi and Scotty!" Billy said excitedly. "We've been praying!"

"This is a lot of people," she said. She looked towards her news van. Roger was covering the story with his cameraman, Chris. Roger would be hating this story, being an atheist and all. She smiled. "Hey, you guys haven't heard anything about my cameraman, Troy, have you?"

They both looked down. "Yeah, Christina," Matt said. "He was in an accident."

"What!?" she stepped back.

"His van went off the road and hit a pole," Matt continued. "He...didn't make it."

She covered her mouth, "Oh Troy." She teared up and looked away.

"When we heard the story," Billy said, "we thought you were with him. Thank God you weren't though. Then you were missing, and..." Billy's voice just trailed off.

Christina looked at her watch and knew there wasn't much time. "Listen guys, I have work to do. Please keep praying for me, okay?"

They both nodded. She smiled at them and headed for the news van.

"Father," Pastor Randy continued, "we ask you to deliver us from the enemy! To give strength to your angels and protect your people from the plans of the evil works of Satan!"

Topher and Clayton stood on either side of Bethany. Her mom and stepdad were seated in the room quite oblivious to the host of angels and demons in their vicinity.

Adam appeared next to Clayton with two other warring angels. "They are restless," he said. "They will attack any minute."

"How many?" Topher asked.

"The hospital is surrounded," Adam replied. "This is Marcus and Chinua," he nodded toward his companions. "There is not enough to overtake us."

Chinua drew his sword and the fire of it lit the room.

Mark's mom looked up. "Did it just get warmer in here?"

"It felt like it," his stepdad said. "Like a burst of energy."

Clayton looked at the clock. Twenty minutes until midnight in Switzerland.

"And," Pastor Randy said, "protect and bring Mark McGee to us, Father. Not only to have him safe, but to destroy the plans of the enemy. Be with him, Gabi, Scotty and Christina, and we pray you will fully and completely heal Bethany…"

When Gabi opened her eyes, she was floating toward the ground, slowly. The pain she'd felt earlier was gone. She saw Scotty floating downward with her. Everything else like rocks, debris and walls, fell at normal speed, but they were falling in slow motion. And what was that blinding light below? Were they dead? She knew that couldn't be the case. They would be soaring up, not floating down. As her eyes adjusted to the light, she saw someone. A soldier. He was huge, muscular, in armor with a shield and sword. He was smiling at her, really big, and goofy like.

"Mark?" Her own voice sounded strange, muffled. "Is that you?"

He held out his arms. "In the flesh!"

Scotty hit the ground running right up to Mark, looking up at him. "Dude! No way!"

Gabi followed him. "What in the world, Mark McGee?" There was a bright ball floating above him.

"I found it, Gabi!" he beamed. "I found the Gateway!"

"Well, it's about time!" She smiled.

Mark towered over them like a Philistine giant. He knelt down. "I was there, Gabi. I stood there as he hung on the cross. He spoke to me." Mark choked back a sob. A tear slid down his cheek. "He whispered two words in my ear."

"What did He say, Mark?" Scotty asked.

Just then a loud horn blew and shook the walls around them. More dust and debris fell. Mark stood. They all covered their ears.

"What was that?!" Scotty yelled.

"The call to battle!" Mark said. The ball of light floated down between them and the wall to their right. They each turned to face it.

"Guys," Mark said. "Meet the Holy Spirit."

Gabi covered her mouth and began to sob. That in turn made Scotty and Mark cry too. Scotty reached over and took Gabi's hand and as soon as he did, the ball of light shot through them and vanished. The room went dark. The ground shook.

"And Father God!" Pastor Randy yelled over the insanely loud horn blast, "we place our lives in your capable hands!"

Christina approached the news van. "Hello, Roger!"

He spun around. "Well, there you are!" You have some explaining to do, young lady!" He looked her over, noticing her scrapes and bruises and torn clothes. "Apparently a lot of explaining."

She simply smiled. "It's nice to see you too, Roger."

"Where have you been?!" he shouted. "Did you know Troy was dead?"

"I just found out about Troy." She lowered her eyes.

"So where were you?"

"You wouldn't believe me if I told you," she said.

He stepped closer. "Try me."

"I've been in the castle."

"You've been...what?"

She nodded. "You heard me."

"You're right, I don't believe you." He turned away. "We'll discuss this later with Allen. For now, get cleaned up. You're taking over here. All these Christians are making me sick to my stomach. All this praying and crying and singing and hugging. It's nauseating."

She pulled her hair back as Chris gave her a hug and told her he was sorry about Troy and glad to see her.

"Go home Roger, I've got this," she said.

"Thank God," he said, taking off his mic.

"Thank who, Roger?" she asked, smiling at him. He rolled his eyes and walked away.

Chris handed her a t-shirt. "You can wear this instead of your torn one. Go change in the van."

She looked at the shirt and smiled. "Pray for Bethany."

"Bring Mark to us, in these final moments, Lord," Pastor Randy continued. "You have shown us your mysteries, we have seen your enemies, your allies, and we have experienced your glory! Now, we pray, show us your strength!"

CHAPTER TWENTY-ONE

THE BATTLE

C layton and Topher looked at each other when the war horn sounded. Adam and Marcus drew their swords along with Chinua. There was movement in the hall, outside the window, below them and above them. They were greatly outnumbered.

"Can you feel the prayers?" Clayton asked.

"Yes!" Adam said. "The prayers are our strength!" His sword burned with a holy fire.

"It really is getting warm in here," Mark's mom said. "I'm going to ask someone to turn the air down."

"I'll do it honey. You stay with Bethany," Mark's stepdad said. He left the room.

"Let them come," Chinua said. "I will litter the ground with their blood!"

As the door closed, it exploded inward and demons poured in with swords drawn.

Mark's mom got up and closed the door, thinking it was strange how it had swung open. She rubbed her arms at how cold it had suddenly gotten.

There was a flash of light that filled the room. The clanging of sword on sword. Marcus and Chinua cut them down as they entered. Adam got them as they came close to Bethany from any and every direction. Hundreds of demons replaced each one they cut down. They were outnumbered. These demons wanted her dead. The angels stood their ground.

The demons were moving up the mountain. Some running, some flying, some leaping. All were moving toward the top, very fast, on all sides.

Their screams were terrifying. Ear splitting. Pastor Randy, Pastor Joshua and Mr. Hoffman covered their ears.

Topher appeared with two men. "I brought more prayer warriors!" he said. "Hold your ground!" Pastor Eric and Larry stood there extremely confused. One second they'd been praying outside the hospital, the next they were on a mountain top.

"Pray!" Topher shouted. "The time is now!" And he vanished.

Each prayed silently, watching the hordes of hell ascend. The angels remained silent and still. "They're getting close!" Mr. Hoffman shouted. "Halfway up the mountain already!"

"That's still slow for demons!" Larry said. "Aren't they as fast as..."

There was a loud explosion that blew out one whole side of the mountain. The ground shook below them. Demons went flying, screaming as they fell. A bright light shone from the mountain for just an instant. The demons covered their eyes. The angels above drew their swords. It was quite an impressive sound.

"What's happening!?" Pastor Eric shouted. They were all straining to see. He looked up. The lead angel held up a fist to hold his army back.

When the dust cleared below, there were three giant warriors that emerged. Two were male and one was a female. They were in full armor swinging swords as big as motorcycles and shields the size of a car hood. They sliced demons as they charged out.

'Hey!" Larry said, is that..." he leaned out for a better view. "Gabi?" He could see her hair coming out the back of her helmet.

"Is that Mark and Scotty with her?" Pastor Eric asked.

"Wow!" Pastor Joshua said. "They've been working out!"

"They're giants!!" Pastor Randy yelled.

"Demon killing giants!" Pastor Eric added. "Let's pray!"

Just then an icy cold wind blew over the mountain. They all looked to the south. A giant dragon was heading towards them. The angels faced him. It began to laugh as it circled the mountain. "It is too late, you fools!" it shouted. "You have only seconds to complete the circle and Mark McGee will never make it!" Again he laughed. "You have failed!"

Clayton had joined the fight as more and more demons entered the room. They came from every direction. It was like an infestation of ants. Marcus flew in and out of the room sending hordes of demons to the pits of hell as he swung his sword.

"Honey, the nurse needs to ask you some questions out here," Mark's stepdad said, holding the door open. His mom walked out.

Chinua stood facing the door. "You will not have Bethany!" He shouted slicing four demons every time he swung his sword.

Just then, there was a flash of brilliant light that blinded everyone. Demons covered their eyes. The angels blinked back the light and when they opened their eyes...the demons were gone."

"What happened?" Adam asked, turning to face the others.

"I have no idea," Marcus said. They looked around expecting a surprise attack.

"Have the cowards fled?" Chinua asked.

"No, they didn't," Clayton said, standing there staring at Bethany's bed.

"What is it Clayton?" Adam asked, approaching. The four angels stood around her bed, staring. Bethany was gone.

"Hello, this is Christina Bulford with Channel Six news in Gateway, Florida. I'm here at Gateway Community Hospital where hundreds of people have gathered to pray for a little girl, Bethany McGee. Bethany is six years old and fighting for her life with a rare heart condition that doctors cannot explain. We've been told that the next few hours are vital and things are not looking too good for young Bethany." (Bethany's picture came up on the screen.)

People were watching this all around the country. The gathering had gained national attention. Several news organizations linked up with Channel Six to give Christina a live feed all over the country.

"For right now, we're going to leave Bethany in the hands of these prayer warriors." The camera panned over the crowds. Heads were bowed, candles were being held. Some held hands in groups, others stood silently praying. "And the God they are praying to."

Christina adjusted her mic and cleared her throat. She was about to throw her career away on national news. "The real story tonight is not Bethany McGee. The real story is you. Each and every one of you watching this broadcast. You see, when this whole adventure began, I, like many of you, believed we were in this thing called life, pretty much on our own. With nobody to please but myself and those I care about. With NOBODY to answer to, in the sky." She pointed up. "That's right, I wasn't exactly a church goer." Her cameraman, Chris, was giving her a strange look. "But over the past several hours, I've experienced some things. Some...unexplainable things. I won't go into any details, but I will say this...there is evil in the world. It is real. It is fierce, and it wants to destroy us. All of us. It wants one thing. Our souls...in hell." Chris touched his ear like he was getting a call through his ear piece. "But," Christina said, "there is also a God...a God who loves you so much, He died for you. He died to destroy that evil." Chris shook his head. "His name is Jesus Christ and..."

"Christina!" Chris called, "they unplugged us. You're off."

Mark, Gabi and Scotty, each still over ten feet tall and dressed as Roman warriors, were slicing demons down like corn stalks. Arrows were bouncing off their shields and armor.

Still, more demons came, by the thousands. Mark looked up above where the dragon flew. The angels remained in place.

"There's too many, Mark!" Scotty yelled. "We can't hold them off!" He cut the arm off a passing demon and turned it to dust.

"Why aren't the angels helping?" Mark asked. "What are they waiting for?"

The demons formed a circle around them. Laughing, taunting, and swinging their swords at them.

"You're supposed to be on the mountain top, Mark!" Gabi said, cutting a small demon out of the sky. "You need to complete the circle before they can fight!"

"It's too far away!" He shouted, looking up. He could barely see the top from where he stood.

The dragon swooped down close to them and roared. Mark could hardly believe it was the same dragon that had fit in his room or even in the castle. He was as big as a battleship now. "It is too late, Mark McGee!" He roared with a laughter that shook the mountain. "You have failed! The castles are secure!" More laughter from him and the demons. They lifted their swords high. "Once again, Satan is victorious. The circle is incomplete!" The demons cheered.

Scotty reached over and sliced the head off of a demon that stood too close.

"Your time is up!" The dragon swooped again. "Now you will feel the sting of our blades and our arrows!"

At that moment there was a brilliant flash of light on the top of the mountain. The dragon covered his eyes with his wings, turning his head.

"Not so fast, Anansi!" Topher yelled from the mountain top. The cheers of the demons were silenced. "We are not too late!"

"The hour is now!" the dragon roared. "Do not lie to me! McGee has failed!"

"Yet the circle is complete!" All eyes turned toward the circle.

Pastor Joshua Guillemette, Pastor Randy Scalise, John Hoffman, and ...Bethany McGee.

"Bethany!" Larry shouted. "You're healed! Praise Jesus!"

She was thoroughly confused but smiling from ear to ear. "I see a dragon!"

"Bethany?" Pastor Eric asked, "Would you like to ask Jesus into your heart?"

She shook her head no and the dragon roared with laughter. Everyone stared in stunned silence.

"I already did in Children's Church," she beamed.

"You failed Anansi!" Topher shouted. "Let the hosts of heaven descend upon you!"

It was all Daniel needed to hear. Within seconds, hundreds of thousands of angels descended on the mountain. They were joined by Chinua, Marcus and Adam...who personally destroyed the dragon with one swipe of his blade. The demons couldn't flee fast enough.

Mark, Scotty and Gabi chased them down the mountain.

Topher turned to those in the circle. To Larry and Pastor Eric he said, "Come." They vanished. Only the circle remained, hands held, heads bowed, leading the hosts of heaven to victory.

As they fought, castles crumbled in Porte, France... in Ingresso, Spain...in Einfarht, Germany...and in Gateway, Florida. Stone by stone they fell to the ground.

The demons were either routed or destroyed. The angels soared, circling the mountain, chasing or killing any stragglers.

Daniel landed next to Mark, Scotty and Gabi. When they looked down they noticed they were normal size again.

"Hey what happened?" Scotty yelled, "I liked being big!"

"Yeah, why WERE we like that?" Mark asked.

Daniel smiled, "You were able to see yourselves as the demons see you when you've been in the presence of God."

"Wow!" Gabi said. "That's awesome!"

"Punk demons!" Scotty yelled into the air.

"Daniel!" Adam called from the sky. Daniel and the others looked up. Adam pointed to the hole where Mark, Scotty and Gabi had come out.

An enormous angel stood there, glowing like a light bulb. He was holding onto someone. A child...David.

"What do you have there, General?" Daniel asked. Mark noted that he said what, not who.

The angel smiled brightly. "The troublemaker." Daniel and Adam joined the larger angel.

"A worm." Adam said. "Let me split him open!"

Mark, Scotty and Gabi ran up to join them.

"In your dreams, angel!" David said. "This is my realm."

"Yeah, well, you've lost your precious castles," Daniel said.

David squirmed. "Let me go or you will suffer!"

The angels laughed. "Suffer?" Adam said. "How? Will you bleed on us? Stain our robes with your fear?"

David calmed, and looked at Mark. "I am a part of you, Mark McGee. We are one. Enjoy your new God for now. I'm not finished with you. I will destroy ALL you hold dear."

There was a loud explosion like thunder after a lightning strike. They all jumped back. David was gone.

CHAPTER TWENTY-TWO

TWO WORDS

I t was Sunday afternoon the following day. Oh what a Sunday celebration they'd had at Lighthouse Christian Center. Pastor Randy and Pastor Joshua had joined the service there instead of at their own churches. John Hoffman had even been there. The celebration continued at the end of the service when Mark's mom and stepdad went down to give their lives to Christ.

Now, along with all the pastors, Mr. Hoffman, the McGee's, the Motes, the Morgan's, Christina, Matt and Billy were all gathered in the fellowship hall. They were having fried chicken and all the trimmings they could each bring.

They were all laughing and patting each other on the backs. They'd been through so much together. It was great to be able to laugh about it. Of course, there were tears too. So many had died, Todd, Angel, Troy, Bethany's doctor. It didn't dampen their joy though. They even voted to have this same celebration every year on this day. They would call it the castle celebration.

Bethany was all smiles sitting in her mother's lap. Her mom would hardly let her out of her sight. She had been hailed the hero of the night.

"So, what are your plans now Mr. Hoffman?" Pastor Joshua asked.

"I have no idea." He laughed. "Maybe I will start a church in Einfahrt." They all laughed. "With a children's ministry that is second to none."

"Amen!" Pastor Eric said.

"I still can't believe everything that happened," Christina said. "It all seems like a dream."

"Well, your little sermon on the news went viral!" Pastor Randy said.

She blushed. "About that, my studio manager wants to meet with me in the morning. I'll probably be fired... but that's okay."

"Let me know if you do," Pastor Eric said. "I have connections."

"Speaking of trouble," Christina said. "It's good to see that Matt and Billy weren't killed by their parents." Everyone laughed.

"Our parents agreed that considering what we did, and being on the news and all, we were not acting self-ishly, but to help others." Billy said.

"And my dad wants to sit down and tell me every-thing he knew about the castle," Matt added. "Not sure if even matters now."

"Oh, I could tell him a few things about that castle!" Scotty said. They all laughed. "Every nightmare that ever existed was in there."

Mark and Gabi nodded, along with Christina.

"Well, I have a confession to make," Mark said. "To Gabi."

Gabi gave him a look. "What?" She looked concerned.

"Sorry Mark," Scotty said. "She's in love with me!"

"I am not in love with you, Scotty Morgan!" she yelled, shoving him lightly.

"You sure were crying when you thought I was dead." He smiled.

"Ugghh!" she said and everyone laughed. "Anyway, back to Mark."

He paused for a moment and everyone was watching him. "I just wanted to say that I was sorry for lying to you."

She looked confused.

"It was me that did those things to Todd and Eddie and Andy. Even the thing that got them expelled."

Gabi nodded. "You didn't actually think I didn't know that, did you?" Laughter erupted again. "Those boneheads deserved all of it."

"Yeah, well," Mark said, "from now on, I'm leaving vengeance to God."

"It's better that way," Pastor Joshua said.

"Are you telling me there's a party going on and I wasn't invited to it?!"

"Topher!" They all yelled, and went to give him a hug.

He patted Mark's mom and stepdad on the back. "I was at your salvation party this morning!"

They both smiled. "Congratulations."

"So, what brings you here, Topher?" Pastor Randy asked. "Or did you come to give us another mission?"

"No mission!" He smiled. "I come bringing gifts." At that moment, Clayton stepped in the door and a little black mutt dog ran in, tail wagging.

"Gameboy?!" Scotty shouted and almost tripped over a chair getting to him. Gameboy covered Scotty's face with kisses. Everyone laughed and awed. "He's alive!" He looked at Topher, "How?"

"He had a friend," Topher said and looked back at Clayton who was blocking the door. Clayton stepped aside and a young woman stepped in.

Gabi gasped, "Tammy!" She ran to her and gave her a hug. "You saved our lives." Scotty jumped up and hugged her too.

She smiled and hugged them back, but she was scanning the group. Looking for...the old man who was wiping his eyes. His whole body shook.

"Mr. Hoffman, are you okay?" Pastor Eric asked.

"My Tammy!" He cried. "My baby!" He could barely stand.

"Papa!" She ran to him. They embraced.

There was a collective gasp in the room. Nobody was breathing and everybody was crying.

"Ohhh, my baby!" Mr. Hoffman cried. "Thank you, Jesus!"

They both cried and held each other.

"So, as it turns out," Topher said. "She was given a task to do in the castle, like you were Mark. After a while, she gave up. She found a room and made it her home. Gameboy found her and they took care of each other."

"That's amazing," Gabi said through her tears.

"Its's unbelievable," Scotty said.

"That's God!" Topher said. "Amazing and unbelievable." He and Clayton were gone.

Everyone was quiet, other than the sobs of Mr. Hoffman and Tammy, and the sniffing of everyone else.

After a few minutes, Gabi spoke up. "So Mark, you mentioned that when you got saved you saw Jesus?"

Mark nodded, looking up, remembering. "It was like I was there when he was being crucified. I mean really there. I could see it, hear it, and smell it even. The mobs, the soldiers, the others on the cross.

"Yeah," Scotty said. "You said he said something to you...two words...what were they?"

Mark looked up. All eyes were on him. He smiled... "For you, He said FOR YOU."

The End

Mark McGee and the Gateway to God is a fictional story based on a Biblical truth…"for all have sinned and fall short of the glory of God" (Romans 3:23 NIV). "For the wages of sin is death, but the gift of God is eternal life in Christ Jesus our Lord" (Romans 6:23 NIV). If you have not made Jesus Christ the Lord of your life, I sincerely encourage you to do so. See your Bible for details. Topher cannot wait to celebrate at your salvation party!

CPSIA information can be obtained
at www.ICGtesting.com
Printed in the USA
FSHW020015230721
83461FS